The Road of Vultures

Luka Vernik – The Vengeful Warrior Trilogy

Book I

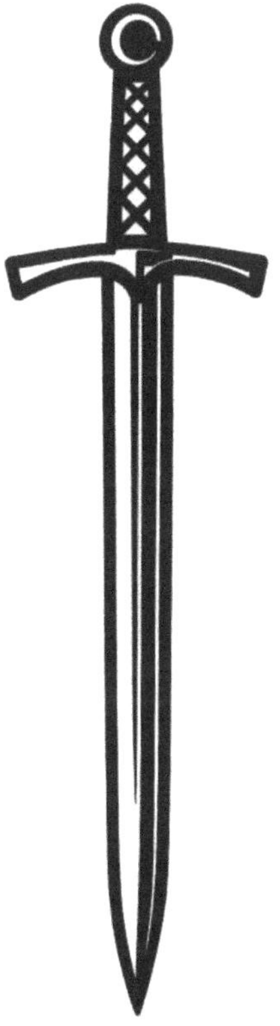

Albert Lord

Contents

Dedication i

Acknowledgments ii

About the Author iii

Chapter 1 Night Terrors 1

Chapter 2 The Champion 9

Chapter 3 A Difficult Lesson 15

Chapter 4 The Streets of Vernikport 24

Chapter 5 The War Room 35

Chapter 6 The Flag of War................................... 44

Chapter 7 General Warwick 54

Chapter 8 The Calm 59

Chapter 9 The Storm 67

Chapter 10 The Battle of the Families 81

Chapter 11 Ruin 89

Chapter 12 The News 98

Chapter 13 The Insurgency 107

Chapter 14 Awakened 114

Chapter 15 The Blood Oath 123

Chapter 16 Vulture Road 136

Chapter 17 Unwelcome Visitors 141

Chapter 18 Glazben 150

Chapter 19 Martial Law..................................... 162

Chapter 20 Privagrad 169

Chapter 21 The Archlord and Archlady.................. 180

Chapter 22 Prayers of the Widows....................... 185

Chapter 23 The Healer 193

Chapter 24 The Rasko Inn 198

Chapter 25 Reflections of Power.......................... 202

Chapter 26 The Magic Tavern 209

Chapter 27 The Wizard of Jetsac 216

Chapter 28 The Meadows 225

Chapter 29 The Warrior and the Wizard 230

Chapter 30 The Invasion of Exeter 236

Chapter 31 The Sova Woods 245

Chapter 32 Rumors Travel Faster than the Wind 254

Chapter 33 Holy Matrimony 267

Chapter 34 Rys 278

Chapter 35 The Queen's Journey 284

Chapter 36 The Cavalcade 292

Chapter 37 The End of the Road 299

Chapter 38 The Siege 305

Chapter 39 Reishi's Plan 312

Chapter 40 Plan in Motion 320

Chapter 41 Into the City 327

Chapter 42 The Duel 339

Chapter 43 Rage of the Phoenix 352

Chapter 44 Battle at the Mountain's Gate 357

Chapter 45 Vengeance's Burn 366

Chapter 46 Corpses 376

Chapter 47 Battle Scars 382

Chapter 48 The King's Address 388

Chapter 49 Farewell 398

Chapter 50 The Final Lesson 403

Dedication

Dedicated to Ana—the book's first reader, my number one supporter, and my best friend, always.

Acknowledgments

I first conceived of this book in 2018. It's been a long journey since then—not quite as difficult as Luka's in this book, but certainly with its own twists and turns. Throughout that journey, there have been a lot of people who have supported me, and this book would not be possible without them.

First and foremost, I need to thank Ana, who once told me early when we were dating that she would love to read something I had written. *Oh boy, do I have something for you,* I thought. The next day I handed her a very rough draft of *The Road of Vultures*, much to her surprise. That was about five years ago to this day. Since then, she has been a huge advocate for this project, and I probably would have just given up without her.

I also want to thank my parents and my brothers, who provided their own steady encouragement throughout this process. Growing up, my mother, in particular, encouraged my creativity and imagination, making sure those instincts were never stifled.

My writer's group, consisting of Drew, Kenny, Julia, Stephanie, and Andrew, also had a significant impact on this novel and my writing journey. Their thoughtful feedback week after week helped me sharpen each chapter, all the while producing compelling work of their own.

If you are impressed by the cover, the formatting, or marketing of this book, all credit is due to the great team from The Curtis Publishing Company. I owe them a debt of gratitude for their phenomenal work to bring this book out to the world with professionalism and a killer design.

Lastly, I want to thank *you.* If you're reading this, then you've taken a chance on a first-time author. It means a lot to me, and I sincerely hope you enjoy the ride.

About the Author

The Road of Vultures is Albert Lord's debut novel, and the first installment of *The Vengeful Warrior Trilogy*. He lives outside of Philadelphia with his wife, daughter, two dogs, and a crazy cat. Outside of writing, he enjoys reading (of course!), golf, whiskey, and fervently rooting for Philadelphia sports teams. Find out more at albertlordauthor.com.

THE KINGDOM OF ESTRAVIA

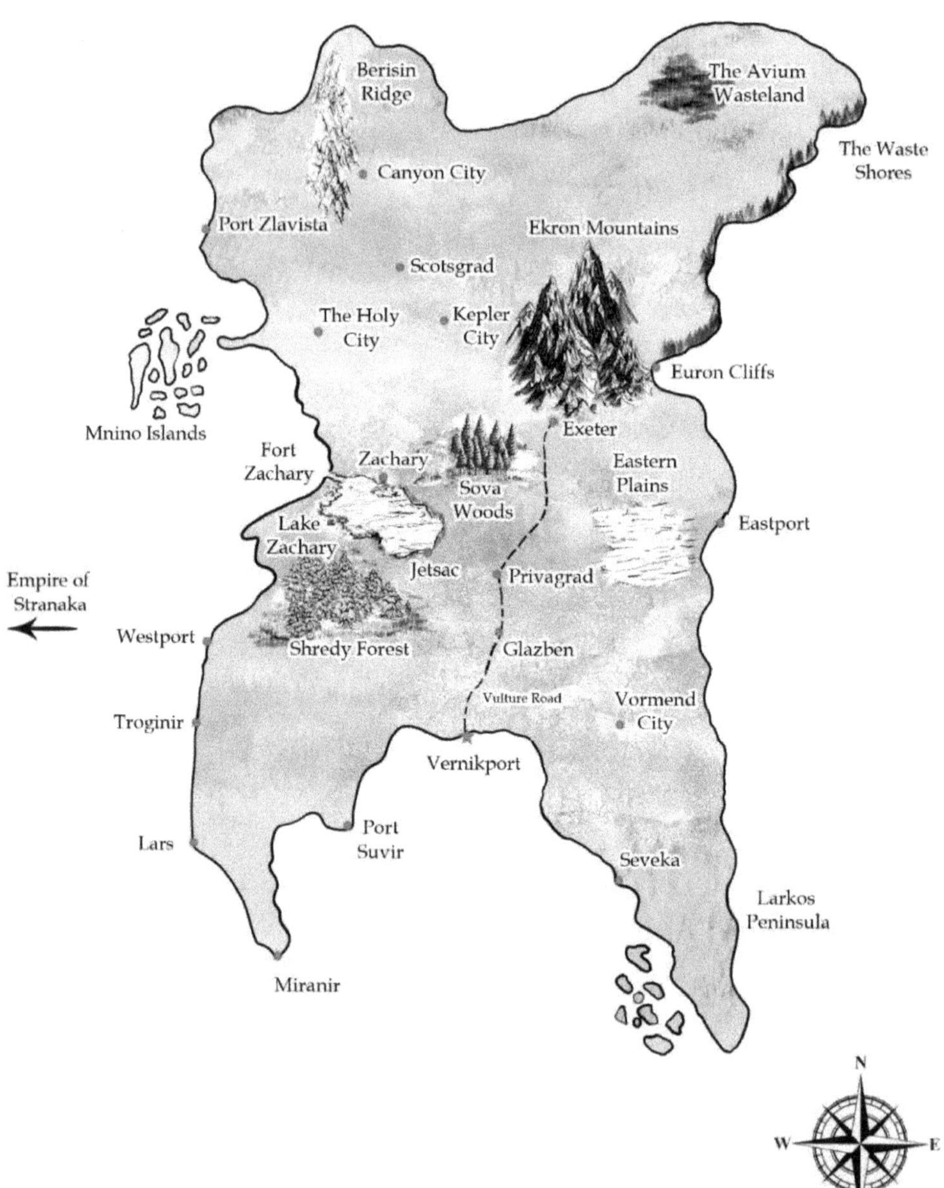

Chapter 1
Night Terrors

Geffen circled the camp again, long into a nighttime patrol that he assumed would be as dull and uneventful as it always was.

The camp sprawled in a wide circle with dozens of soldiers asleep in the middle of the vast Shredry Forest. It was scarcely visible—the only illumination came from the moon and stars above, but even that light was restricted by the thick canopy of trees overhead.

The humid, summer night air sat heavy on him as he patrolled. Halfway around, he came to his spot on the forest floor, where a makeshift nest of blankets served as his bed. He strained his eyes in the darkness, staring at it longingly. With a sigh, he moved past, knowing his shift would not be over for several more hours. Only then could he rest.

As his patrol continued, his mind drifted to thoughts of his own bed at home. Almost nothing seemed more appealing than his own comfortable mattress and sheets. But more than that, he thought desperately of lying next to his wife, Nika, longing for the touch of her skin and the warmth of her presence. Only three months remained on his tour of duty, but he felt like he would never escape the limitlessness of the Shredry Forest.

He reminded himself that he had enlisted for her. The good wages and the prospect of a pension made the struggles and the dreary patrols worth it. Soon enough, they'd be able to start a family together, leaving all of this behind.

The sound of alien rustling close at hand interrupted Geffen's thoughts. He froze, straining to catch the sound again. Crickets filled the night air with their rhythmic chirping. A gentle summer breeze whistled through the trees like a ghostly whisper, but that was all he heard. After no other disturbances, he let the moment pass and proceeded with his patrol, unbothered.

Moments later, Geffen heard rustling again. This time, it was unmistakable. "Please don't be a Giant Werdal," he muttered under his breath. The appearance of one of those armored beasts would be disastrous for everyone in the camp.

Hushed voices became audible, and Geffen looked around at his unit. They were all sound asleep, meaning that none of them could have been the source of the noise.

The human voices eliminated the possibility of a Werdal—which itself was a great relief—but much concern remained. Geffen began to consider whether it was worth waking up the other soldiers. Though bandits were known to hide in these woods, Geffen would earn only scorn if he roused the camp over something trivial, like a few lost travelers.

When the sounds grew nearer still, panic churned within Geffen's stomach. He opted for caution, hurriedly darting from soldier to soldier, trying to shake them awake. "Get up, someone's coming," he said to them. At best, the men were slow to stir. At worst, they ignored Geffen altogether in favor of remaining in their satisfying slumber.

By the time Geffen had shaken all his fellow servicemen, the source of the commotion was directly upon them. An incalculable number of silhouettes now stood in the dark forest. Faint chattering came from the shadows. Geffen went silent, straining to hear.

"I still do not know whether it is wise to place so much trust in our supposed ally," came a muffled, raspy voice. "This could end up being a trap for us, rather than for them."

"There's no need to talk of a trap, Privus. You worry far too much," said a lighter, second voice.

"You don't worry nearly enough, Drugi," shot back the first voice, now identified as Privus. "You want everything to be fine and dandy without the effort of considering all of the possibilities. Especially the dangerous ones."

A third voice—distinct and much deeper—spoke then. "Privus, I share in your concern, but we discussed our contingencies, should we need them. However, I am confident they will be unnecessary. We are giving our contact everything, including the chance to shape the new world. That is enough incentive."

"Fair point, brother," said Privus.

The soldiers in Geffen's camp could hear this too—and a half-awake young soldier rose and lit a torch. "What? Who's there?" the young foot soldier said, holding up the light in one hand and wiping the sleep away from his eyes with the other.

Now, with that single flame ablaze, much of the camp became visible, both parties coming face to face in the dancing firelight. The strangers consisted of scores of armed men. Geffen knew of no other patrols in the Vernik Army stationed in the Shredry Forest. It was also unlikely that one of the houses would have sent a patrol of their own. That left very few pleasant possibilities of who these men could be.

"Who's there?" repeated the soldier, squinting as hard as he could.

The band of strangers came closer and stepped into the light, with three men at the forefront. A black batlike emblem adorned the center of their armor. The three men were all quite tall, but one of them stood above the other two—the man with the deep voice. He had a hulking frame and heavy armor, but he was helmetless, revealing a thick black beard and a bald head. The man was flanked by his two brothers, who had been referred to as Privus and Drugi.

The younger brothers kept their faces clean-shaven and had dark hair. The man, identified as Privus, kept his hair short and orderly like that of a military officer. Drugi's hair was longer and unkempt.

"This area is under official Vernik army patrol. We need you to state your name and business here," said the soldier, but his voice severely lacked the authoritativeness he had hoped for.

The hulking man stepped forward now, his imposing frame towering over the young soldier. "And why do I owe you that information?" he asked, his voice low and menacing.

"It is the King's business. We are under official order in this—"

"The King's business!" the large man guffawed, his laughs even deeper than his voice. "I am quite confident you know nothing of the 'King's business.' I am quite confident you have never even met him. But I have. And I will meet him again soon."

The young soldier stammered again. "Sir, if you do not cooperate, I will have to arrest you on suspicion of banditry."

The large man's gaze became fierce and focused upon the young soldier. "So be it. I am Omarius Zlikrej, the firstborn son of Lord Diocretin and the rightful heir to Canyon City. I am joined by my younger brothers, Drugi and Privus. We also boast several hundred loyal soldiers in our ranks with us. Our business is to avenge our parents, wage war on the Vernik Family, and take control of the Kingdom of Estravia." The hulking man paused for a moment, watching the reaction of the young soldier in front of him. "Are you satisfied? I have stated our names and our business."

Before the private had a chance to respond, the man—now identified as Omarius—unlatched a mammoth war hammer from behind his back. The young soldier attempted to evade the attack but was much too slow, the giant weapon coming down upon his neck swiftly.

The soldier did not even have time to let out a scream. Blood exploded from the point of impact. When Omarius pulled back his hammer, the young soldier's head was crushed to a pulp, leaving behind a deformed, inhuman body.

The onslaught followed immediately.

As soon as the soldier fell, the rest of the strangers began to attack in unison. Geffen's unit was not prepared for the attack. He turned to flee, but an arrow snapped in the darkness, piercing his right shoulder and sending him to the ground. He lay on his left side in agony, keeping his eyes shut for several moments.

When Geffen could bear it, he opened his eyes, trembling in terror. From his low vantage point, he watched one of his fellow soldiers fall on his back. His blade landed on a tree root only a meter from Geffen's face. He then saw a pair of black-armored legs standing above the soldier, followed by a sword slicing down into his throat.

Though he could see little else, Geffen knew the carnage was still going on from the screams around him. He could hear the frantic pleading of one man begging for his life, but the sound of steel meeting flesh silenced his cries.

Near Geffen, the metallic clangs of swords and spears clashing in a duel rang out, only for a flesh-squishing, bone-crushing noise to put an end to it. The source of the horror could only have been Omarius's war hammer.

More screams echoed out in the night, but they grew quieter and soon became silent like the ending of a tragic song. The enemies had made quick work of the patrol.

"I think we've got all of them," said one of the men, a moment after the skirmish had settled.

"Excellent work, as always, My Lords. I have the utmost admiration for how you conduct combat and how—" another voice said.

"You can stop licking our boots, General Klacan," Omarius said. "I am not convinced we killed them all. What about the one Drugi shot with an arrow earlier?"

"I shall check on him, but I think I killed him," said Drugi.

"Do that. It did not look like a fatal blow to me," Omarius replied.

Geffen's heart pounded faster than before, hearing the footsteps of Drugi Zlikrej coming towards him. He had only moments to act.

Silently, Geffen reached for his dagger. He shut his eyes and lay with his fingers enclosed on the weapon. He would only be able to feign his death for a split second, and he needed to make the most of it.

"Found him," announced Drugi, the archer. He stood above Geffen, holding a large bow in his hand. "Looks like he's dead," he added before beginning to reach down to check on his work.

Geffen seized the moment. He sprung upward swiftly, smacked the archer's bow out of his arms, and grabbed him. He pressed the knife threateningly across the man's throat and held him before all the other assailants. Drugi yelped like an animal in his arms.

"Stop! Stop, or I will kill him!" Geffen screamed.

There was no clear plan of escape, and the arrow was still lodged in Geffen's shoulder, but now he had leverage. He had a chance to survive and return home.

"Stop!" Geffen repeated, his voice shrill.

Privus and Omarius Zlikrej stared intensely at Geffen, who was holding a knife against their middle brother. Privus wielded an arming sword with a black hilt while Omarius held his massive war hammer, both weapons wet with blood. Behind them loomed a small army of soldiers, a force of what looked like hundreds strong.

"What exactly do you want us to stop?" said Privus. "If you mean you want us to stop killing your comrades, then I think that's already done."

"Brothers, help! Make him let go of me," pleaded Drugi.

"You must be more careful, Drugi. There are ways to check on bodies without falling captive," said Omarius.

"Put down your weapons. Put them down, or I *will* kill him," Geffen ordered.

Omarius nodded to Privus, and both brothers dropped their weapons, with the soldiers behind them following. Hundreds of steel blades falling to the ground rang out in a metal harmony in the forest night. The hammer made a distinct, sizable thud when it landed.

With everyone disarmed, Geffen stole a quick look behind him. The black abyss of the forest was all that lay around him, much of it uncharted territory. Geffen did not have a sense of which direction would lead him out of the woods the fastest. He only knew he had to get away. When he made it to safety, he would make sure word of this reached the crown. But most importantly, he would get home to Nika.

Geffen turned back to the two brothers. There was no expression on Omarius's face, but a twisted smirk covered Privus's. He was reaching for something.

"I said weapons down," repeated Geffen.

"You did say that, and I obeyed. I put my sword down. Why do you assume that this is a weapon, too?" answered Privus. The object he produced was a golden staff, thin at the bottom and thicker at the top, where a golden eye eerily sat in between two wing-shaped protrusions.

"Put it down, I said."

"If I put the staff down, then you will not get the privilege of witnessing magic. Real magic. You wouldn't want to lose the chance to see that, would you now?" responded Privus.

"Privus, be careful," Drugi said. "I don't want to get burned."

"What? Burned?" Geffen asked with panic. "Put that staff down!"

Privus defiantly hoisted the staff up, aiming the eye directly at him. Geffen flinched hard, anticipating something to happen. He heard and felt a rush of wind around him, but as far as he could tell, he was unharmed.

"P..p..p..." Geffen tried to repeat his command, but suddenly, he couldn't find the words nor the air. He had seemingly lost the ability to inhale. *It must be nerves, Geffen thought. I must get it together.* He tried to take a deep breath to calm himself but again could gather no air.

Privus began taking steps towards him, his grin stretching even wider. "You thought you were so clever, capturing my brother so that you could escape from this. But you are merely a fool. I am your fate, and there is no escape from fate."

More frantic now, Geffen made another effort to inhale, but nothing filled his lungs. The act of breathing, something so automatic and taken for granted, was now an impossibility to him. His chest began to ache. His body began to fill with dread.

Geffen stumbled back, lightheaded, and released his captive. Drugi teetered forward, now a free man. As Geffen retreated, his heel connected with a large tree root. When he fell, the arrow was pushed deeper through him. It now protruded all the way through his shoulder and his chest. The hole in his body throbbed uncontrollably, matching the rhythm of his racing heart.

Laying on the ground, Geffen's lungs cried for air like starving dogs. Geffen wanted to scream in pain, but with no breath, even that was futile.

The desperate foot soldier closed his eyes and started clawing at his throat, struggling to draw a single breath. Each tug on his throat grew weaker as his body began to lose energy. He opened his eyes for a waning moment to see Privus standing above, the sinister golden eye still pointed at him.

The last of his breath and his life soon faded away. Privus's smirk was the last thing Geffen ever saw.

Chapter 2
The Champion

Thousands rose from their seats, applause bursting out in the arena like the sudden arrival of a tempest. In the center of the sand-covered battleground, the young warrior had delivered a brutal blow to his opponent, who now lay still. He walked over to the man he had downed and stood above him menacingly, his shadow stretching long under the glaring sun and eclipsing his rival. He waited, watching through the slits in his helmet, looking for any signs of movement.

The official ran over and began counting down, the crowd joining in.

"Ten! Nine! Eight..."

The man on the ground groaned and strained but could not lift himself up.

"Seven! Six! Five..."

The young warrior began to relax his stance. Both men understood that if the downed contender dared to rise, a blow more powerful than its predecessor would be his only greeting.

"Four! Three! Two! One!" The crowd's volume crescendoed. They could not hear the officiant's next declaration, but they knew what the words would be all the same.

"For the fourth year in a row, Prince Luka Vernik is the champion!" The official held Luka's arm high in the air. With his other hand, Luka removed his helmet, revealing his triumphant yet battleworn face.

Luka rotated his body around, facing each section of the crowd, pumping his fists. He glanced pointedly at the Royal Suite, which appeared to be empty, but he wasn't certain. If he had been sure of that, it would have dampened his triumphant moment.

When he finished celebrating, Luka turned to his defeated opponent and offered him a hand. The other warrior took it and allowed Luka to lift him. "Thank you for a worthy match," Luka said once they were both standing.

"Th-thank you, Prince Luka," the opponent said, his voice strained by the pain of damage he had taken during the duel. "C-congratulations."

A handful of nurses and arena workers rushed over to the runner-up and carried him away, disappearing beneath the battleground. He would not be present during the trophy ceremony.

*****

An hour later, the arena sat empty. Alone in his private training room beneath the coliseum, Luka Vernik admired his new silver chalice. In the space between the rubies and the gems, he could make out his reflection, an image of the young, blonde-haired prince distorted by the curvature of the trophy.

While the chalice was a fine prize, it would simply end up as the latest addition to Luka's vast collection. His opponent earlier that day was now merely another name on the long list of Luka's defeated adversaries.

In the privacy of the training room, Luka examined his own body. He could see the spots where new bruises would form, adding more texture to the tapestry of purple and yellow that covered his body from the days of dueling. It was a prize very different from a chalice, but a prize nonetheless.

Luka returned his armor to the chest in the corner of the room and locked it. Donning his informal, tan-colored pants, shirt, and vest, he left the training area with his sheathed sword and dagger latched to his belt.

As he walked back towards Vernik Palace, Luka's legs were already beginning to stiffen. Walking tomorrow would be uncomfortable, but tonight, Luka still felt light on his feet, the victory an hour earlier carrying him at an excited pace.

Two guards in crimson acknowledged Luka as he reached the western entrance. Each guard swung open one side of the large black door, letting him inside. From there, he walked through the candle-lit hallway until he found his family's secondary dining room, the buzzing of dozens of conversations seeping through the doorway.

Nearly eighty people were gathered in the dining hall. The bar area sat in the back corner of the room. Shelves of fine wines, rare whiskeys, and other expensive spirits loomed over the counter. Several servants stationed behind the bar attentively met the needs of the patrons.

Luka's father, King Var, stood against the marble counter, amidst a lively discussion with Xander, Luka's elder brother and heir to the throne. Both had hair of a darker shade of blonde than Luka. Beside them, though not as engaged, was General Warwick, commander of the Vernik Army.

Luka entered the room, heading straight towards them. It took only a moment for the partygoers to notice him, rowdy applause erupting as he walked by. He smiled proudly and held up his chalice for the room to see, which only enthused the crowd more.

"It looks like the mighty champion has arrived," Xander exclaimed as Luka approached. "I heard it was a rather quick unhorsing," he added.

"You *heard* it was a quick unhorsing?" Luka asked, surprise in his voice.

King Var and the General let the floor suck their eyes in, but Xander held his gaze. "Yes. I am sorry, Luka. I would have come, but we had a meeting. Believe me, I certainly strategized how to get out of it. It was rather dull."

General Warwick opened his mouth to reprimand Xander for referring to the meeting as "dull," but Var jumped in first.

"Yes, Luka," his father said. "It was no pleasure to hold this meeting during the finals today, but as you know, Lady Melina was in the city, and she had to leave well before sundown. It was my duty to attend, but it pains me desperately to have missed your third tournament win in a row."

"My *fourth* win in a row, Father," Luka corrected quietly.

"That's right! Four consecutive championships. That is truly a most impressive feat! You should be very proud." Var heartily patted Luka on the back, but Luka's wide smile had disappeared.

"Well done indeed, Luka," General Warwick added. "I also would have much liked to have seen your victory today, though I am at least pleased to have witnessed your hard-fought win in the semi-finals."

"Were you in the meeting too?" Luka asked.

"I was," Warwick acknowledged, turning to the bar. "Barman! More whiskey!"

"Should I have been at this meeting?" Luka asked Var and Xander. "I am a prince, after all. Shouldn't my duties there come first?"

"No, Luka. You had a tournament. And trust me, the meeting was a bloody waste," Xander said.

"Xander," Var scolded shortly.

"Anyway, show us your prize," Xander said, ignoring his father and reaching out for the chalice. Luka reluctantly relinquished it. "Looks magnificent, but wasn't last year's gold and much bigger?"

"So, did anyone see my win today?" Luka asked, unconcerned with Xander's evaluation of the trophy.

"Your mother did. She met with Lady Melina separately in the morning and saw the entire match," Var answered, pointing behind Luka. The prince turned to see his mother Vanessa, Queen of Estravia, entertaining a large circle of wealthy citizens with her usual, graceful command. Beside her was Princess Amelia, Xander's wife. Vanessa, noticing Var's gesture, excused herself and approached Luka, with Amelia following.

Vanessa wrapped Luka in her arms when she reached him. "I am so proud of you," she said. "What an incredible win today. You were absolutely magnificent in the arena. I hardly even felt scared or nervous for you this time." Luka felt the urge to smile coming back.

"Congratulations, Luka," Amelia echoed. With her light hair, she already looked like a Vernik—only lacking in the height that the rest of them had.

Luka had assumed that Amelia had been with Xander during the match and thus had not witnessed it. Before he could ask her as much, Xander shoved Luka's chalice, now brimming with red wine, in his face. "Drink up, Luka."

"Xander!" Luka exclaimed, "That's a trophy, not a bloody drinking cup!"

"Oh, be merry, Luka. Chalices are for drinking, you know that. Besides, you must have a hundred of these by this point."

Luka rolled his eyes but ultimately relented, sharing a drink with his family. "To Luka!" Xander cheered, their glasses clinking together.

The merriment seemed short-lived after that, with Vanessa excusing herself for bed and Var following. Xander left with Amelia to mingle with the other esteemed guests but promised to return.

Only General Warwick remained, who had a few sips of whiskey remaining in his glass.

"Luka, I hope that you have done your reading for tomorrow," Warwick said with a subtle grin beneath his distinct mustache. "You may be a champion, but that does not excuse you from your assignments."

"Do not fret, General Rory. I completed the reading yesterday, well in advance of my match. I look forward to discussing it with you tomorrow."

"Very good. Historical military knowledge is critical of any high-ranking member of our army, especially for a Vice General. You know—"

A commotion interrupted the general mid-sentence. A large man with a thick white beard burst into the room, accidentally knocking over a guest and her wine. The cause of the disruption was Admiral Mormar, the leader of the Vernik Navy. Mormar hurriedly helped the woman back to her feet and rushed over to General Warwick. More than half the eyes in the room followed him as he did so.

Luka could see concern on the admiral's sea-wrinkled face before he leaned in to whisper in Warwick's ear. From his proximity, he could make out the words, "message," "from the north," and "potential threat," but nothing else. When he finished explaining, the admiral handed a letter to the general.

"Admiral," Warwick said aloud. "You must go now and discuss this with no one. Not a soul. I shall inform the King at once."

The admiral consented and bid farewell to Warwick. He turned briefly to Luka and said, "My Prince, congratulations to you." He rushed out of the room before Luka could thank him.

The general guardedly read over the letter in his hands, ensuring no one could see over his shoulder. When he was finished, he folded and pocketed the letter. "Luka, I must be going. I will see you tomorrow."

"What does that message say?" Luka asked.

"Nothing good."

Chapter 3
A Difficult Lesson

The following day, Luka traversed across one of the palace's highest balconies, hundreds of feet above the ground. From this perspective, it felt as though the whole world was in view. To the south lay the vast blue ocean. To the north, the rocky hills beyond the city walls. Vulture Road, the main corridor through the center of the country, faded out into the northern horizon. A few travelers and merchant caravans were visible as specks on the ground, coming and going to and from the capital city.

Just above Luka, at the pinnacle of the palace, the flags of both Estravia and The Royal House Vernik fluttered in the morning breeze. The nation flag bore a golden crown on a sable background surrounded by thirty-three stars. Each star represented one of the city-states that King Okupi Vernik, the Uniter, brought together nine hundred years ago. Beneath it flew the grand flag of the Vernik Family, adorned with a majestic golden phoenix, its wings spread proudly over a crimson background.

The coastal breeze died away as Luka returned inside and down a stairway. He followed it five floors to the ground, his legs stiff from the previous day's tournament. At ground level, he walked past the gardens towards the western wing of the palace. In the early summer, the flowers were in bloom and full of color.

Several paces beyond the gardens, Luka arrived at the western wing, where the general's office was located. He knocked three times on the general's door when he arrived. "It's Luka."

"One minute!" the general called back from inside the room. After a moment, he said, "Come in!"

General Rory Warwick had led the Vernik Army for decades. He was a longtime friend of the king and seemed to possess infinite knowledge in military matters. The general was beginning to gray and wrinkle, but he still had formidable skill in swordsmanship and combat. His skin hued slightly olive, and a thick mustache sat on top of his lip with prominence.

"Good morning, General Rory," said Luka upon entering.

"Welcome, Luka. I'll just need one more moment, and then I'll be ready." The general was busy steeping a cup of tea, the steam rising all the way to the ceiling. When the flavor had been distilled to his satisfaction, he set it down on his desk. He then fiddled with a few items in his drawers and produced some parchment and paper.

As he got his materials ready, Warwick asked, "How are you feeling after your big victory yesterday?"

Luka shrugged. "I lost my footing at one point in the duel. I was off balance for a good bit."

"That is no matter. I'm sure it will not be remembered by anyone save for yourself."

"I'm sure you're right," Luka said, the general not detecting the bite in his words.

"Now let's see. Where did we leave off in our last lesson?" Warwick said, now flipping through Luka's book.

"The Siege of Seveka, General," Luka answered.

"Yes, that is right. Our final lesson on Zachary the Fierce, otherwise known as 'Prince Luka's favorite.' Let's begin. Now tell me, Luka. From your reading, what were some of the major flaws in Zachary's siege approach?"

"I think his biggest problem was trying to sneak into the city via—" Luka began.

"Slow down, Luka. You are getting at what is ultimately the biggest issue here, which was Zachary's impatience and his foolish attempt to break into the city. But you are also getting a little bit too far ahead. I am referring to the siege itself. There were a number of flaws as he tried to hold the city. Can you name them?"

"Yes, General. Zachary began the siege too early. After his eight previous consecutive victories or 'liberations,' his men were tired. They were low on supplies and low on energy. They could have taken a day to rest without yielding any additional advantages to their target."

"Most astute. Aggression is a positive trait in a military leader, but not if it pushes forces past the point of exhaustion. Or if it pushes the strategy beyond a reasonable level of risk." The general paused for a moment. He brought his tea close to his face, the steam enveloping him. He put his lips to the cup and took a miniscule sip.

"That is still too hot for me," General Warwick said to himself. He put the tea back down on the table.

"General, what was in that message last night?" Luka asked, taking advantage of the break in the lesson. "The one Mormar gave you?"

Warwick's mustache seemed to twitch, his demeanor souring. "It really is nothing of concern, Luka. Let's get back to the lesson."

"It most certainly seemed like something of concern. You and Mormar looked *gravely* concerned."

"Right now, you are not to be privy to that information. Your father and I do not want the contents of that message to be spread beyond the few who already know."

"Does Xander know?" Luka asked. The question was met with silence.

"So, you can tell Xander, but not me?" Luka said.

The general's reply came muffled through his gritted teeth. "Your *father* told Xander. Against my council."

"Does this message involve military concerns?" Luka asked.

"More or less."

"Then I should know! I am Vice General!"

"Enough!" Warwick said, matching Luka in tone and force. "You are nineteen! You have so much still to learn! You do not yet need to know all kingdom information."

Luka sank back into his chair, feeling both like a chastised puppy and a provoked hornet. The room fell into a tense silence.

Appearing to notice the emotional wound in his pupil, Warwick said, "I admire your ambition and your passion, Luka. When I was your age, I would have reacted in an identical manner. But I am far older now, gifted with the wisdom those years have bestowed upon me. I need order to be effective in my position. And I can't have order without controlling the flow of information. If you are to follow in my footsteps, you will learn that for yourself one day. Consider that a difficult lesson. But an important one, no less."

Luka nodded and softened. He leaned forward, but not all the way back to the attentive pose he had begun the lesson with.

Warwick resumed his discussion of Zachary, and the rest of the lecture dragged by. Luka now kept his participation to a minimum as Warwick recounted the tactical blunders that Zachary had made trying to conquer Seveka, including trying to sneak into the city through a narrow opening. Those mistakes led to the warrior's capture and execution.

"You can have a lifetime of successes, but one failure can wipe it all away," Warwick said.

"Would you really call Zachary a failure?" Luka asked.

"While his efforts did spark the end of slavery in this country, he never lived to see the free world he helped create," Warwick said.

Knocking interrupted the discussion. "Who is it?" Warwick asked.

"It's Admiral Mormar, sir," came the voice calling through the door. Warwick beckoned him in.

"General, do you think this is a good time to discuss, um, the latest correspondence?" Mormar asked hesitantly.

The general seemed annoyed but said, "Yes, yes, just one second. Luka, I think this is an opportune spot to end today's lesson. You are dismissed. Go and enjoy the rest of your afternoon."

Luka muttered a reluctant "okay" and got up to leave. He resisted the urge to slam the door behind him.

He maintained a brisk pace back to his quarters, keeping his head down and clutching his books tightly against his chest.

As he was walking past the gardens, he spotted Priestess Teya from the corner of his eye. She wore her usual white robe with sable accents, with the Divine Circle of Sila the Creator and his Agents affixed above her heart. The priestess led all religious matters both for Vernikport and for the Vernik family privately.

Teya was tall, able to meet Luka at eye level when she stood, but now she crouched down, tending to a rare young phoenix. The creature's appearance resembled the bird on the flag of House Vernik, but instead of its gold and crimson feathers stretched out in flight, the bird held its wings in timidly on the ground.

Luka tried his best to continue his pace, but she called out to him. "My Prince, you appear to be in a hurry."

He stopped his fast walking and replied, "A little bit. I just have some letters to attend to." As he spoke to the priestess, he noticed that the bird's wing appeared to be injured, its feathers in disarray.

"This is Naka, correct?" Luka asked. "What happened to her? She appears to be hurt."

"You are correct on both accounts, Luka. Last evening, a wake of vultures attacked Naka. It is most unusual and concerning."

"I didn't think vultures attacked other birds," Luka said.

"They usually don't. They typically only bother with what is already dead," Teya said. "It will take poor Naka time to regain her confidence as well as her self-healing abilities. It could be many days before she takes flight again."

Luka approached and put his books down. He knelt next to the phoenix and reached his hand out gently to pet the bird. The bird reacted with a threatened peck, causing Luka to retreat.

"Naka is still very scared," the priestess said. "I expect her to need time before she can welcome much attention again."

Luka nodded and stood up. "I am very sorry to hear that this happened. I hope Naka is able to recover soon."

"Thank you for your words. I pray that everything will be okay. Be well, Luka." Her words were soft and comforting, and she looked into his eyes deeply, seeming to scan him on an inner level.

By the time Luka reached his bedroom, he had largely forgotten his encounter with the priestess, finding himself caught up in wondering what the contents of that mysterious letter held. When he entered the room, he slammed the door shut behind him. The noise would carry far, but he cared little.

The young prince's quarters were spacious and majestic, featuring several chairs, a work corner, a small armory, and his multi-story trophy shelves. The chalice from the previous night stood proudly now as the centerpiece.

Luka set down his books and sighed as he sat. A stack of letters loomed on his desk. On Warwick's behalf, he was to read each one and draft replies as necessary. Some letters would require escalation to the general, but typically, the letters were administrative in nature.

He had started on one such message to be addressed to Officer Dunjak, who led a unit stationed in the Shredry Forest. They had not heard a status update from that unit in a long time. Officer Dunjak would face disciplinary measures if he did not have a valid reason for the absence of reports.

As Luka put a quill to the parchment, Queen Vanessa entered without knocking. "Luka, is everything alright? I heard a door slam."

Luka turned around to face his mother. She stood tall with a confident posture, wearing a floor-length golden dress that nearly matched the color of her long, wavy hair. "Yes, Mother," Luka replied, knowing that concealing the truth would be futile. "I slammed the door in frustration. I know that I should not have."

The queen approached her son and put her arm on his shoulder. "What frustrates you?"

Luka hesitated for a moment, debating whether to fabricate an explanation, but ultimately decided against it. "Admiral Mormar and General Rory received some strange message, and it seemed to worry them. When I asked General Rory about it, he refused to share any details, despite the fact that I should be informed about such matters."

"Believe me, Luka, I know that is terribly frustrating. I understand what it's like to feel excluded from information. I've been around your father and Rory longer than you."

Luka shrugged. "Yes, but I am the Vice General. I need to know what is going on in this kingdom's military affairs, yet I am almost always kept in the dark. I must learn things from Xander, if I am lucky."

"Luka, there is a chance that this is nothing serious. I've seen the general and the admiral overreact many times before. I would not trouble yourself with this, especially today," Vanessa said.

Luka shrugged again, but this time, his gesture was more sincere.

"Your performance in the tournament was fantastic, by the way," Vanessa said, strategically shifting the subject. "You are so skilled that I know you can defeat anyone in the kingdom."

"Thank you, Mother," Luka replied. "The semi-finals actually presented more challenge for me. I know I have room for improvement from that match. I plan on training with Xander in the next day or so, with the goal of focusing on a few week areas."

"You are far too harsh with yourself, Luka. At least revel in your victory and recover from your wounds first," Vanessa suggested.

"If I don't continue to improve, then I will only be faced with more wounds in the future," Luka answered. He glanced back down at the letter in front of him and then back at Vanessa.

"Mother," Luka continued, looking her deep in her eyes, "Why didn't anyone else come see my match? I know I've won so many, but this was still the Vernikport Cup."

"Luka, you know that they had to be courteous to Lady Melina and her people. Believe me, they all wanted to be there."

"I believe that *you* wanted to be there. You made certain that you went."

"That's right. And I am very happy I did so."

"Why couldn't father have done the same thing?"

"Your father constantly has his attention pulled from every end of Estravia. I selfishly want more of him to myself as well, but he has duties to uphold. It's not easy being a king, Luka."

Luka smiled ironically. "I guess I will never know."

"And maybe that's what is best for you. Besides, you are already Vice General and one of the fiercest warriors in the land."

"Neither of which seem very important in anyone's eyes."

"You mustn't say that, Luka. You are so important to all of us. We love you." Vanessa planted a motherly kiss on his forehead and then gestured towards the doorway. "I must go speak to Priestess Teya now. We have arrangements to make for the High Summer Ceremony."

They bid farewell, and Luka turned back to his letter.

Out of boredom and frustration, Luka rushed to finish his message. There was likely nothing noteworthy regarding the status of Dunjak's patrol anyway. He sealed the note and deposited it, thinking little of the fate of Officer Dunjak and his men deep in the Shredry Forest.

Chapter 4
The Streets of Vernikport

The two duelists circled each other amidst a temporary pause in their intense match. They both breathed heavily and audibly, their eyes fixed on one another. The brief intermission suddenly ended, and they engaged again, their wooden training swords connecting high with a loud wooden "thock."

They traded blows at a blistering pace, but they both found only a parry and a counterattack in response to each move. After another intense bout, the duelists separated again.

Circling the boundaries of the old Vernik training arena, Luka and Xander stared at each other with intense focus. Sweat ran down their backs from sparring for so long. A small crowd of young boys looked on at the two princes from beyond the outskirts of the grounds. They knew that to witness this was a supreme treat. They eagerly wondered if this would be the moment the elder brother finally bested the younger—a feat that hadn't happened in years.

Xander moved in this time, unleashing a flurry of blows in succession. Luka was prepared for each one, not yielding so much as an inch of ground.

Towards the end of Xander's sequence, Luka jumped ahead of one of Xander's attacks and delivered a stab to his chest plate. Xander's next strike came in wide as a result, and Luka parried it back hard. The younger brother wasted no further time and struck again, this time connecting with the elder's hand.

Xander dropped his training weapon but immediately dove to the ground, ducking an overhead strike as he did so. He quickly recovered his sword and thrusted upwards with it. The wooden blade found Luka's chest plate, pushing the younger brother back forcefully. Xander used this momentum to regain his footing.

With the ground now safely back under his feet, Xander resumed the offensive. He drove Luka backwards towards the edge of the arena. If he could push his younger brother beyond the white perimeter, victory would be his. He gritted his teeth and pressed harder.

Luka caught on to the strategy and glided backwards, allowing his brother to push him towards the edge. Then, with the end seemingly at hand, he parried Xander hard and immediately spun around in the other direction. In one motion, he slashed downwards, reaching the backside of Xander's calf. That leg gave in, bringing Xander down to only one knee.

The elder brother was powerless to resist Luka's next two blows, which brought him all the way to the ground.

The tip of a wooden blade now hovered only inches from his face. "You bloody ratwagger," Xander said.

Luka had won again. The boys in the audience applauded vigorously. After a moment, Luka extended his arm and lifted Xander off the ground.

*****

"One of these days, I'll unravel how I can best you," Xander said, as they removed their training armor together after the match. "I used to be able to all the time."

"Yes, but that was when you were far taller than me. Now that we are the same height, you have no advantage," Luka responded.

"Maybe that's the trick," Xander said, donning his crimson jacket. "I just need to get much larger than you again."

The two brothers put away the rest of their equipment in thick wooden cases. "Are you still planning to join me on my daily patrol?" Xander asked.

Luka nodded. "Are you planning to tell me what has been going on since Admiral Mormar received that message?" Luka asked.

"Yes, but not here. I'll tell you when no one is in earshot," Xander said, glancing around. They departed the training yard, cobblestone meeting the underside of their boots as they walked towards the city sprawl. Two guards tailed them for safety, but they kept a distance away, letting Xander feel comfortable enough to talk.

"I had to hear all of this from Father, but even he could scarcely speak of it. And obviously, do not tell a soul that I was the one to divulge this to you," Xander began. He waited for Luka's nod to continue. "The message that Admiral Mormar received was from Lady Dija in Exeter. One of her scout patrols spotted a small insurgent force led by the Zlikrej brothers."

"Who did you say?" Luka asked.

"The Zlikrej brothers. Do you remember hearing about Lord Diocretin, the man that Father had executed many years ago?"

"Yes, that's right. Father does detest speaking of that," Luka said.

Xander nodded. "Well, the letter mentioned that his three sons, Privus, Drugi, and Omarius, who were formerly in exile, have raised a small army and are marching from the Avium Wasteland through the Ekron mountains."

"And they're headed for us?" Luka asked.

Xander shrugged. "Apparently so. Presuming that all of this is true."

Luka thought for a moment, visualizing the territory this theoretical enemy was traversing, "Through the Ekrons, you say? Won't the dragons get them?" he asked.

"I had wondered the same thing. I suppose they've managed to avoid the dragons so far," Xander said casually.

"I must say you don't seem nearly as concerned as Admiral Mormar and General Rory do."

"It's not that I'm unconcerned," Xander remarked. "It's just that this information is so preliminary, yet everyone is acting like a bee-stung Werdal over it. And even if the reports should prove true, we're not dealing with an all-out war here. The letter described a few thousand men at most—a small issue that could be handled by the lords in the north. Admiral Mormar, on the other hand, wants to wage a nationwide military campaign around this. Bloody lunacy."

Luka absorbed this, now feeling free of a heavy weight, despite the potentially treacherous situation he had just learned of. To him, it was a far better alternative than being kept in the dark.

They departed from the northeastern corner of Vernikport, a quieter area of the city. Blacksmiths were the primary retailers in this location, given the proximity to the training arena. "I must stop at a smith later on this patrol. I am in need of a new dagger," Xander said. "But obviously, we will be going to one of the superior ones downtown."

"That's wise," Luka said. "The wares over here are always poor."

The princes soon reached Andeo Square—the heart of the city. A golden statue of King Okupi stood triumphantly in the center. The square was broad and spacious, designed to accommodate large gatherings. Sitting adjacent to the southern gates of Vernik Palace, it was often a place where King Var would address his citizens. The other edges of the square were lined with shops on the ground floor, with high-end apartments sitting above.

The two princes walked through the light morning crowds of people that greeted and bowed to them, past the statue of King Okupi, and then down Glavin Street, which served as the main commercial artery of the city. It led from Vernik Palace all the way out to the ports and the sea, with a plethora of shops lining each side of the road. The street was almost perfectly straight—nothing obstructed the view of the ocean on one end or Vernik Palace on the other.

In the midst of Glavin Street, Xander waved and smiled at dozens of people. Luka followed suit. The crowds grew steadily as they progressed further down. "How can you get your patrols done every day with all of this?" asked Luka.

"Don't act as if you don't love this, Brother," Xander chided. "Don't worry, it gets easier down the side streets."

About halfway down the street, Xander motioned to a limestone-colored building coming up on their right. A rectangular sign with an anvil in the center hung over the entrance. Xander signaled to the guards to wait outside while the brothers entered.

The air in the shop was thick with the nostalgic scents of metal, fire, and sweat. The sensation pulled him back to childhood visits with his father—especially the fondest ones, when he'd leave with a new toy sword or dagger to brandish proudly.

A young lady, likely about a year apart in age from Luka, nearly gasped when she saw the two princes. "My.. My Lords.... G- good day to you both..."

Xander smiled warmly and said, "Good day to you, young madam. Is your father around? I was hoping he could show me some of the daggers in his stock."

The girl stammered more before replying, "Y-yes, he is just back in the forge. I will get him at once."

Luka eyed her as she rushed off to fetch her father, her beauty evident. He found himself wondering if she would be worth the risk of pursuit, despite the scandal it would cause if Luka was seen courting someone so lowborn. It was a foolish idea, he decided, so he let the thought pass.

She returned shortly with her father, a seasoned blacksmith, donned in short-sleeved, sweat-drenched clothing. "My Lords, it is an utmost privilege to see you both today. My daughter tells me you wanted a look at my dagger selection?"

"That is correct," Xander replied.

"I am most certain that I can be of service, My Lord!" He disappeared into the back, the sound of jingling keys and clinking locks audible from that area. He returned soon after with a bundle of daggers wrapped in cloth.

"Got my finest wares right here," he said, laying the cloth open on a wooden countertop. Three long knives glistened against the fabric backdrop.

The first dagger glimmered the brightest, though it had the shortest blade protruding from its golden hilt. The second weapon was plain, other than a jagged section at the edge of the blade. The third dagger had a smooth, long blade with a slightly curved crimson handle. Elegant wings were subtly molded into the weapon's hilt.

Luka's eyes were immediately drawn to the golden dagger—the most opulent of the three. He reached out to touch it, but Xander's hand shot down and picked it up first. The elder Vernik lifted it into the air delicately and practiced a few slow, imaginary cuts with it. When he was done, he did the same with the other two weapons.

Xander held the winged dagger for the longest, examining it multiple times. "I will take this one," he announced as his evaluation concluded.

"That's the worst one," Luka mocked. "How can you pass up the gold one?"

"It is the *best* one. Feel it."

Luka turned the winged dagger in his hand gently but then promptly laid it down for the golden one, admiring its glamor. "Xander, that is absurd. It matters little what difference in functionality you think you've uncovered. Get the grandest weapon. Daggers see little use in real battle, anyway."

"Your brother is right, My Lord," interjected the blacksmith, "That is the highest quality dagger in our inventory. Certainly, fit for a prince. In fact, I have had inquiries all the way from Marlinus about it."

"And you're not saying this because it also happens to be the most expensive one?" Xander said.

The blacksmith hesitated for a second and then said, "Given its stature as the finest of the three, it does in fact bear the highest price."

"I knew it," Xander said, folding his arms across his chest.

The blacksmith awkwardly grinned at Xander and Luka, and a brief silence hung between them. "How much for this one?" asked Xander after a while, picking up the weapon he liked best.

"That one is two hundred and sixty Novaks, My Lord," answered the blacksmith.

Without looking, Xander pulled out a handful of coins from his pouch. A small pile of gold, silver, and bronze formed in his left palm. He sorted through his pile with his right index finger and placed two gold coins on the table in front of him. Six silver pieces joined the gold ones and completed the payment.

"Excellent! It is an utmost honor to do business with The Heir to the Throne of Estravia!" exclaimed the blacksmith. His joy did not stop there as Luka began fiddling with his money pouch as well.

"Since the golden dagger is now officially available, I think I must buy it," he said. "It would be a shame to see it left behind while my brother takes a lesser weapon. How much for it?"

"The gold one is four hundred and fifteen Novaks, My Lord," answered the blacksmith, hardly containing his excitement.

Xander rolled his eyes, while Luka began counting out gold pieces. He placed four gold coins on the table, then one silver piece, followed by five copper pieces.

"Are you really going to buy that? Don't you already have two dozen daggers?" said Xander.

"No, I have *less* than two dozen daggers." Xander rolled his eyes again.

The two princes wrapped up their business in the shop and departed. Luka immediately unsheathed his new dagger so he could admire it. "I can't believe you passed this up, Brother," he repeated.

"I can't believe you overpaid for a weapon just because it was shiny."

"Look at it. It's fit for a prince. Even a king!" said Luka.

"And my dagger is fit for combat, which is the whole bloody point of it."

Luka grunted. "Don't be so dull, Xander. A good warrior should be able to do battle with any dagger he pleases."

The two brothers continued their path down Glavin Street, which hosted a larger crowd than before. Horse-driven carriages, merchants, and pedestrians filled the streets, leaving little open space. More of the outdoor foot stands and small markets had opened, the smells of fresh bread, vegetables, and spices wafting in the air.

As Luka breathed all of this in, he couldn't help but think of his father's words. *We are living in grand times*—something The King of Estravia said whenever he would hear his children complain.

Though his sons grew sick of hearing it, King Var's favorite phrase contained only truth. Estravia's economy was growing and prospering, even well beyond the wealthy capital city of Vernikport. The nation boasted its longest run of peace, with nearly two hundred years since the last real war. During that time, there had only been infrequent rebellions or small conflicts, all of which were resolved swiftly and relatively painlessly.

The patrol led the princes to Vernikport Temple, the second largest structure in the city, after Vernik Palace. Citizens filed into the pearl-colored stone building for the daily ceremony through one of the three golden arched doors evenly spaced below the spectacular facade. Above that, the central spire rose hundreds of feet in the air, surrounded by twelve smaller spires, representing the all-mighty Sila, the creator, and his twelve divine agents. Each agent was responsible for a different aspect of reality, from the harvest, which the agent Usjvei oversaw, to the underworld, which the agent Cuvar oversaw.

The underworld had formerly been the domain of Vragr, until he was expelled and cast out by Sila for attempting to take control of reality itself.

"It looks like Priestess Teya did not lead the public ceremonies today," Xander commented as they turned down an alley that ran off Glavin Street and alongside the tremendous temple.

"I saw her tending to Naka the Phoenix the other day," Luka said. "Apparently, she was attacked by vultures."

Xander nodded. "Teya is resorting to using her own healing powers on the bird, since Naka is unable to heal herself right now."

"Do you really believe she has actual healing powers?" Luka asked.

"I *know* she has those abilities, Luka. I've seen wounded people make startling recoveries that could only have been conceivable with the aid of magic."

"Yes, but medicine does those things as well, Xander."

"Luka, I can't believe we are having this discussion yet again. Are you seriously telling me you do not believe in magic?" Xander asked.

"Of course, I *believe* in it. I know what the history books say, at least. I just don't think all that bloody much of it. I ascribe value to swords and the warriors who wield them. I can't say the same thing about magic and wizards."

"Luka, one wizard can vanquish an entire squadron of great warriors. No blade can defend against a burst of fire."

Luka scoffed. "If wizards have so much power, then why isn't a wizard on the throne right now? Why isn't someone trying to take over this country with their abilities to summon fire?"

"We are fortunate that wizards are seldom born, and the ones who are alive today have no desire for chaos or war," Xander replied. "Not since the Pre-Unification ages, at least."

"I find that to be unlikely. If there are wizards out there, then I can't imagine them wanting to do anything other than conquer," Luka replied.

"I know of one such example of a wizard who lacks that desire. I suggest you pay a visit to the Magic Tavern in Jetsac. The wizard who performs there will change your mind about a great deal of things."

"I'm sure this wizard's 'performance' will rival that of our court jesters," Luka said.

Xander rolled his eyes and kept moving along. The rest of the patrol looped around the narrow side streets and alleys of the capital city. Xander would occasionally stop to peek into a shop here or there, or to greet some of the passersby, but otherwise, they made quick pace.

At last, they emerged from the city's southeastern outskirts, passing a cluster of palm trees. The urban sprawl gave way to a rugged shoreline, where patches of white sand dotted the rocky beach. The secluded stretch was devoid of any other visitors. Before them, the calm, crystal-blue water gently lapped at the shore, its surface glistening in the sunlight.

"Every day I end my patrol here," said Xander. "A fitting and peaceful conclusion to my duty."

Luka and Xander both stood silently while the waves lightly crashed against the rocks. A large merchant ship appeared on the horizon after some time. It looked like a black bird from far away but gradually grew in size as it drew nearer.

The ship had taken its shape and was fast approaching when Xander sighed and said, "I can't stay much longer. Today's patrol is not my only duty. I have a council meeting later this afternoon."

"The War Council?" Luka asked.

"Indeed. I know you would like to be on it. I am still trying to convince Father and Rory to put you on."

"Don't waste your effort," Luka replied, looking into the distance.

Chapter 5
The War Room

Submerged in an early morning grogginess, Luka sifted through a pile of letters, most of which were military updates addressed to General Warwick. Luka remained unstimulated performing his mentor's administrative work.

He was through nearly a dozen mundane responses when one message made his eyes nearly burst from his sockets. The letter was addressed directly to him. The sender was Serena Tomkins, the daughter of the Lord of Privagrad and someone Luka had spent much time with in their teens.

Luka tore into the note.

Dearest Luka,

I wanted to send my congratulations on your recent tournament win. I regret that I missed it, but I heard the crowd had the privilege of witnessing your usual spectacular performance. Of course, you were fortunate that I was not there to compete against you!

I hope that everything is well with you, beyond just your swordsmanship endeavors. Please give my regards to the King and Queen as well as Xander and Amelia. I hope that we will all have a chance to see each other soon, but I do hope you at least know you will all be invited to my wedding next spring. It will be so beautiful- I really hope you can make it. I know that Brooks is just dying to meet you as well. I've spoken much about you (not too much, don't you worry).

One more exciting thing to tell you about is that we have commissioned a historian to look at Strujaza in a few weeks' time. We're going to record stories about our family sword and how it ties back to the age of The Unification. I know you love that blade. I'll try to have a copy of the work made for you when it's completed. I thought of you when I heard about this, as I often do.

Wishing you the best and hope to see you soon.

> *Sincerely,*
>
> *Serena*

A smile appeared across Luka's lips, but it faded as he reflected on Serena's upcoming wedding. In time, Luka would need a princess at his side, but it was evidently not the will of Sila or his agents for it to be Serena.

Setting his other letters aside, Luka eagerly picked up his quill and began drafting a response on fresh parchment. He was midway through his reply when a familiar voice suddenly broke his concentration.

"Oi, Luka." The two words made his heart leap from his chest.

Xander stood in Luka's doorway, his face bearing a smirk. "What's that letter you're writing there?" he asked.

"Nothing of interest, Xander. Just doing my job," Luka replied hastily. "You are aware that it is common courtesy to knock before you enter someone's room, right?"

"Yes, well, I'm sure you'll forgive me rather quickly."

"Shouldn't you be at the council meeting?"

"Not yet," Xander replied. "It's been delayed. And that's why I am here. You're coming with me."

"What?" Luka replied, stunned and waiting for Xander's cruel joke to play itself out.

Xander just stood there smiling.

"You can't just bring me along with you..." Luka added, beginning to realize this was no jest.

"Don't worry, I obtained father's permission."

"You did?" Xander nodded and ushered him along. Luka enthusiastically obliged, putting his half-written response to Serena securely in his desk drawer.

The council room was a dimly lit and secure chamber in the western wing of the palace. The mood was stern when Luka and Xander arrived. King Var and General Warwick were not yet present, but the rest of the advisors were. Admiral Mormar tapped nervously with one hand while writing notes down with the other. Confusion twisted across his face when he looked up to see Luka enter but otherwise remained silent.

Xander walked past Mormar and took his seat next to Sir Jesec, the oldest knight in The Royal Guard. He pointed to the chair to his immediate right, which Luka took. Sir Jesec acknowledged Luka with a subtle nod as he sat.

The other side featured two empty chairs as well as Lieutenant Alexander—the third highest ranking member of the military—Lieutenant Baciti—one ranking below Alexander—and Milo Pametan, the bald and bookish Minister of Finance. They eyed Luka suspiciously but said nothing beyond a simple greeting.

Luka sat still while Xander leaned back in his chair, twirled a quill, and cracked jokes with Sir Jesec to pass the time. The tension in the room died mercifully when King Var entered the room, General Warwick following close behind. All rose to their feet for their king.

"You all may be seated," Var said. His eyes met Luka's briefly, offering a small smile before beginning his remarks.

"I hope this afternoon finds you all well. I take no pleasure in assembling you all on such a pleasant day, but the circumstances have forced my hand.

"Before we get started, I would like everyone to welcome my youngest son, Prince Luka. He is joining us for his first War Council meeting. He will also be a permanent part of this council going forward."

The men around the table politely clapped for Luka. Outwardly, he tried to remain stoic and calm. Inwardly, he was beaming.

"Rory, please begin," King Var said, after the applause had died down.

The general cleared his throat, everyone's attention immediately shifting to him. "We have more news of the Zlikrej invasion. Another one of Lady Dija's scouts spotted a force of about one to two thousand men, several leagues southeast of Exeter. This is the second report of its kind, confirming they are drawing closer. We must act swiftly to address this threat."

General Warwick then rose and motioned to the large map of Estravia that hung on the wall. He stuck two bat-like emblems onto the map with hot wax on two spots just below the eastern side of the Ekron Mountains. The emblems were Mithacors, the house symbol of the Zlikrej Family. They were large black-winged creatures that inhabited the lands near Canyon City.

"These are the two locations where sightings have been reported, only four days apart. This shows a rapid southern progress," Warwick said.

"What route do you think they will take from here? Anticipating this will be paramount to how we approach this, and how many resources we will require," Minister Pametan chimed in.

"I think we can rule out any path along Vulture Road. They would face too much opposition in that part of the country. They are likely planning to take a far less direct path," said Sir Jesec.

"That narrows it down quite a bit," said Xander.

Sir Jesec gave a small chortle at the prince's humor. The old knight was difficult to offend.

A handful of others at the table attempted to chime in after that, but the general pressed on. "We do not know their exact trajectory, but we can make assumptions. It is likely they will avoid the coast, as that is too indirect and is more likely to lead to resistance from eastern cities. As Sir Jesec mentioned, that same principle applies to Vulture Road, so that leaves their route in between.

"My proposal is to send two battalions to block their path. One by land, the other by sea." The general then swapped his dagger for a wet quill and drew a path from Vernikport up to a point west of Eastport. He then took his quill back to Vernikport and drew a line around the sea all the way to Eastport again.

Admiral Mormar nodded vigorously throughout the general's proposal.

"How many soldiers do you suggest sending?" Xander asked.

"I would like to send twelve thousand in all. Ten thousand by foot and another two by sea."

"What? Twelve thousand? Is that a jest?"

"It is not a jest, Xander. It may be difficult for you to realize, but not everything in this kingdom is light-hearted," the general shot back.

Xander did not back down. "Twelve thousand men is outrageous. That's most, if not all, of the forces we have stationed around Vernikport."

"General," Pametan spoke up. "I do share Prince Xander's concerns. Twelve thousand does seem like a great deal. How did you arrive at that estimate?"

"I did exactly as Prince Xander said. I assumed we would deploy all of the men we have at our disposal here in Vernikport and the nearby regions. We can gather more as necessary," said the general. "If the reports are correct, and the Zlikrej force consists of at most two thousand men, then we will have strength in numbers. We should use that to our advantage. There is no need to be delicate with this."

"So, we plan to leave Vernikport completely defenseless, without any military resources?" Xander asked.

"Yes, Rory," Var said, "That does make me uncomfortable."

"It is something I have considered, and I agree that it is suboptimal—but it will be temporary, and the city will not be completely unguarded. We will leave a sufficient amount of defenses, perhaps two hundred infantrymen, to remain stationed here. I also have already made arrangements to request reinforcements from other cities to be deployed here. At worst, the city will have diminished defenses for perhaps a matter of a few weeks.

"What are we so worried about?" Mormar interjected. "We've had almost a century without a real conflict. We know exactly where the only possible threat is, and they're outside of Exeter right now. Let's go and get them!"

"You can never be too careful," Xander said. "But I'm comfortable with the defensive plan the general laid out. I'm still just not seeing a reason for the *offensive* plan. Not to this extent."

"I worry about creating a bit of a panic with a deployment of that size," said Sir Jesec.

"People won't panic. There is no harm in taking these actions," said Admiral Mormar.

"Tell that to Pametan, who is responsible for financing all of this," quipped Xander.

Pametan nodded, content to say nothing at first. But King Var looked directly at him and said, "Milo, what do you make of the cost of Rory's plan?"

"It will surely be expensive..." he began.

"Can we afford it?" asked King Var.

"Well, yes. I will likely have to draw on a loan to do so, however. We don't want to expend any of our reserves."

"Is this conflict worth the trouble of borrowing so much money?" Xander asked him.

Pametan sighed. "My judgment is by no means perfect, but I must agree with General Warwick. From a financial perspective, a drawn-out conflict, even on a small scale, shall end up being far more expensive than a swift resolution. If we believe these reports, then it is logical to be aggressive with this issue."

"Twelve thousand men is not aggressive—it's *excessive*," said Xander. "And need I remind everyone that we are basing this on only two unreliable scouting reports? Simply an absurd level of reactivity from all of you."

"May I see the reports?" asked Luka. His interjection surprised everyone, as he had not yet spoken. Lieutenant Alexander brought the original copies and laid them in front of Luka. The youngest member of the council read the reports while the others continued to bicker at the table. It was an odd feeling to finally lay eyes on the letter that he had originally been shielded from.

The reports, stamped with Lady Dija's official house seal of Exeter, expressed extreme concern, but more so for the rest of the country. Exeter, the most fortified city in Estravia, had never been conquered in its entire history. As such, they had scant need for armed services, employing a little over five hundred active soldiers in their guard and another five hundred or so in civilian reserves. They could do little against a Zlikrej force of equal or greater size, but the threat had little chance of ever breaching their walls in the first place.

Luka looked up to reorient himself to the conversation. Xander kept going. "We have two reports from only one city. That is all. Yet we're prepared to spend an exorbitant sum, deploy a massive number of troops, and throw everyone into the panic of war. All because of two reports. Two!"

"No one will panic," repeated Admiral Mormar.

Before Xander could fire back at Mormar, King Var spoke. The room quieted immediately. "We may only have two reports, Xander, but we must act swiftly if they are true. The Zlikrej are an old threat that you never knew. I put Lord Diocretin to death for committing unspeakable evils against his people. I had hoped any spirit of that would never again find its way to me. Unfortunately, it appears that I made the mistake of leaving his kin alive. And now they are back."

"I warned you that you should have killed them too," interjected Warwick.

"You did—and perhaps you were right after all—but I could not bring myself to. The eldest of them had not even reached a decade in age. Their youngest was an infant."

The general remained silent, and Var turned back to Xander. "But it is not too late. We must vanquish this threat before it grows further. If only you knew, Xander. If you knew the horrors their father was capable of... the things that I've seen... You would think differently."

Xander actually stopped arguing for a moment. He sat back in his chair, crossing his arms over his chest.

"I would like to put Rory's plan to a vote," said King Var. According to what Xander had told Luka, there were times when the king would rule unilaterally if the decision warranted it. When the king did not have his mind made up, he would request a vote from his council. Most decisions required five out of seven, or four out of six, if Var abstained. Many times, however, their father merely desired validation for decisions he had already made.

"All in favor of General Warwick's plan, say 'aye'," instructed Pametan.

All but Xander and Sir Jesec voted in the affirmative. Luka stayed silent on both the 'aye' and the 'nay' but did not think his vote counted anyway.

"Looks like the decision's been made. I have preparations to make now," said Admiral Mormar. He began to get his notes in order so he could leave.

"The decision has not been made," Var replied firmly. Mormar stopped in place, his eyes scrunched together in befuddlement.

"My youngest son has not voted yet," Var said. "Luka, what do you think of this?"

All eyes fell on Luka immediately. His heart began racing in turn. He turned his head sideways and locked eyes with Xander. Then he turned back to his father and said, "I vote 'Aye'. Send the men."

Chapter 6
The Flag of War

One week after the War Council made their decision, two servants were busy at work on the roof of Vernik Palace. Their efforts would be the first to mark the momentous day. The crown had invested considerable effort into ensuring the departure of thousands of soldiers would be seen as a celebration and not a cause for concern.

The flagsmen roped a new banner to fly just below the phoenix flag of the Verniks. The third flag was blood red as opposed to crimson, depicting a white sword in the center of the ring of thirty-three stars.

When they were done, they took a step back to admire their work. In the high seaside winds, the new flag of war waved just as proudly as the flags representing the Vernik family and the nation above it.

*****

Outside of Luka's bedroom, General Warwick froze nervously. He hovered his knuckles over the door and hesitated before finally knocking.

"Come in."

When the General entered, he found Luka in a flurry of activity, preparing his things for the long journey he believed he had ahead of him. At that very moment, he was organizing his daggers, deciding between an older black one and a newer, gleaming golden one.

"Good morning to you, Luka," Warwick said.

"Good morning to you as well, General. It is a fine day. I can feel a buzzing in the air."

"Yes, indeed. Sir Jesec was worried about creating a panic. As I predicted, those feelings were unfounded. Excitement is the only sentiment I can sense in the people. We've handled this well."

"The only thing that will be more exciting than this will be the celebrations and feasts when we return victorious from our expedition," Luka said.

Warwick was uncomfortable for a moment, meeting Luka's last comment with silence.

"What is it, General?" Luka said, looking up from his dagger collection.

Warwick took his time before answering. "Luka, there is something I must tell you... I fear that you will not like it."

"What?"

"I have decided that your talents will be best suited here, back in Vernikport, rather than alongside me on the campaign," he said at last.

"What on earth do you mean? I am coming with you for this."

"Luka, no, I am afraid you are not coming. I am truly sorry—I know how much you want to taste battle, but you must remain here. I have decided I do not want the responsibility of a young prince at my side."

"That's absurd," Luka said in a rising volume. "I am more capable than anyone else in that army. And I am not 'your responsibility.' I am the *Vice General*."

"You have no battle experience. No *real* battle experience, that is, and I am afraid that this is a far more serious matter than some, including your brother, are making it out to be."

"I *do* have battle experience," Luka shot back. "And anyway, how in Sila's wrath am I supposed to *get* experience if I am being excluded from one of the only 'real' battles of my lifetime?"

"Luka, I know, I know," Warwick said, putting his hands up defensively.

"This is ridiculous!" Luka stood up now and faced the general. "No one takes me seriously, just because I am the youngest brother. This Vice General position is a load of horseshit!" Luka exclaimed, slamming his fist on his desk.

The general sighed and tried to ease his mentee who was hot as an iron in the fire and was not cooling down. The two went on for a while with no resolution in sight.

"Luka, I know you are upset. Here is my promise to you then—I will make sure to bring you on the next battle of your lifetime, when you are older. For the time being, I will leave you in charge of the two hundred or so remaining Vernikport soldiers stationed in the city. You can lead their training sessions, run all meetings, and fulfill my other duties while I am gone. It's part of the reason I am leaving you behind.

"Being a leader of an entire army is not merely about battles and glory. It is about organization and patience. I know you have those qualities within you.

"The time for battles and glory will come one day for you, Luka. You may find that they are not what you dreamed they would be."

Warwick then turned his back and left the room, leaving Luka fuming behind him.

*****

Amelia soothed Xander, gently rubbing her fingers along his back. He had just finished his role in a large military ceremony and had come up to his quarters. His heavy frustration eased out of him the more Amelia touched him.

From their bedroom window, the prince and princess watched the procession below them. Beyond the city walls, a mammoth mass of men slowly crept away from Vernikport. It was a sight to behold, one that had not been seen for many generations.

The last time occurred when King Var was only a young prince—the crown had dispatched a small army of soldiers to the west, fearing invaders from the far away rival nation of Stranaka. The threat never materialized, and that campaign had a mere fraction of the forces that were marching out today.

"It seems obvious to me that General Rory is a bit war-hungry," observed Amelia.

"War hungry is spot on, dear. Rory wants his fix of combat and is going overboard to get it. He and the Admiral. Luka too. I can't help but think that the reason he voted against me was just so he could get a taste of conflict. How ironic that Rory won't even bring him along now. Luka will learn, though. He has my sympathies."

"Luka *will* learn," Amelia agreed. "The more time he spends with you, the better he will be. And like you said, they probably will not find anything out there if the reports are mistaken."

"Yes, and everyone would look quite foolish. Thank Sila and his agents that I am not going with them."

"Yes, thank Sila indeed," she said. "With you home, maybe we can focus on building our family again."

Xander glanced away from the march, turning to his wife with a smirk and said, "I think you are quite right. Even though it has not worked so far, I do not mind all of the attempts."

Amelia giggled and then put her arm around Xander, bringing him in closer. They angled themselves, one arm around the other, and faced the procession again.

After some silence, Amelia asked, "Xander, would you still love me if I cannot bear any children?"

"Of course, my sweet. I love you for the woman you are, not for the promise of children. Either way, I see no reason to worry about that."

The complete absence of hesitation in Xander's response caused Amelia to relax. Xander then added, "Just make sure you give me a son for my first-born. I will not tolerate a daughter."

Amelia jabbed him in his ribs, and Xander laughed. "You know I do not care for that jest," she said.

"I know, I know. One day, I will stop saying that."

Below them, a sea of armor marched towards a threat that Xander did not believe in.

*****

Luka threw a stone half-heartedly and half-watched it plop into the crystal blue ocean. Like Xander, he had departed the military ceremony as soon as he could. He now sat cross-legged on a short seacliff with one arm used to prop up his face and the other to toss rocks into the water. Another stone absently found its way into Luka's hand, and he threw it again, creating another plop below him.

He made sure to keep his head down to avoid the sight of the Royal Navy Warships that were slowly getting smaller on the horizon as they departed for their journey.

I am never going to have a real purpose in this kingdom. Can't be king, can't be general... he tossed another rock. *Can't go to war. Can't hear war reports unless I beg...* he stood up now with a coconut-sized stone. *I'll never matter. I can't stand this.* He heaved the rock forward with anger behind the throw. The water splashed several feet high, leaving the sea's surface unsettled and rippling.

"Well thrown, Luka," came a voice behind him. Luka turned around to see Xander and Amelia.

"Luka, is everything alright?" Amelia asked when they had approached.

Luka looked down at the stone ground beneath him and said, "Yes, thank you, everything is alright."

"It is quite apparent that everything is not alright with you," Xander quipped. "To be frank, Luka, you are very fortunate to be left behind. Long marches are grueling. The food is terrible, the days are long, and it smells like Vragr's underside. Imagine going through all of that, only to find the threat non-existent."

Luka looked away, annoyed that Xander had diagnosed his trouble so quickly. "Even if you're right, I should still have been included," he said, turning back to his brother. "I am the Vice General."

"That's fair," Xander admitted. "One day, though, you will be the outright General, and you can handle everything yourself."

"That day seems like it may never come." Luka turned away again and picked up another handful of stones to toss.

Xander opened his mouth to protest but held onto whatever he was going to say. Instead, he joined Luka, picking up his own handful of stones and handing a few to Amelia. They remained silent while they plopped and splashed away. Above them, a flock of seagulls flew overhead and squawked eagerly.

As with many things between the two princes, the stone-throwing morphed into a competition. First, it was who could throw farther. Both brothers launched stones far out into the sea—far enough that neither brother could appropriately judge the distance or claim clear victory.

Finding a competition in which they could identify a clear winner, Xander and Luka took to skipping the stones. They took turns, Luka starting the contest with three skips. Xander followed, matching Luka's throw with three skips of his own, setting the stage for another round.

For the next turn, Luka picked up what appeared to be the perfect skipping stone. He threw it side-arm and counted the skips—one, two, three, four, five, and six. A brilliant toss.

Xander shook his head and looked for a stone of his own. He picked up two and evaluated which one was more likely to match his brother's total. He chose one and tossed it. It made one skip, then two, three, four, and finally plop. A total of only five skips.

Before Luka had the chance to gloat, Amelia stepped forward. They watched her throw a stone that skipped one, two, three, four, five, six, seven, and then eight times. Amelia threw her hands up in victory and cheered.

"Thanks for ruining our game, Amelia. I don't remember inviting you to play," said Xander, with half-feigned annoyance.

"Sorry, I couldn't bear watching you two skip rocks so poorly. I had to show you how to do it properly."

"Maybe just Amelia and I should do this ourselves next time," said Luka.

"Oh, don't you start now. You just got lucky you went first, otherwise I would have chosen that exact rock. I was eyeing it, and you know that."

"There is no need for the second and third-place finishers to be bickering, when I should be getting all the attention, because *I* won," bragged Amelia.

"Okay, okay, we get the idea. You won, *my love*. Come, let's continue onward," Xander took Amelia's hand gently. "Luka, I'll even let you come along."

Luka's first instinct was to decline so he could be left alone again, but he ultimately decided against it. Sulking would get him nowhere, especially on a day like today.

*****

Vengeance was one morning closer when Privus Zlikrej awoke that day. The Zlikrej unit had finally cleared the Shredry Forest and only a few weeks remained before they reached their destination.

The insurgents had slept in an uninhabited, grass clearing that sat just southeast of the forest. They knew no one would be looking for them there. Throughout the journey, they continued to eliminate any witnesses they encountered and disposed of the bodies methodically.

Moments after Privus had awoken, Omarius emerged carrying a large elk and a bow over his shoulders. Breakfast. The sight caused quite a commotion amongst the hungry travelers, enough noise to finally get Drugi to stir. The middle Zlikrej brother was not nearly as pleased as everyone else.

"Omarius, is that my bow?"

"Yes."

"Did I say you could use that?"

"You didn't say anything. You were still asleep. Perhaps next time, you can wake at a proper hour and hunt yourself."

"Why couldn't you have used someone else's bow? There are dozens here in the camp," Drugi asked.

"Your bow is the highest quality and the most reliable. I can see why you like it so much," Omarius stated.

"Would you like it if I used your hammer?"

"I'm not sure that's a relevant question. You would have to be able to lift it first."

"I can lift it," Drugi protested. "And I just may use it without your permission and see—"

Privus unlatched his dagger and jumped into the dispute, cutting his middle brother off, "Drugi, shut up and help me skin this."

Though Privus asked for Drugi's help, little was required as he handled much of it himself. After some time, the elk was ready to be cooked. Privus aimed his golden staff at a pile of wood, a small ball of flames flaring out. The kindling ignited in a small fire.

"Careful using your staff for trivial matters such as these, Privus," Omarius warned.

"It has a great deal of magic still in it, Omarius. You need not worry."

Once the elk was cooked, the men gathered around and used their daggers and their hands to tear off meat. In short order, everyone had full bellies, and it was time to move again.

Drugi seemed less than enthused to mount his horse and restart the journey. The middle brother took his time packing his things and took a long moment to clean his bow. He was scrubbing the same inch near the handle of his weapon over and over again when Privus noticed.

"Drugi, what are you doing?"

"Cleaning my bow after Omarius used it."

"It is clean."

"You do not know that for sure."

"I do know it for sure. And since when do you care for cleanliness? This is a ridiculous moment for you to do this. Time is of the essence."

Drugi shrugged and simply moved to another inch along the bow, scrubbing with equal intensity. Privus tensed his eyebrows and was beginning to grow angry when Omarius approached.

"Drugi, you must treat our timeline with more earnestness," he said. Before Drugi could attempt a retort, Omarius continued, "You were too young to truly appreciate the spoils of our lives before we were banished. We lived in one of the finest castles in Estravia, overlooking a tremendous rock valley. Our father was one of the greatest lords in this country. He loved us dearly and had a vision of raising us all to be great lords of our own, as is our birthright. Instead, the tyrant Var came to our home and took everything away, and we grew up as outcasts in a barren wasteland.

"Though we were robbed of many things, the tyrant king did not revoke our destinies permanently. We are going to reclaim them. We are riding to his home to collect our debts before taking our rightful places as archlords in this kingdom. But you need to stay focused and keep all of this at the top of your mind. These are serious matters, and we have no margin for error."

Finally swayed by the words, Drugi mounted his horse, though he didn't back down completely. "And when we get there, we may find an army waiting for us," he warned.

"Not if we see the red flag of war flying when we arrive," said Privus. "Then we will know that they are defenseless."

Chapter 7
General Warwick

The pace of the army's march frustrated General Warwick. The possibility of real conflict awaited them, and their timeline was tight. Each day, they had covered less ground than their schedule had projected. The majority of these soldiers had never taken part in a military campaign, but that was no excuse. A good soldier should always be disciplined and prepared regardless of the circumstances. Maybe these weren't good soldiers.

They were already nearly a week behind schedule when they came upon Moste Bridge, a giant structure that connected two rocky plateaus and arched over the vast blue Mijek River. The bridge stood tall, hovering hundreds of feet above the water below, but only stretched a few feet wide. The army of ten thousand men would have to filter into rows of only a dozen in order to cross.

General Warwick sat on his steed, barking orders at his men to hurry their pace as they tried to get in formation. With no tree cover and little breeze, the summer sun beat down on Warwick and his men. Sweat covered their bodies, but if Warwick overheard the men complaining, he shot them down and issued a warning. Fighting for one's country was a privilege. Even something as small as giving sweat for one's cause could be glorious.

Lieutenant Alexander, who sat at the general's side, said, "We'll get them into shape, sir. Just give it time."

"I hope so," Warwick replied. "I am not sure these men were born to be soldiers. Not the way I was."

General Rory Warwick reflected on his own life as a soldier, coming from the lowest echelons of society. He had never known his father, and he lived with his mother and a rotation of her surly lovers in the small, poor town of Bethafis, only a day's ride from the capital. The boy hated nearly all of those men except for one—a young officer in the Vernik Army named Obadiah. Instead of treating Rory with disdain or even violence like the rest of the men, Obadiah took an interest in the boy and taught him about the excitement of being a soldier.

The great ambitions and glories that battle presented seized hold of the young man and never let go. He began spending all of his time reading as many military texts as he could get his hands on or practicing swordsmanship with a stick in the streets. Obadiah often mentored him in these hobbies.

Though Obadiah was more than a decade younger than Rory's mother, it seemed that they were destined to be married and that Rory would finally have a father in his life. But at an inconvenient time, Obadiah received a summons and had to promptly return to his base. Rory and his mother never saw him again. The young boy, not even a teenager yet, was left wondering whether Obadiah had been killed in action or whether he had simply abandoned them.

Nevertheless, Obadiah's presence had left its mark. He had helped Rory become a man. From that point on, he began to resist the attacks that his mother's successive lovers laid on him. As soon as he could pass for the minimum age to join the military, he left home and enlisted (the required age was sixteen, but Rory was only fourteen and managed to get away with the lie).

Many of the young trainees in the military were not there by their own choice and had a miserable time adapting to the harsh daily life of being a cadet. Rory was an exception. He enjoyed the pain and toil of the hard work, and he was certainly no stranger to being picked on by older men. He was soon the shining diamond in the group and found himself assigned to an important unit. Within weeks, Private Rory Warwick was appointed as the youngest member of the Vernik Special Infantry. Given military robes and accompanying armor, as well as a sword and shield emblazoned with the Vernik Phoenix, pride had surged within him. As he sat atop his horse, overlooking the vast canyon below, he reveled in the significance of that moment.

Shouting and commotion interrupted Warwick's reminiscing. The general surveyed the situation and deduced that one unit had gone out of order and jumped in front of another unit. The second unit took this personally, causing two officers to yell in each other's faces, with some of the foot soldiers joining in, too.

Warwick interceded, marching his steed into the crowd. "What is this all about? You've completely halted progress behind you."

The second officer had probably not expected this altercation to reach the highest level. "General, sir, this unit is scheduled to follow us across, but they have erroneously jumped ahead."

Warwick didn't say anything at first. He scanned the face of the officer from the first unit. He did not seem to protest. Warwick turned back to the second officer. "Just let them go ahead and get on with it. We don't have time for this. And you," Warwick said, turning to the first unit. "Don't *ever* break from alignment again. There will be hell to pay next time you do."

The first officer looked as if he had a cork stuffed in his throat, but he nodded and obeyed. Soon, order had been restored, and the march across the bridge went on.

As they continued to wait, Lieutenant Alexander said, "General, sir. You never did quite finish that story about you and The King in the forest. Seeing as it'll take a while for everyone to cross here, now seems to be an appropriate time for it."

Warwick glanced at his second in command from the side and then looked back at his men. Only about half of the army had crossed the bridge so far. "I suppose you are correct," he said. More reflections rushed back to him. He recalled how standoffish his best friend was when he first met him. Young Var, a prince at the time, largely kept to himself or his two royal knights who accompanied him and served as personal guards.

"General, sir, I believe you said the moment you first bonded with The King was during an ambush. That's more or less where you last left it," Alexander said.

"Oh yes, indeed," Warwick acknowledged. "Var was included in our Special Infantry Patrol, because King Gregor deemed it a fitting duty for the future regent of our nation. We were hunting down the Vorn Raiders, one of the fiercer groups of bandits in those days. Cunning and deadly. A pack of tough buggers."

By this time, a scattering of other lieutenants and high-ranking officers crowded in, making sure to catch their leader's story.

"On one memorable night, when we were drawing nearer to our targets, or so we had thought, our unit became separated. My half of the unit, which included Var, was ambushed. Most everyone fell to them quickly, including two knights of the Royal Guard who were sent with us on the mission. Soon, it was only Var and me, standing back to back, fighting like hell. Our very lives depended upon each other.

"At the time, I was young and at my peak in swordsmanship. To my surprise, young Var was also adept. Together, we slayed many bandits and escaped, holding onto our lives. I gained enormous respect for him that night. And I know he felt the same about me.

"I'll never forget how we both looked after we were finally safe. Drenched in blood and sweat and dirt. Few things build stronger bonds between men. Something those in our ranks fail to appreciate, apparently."

"That's bloody amazing. Absolutely glorious," came the voice of Lieutenant Baciti, who had caught the end of the story.

"Yes, General," Lieutenant Alexander replied, holding back an eye roll towards the third in command. "I am glad that *I* made sure to ask you about it."

"We have much riding still ahead of us," Warwick said. "I imagine we shall share many more stories together in the days to come. But what is more important is being able to live through some new ones."

By this point, the march had achieved an organized flow, slowly getting its men across the bridge. The heat had begun to soften as the sun lowered across the sky. Moods slowly improved.

Eventually, it became Warwick's turn to cross the bridge. At the end of the ten thousand army march, he rode at an easy pace with his highest-ranking lieutenants flanking him.

He spared a glance over the bridge's stone railing and down at the river far beneath him. As they reached the midpoint of the bridge, Lieutenant Alexander turned to him and asked, "Did Prince Luka not want to come along? I know others have asked, but this seems like it would have been a good experience for the young lad."

"He very much wanted to come," Warwick replied, earnestly. "I told him he was to stay. His father did not want him here, either."

"Why, General?" Alexander asked, then politely added, "If you don't mind me asking."

"I am easing my good friend's conscience by leaving him at home. But moreover, it's far easier for me. I don't have to worry about having the Prince of Estravia at my side. Though he is capable and bright, I could not worry about the distraction or liability if something were to befall him."

They all fell silent for a moment, nearing the solid ground past the end of the bridge. Then Warwick added, "Perhaps it was an error to leave him behind. The boy has a fire that reminds me of myself. I am quite fond of him. But, at this point, there is no sense in doubting my decisions."

Chapter 8
The Calm

Gray clouds threatened above as King Var strode towards the city gates. The palm trees along the gravel path blew and tilted from the wind of the coming storm. Six crimson-clad royal guards trailed the king as he traveled the city these days, thrice the usual amount.

Between the urban sprawl of Vernikport and the city gates lay a vast greenery, completely open, save for a few trees and garden areas. Two hundred or so Vernik soldiers and one prince currently occupied the space, performing rigorous drills and maneuvers. Var stood off to the side, watching his youngest son as he led the soldiers and shouted out orders. The king had witnessed this before, but today, he noticed Luka's voice lacked the zeal that it usually contained.

In the middle of one drill, Luka glanced across the greens and met his father's gaze. Var noticed him look away almost instantly. The drills went on for several more moments but concluded soon after that, as Luka announced the session was over and dismissed his men. He darted off in the opposite direction with haste. Var hurried after him, his guards trailing.

Var's pace was nearly a jog, trying to keep up with Luka's brisk movements. Finally he had closed within a reasonable distance and called out for his son. Luka ignored his father for a split second but then relented.

"Luka, I have been meaning to talk to you," Var said when they finally caught up.

"What is it, father?" Luka said with icy formality.

"That training session was well run, Luka. The men stationed here are fortunate for your leadership and your influence."

"You only saw maybe ten minutes of it. I led them for hours. Is that really all you wanted to talk to me about?" Luka started to walk away.

Var grabbed Luka around his shoulder, preventing his departure. "Luka, I know you are upset. I know you wanted to go on the Zlikrej Campaign."

Luka's face twisted for a moment, but he remained silent.

"I need you to understand that this goes well beyond you. Do not take it as a personal slight. To me, the Zlikrej brothers are a nightmare come to life, a reminder of terrible things from my past. I want them vanquished as soon as possible, and I don't want my family involved in any fashion.

"All those years ago, when I went to Canyon City, I saw the work of Vragr himself in my own country. After I put Lord Diocretin to death, I had hoped to never have to think of this again. Now, I can hardly sleep at night, knowing that this evil has resurfaced. I would sleep a great deal less knowing my son was on his way to face them without me. No matter how much we may outnumber them.

"Luka, you are a great warrior. You are also a great leader. You need not worry about proving that to me, or anyone. You have marvelous things ahead of you. One day, you will lead our army, and you will do so remarkably."

Var had kept his hand on Luka's shoulder for their entire conversation. By the time he finished talking, he could feel Luka's body soften, and the scowl on his face went away.

"I am proud of you, my son," Var said. He pulled Luka in, wrapping both arms around him. Luka returned the gesture.

Luka replied quietly, "Thank you, Father. I understand. I'm not pleased, but I understand." At that moment, thunder roared above, and the sky opened up. A torrent of rain fell on Luka, Var, and the citizens of Vernikport.

*****

A hand shot out at Var, grabbing at his leg. Instinctively, he yelped and danced away. When he was clear, he looked towards the source of the hand—an emaciated young boy in a prison cell.

The boy was silent but looked at Var with a sense of helplessness and pain. "What is your name, child?" Var asked after composing himself for a moment.

Rory grabbed him by the shoulder. "Var, we must keep moving. Our men will be down here shortly to free them," he said.

"I'd like to help this one," Var replied, turning to his general.

"You have helped him," Rory said, releasing Var from his grip and patting him on the back. "We saved his city and rid him of the one who put him here."

"I'd like to help him find his home. His parents," Var trailed off.

Rory pulled him in close and whispered in his ear. "His parents are almost certainly dead. You know that."

Var sighed and softened his body. He met the boy's sad eyes, wondering if he had heard what the general had said. Thankfully, it appeared that he hadn't. "Just give me a minute," he said to Rory.

He went over to the cell and stood before the boy. "You are safe now. I promise you that. Good soldiers will be down here soon to free you from this prison."

Var bent down now, meeting the boy at eye level. "Here, take this." He gave the boy a pendant bearing a phoenix from his jacket. "Remember that The King gave this to you." The boy took it in his trembling, bony hand.

As they walked down the hallway of the dungeons, a deeper sense of despair loomed ahead. Var held back shivers and his stomach twisting as if it might plummet straight to the floor.

Everything he had seen so far in Canyon City had matched the reports they had acted upon. Children in cells, gallows set up in the middle of busy streets, and homeless people of all ages scattered about. If those elements had been accurate, then that likely meant the worst of it had to be true as well—the mass grave.

Var became aware of the vile stench at the end of the hallway, before the door even came open a crack. Beyond the door, a narrow pathway jettisoned over a gorge in the canyon. Var could not fight the wretch in his stomach at what he saw below.

After he finished vomiting onto the platform, he glanced only one more time at the sea of bodies, dozens of feet high at the bottom of the canyon.

He had never seen so much death before.

*****

Var woke from his familiar nightmare sweaty and nauseous, his heart racing as if he had completed a full sprint. It was well before dawn, and the day ahead of him tomorrow would be long, as all the days were now.

He tossed and turned, fighting a battle against anxiety that impeded him from returning to sleep. After more than an hour of this, he accepted that this was a fight he could not win.

He got up and headed to the beach alone and unarmed, not bothering with guards for protection. The sky held charcoal gray but had a glimmer of pale orange that marked the coming sunrise.

When he reached the sand, he took off his boots and walked to the ocean. More foul memories of Lord Diocretin Zlikrej slipped into his mind, but he fought them off. With a few deep breaths and the feel of the gentle morning waves against his feet, he was able to relax.

Against the soft noise of small waves breaking at his feet, Var heard footsteps behind him. Dismay swept over him. Company was the last thing he wanted, but when he turned around to see that it was Vanessa, the dismay vanished instantly.

"You could not sleep?" Vanessa asked him. She was donned in a crimson night robe, walking over to him and taking his hand.

"Hardly," Var confessed. "I hope I did not wake you."

"Don't worry, love. I am just as strong on little sleep as I am when I have had a full night."

"Aye, I envy that about you," said Var.

Vanessa began to gently rub Var's back, further alleviating his tension and anxiety. "This will be over very soon, Var. At least Luka is no longer being cold with you."

"Yes, and you were right about him. I was honest with him, just like you said. He is still displeased that he is not with Rory, but he is no longer taking it out on me."

"See? Exactly as I said."

"Exactly as you said," Var admitted. "Your counsel has never led me wrong. You got me through the first Zlikrej episode, and I know you will get me through this one, too. I am so lucky you are My Queen."

"And I am so lucky you are My King," Vanessa responded. They drew in together, their arms circling around each other's waists and their lips locking. They stayed connected like this for several long moments as the sun became visible over the horizon and climbed into the morning sky.

"I think we should accelerate our retirement," Var said, finally pulling back. "When this nasty Zlikrej business is over, we should start planning our move to the Mnino Islands. I think I am ready. I think Xander is ready. Nearly ready, at least."

"I love that thought, dear. We can take a long trip, exploring all of the islands. Decide which one is best. Which one we want to spend the rest of our lives on," Vanessa said.

"Well, it'll likely be Ugojno. You know that is my favorite."

"Yes, I know, you've said so many times. But you must be more open-minded. There are more than a hundred islands. My brother and I spent many summers on dozens of islands. You've only been to one," Vanessa said.

"Very well," Var said, a smile stretching from one side of his mouth. "I will let you take us on a trip and try to convince me that there is a better island than Ugojno."

"I accept that challenge," Vanessa said.

Var and Vanessa kissed again, momentarily shedding the weight of their titles as king and queen. In that fleeting moment, they were nothing more than two lovers lost in each other.

*****

Luka shifted his gaze from the dark red wine in his glass to the light-haired young woman sitting across from him. The blacksmith's daughter took a long sip from her glass. When she put the cup down, her face beamed with glee. "This may be the best wine I've ever had!" she exclaimed.

Luka shrugged. "I am pleased you like it. This is the kind of wine we have nearly every night."

"Every night? That is so incredible!"

"Well, I don't know. I certainly like it, but I think I've grown accustomed to it." He filled both their glasses all the way despite the fact that neither was quite empty. "We have even better wine on special occasions."

"I couldn't even dream of wine that could be better than this," she said. Luka just smiled back at her politely, realizing that this had not been his best idea. The differences between them were wider than the ocean between Estravia and Stranaka.

"How are you enjoying my father's dagger?" she asked, trying hard to keep the conversation afloat.

"Well, it's my dagger now," Luka responded.

"Oh yes, of course, I'm sorry. I did not mean—"

"Do not fret. It is a marvelous weapon. Look at it." Luka unlatched it from his belt and unsheathed it. Even at night, it glistened, reflecting the light of the lanterns around them. "My brother made the mistake of buying a far less glamorous weapon. He will be king one day, and though kings rarely go to battle, they should still have the grandest weapons."

The blacksmith's daughter nodded in agreement, as if she could sincerely relate to the dynamic that Luka was describing.

"It is no matter. I'm sure far more people will be slain at the hands of my dagger than his."

"What do you think of this war?" the girl asked after they each had another sip of wine. "Sending off all these troops to fight the Zlikrej brothers?"

Luka's smile vanished. "It is not a war. It is only a small rebellion, if that. My brother even thinks that it all could be a massive mistake and that there could actually be no rebellion at all. If it was a real war... well, then I would certainly be there."

"Oh... That's good news then, isn't it?"

"Yes. It is good news."

A server interrupted their conversation, bringing two plates of steaming hot noodles and fresh fish.

Vernikport, as both the capital and wealthiest city in Estravia, was unique to other cities, boasting fine dining options that were far superior to the taverns and inns commonly found elsewhere. Tonight, without his father's knowledge, Luka had reserved the entire establishment for himself and his female companion. They ate in a narrow, quiet alley. It was private and quaint, just the two of them, save for the restaurant's staff.

As Luka began to fork another bite of fish and noodles into his mouth, his skin prickled at the sound of distant screaming. He wanted to think nothing of it, but he noticed his companion was looking around for the source of the very same noises. An unmistakable shriek and crash followed, those sounds much closer at hand.

"Do you hear that?" he asked.

She nodded slowly. "I think so..."

He threw down his fork and stood up. "I must go," he declared.

The young woman tried to stop him, but he was already rushing to the palace. With futility, she tried to follow, leaving the two plates of food alone, almost completely untouched.

Chapter 9
The Storm

The sentry yawned widely and stretched his arms, his uneventful job providing little stimulation during a long evening. This night would be spent like all the other nights—sitting in a cramped watchtower looking down upon the city's dormant gates. It was seldom that anything unusual ever happened at the entrance to Vernikport.

Following the recent military campaign, the Vernikport gates were sealed from sundown to sunrise. During the day, they remained open, but under strict watch by the guards on duty. Despite the heightened security and growing tensions, the sentry remained convinced that any real danger was distant.

The guard sat down in a stiff wooden chair, his eyelids heavy. Regrettably, he had spent too much of the day awake with his friends rather than resting up for the night ahead of him. As a yawn came over him, he decided it would be forgivable to doze off for a few minutes. He closed his eyes, hoping that no one would check on him for a while.

Before sleep could arrive, he heard people approaching, a rather large group from the sound of it. This was strange—no merchant convoys were scheduled to arrive tonight. The sentry stood right back up and peered out of the narrow window in his post.

The sight below made the sentry question whether he had indeed dozed off and was witnessing the surreal fabrications of his own subconscious. Hundreds of heavily armed men stood outside the city gates. Even when he realized that he was not dreaming, he could not make sense of what he was seeing.

One man on each side of the formation carried a black flag with a silver bat-like creature emblazoned in the center. The emblems on the flags were Mithacors—the large, nocturnal, dark-winged creatures that inhabited the areas in the northwest of Estravia. Typically, they attacked only in rare cases, but they had razor-sharp teeth and enough venom to kill a score of men if they ever did turn violent. Only one house used that creature as its sigil.

Before the sentry could process all of that, he heard the snap of a bow. He fell seconds later, an arrow protruding through his throat.

*****

"Excellent shot, Drugi," said Privus, when he saw the face disappear from the window. Drugi nodded and suppressed a smile.

Omarius stepped forward now. "It is time," he said, stepping forward. "Time to enter the home of a tyrant and avenge our parents." He pulled his hammer from his back scabbard and approached the entrance. When he came to the gate, he took a great swing at it, creating a craterous dent in the center. It only took a few more blows for it to fly off its hinges.

With the gate lying broken and bent on the ground, Privus and his brothers paused for a moment. They looked at each other, sharing unspoken excitement and appreciation for all it had taken to reach this point. Years of planning, mostly by Omarius, had led them to the door of their enemy—a door that was now wide open.

When they were ready, the Zlikrej brothers led the way through the broken gates, with their men following close behind. A vast green area greeted them when they entered the city, with the urban center of Vernikport sitting just beyond. The field was empty save for seven Vernik guards.

Privus watched as the guards quickly realized the threat. One of the members dashed away, likely to alert others in the city of the invaders.

The rest drew their swords and prepared to stand their ground. Brave of them, but foolish.

"Drugi, handle the runner, would you? I'll dispose of the rest," Privus said.

Drugi nodded, stepping aside to make room. He pulled an arrow from his quiver and got down on one knee, loading his bow and aiming it at an upward angle. His eyes shifted back and forth from the tip of his arrow to the fleeing soldier. When the moment was right, he released.

The arrow launched high in the air and flew in a magnificent arc in the Vernikport night sky. Privus could see the soldier glance back once quickly, wondering if he could recognize the black streak that was hurtling towards him. The arrow came down only a moment later, the soldier collapsing on the cobblestone street from the shot.

"My turn now," Privus said, suddenly feeling excitement well up in him. He had been using his staff on unsuspecting enemies for the last several weeks, but now he would get to do so on a scale much grander and on victims much more deserving.

The remaining soldiers in the field watched, clenching their weapons tightly. Privus considered insulting the futility of their supposed bravery but decided against it.

He held out his staff and smirked, standing apart from his small army. A torrent of fire burst from the weapon, lighting up the night sky and flying through the air with violent speed. The inferno lasted little more than an instant, but long enough to leave six smoldering bodies on the ground.

As the Zlikrej men passed by, most of them looked down at the deceased. There would be plenty more of that to come.

The unit finally reached the end of the greenery and the beginning of the urban sprawl. "General Klacan," Omarius ordered. The summoned general filtered out of the pack and stood at attention. "You know what to do."

"I certainly do, Archlord Omarius," Klacan said with a grin.

From here, the general split the forces into three groups and sent them to wreak havoc on the capital, each assigned to a different section of Vernikport. Klacan himself would be leading the largest unit. The only part of the city closed off to the soldiers was Vernik Palace. Omarius, Drugi, and Privus were the only ones permitted there.

Privus watched the soldiers depart in an orderly manner while he and his brothers stayed behind. He knew well that the moment they dispersed, they would become a chaotic force of destruction.

"I can hardly believe this is real," said Drugi. "We are finally here."

"I share that same sentiment, Drugi," said Privus. "This is such revelry."

"I *can* believe this is real. This is exactly how I envisioned this for many years," said Omarius. "Onward, brothers. We have a king to kill."

*****

A few candles danced gently in Amelia's bed chamber, providing the only dim lighting in the room. The princess lay face-down on her bed, as a servant lady massaged her upper back with intense focus.

"Is this good, My Lady?" the servant asked.

The princess groaned with satisfaction before responding. "Yes, that is *very* good."

When the servant had finished with the shoulder area, Xander burst into the room, disturbing the peaceful moment. He did not immediately address his wife or the servant, rustling around the room with visible worry on his face.

"Xander, what's going on?"

"Amelia, hello, my love. There appears to be some sort of problem. Some sort of attack."

"An attack?" she asked, now sitting up. "Is everything okay?"

"Yes, my love. I'm sure it will be okay. It seems we may have some arsonists or some raiders in the city, but hopefully that's all."

"Are you going out there?" she asked, a sense of dread expanding within her.

"Without our army here, we need everyone's help to deal with it. Myself included," he replied. By this point, he had grabbed his sword, most of his armor, and his new dagger. "Dammit! I can't find my helmet. I swore I had it with all the rest of my armor. Where in Sila's wrath is it? Amelia, have you seen it?"

Amelia remained wide-eyed, all serenity from the massage now completely gone. "No Xander, I haven't seen it. You may have left it at the training grounds."

Xander groaned and looked up as he considered this.

"Is the attack serious? Are you sure you should be going?" she asked again.

"Yes. I mean, no. I mean, yes, I should be going, but no, I don't think the attack is serious," he replied. Then, mostly to himself, he said, "Shit. I don't have time to go to the training grounds. I'll be fine without it."

"Xander, don't go. This sounds dangerous," she pleaded. "Stay with me."

He came over to her, the masseuse stepping aside. She looked directly into his eyes and sensed more fear than he was letting on. He kissed her and said, "Amelia, it is my duty to protect my people. After this is resolved, I promise I will return. I love you."

"I love you too, Xander. Please be safe." Her stomach twisted with fear inside, resisting the urge to hold him back in spite of his promise.

"Of course, my love. I will see you soon."

*****

King Var marched briskly through the palace with Pametan and Sir Jesec at his side. Between gasps of air, Pametan explained, "I don't know who or what it is. All I know is that there are anywhere from a few dozen to a few hundred invaders within our walls. In the chaos, I can't get a good estimate, but they must be equipped with incendiary weapons. Much of the city is already on fire."

"It's them. I know it is," Var said. "We've been fooled. Utterly fooled."

They reached the small palace armory, where Var quickly donned golden-colored armor and picked up an arming sword. Pametan began to do the same.

"Men," Var said, turning to Pametan and Sir Jesec. "I need you to go find my family. This could be a dire situation. Once they are safe, rejoin me in our counter-offensive. We can still fight with the forces we have left in this city."

Sir Jesec hesitated before replying, "Yes, My King. We will go at once." The elderly knight hurried off with Pametan scurrying to follow.

Var watched them go as he finished armoring himself, donning his helmet and lowering the metal visor. He took a deep breath in between the slits of the mask. He could still try to run for safety with his family. He was one man, and he would make little difference in the conflict. He could easily make the argument that, as king, his principal responsibility was to survive this battle so he could continue ruling the nation. The possibility lingered only for a moment longer. Every time he had been conflicted on a decision, one thing always won out—duty.

Var stepped outside the palace, seeing a small group of royal guards running towards the outer walls. Beyond them, the clash of steel and the cries of battle echoed through the night. Flames licked the sky, casting an eerie glow over the chaos. Without hesitation, he rushed forward, straight into the fight.

Before Var made it halfway across the courtyard, three enemy figures emerged from around the palace wall, clad in black armor. The largest of the group carried a massive war hammer, much too big for an average man to wield in battle. The other two were tall, but not nearly as wide and bulky. One carried a bow, the other a golden staff. Var did not have to see the silver Mithacor on their chest plates to know who they were.

The man carrying the staff pointed it at the Vernik guards who were advancing toward them. The staff produced a fire stream that engulfed the forwardmost men. Var froze, his mouth dropping in horror underneath his helmet. He was far enough to remain safe, but the heat made his body sweat even from a meaningful distance.

Ahead, the surviving men halted their advance and turned around in panic. Var's instinct was to order them to stay on the offensive, but good sense came over him, and he spun around as well.

With his back turned in retreat, Var heard a strange watery whoosh followed by a whistling noise from behind. A large, jagged ice shard landed directly in his path, giving him no time to avoid it. His shin connected with the icicle, sending him tumbling. When he fell, Var lost the grip of his sword, and his helmet came loose. It rolled away and became impaled by another ice shard—one of several that were still falling from the sky.

Var lifted himself slightly off the ground to see a scene of death around him. Ice shards had cut through the backs of most of his men like pikes through fish. Only two soldiers had survived, picking themselves up from the ground. Each one was met with an arrow, their bodies dropping back down instantly. Terror flared inside him as he realized that he was next.

The archer noticed him and drew his bow back again. Var covered his face and braced himself when he heard a thundering voice command, "Wait!"

The bowman turned to the soldier with the hammer in confusion. "I think we have found our tyrant," said the deep voice again. "Let's have a look."

The three men weaved their way through the carnage they had created until they reached Var, standing over him menacingly.

"So, *this* is King Var? I'm unimpressed," spat the man with the staff.

"You must be Diocretin's sons," Var said.

The man with the staff kicked him in his ribs. "You will *not* speak our father's name." Var winced in pain.

"You are correct," The large man with the hammer bellowed. He spoke through the slits of his barbute helm. "As you know, our acquaintances were first made many years ago. I still remember it vividly, but for the sake of reintroducing myself, I am Omarius Zlikrej, the first-born son of Lord Diocretin, and the rightful heir to Canyon City, a birthright you have taken from me. My brothers Privus and Drugi are with me as well, though they don't remember the home you took from us as well as I do.

"I know you remember us."

Var's heart pounded as Omarius continued. "When I was merely a boy, you marched into my home and murdered my father. Then you sent us to a dreadful prison city in the Alium Wasteland. The journey of exile made my mother deathly ill—another thing you took from us. We spent our childhoods parentless in a horrid, desolate place. Your actions were cruel and unjust.

"But now we have marched into *your* home to avenge our parents. You will know what it feels like to lose everything you hold dear. And when we are done here, we will not only reclaim what we lost, we will conquer the entire country. Our campaign will end the Vernik line of tyrants and establish a new order in Estravia."

Omarius continued, cocking his head to the right. "Tell me, tyrant, what were the last words you spoke to my father before you had him killed?"

Var thought for a moment, but didn't respond at first. Privus kicked him again. "Answer my brother," he barked.

"I... I told him he had to pay for the crimes against his city with his life," he answered, truthfully.

Visible anger flashed through the slits of the Zlikrej brothers' helmets. "Well, Tyrant Var," Omarius responded sternly, "You are going to pay for the crimes against *my* family with *your* life. Privus."

Privus pointed his staff down at Var. It began to heat up and emit a red glow. Var realized he was going to perish at the hand of a magic he had no explanation for.

At that moment, a familiar voice echoed out from across the palace grounds. "Oi, ratwaggers! Welcome to Vernikport! Here's a gift!" The four men turned to see Xander standing in his armor, sans his helmet, next to a large catapult. The grinning prince pulled back the lever, launching a massive boulder into the air.

Seizing this moment, Var scrambled to his feet, retrieved his sword, and rushed toward the far corner of the grounds, where a safe exit awaited. The Zlikrej brothers were preoccupied with the projectile and could not stop the king from escaping.

Var turned to see Privus aiming his staff at the boulder while his brothers ran for cover. As the rock began its descent, Privus seized control of it. It was only meters from crushing Privus's body when it exploded into hundreds of pebbles that landed all around in a soft rainfall.

Then, without explanation, the pebbles began to rise off the ground, seemingly at Privus's command. Privus waved his staff, and the rocks bulleted towards Xander. Var froze, watching dozens of stones pelt Xander on his armored body, eventually knocking him down.

Privus's staff now glowed again with the redness of imminent flames. Var considered turning back to save his son, but to his relief, he watched Xander pull himself up, using the catapult as support. A wall of fire hurtled towards Xander, but the prince was on his feet, trying to outrun it.

As Var continued his escape, he turned back to see Xander's body disappear past the palace walls only seconds before the blast of fire arrived.

*****

Luka scurried through the chaos of Vernikport, armed only with his new golden dagger. It wasn't much, but it was a welcome alternative to being unarmed.

As he sprinted up Glavin Street, he noticed a half dozen soldiers just ahead. Clad in black and silver, they were brutally stomping a father who they had just torn from his family. Luka's heart jumped in his chest in shock and rage. He wanted to charge right in, trying to save the man. But good sense won over, and he ducked into an alley out of sight. It was already too late for the man, and Luka needed to assess his options.

Leaning against the alley wall, Luka pressed a hand against his chest, his heart pounding inside like banging against a door. He tried to gather his thoughts—tried to make sense of what he was seeing—but could not. All he knew was that he needed to fight. He just needed to do that in the most prudent way possible.

He waited until the six soldiers drew even with the alley, remaining hidden with his dagger ready in his fingers. He overheard some chatter, and one of the soldiers filtered away from the pack and into the alley. When the soldier came within reach, Luka sprang from the shadows, yanking the target into the darkness. The dagger pierced his throat before he could even utter a sound.

Luka wiped some of the blood off of his fingers, not having time to reflect on the life he had just taken. He quickly collected his victim's sword and spear and emerged from the alley, focused on the remainder of the group. They had pushed past, their backs now turned away from him.

He capitalized on this, heaving the spear through the neck of one of the men and charging another, thrusting the short sword into the soldier's back. He quickly picked up the arming sword from his latest victim, leaving the other blade buried in the dying man's innards.

The remaining three soldiers turned in unison. They were wide-eyed in surprise, but with their blades already drawn, they wasted no time advancing on Luka. Without any armor, he was one blow away from death, but still not at a disadvantage. He was Luka Vernik—the champion—after all. With his stolen arming sword, he danced gracefully around the soldiers, evading and parrying, always one move ahead.

As the dance progressed, he was quickly able to angle one soldier several steps away from the others, opening enough room for an offensive. Two flashes of silver—one to disarm, one to kill—narrowed the enemies down to two.

The remaining soldiers came upon Luka from both sides. He ducked out of the way as they struck simultaneously. With their target not there, their blades struck each other on their chest plates. One fell to the ground, taking a more direct hit. The other took a step back, trying to regain his balance—something that Luka did not allow.

It took three swift strikes—two to knock off the helmet and a final slash across the neck to end the penultimate soldier. He collapsed beside his comrade, who was still stirring, desperately reaching for his blade.

"Surrender now," Luka warned, turning to him.

The soldier did not comply. He had only just begun to lift himself from the ground before Luka slashed down with predatory precision. That time, it took only one strike.

Luka looked back at the enemy soldiers that now lay lifeless on Glavin Street on his account. A sense of guilt and disgust filled his insides, but he pressed on. He had only one choice in that matter.

As he continued north up the main road, he passed the body of the father he had seen earlier. The feeling of guilt burned away instantly at the sight.

These bastards. They deserve it.

After that point, he encountered far less resistance but far more destruction as he dashed towards his palace. Many of the enemy forces had already moved past this area, leaving behind more dead bodies and buildings set ablaze.

He weaved through debris that covered the once pristine street until he could see the statue of Okupi Vernik standing majestically in the center of Andeo Square. Above the statue, a bright flash of light appeared in the night, and fire seeped over the palace walls. The figure of a man burst from the walls only a second later, clearly trying to outrun the flames.

"Sila's wrath, is that..." Luka muttered to himself. The figure was his brother, who barely had outpaced the stream of fire that was flowing after him. "Xander!" he yelled out.

Luka ran across the square, meeting his brother near the statue of their ancestor. "Xander, what the hell is happening?"

"Luka!" Xander exclaimed, not halting his sprint. Luka spun around abruptly so he could run alongside him. The way his elder brother was moving indicated he had been wounded.

"We're under attack!" Xander exclaimed.

"I know! By whom?"

Luka followed Xander into an empty shop within the square. They both caught their breath and peered out of the window, hunched down. Three black-clad men, two slender and tall figures, and one larger and thick, emerged from the gates. Xander pointed to them and gasped. "*They* are attacking us. The Zlikrej brothers."

"That's them?" Luka asked.

Xander nodded.

"How? I thought they were well up north?"

Xander ran his hands back through his dirty blonde hair and rubbed his eyes. "Well, they're not up north," he said. "They're right here. We've obviously been fooled. And they have a staff that can shoot fire and stones. Probably other things, too."

"Elemental magic?" Luka asked, incredulously.

Xander nodded.

As they spoke, the man with the staff began indiscriminately lighting buildings on the other side of the square on fire. Luka thought he could hear a maniacal laugh echo out to them.

"How is that possible?" he exclaimed in horror.

"I do not know, but I think that's Privus, and we need a strategy to stop him," said Xander. "If we can't get that staff out of his hands, we don't have much of a chance."

For a moment, it looked as though Privus was peering in their direction. The Vernik brothers clenched their jaws in tandem, expecting to fight or to flee, but Privus's gaze swept around and became fixed upon a different target. They could hear him snicker aloud as he pointed his staff at the grand statue of King Okupi Vernik.

The ground trembled, and cracks spread beneath the statue. The earth gave way, opening up and swallowing the statue into it. Only the top half of the Uniter's head and his crown were in view, his body now entrenched in the newly formed chasm.

"I'm going to kill these bastards," Luka said, under his breath. He stood up now, sword ready, no longer caring for stealth as he had before. Xander pulled him back down immediately.

"Are you mad? We can't rush in there," he said.

"They just disgraced King Okupi. That cannot stand."

Before Xander could respond, another figure emerged into the square from another gate. The Zlikrej brothers noticed this figure at the same time Luka and Xander did. Privus pointed his staff in the direction of the newcomer.

The figure was their father.

This time, Xander did not hold Luka back.

Chapter 10
The Battle of the Families

The two princes dashed out of the shop. Luka's gaze stayed fixed on Privus's staff, his fingers enclosed around his dagger tightly as he ran. The staff began to emit a red glow, causing Luka to propel himself even faster. Just before the flames erupted from the weapon, he hurled the dagger.

The weapon spun vertically through the air across the courtyard. It found its mark, cutting across the back of Privus's wrist. The staff fell from Privus's hands, sparing Var from a blanket of fire.

Three Zlikrej heads turned towards Luka and Xander, who now stood battle-ready, meters away.

"Ah, Prince Xander and Prince Luka. Thank you for joining us," said the large man with thick armor and a black beard spilling out of the bottom of his barbute helmet. Luka knew that he was Omarius. "We now have all three Vernik men gathered in one place. This is true serendipity!"

There was something unsettlingly familiar about the towering warrior, a nagging sense that Luka had seen him before. He brushed the eerie feeling aside and shifted his focus, his eyes oscillating between the three brothers and the staff that lay on the ground.

"You are all going to pay for what you have done tonight!" Xander exclaimed.

Privus laughed. "You are just as naïve as your father. You fail to see that *you* are the one already paying, discovering what the cost of tyranny really is! Tonight, we are collecting your debts and ending the oppressive Vernik bloodline!"

As Privus spoke, Luka whispered in a volume that was only perceptible to Xander. "When I go for it, cover me."

Great uncertainty sat behind Xander's eyes, but he nodded subtly in tacit support.

Off to the side, Var drew nearer to the group, holding his sword in front of his face. Drugi slowly put his arm behind his head, angling towards his quiver. Privus continued his tirade. "But tyranny is not the only reason for your downfall. You are also paying the price of your foolishness. This entire city is a monument to a regime that is so inept, it sent almost all its defenses far away. That is why it will burn, and you all with it!"

Privus then abruptly turned away and made for his staff. Luka sprang forward, darting in the same direction. Omarius tried to intercept Luka, but as they had planned, Xander covered for him. The Vernik blade clanged against the handle of the Zlikrej war hammer as Luka went for Privus.

Luka quickly closed the distance between them, forcing Privus to abandon his pursuit of the staff. Privus spun around to engage Luka, swinging his black-hilted arming sword to parry an attack.

Their blades stayed connected for a moment, sliding and scratching against each other, until Privus pulled away and struck once more. Their blades clashed again, exchanging the sacraments of steel with one another.

The youngest Zlikrej brother took the offensive quickly, clearly sensing an advantage. Since Luka was unarmored, he was only one strike away from death.

The flow of Privus's attacks pushed Luka backwards, each blow aggressive and visceral. Luka could hear hateful grunts and snarls beneath Privus's black helmet as he fought.

Many of Luka's past opponents shared this aggressive style. Though Privus's strikes displayed notable speed and power, Luka knew his window to exploit his enemy's weakness would open up soon. All he had to do was defend long enough, and he could turn his opponent's aggression on himself. In the meantime, Luka kept parrying and retreating, drawing nearer to where Xander and Omarius were now dueling.

Coupled with another violent grunt, Privus struck forcefully from up high—the opening that Luka needed. Rather than trying to parry, he side-stepped, causing Privus to connect with only air. The forward momentum threw him off balance, nearly tripping him up.

Luka struck his off-balance enemy twice on his helm, a crack appearing on the armor as he fell to the ground. He readied himself to deliver another fateful blow, but as he reared back, he heard his father scream.

He turned back to see Var on the ground of Andeo Square with arrows protruding from his chest plate and knee guard. While Luka had been dueling against Privus, his father had been trying to recover Privus's staff, which was evidently when Drugi had noticed and shot him. Luka watched the middle Zlikrej brother load another arrow onto his bowstring. He abandoned the youngest and bolted straight for the archer.

As Drugi drew the string back behind his ear, Luka arrived, swinging his blade desperately. The arc of his strike split the bow in half before the arrow could be loosed. The sword continued its path through the bow and into Drugi's helmet. The middle Zlikrej brother fell, the back of his head smashing into the pavement below. Drugi's body didn't move—Luka had presumably knocked him out.

Briefly, Luka stood over the still body, contemplating whether to finish him off. His window to decide closed quickly. A helmetless Privus sprang up behind him, forcing Luka to resume his prior duel.

The Zlikrej swordsman was covered in bruises and scrapes but attacking with equal or greater fervor than before.

*****

Meters away, Var sat up and removed the arrows that were lodged in his armor. They had broken the skin, but not deeply enough to cause serious harm.

Var rose and surveyed the scene. To his left, his eldest son battled Omarius. In his golden armor, Xander danced around the war hammer, striking only when safe. To his right, his youngest son dueled with Privus. Luka appeared to be in control of their battle, but he was armor-less, and therefore completely vulnerable.

In the middle of it all lay Privus's staff. Images of his men dying from ice shards and fire blasts flashed into Var's eyes. The staff was the real danger and the key to overcoming this threat. He sprinted straight for it, resuming his mission from before he had been shot.

As he came upon the mystical weapon, Var noticed that Privus was rushing towards him. Somehow, he had broken free of his fight with Luka. Var arrived the moment before Privus did, hurriedly picking up the staff. He held it threateningly in Privus's direction, preventing him from coming any closer. The old king and the young insurgent stared each other down.

Var glanced around again. He saw that Xander and Omarius had also separated temporarily, both watching on. He turned his gaze back to Privus who was now taking half steps towards him.

"Don't you move," Var ordered. He concentrated hard and waved the staff at Privus, but nothing happened.

Privus defied Var, continuing to slowly draw nearer. "What's the matter?" he taunted. "Does the staff not obey your commands? Aren't you a king? I thought your will was ordained. It must be so strange that you're not getting your way."

Var doubled his focus, ignoring Privus's taunts and trying to urge the staff to unleash its magic. Thick beads of sweat rolled down his face. It was clear that this would not work. He began to lower the staff and reached for his sword, which he had sheathed at his left side.

Privus did not allow him enough time to draw the weapon.

*****

Luka tried to act, but he was too late. He realized what was about to happen only seconds before it did. As he sprinted towards the scene, he saw Privus lunge forward. A flash of silver disappeared into his father's throat and reemerged from the other side.

Blood seemed to drown Luka's vision as he screamed in anguish. Privus pulled back his sword, leaving Var's lifeless body to fall to the ground. The staff fell from the king's dead hands and rolled away to the tune of Privus's jeering laughter.

From somewhere behind, Xander screamed with equal measure and joined Luka in his pursuit of Privus. There would be no more caution, and there certainly wouldn't be any mercy.

Luka arrived first. This time, he was the aggressor. His strikes were wild and ferocious as he slashed at Privus. With each blow, his throat turned rawer as he screamed in rage. He forced his father's killer into a retreat, pushing him backwards and landing several blows to his armor.

As Luka continued to cut away, Xander joined him. The Vernik brothers tried to hack away at Privus like two crazed carnivores. They quickly overwhelmed him, causing his footing to give way, knocking him to the ground.

Luka reared back to strike Privus from above, when he became aware of a threatening presence. That sensation was followed by a swing of a massive war hammer, which Luka evaded just in time. The weapon's gravity was palpable as it flew by, missing his head by mere inches.

The two princes instantaneously shifted their focus to Omarius, creating a new locus to the battle.

For a time, they engaged in a synchronous pattern, darting around Omarius, moving in and out in a perfect rhythm. Each brother alternated dodging Omarius's hammer while the other landed a solid, hate-fueled blow. After several sequences, cuts and dents covered their adversary's thick armor. Omarius grunted with frustration, unable to find an opening against the Vernik brothers' attacks.

Out of the corner of Luka's eye, he noticed Privus lift himself from the ground. Luka landed one more blow to Omarius's pauldron and ducked away. Xander would have to duel with Omarius alone. He re-engaged with Privus only a moment later.

Privus didn't hesitate, giving Luka an instant blow that he parried. Their swords clashed and locked in midair, muscles straining as they pressed against each other. Their faces hovered just behind the blades, eyes burning with rage and hatred. But Luka's hatred was far more recent—and far more savage.

They broke free of their block and struck again and again, the clanging of their blades creating a violent symphony of metal.

The duel did not stay even for long. Amidst the exchange of blows, Luka feigned a downward strike, only to strike upwards like a viper. The attack connected with Privus's wrist, causing him to drop his sword.

Privus's only defense was to throw up his arms in front of his face. The next attack shattered one of Privus's arm bracers.

Luka roared as he brought down savage blow after savage blow, his sword feeling more like a blunt instrument in his hands as he knocked his opponent down. He did not care about the inefficiency of his method. He was content to strike away through Privus's armor, flesh, and bones until he reached the very heart of his father's murderer.

A startled yell from behind made Luka stop his onslaught. A weak cry followed, one of resignation and fear. Luka turned to see Xander holding up a bent sword, crushed by Omarius's war hammer.

The crooked sword would not be able to defend against anything, let alone a weapon of such size. Inevitable dread swept over Luka as Omarius brought his weapon back down. A scream burst from Luka's throat, and his legs seemed to become weak noodles under him as he watched his brother's head disappear beneath the weapon.

Just like that, Xander was dead.

Luka had lost his father and brother in the span of mere minutes. Hot streaks flashed through his body and his line of vision. His thoughts were held in abeyance somewhere beyond.

Privus capitalized on this and scurried away.

Feebly, Luka held his sword back in front of his body. On one side, he saw Omarius turn towards him, Xander's dead body lying deformed at his feet. On the other side, he saw Privus rushing towards his staff, which lay next to his father's corpse.

No strategies came to Luka now. He couldn't think of any options. But he had to fight. His shock faded, and rage filled him, his body stiffening again. He clenched his sword tightly, screamed again, and charged towards Privus.

By this point, the youngest Zlikrej brother had already reached the staff. He pointed it at Luka as he ran towards him.

Before he knew what was happening, a heavy wall of wind smacked Luka head-on. Instantly, his direction reversed, the blast of wind lifting his body violently and hurling him across Andeo Square.

The back of Luka's body slammed into one of the burning buildings at the edge of the square, then fell onto the cobblestone ground at the foot of the building. Every bone in his body howled in agony, overtaking all his other senses.

Though it was barely perceptible to Luka, the ground below him began to shake forcefully. The burning building next to him began to wobble. Luka was able to open his eyes for a brief moment, just long enough to see a glimpse of the fiery structure as it came crashing down on him.

Everything went black amidst the torrent of ash and debris.

Chapter 11
Ruin

Wearing only her sable-colored nightgown, Queen Vanessa flew down the main staircase of Vernik Palace.

Only moments earlier, she had been lying in bed, waiting for Var to join her, when bright lights through the open window caught her eye. The city was on fire. Panic jolted through her as she darted out of her bedroom, heart hammering. She needed to find her husband.

On her way down the steps, she nearly stumbled, stopping in place on the mezzanine, where a fearful Princess Amelia stood frozen.

"Vanessa! What's going on?" The princess's voice nearly cracked as she spoke.

Below them, the rest of the palace seemed to spin in disarray, palace staff scurrying about, yelling in confusion. The buzzing of the mayhem rose all the way up the stairs.

"Come with me," Vanessa replied, ushering her daughter-in-law down the stairs. "Where is Xander?"

"He went off to fight, but he didn't know who he was fighting against—" her voice broke off. "What's going on?" she repeated.

"I have no bloody idea!"

They reached the ground floor where Sir Jesec and Minister Pametan greeted them.

"My Ladies!" Sir Jesec said as the four of them converged at the bottom of the stairs. "We must get you both out of the city." The older knight looked stern but otherwise remained calm amidst the chaos. The finance minister did not look so composed, his face white.

"I'm not going anywhere until I find out what's going on," Vanessa replied.

"We are being attacked," Jesec said. "His Highness fears that it is the Zlikrej brothers."

"You were with my husband? Where is he? I need to find him and my sons," Vanessa insisted.

"Yes, we were just with your husband, My Queen. He ordered us to get you to safety," Pametan replied.

"No, I must find them," Vanessa protested.

"My Queen, I implore you to come with me," Sir Jesec said. "When this situation settles, we will reconvene with your family. I swear this to you, but you must come with us for now."

"What about your wife?"

"I will find her as soon as this is over. For now, my duty is to the crown," Sir Jesec responded.

With that answer, Vanessa relented. They reversed course and exited out the back of the palace.

Just a few blocks from the palace grounds, panic filled the streets as terrified people ran in all directions, some attempting to bring belongings with them, many not bothering. The violence seemed like it hadn't reached this part of the city yet, but it was close enough to have struck fear into the hearts of these citizens.

"This way," Sir Jesec said, continuing to lead the group southward.

"Why are we going this way?" Vanessa asked.

"The attackers must have come through the north gates. Our best bet for escape is south, by the ocean."

The group ran for several blocks until they came across nearly a dozen soldiers clad in dark armor. They halted and watched on as one of the soldiers brought a longsword down upon a defenseless old man, his body then tossed unceremoniously onto a pile of corpses.

Amelia shrieked audibly, attracting the attention of the soldiers who were eagerly looking for their next target. They looked like ravenous beasts when they spotted Vanessa and the group.

Sir Jesec didn't hesitate. "This way!" he commanded, immediately pulling them to the side, taking them on another route. About half of the Zlikrej men pursued them, and the other half stayed back to murder citizens that they didn't have to chase.

Vanessa held onto Jesec tightly while Amelia held onto Pametan. They dashed through the bedlam, no one even having a moment to notice who they were. Many street corners were filled with other soldiers deep into their acts of slaughter. Jesec continually tugged Vanessa, steering them in another direction.

After several tense minutes of sprinting down alleys and through scared crowds, the group reached the Vernikport shore. Jesec led them over to one of the piers, where two canoes remained. Only seconds later, the Zlikrej men that had been pursuing them appeared, joining them on the shore.

"Sila's wrath," Pametan said when he noticed them. "They've found us."

"Go now and get the boat ready," Sir Jesec said, turning towards the enemy. "I shall hold them off."

"Let me fight with you," Pametan said.

"Your priority is to get the Queen and the Princess out of here. Help them with the boat." Pametan willingly gave in and joined Vanessa and Amelia as they began unlatching one of the boats.

Vanessa looked back as the final knot on the canoe came loose. Sir Jesec had drawn his sword and stood at the beginning of the pier before six Zlikrej soldiers.

"How darling. An old man with a longsword," one of the Zlikrej soldiers said, an arrogant snarl across his face. He pressed forward with a sharp cut aimed at Sir Jesec. The knight blocked the attack easily with his wide blade, kicked the shin of his younger opponent, and then shoved him off the pier. The water was shallow and made a mild splash before the soldier's armor and bones crunched against the rocks beneath.

Only a few feet from Vanessa, the other men moved in, this time not making the mistake of taking the old man for granted. Sir Jesec dug in and defended as best he could. He spun around in many directions, trying to block several flashes of silver at once. The battle moved him backwards along the pier, closer and closer to the ones he was trying to protect.

"Get away from here," Jesec urged to them as he fought.

Pametan held the boat as it began to float away, allowing Vanessa to climb in. She kept one eye on Jesec, as she steadied herself in the canoe. She held out her arms to help Amelia climb in after her. Pametan climbed in last.

As the boat bobbed on the water, they looked back at the dock to watch Jesec. The knight continued to fight valiantly, landing blows and fending them off, but the Zlikrej men were now in sync as a group. Squeezed on the tight pier, one soldier would spring forward as soon as another struck. This strategy finally overwhelmed the old knight, who was unable to keep up. One of the soldiers stabbed, this time too fast for Jesec to block. The blade buried itself into the knight's stomach, dropping him down first to his knees and then down into the water.

Vanessa screamed in anguish. The Zlikrej men began running over to them now, wasting no time finding new prey.

"Let's go! Start rowing!" Pametan called out.

They began rowing backwards as fast as they could, creating a gap between the boat and the danger. It didn't take long to reach a safe distance away from the dock, away from their enemies, away from Vernikport.

Vanessa looked back at the Zlikrej soldiers standing at the edge of the dock, watching them ominously.

*****

"Should we swim after them?" One soldier asked from the dock.

"No, not bloody worth it," another replied. "We've killed plenty of people already. No harm in three getting away."

"It looked like they had a knight protecting them," the first soldier said. "They may be important."

No one said anything for a moment, considering that fact. "Well, too late now," said a third soldier. "Can we agree that no one shall speak of this to Omarius? He was serious when he said absolutely no survivors."

The black-clad soldiers all agreed. Omarius could be harsh, even in response to the smallest of failures. The soldiers quickly pushed any thought of the three escapees out of their minds and headed back to the city to inflict more havoc. On their way off the dock, they spat at the floating corpse of Sir Jesec.

*****

After several minutes of rowing on the canoe, Vanessa began to lose her vigor. She glanced back at her home, seeing an orange glow against the night sky with smoke rising above. Bile sat in her stomach like a heavy molten rock. Her family was back there. Sir Jesec had promised to save them after Vanessa was safe, but then he died. Her family was on their own.

Her grip loosened, and she let the oars rest on her lap, overcome by the weight of it all.

"I can't abandon them...," Vanessa said, almost faintly.

Pametan seemed to recognize what she was thinking. "My Queen, we must keep rowing away. We need to ensure your safety. That's the only action we can take right now."

"I can't accept that. I need to save my boys. I can't leave them."

"They are strong warriors in their own right," Pametan said. "They can fend for themselves."

"Vanessa, please stay with us. Please stay with me," Amelia implored.

"I can't," she said, setting her paddle aside. "I must do this."

Both Pametan and Amelia began protesting more fervently, but their efforts were futile. Vanessa jumped into the ocean. She swam at a rapid pace towards the city, quickly putting a large degree of space between her and the boat.

Vanessa hoped that they wouldn't follow her. She spared one glance behind to see Pametan and Amelia sitting still in the boat. In the low lighting of the night, she couldn't make out their faces, but she could tell they were unsure of what to do.

Just go get to safety, she pleaded inwardly. *And leave me be so I can find my sons.*

The queen got her wish.

Vanessa was completely drenched and chilled when she reached the shore. The long swim had tired her out, especially after rowing so vigorously just prior, but she pushed through.

She rushed back into the city once again. The buildings in the southernmost part of Vernikport were now almost completely on fire. Corpses littered the roads and, in some places, were stacked several bodies high.

As Vanessa ran through the streets, she felt the heat from the burning structures. A building behind her collapsed and released piles of ash and clouds of smoke into the air. She choked and wheezed but continued forward.

She reached a small square where shadowy soldiers circled around a frightened family of four, perverse glee in their voices. They did not notice her. Vanessa could not think about what would happen to that poor family. She had no power to stop it—but perhaps she still had hope to save her own family.

A few streets later, Vanessa reached a block of buildings entirely immersed in inferno. The flames danced high in the sky and prevented her from moving further. To her left and her right, she could see Zlikrej soldiers. It would only be a matter of time until they came her way. Her only option was forward, even if that meant jumping through the fire.

At that critical moment, Vanessa became aware of a figure that had emerged from somewhere behind. "My Queen!" the figure called out. It was Priestess Teya, sweat and fear covering her face.

"Teya! Thank Sila, it's you! Do you know where my family is?"

Teya's face sank, but she did not hesitate to tell her the message. "My Queen, they have been killed. I saw it from the bell tower in the temple. They are gone. I am sorry, but we must go."

"No... No... No..." All the energy left Vanessa's body, her heated face turning ghost white. She felt herself being grabbed and pulled away. Vanessa had lost her will, but the priestess was still able to lead her. They dashed through the burning, dying city.

It felt as though it were happening to someone else, but Priestess Teya led her back south, then west. They eventually were able to flee the city from its southwestern-most point. Only rocky hills and light forests lay beyond. Neither spoke as they continued their escape. Vanessa couldn't have uttered a word even if she had wanted to.

Their way through the hills and the forest lasted for an indiscernible amount of time. Finally, they reached a grassy area where several farmhouses sat. A husky farmer and his family were standing outside watching the orange hue and dark smoke coming from the east.

When they came to them, Priestess Teya spoke. The whole conversation was a blur, with Vanessa continuing to say nothing. Soon, she found herself being led towards a cottage-like home. The farmers said that Pametan and Amelia had made it to the same farm only a short while earlier.

Vanessa was given her own bedroom and left alone. When she sat in her bed, the silence struck her like a hammer. Her ears rang as her mind struggled to process what happened.

Var gone. Xander gone. Luka gone. It wasn't possible. Her body began to shake, streams of tears running down her cheeks.

Priestess Teya came into her room at some point around noon the next day. She had spent the night between the terror of nightmares and the horror of reality, not sleeping much in either state. Exhaustion and pain weighed heavily on her, leaving her without the strength to offer a greeting.

Teya spoke up quickly, not waiting for an invitation from the queen. "Luka is still alive, I can feel it," she announced.

"What?" Vanessa uncovered her face, revealing red eyes and streaks of tears down her face.

Teya nodded. "He is not well, but I believe we can still save him."

"Is this true?" The words had a coloring of hope, but they fought heavy gravity to rise out of Vanessa's throat.

"Yes, My Queen, but we must go immediately. I will lead you to him."

They went at once. Pametan joined them on their expedition, but Amelia was inconsolable about the loss of Xander and stayed behind.

It took almost two hours, hiking up and down several large rocky hills to reach Vernikport. Though the Zlikrej force was now long gone, thick, dark ash filled the air, and the city was still smoldering in many areas. Few buildings still stood, including Vernik Palace, where only a ghostly fraction of the great structure remained above the dead city.

They kept silent as Teya led them through the rubble to the remains of Andeo Square. Even the statue of Okupi Vernik was gone.

Teya pointed to a charred pile of debris that had formerly been a multi-story building. The group rushed over to it and began lifting big chunks of stone off the pile.

After an arduous effort, they had dug far enough to see a body. Vanessa hurriedly pulled off the remaining rocks until she could see the back of her youngest son's head. It was caked in blood, and his whole body seemed lifeless. The sight was sickening and heartening in equal parts.

"I know how this appears, but I can sense that his soul is still anchored to his body," Teya assured her.

They lifted him from the rubble and laid him on the ash-covered cobblestone. Vanessa pressed her head against her son's chest. She could not detect a heartbeat, nor any breathing. She felt tears begin to well up within her eye sockets all over again, but then she felt a modest, almost infinitesimal rise in her son's chest—a breath.

Luka was alive.

Tears burst from her eyes, but this time not from sorrow.

Vanessa, Teya, and Pametan carried Luka's body all the way back to the farm, which proved to be quite difficult. When they finally reached their destination, they set him down in a bed and waited for him to wake up.

Chapter 12
The News

From his window high above the beach, Donte Zena watched a lizard crawl along the sand. It scattered between a pair of rocks and disappeared from sight. Donte continued to stare, waiting for the lizard to reemerge. Jealousy rose within him as he thought about the small reptile. The creature could simply hide from its problems, not having to bear any weight or responsibility.

"Your Grace," came a voice behind him. One of his assistants stood at the entrance to his room, holding a document in his hand.

"I told you that you don't have to call me that. 'My Lord' is sufficient," Donte answered.

"Yes, Your Grace, but you are now Acting Regent. I feel that it would be more appropriate—"

"There you are again," Donte cut him off. "I do not want to get used to hearing 'Your Grace' or 'Your Highness' or anything of the like. I have no intention of keeping this title or duty. I'm the only one in history who's been given regency over Estravia because his sister married into the royal family. And I intend for that history to be short."

"For what it's worth, Your—"

"Not another bloody time, Marko," Donte cut him off again.

The assistant cleared his throat and restarted. "For what it's worth, Lord Donte, I think you would be well suited to be Estravia's next king. You are the closest to the Vernik bloodline, even if that is only through the late Queen's marriage to their family. But moreover, you act with the wisdom and discipline required of a ruler."

Donte Zena, Lord of Lars and now Acting Regent of Estravia, rolled his eyes. "Yes, Marko," Donte said, knowing exactly why his ambitious assistant was egging this on. "I needn't be reminded so often. Now, I presume you had some other purpose in coming to my quarters today?"

"Yes, My Lord. I received a very peculiar message today."

"Oh, Sila's Wrath, not another bloody war report. Each one is worse than the last. Do you know how sick it made me to read the details of the sacking of Glazben?"

"I do not believe this is a war report, My Lord. It merely addresses you by first name."

Marko handed him a folded piece of parchment, with the word "Donte" inscribed on the outside.

"Peculiar indeed."

Donte dismissed Marko and sat at his desk, his body feeling heavy. He had not slept properly since the news of the attack, almost three weeks ago. Given the southeastern location in the City of Lars, information was slow to reach him. That was especially true when it came to reaching General Warwick. As far as Donte knew, they were still unaware of the tragedy and continued their march toward Eastport, oblivious to what had transpired.

The message shook in Donte's hands as he reflected on this. He wanted to open the letter, but his stomach twisted, fearing only more details of hell ripping through the country that he was suddenly in charge of.

As he hesitated with the letter, a comforting presence entered the room. "You should get some rest." His wife, Lady Crista, said, putting an arm around him.

Donte rubbed his forehead before responding. "Rest doesn't come so easy to me, Crista," he said. "Neither my body nor my mind were designed to bear the burden of suddenly being in charge of this country and this war."

The late King Var lived most of his life as an only child, though it was not always that way. Var was actually the second-born son of King Gregor II. His elder brother, Prince Gregor Vernik III, died at a young age of an incurable plague.

That unfortunate development left Var and his line as the sole heirs to the country. When they all perished in one night, Lord Donte, the younger brother of Queen Vanessa, was next in line for the throne. Donte was horrifically surprised and woefully unprepared for this responsibility.

"What's that?" Crista asked, pointing to the unopened message in Donte's hands.

"Probably more damnable news," Donte said, resigned.

"It looks different from all the other reports you get."

"Yes, which probably means it's *worse* than all the others."

"I really don't think so, Donte. I have a good feeling about it. Open it."

Donte relented and unfolded the message. The man's droopy eyes suddenly widened. He instantly recognized the handwriting.

"Sila's wrath..." he muttered under his breath as he began reading it.

"What is it?" asked Crista, unable to read the words over his shoulder.

"I'll let you know when I'm finished reading."

"Well, who's it from?"

"I'm still reading!"

"I can't believe it," Donte said after a moment.

"What?"

"It's from my sister... She's still alive," he said with bewilderment. "And so is Prince Luka. Well, actually, I suppose that is not right anymore. He is The King now."

"That is incredible news! Is this really true?" Crista exclaimed.

"Yes, I am sure of it. This is Vanessa's handwriting. This changes everything."

"So, what will we do then?"

"Well, according to this, I must carry on for now, retaining my duties as Acting Regent until such time as Luka recovers. He is very badly injured. They are working on healing him, but he is still in a coma. Until he awakens and can carry the crown, the fight against the Zlikrej brothers must go on."

"How long will that be for?" Crista inquired.

"Comas can last ages. But my sister's words were optimistic. Hopefully, he shall rise soon."

Lady Crista hugged her husband tightly. "This is such amazing news! What good fortune."

Donte kept his gaze on the parchment. He blinked repeatedly to make sure his eyes were not deceiving him. Evidently, they were not.

"You seem awfully happy not to be a queen any longer." Still in disbelief, Donte put both of his arms around his wife, holding the letter in his hand behind her back.

"Oh, come now, love. Neither of us wanted the throne. And we both knew this was temporary, even if we did want it," she said.

Suddenly, a chilling thought came over Donte, erasing much of the newfound joy within him. *Some people never wake up from comas. What if that happens to Luka?*

Donte turned and looked back out of his window, not sharing his sudden pessimism with his wife. Somewhere, far along this very same coast, his sister and nephew were there, alive. He could only pray that Luka would awake, and sooner rather than later.

*****

Misplaced mercy, Warwick thought to himself. *That is why we are in this position.*

General Warwick sipped tea in his tent, not far from their destination at Eastport, and reflected on The Battle of Canyon City. There had been high casualties on both sides. The most in Estravia's history since the War of Three Years against the Stranakans before Warwick had even been born. Nevertheless, Var and Warwick emerged victorious. All surviving members of the Zlikrej family and their loyalists were imprisoned in the city dungeons, replacing the innocent civilians who had previously occupied those grim cells.

Lord Diocretin's fate was easy to determine—he was to be executed. It was only a matter of how soon. The rest of the family was more difficult. There were three young children, including an infant and a mother to deal with.

General Warwick knew the solution was simple, even though it was not easy. They would have to join Lord Diocretin when he was laid to rest. Enemies, once spared, could rise again like weeds, posing a renewed threat. This was the message he tried to convey to King Var.

Var would not have it. The idea was abominable to him, and he scolded Warwick harshly for even suggesting it. In fact, Var acted coldly towards Warwick for several months after.

In the end, Var's choice was exile. He banished the Zlikrej children and their mother to the Avium Wasteland, a destination for many of Estravia's criminals over the centuries. Warwick wondered if execution would have actually been the more merciful path to take after all.

Now, decades later, the general was proven to be correct. The Zlikrej brothers had returned with a small force, and the Vernik Army was on their way to battle them near Eastport. *If only Var had listened,* Warwick thought.

Warwick's ruminations were interrupted by an envoy who entered his tent. "General Warwick, I have a message from Acting Regent Donte. I think it is very bad news, unfortunately."

"Acting Regent Donte?" Warwick responded, with heaping doses of incredulity in his voice. "Is this a jest, or have you eaten a sack of Pishi mushrooms?"

"My sincerest apologies, General. I prefer not to speak further. I imagine the message will explain everything."

Warwick took the scroll from the messenger and turned around to read it. After only a few sentences, Warwick sat down on the ground in his tent, almost collapsing. All of the color drained from his face, and the parchment shook in his trembling hands.

An eternity of uncomfortable silence passed. The messenger was clearly resisting the urge to say something. "Is this true?" the general spoke at last.

"General, I was not permitted to read the words, but Lord Donte sent me here shortly after hearing news of an attack on Vernikport. Is that what the message refers to?"

"Yes. All of them... the royal family, Var... They all... They're all... dead?" The last word was agony to push out of his mouth, and it hung out in disbelief for several moments.

"Indeed, General. I am deeply sorry. I did not wish to be the one to tell you. The whole nation is learning of this tragedy. In only a few days, the news will reach Eastport and points north. It is unspeakable."

"We were lied to. The reports must have been false..." Warwick muttered to himself. "I can't believe it. I'm a fool. A damned fool..."

The general closed his eyes for a long moment. Warwick got up from the floor and stumbled over to a table. He reached for a bottle of whiskey and began sipping straight from it. His shaking hands nearly spilled it everywhere.

"You are dismissed," the general commanded after remembering the messenger's presence.

"But sir, I am expected to give a response to Acting Regent Donte."

"I am in no state for a response tonight. You will have my bloody response in the morning. Dismissed!"

The envoy obeyed this time.

The general took another large swig from the bottle when he was alone again. His mind stayed blank, avoiding the painful emotions, avoiding the finality of the news, avoiding the guilt and responsibility that fell on him, as general.

One other tragic thing became clear to him in the torment. *This could have been prevented. If only Var had listened...* he thought with a shudder.

*****

The mare galloped gracefully in the fields outside of Privagrad, its rider reveling in the rush of wind through her long, flowing hair. Though the guards kept a watchful eye from a distance, and her friend trailed closely behind, she momentarily felt the pure bliss of freedom, as if she were alone in the world.

The horse's stride slowed, allowing her friend to catch up to her, riding a majestic steed in its own right. To her slight dismay, the conversation resumed as well.

"So, Serena, you never told me when you plan to get fitted for your dress."

Serena of House Tomkins faked a smile and said, "I am just waiting for my mother to respond to the inquiries. We've received proposals from tailors all over the country. Even as far as Seveka and Lars."

"It's going to be the most beautiful dress ever! You will be the most beautiful bride!"

"Thank you, Dusana," Serena replied.

"Brooks is a very lucky man."

"We are both lucky," Serena said thinly.

"So, have you decided if you're going to invite Luka?"

"Of course, I will invite him. The entire Royal Family is invited to the ceremony." She tried to hide the redness that she could feel rise in her cheeks.

"Ooh-ooh," Dusana teased. "Does Brooks know?"

"There is nothing to *know*, Dusana. And if you're insinuating there is, then you are being highly inappropriate."

Dusana giggled again. It felt like a taunt, but Serena ignored it. Regardless, the words had an effect. She could not prevent her mind from conjuring pieces of her memories with Luka. In the arena. In bed. Craving both but feeling guilty about desiring it. That was all in the past, and it had to remain there.

Changing the subject, she said, "Dusana, when does your sister return from her studies? She will also be invited to the ceremony, of course."

Dusana's fun-filled manner dimmed. "She wrote us just last month saying she desired to stay in Zachary for another year to continue her studies. We thought she'd be back by this time or thereabouts."

While she was listening to her friend's response, she noticed something from the corner of her eye. In the distance, underneath one of the great watch towers that outlined the city, a large pack of men approached on horseback. Their pace seemed hurried.

At the front of the pack, a man rode on a large black steed. From this range, Serena could not make out the man's features with clarity, but she could think of none beyond her father who could be riding atop that horse.

Serena had stopped paying attention to Dusana long before her friend's own words trailed off. Within a few moments, the horsemen were upon them, led indeed by Lord Aros Tomkins himself. The Lord of Privagrad's complexion was so white, it was nearly translucent. His eyes were almost crossed in confusion and anxiety.

Weakly, he said, "Hello, Dusana. Good to see you."

She began to reply, but Tomkins's attention was already on his own daughter. "Serena, you must come back to the palace at once."

"Why father, what is going on?"

"I shall tell you when we are inside. Let's go."

"Have I done something wrong?" she asked.

"No, Serena. You have not. But you must come at once."

She obeyed and rode back to the city alongside her father. They did not speak at all, and Serena rubbed her hand along her horse's neck for comfort.

Once back at the palace, Lord Tomkins escorted Serena to his office, where her mother and brother were waiting. Lady Tomkins, as pale as her husband, sat quietly, while her brother glanced around, his expression a mix of confusion and anxiety. The father bid his children to sit down as he stood next to his wife and addressed them.

"My children, I am afraid I must share some troubling news. The city of Vernikport has been sacked. The King and Queen and the two Princes have been murdered."

Serena put both hands over her mouth. Her attempt to scream was noiseless, as if some creature from deep within her had swallowed up her voice.

But her father was not finished with the dire news.

"These attackers are now headed for us."

Chapter 13
The Insurgency

The next recruit in line came from Stranaka, one of the hundreds of men that Officer Gnusa had been tasked with organizing and assigning to an official unit. Though the Stranakan language was similar to Estravian, it contained distinct dialects and difficult nuances. Officer Gnusa had been educated in Stranakan as a child—a skill that earned him the important but undesirable responsibility of processing hundreds of new soldiers for the Zlikrej Army.

The recruits were gathered in a large, grassy field, just outside of Sastavi, a small town that sat a week's ride south of Privagrad. Under Omarius's command, they had established a three-day recruitment camp, during which they would accept new members for their army. Now, on the final day, their initial force had already expanded more than sevenfold, with hundreds more still waiting to be processed.

"You are from Stranaka, yes?" Officer Gnusa said to the next recruit, in proficient Stranakan. The majority of their recruits so far had been from within Estravia, many of them mercenaries or discontented soldiers from various houses. Gnusa's responsibility was strictly to handle the swaths who had come all the way from Stranaka—a number that was expected to grow.

"Indeed," The Stranakan answered. "I am here to kill the vile Verniks."

Gnusa scrunched his nose before replying. "You are aware that we have already killed the Verniks? Their entire family. Not even three weeks ago?"

The recruit looked confused. Gnusa repeated himself, making sure his Stranakan was clear enough. Now the man understood, but he was not pleased. He took out a letter from his satchel and waved it in front of Gnusa's face. This time Gnusa was the one who could barely understand, as the Stranakan fired off a barrage of words without pause.

"Hey, hey! Slow down, you slimy word serpent!" Gnusa snatched the letter from the man's hand and pointed to a section in the document. It clearly referred to instructions for *after* the Verniks had been vanquished. The Stranakan recruit reread it much more carefully this time.

"Oh..." he said, when he finally realized his error.

"Yes, that's right. *Read* next time, you oaf. How did you come this far without realizing this? Honestly. You're getting put in one of the 'special' brigades. Get over there." Gnusa pointed to where all of the most physically and mentally weak recruits had been sent so far. The man walked away with his head down.

"We just toppled a country, and now I have to deal with these imbeciles?" Though Gnusa said this to himself, it was audible for the next recruits in line.

"At least I get to go back to Glazben after this. Won't have to see you grucknicks for a long time."

*****

On the other side of camp, Privus watched a few more latecomers arrive from a distance. They were reaching their destination on the last assembly day, but that did not necessarily mean they were slow. Some were traveling from far parts of Estravia or beyond. After today, they would allow more soldiers to join them, but they would just have to catch up.

Since conquering Vernikport, Privus and his brothers had only celebrated the victory with more conquest. Dozens of cities along

Vulture Road had met a similar fate to Vernikport, either destroyed or brought under Zlikrej control. That included the city of Glazben, which they had conquered only four days ago. A few dozen soldiers were left behind to rule over the pieces of the city they had left intact.

Ahead of them lay more cities with much stronger defenses like Privagrad. From this point beyond, they would need the reinforcements that were nearly finished gathering. They'd soon have a mass of thousands of soldiers at their disposal.

Privus maintained his watch as another group arrived. He could tell this group was composed of Stranakans by their baggier, light-colored clothing that their people tended to wear. Those garments would soon be exchanged for dark uniforms and battle armor.

As Privus visualized his army clad in Zlikrej colors, Omarius joined him. "General Klacan has a tall order here. I am grateful that I personally do not have to deal with the organization of this haphazard group," Omarius said.

"Yes, but this pales in comparison to how much organization we conducted before we even set out, Omarius," Privus responded.

Under Omarius's direction, they had sent thousands of offer letters to chosen recipients across Estravia and Stranaka, promising the downfall of the Vernik regime and a chance to join them after it occurred. Their targets were those who hated the Verniks, of which there was a particularly large market in Stranaka. Those who arrived from that country were soldiers or citizens acting independently of their own government. Omarius had been requesting more formal support from the Empire of Stranaka without a reply so far. That was no matter. There was a strong possibility that they would not need it.

"I knew that compliance would not come before we had proven ourselves. They likely thought it was madness at the time. I am just pleasantly surprised at how quickly they all mobilized to join us once we delivered what we promised."

"I am also surprised. It amazes me how many men are so quick to be disloyal to their country," Privus remarked flatly, referring to the portion of their army that was composed of Estravian citizens.

"Do you not approve, Privus?" Omarius's voice seeming to thunder even at a low volume.

"Oh no, I certainly approve. I just can't help but feel disgusted with this country. So quick to exile us and so quick to join our side."

"Much of this country still stands against us, Brother," Omarius reminded him. "If anything, this will serve as a valuable lesson. When we seize total control of Estravia, we will know better than to trust our subjects. Or anyone save for each other, for that matter."

"Right you are, Brother."

"These added forces are welcome—enough to get us through the next phase of our mission, but it's only the beginning," Omarius said.

"As long as the individual houses do not rally against us and unite."

"Certainly a risk, but a miniscule one. As I predicted, we've struck enough fear and created enough chaos with our attack on Vernikport. The houses of Estravia will be slow to unite, if they ever do."

"You were also right that Lord Donte was the successor."

"And no one challenged it, because they are terrified we'd come for them next."

"Let them continue to think that. I'm not worried about Donte," Privus snickered.

"Neither am I," Omarius agreed.

Below them their forces continued to organize. "I am grateful we have more conquest ahead of us. Otherwise, I think I would feel... disappointed."

"Disappointed?" Omarius asked.

Privus nodded. "I spent essentially my whole life hating Var Vernik and all his associates. Now that they're dead, it certainly feels good... It's just that there is something lacking without it."

"I understand, Privus. Ever since we were dragged away from our home, I resolved to get it all back. When mother died, that resolve turned to hate, and I spent every moment planning how I would kill King Var. Now that he's gone, I too feel an emptiness.

"But we must keep our drive and our resolve warm. We will need every bit of our efforts and focus for what lies ahead. Killing the Verniks was only half of our destiny. The rest awaits us soon."

After another hour passed, the sun sat in the center of the sky, marking the noon deadline. The forces were now gathered somewhat orderly in the field, awaiting their next instructions. On this cue, Omarius hoisted himself up onto an enormous boulder that gave him an elevated view above the scores of men before him. Privus and Drugi climbed up after him.

With a booming voice, Omarius called out to the soldiers, "Great men, it is an utmost honor to welcome you to join this legendary group. Welcome to the Zlikrej Army!"

Cheering erupted from the crowd. Omarius continued. "Already, with only a few hundred men we have exposed the weakness of the departed Vernik bloodline, showing the people of this country who deserves to rule. Imagine now what we will do with more than three thousand of you!" The applause grew louder.

"It is no small task ahead of us, however. A battalion of the Vernik Army marches in the east. Deception has kept them out of our way so far, but news of our glorious victory will soon reach them, and they will come back to face us. We must be ready for that battle.

"Right now, their army serves the memory of a dead king, through his dead wife's pathetic brother. In time though, and after many hard-fought victories, the people of Estravia will turn to *us*. We are the leaders this country has desperately needed for so long. Welcome to the beginning of a new reign!" The cheers reached a crescendo.

"Now we will march onward to Privagrad. It will fall like Vernikport, only easier. From there, we will only continue to conquer. This is a new day in Estravia. A day that belongs to us!" For a few moments, Omarius held out his muscular arms wide, seeming to soak up the energy of the crowd. When they were satisfied, Omarius and his brothers climbed down the giant rock. Omarius's speech had worked the crowd into a frenzy.

"Well done, Omarius," complimented Privus, when they were on solid ground again.

"Yes, brother, well done. I can sense how excited our new forces are," said Drugi.

"I've sold them our vision," said Omarius. "Now they must help us implement it."

Later that afternoon, the Zlikrej brothers returned to the same rock to watch their once chaotic assemblage march out in order, led by General Klacan.

"This is perhaps the most beautiful thing I have ever seen," Drugi said, watching the spectacle.

"More beautiful than Vernikport burning?" Privus asked.

"Hmm, I don't know," Drugi said, seriously considering Privus's comparison. "There was a lot of smoke above Vernikport at the end there, so it was hard to see. I think this is more beautiful."

"If you think this is beautiful, just imagine what it will look like if we gain the official support of the Stranakans. We could have numbers ten or twentyfold this," Omarius added.

"That would be incredible," Drugi said.

"I still do not know if I trust them," Privus said.

"We do not have to trust them to utilize them. And even if they do not ultimately join us, we know we have a plan to defeat the Vernik Army without them."

The sun had set completely by the time the last brigade marched out of the grounds. In the fading dusk, Privus, Drugi, and Omarius climbed down from the rock and mounted their horses, riding forward to lead their newly assembled army.

Chapter 14
Awakened

The observer became aware in a faint and distant sense, not knowing where he was. He did not even know *who* he was. There were no sounds. There were no thoughts. There was no understanding of time, other than the feeling that much of it had passed.

The abeyance persisted, until gradually, an indistinct aura of light appeared. With that, a vague understanding of identity came into grasp. One word appeared to him. Luka.

His name.

The name carried no memories, but there was a sense of despair and pain attached to it.

Time continued to pass in unknown quantities. Luka's vision wavered, reality coming back in fits of white fog. The fog settled, and with it, a faint ringing that seemed to come from everywhere and nowhere.

The ringing grew as memories seemed to pull from his mind like a splinter buried deep in the skin. Shapes took form in the mist. On one side, two men—one friend, one foe. Then the flash of a sword. On the other, the same number—one friend and one foe, the latter with a hammer.

Names surfaced. Father. Xander. He remembered. He recalled the last thing he saw and felt a cold horror. Father and Xander were dead, killed right in front of him. Was he dead too? The question drifted in the dark. He didn't know the answer, he only knew he needed the pain to stop.

Luka strained in the void, but the ringing only intensified. Pain throbbed, distant but relentless. The fog darkened as he struggled further. Moments later the darkness closed in on him completely, and all went black.

*****

The next time Luka became conscious, he found himself awake on a late summer morning. The little light that leaked between the curtains in the bedroom was enough to pain his sensitive eyes. When the ache and blurriness cleared from his vision, he found himself inside a small bedroom he did not recognize.

With great effort and great agony, he sat up in bed. His entire body felt weak, seeming to vibrate in tune with the ringing in his ears. His mind had not fully come to life, but something within Luka wanted to keep it that way. Something within him knew he stood perilously on the edge of mental torment.

Luka stared blankly at the wall in front of him. Dozens of cracks and hidden textures kept his vision and mind occupied. He allowed his eyes to glaze over, the wall blurring as he lost focus. It was like a temporary oblivion.

The sound of a doorknob turning yanked Luka back to reality. The door creaked open, and a servant entered the room. The woman's mouth gaped like a fish when she saw Luka awake.

After the servant regained composure, she bowed awkwardly and said, "Your Highness."

Luka stared at her blankly. Being called that was foreign to him. It didn't make any sense, but he didn't ask for clarification.

"Your Highness, I have come to deliver you something." She pulled a folded white cloth from a brown sack. "This dagger was found in the city rubble. I was told that it belongs to you. I was instructed to place it next to your bedside, but since you are awake, I can give it to you directly."

The servant walked over to him and placed the cloth in Luka's outstretched hands. She excused herself and departed without Luka uttering a single word.

The fabric-wrapped parcel felt heavy in Luka's hands. He carefully unwrapped it, peeling back the cloth one layer at a time. The moment his eyes fell on what lay beneath, his heart lurched, and a wave of agony crashed over him, seeping into every fiber of his being.

It was not the golden dagger that he was expecting. The handle was crimson with wings molded into the hilt. It was Xander's dagger.

Xander, Luka thought. He remembered how they were together when his elder brother purchased the weapon. He remembered their friendly debate about who had the better dagger. But more than anything, he remembered that he would never see his brother again. His whole body seemed to shake as he recalled the image of the wicked war hammer.

Father, Luka thought. If Xander was gone, then so was his father. It was not a dream. He had watched that sword go through his father's throat, something no son should ever have to witness. He remembered how sick that sight made him feel. It was making him feel even sicker now.

Thick beads of sweat began to accumulate on Luka's face. His heart felt like it would explode from his chest while an electric current of panic ran through his veins. He wanted to cry, but he did not think that tears would be of any help.

The anguish soon turned to rage. Three men that Luka had never even met before had stolen his father and brother from him. He remembered their names. Privus, Drugi, and Omarius. He remembered their taunts before they took Var and Xander away. Luka wanted to scream, but the scream stayed confined within him like a prisoner. The ringing in his ears reached a crescendo as his whole body boiled with fury.

Then Luka remembered something else.

Mother, Luka thought. He had no idea if she was alive. He needed her to be. *Otherwise, I would have nothing left.* But the words of the servant rang out to him. "The city rubble," she had said. That meant Vernikport had been destroyed. How could his mother have survived?

For a moment, Luka wanted to go back into his coma. Or even better—simply pass away.

Before Luka's despair could build further, the same servant reentered Luka's room. This time she was not alone. She was accompanied by Queen Vanessa. In a mercifully short amount of time, Luka's silent prayer had been answered.

Vanessa immediately rushed over to her son. She held him gently to avoid hurting him, but it felt soothing all the same. Luka's heart rate slowed, and the panic in his body eased slightly.

"Mother," Luka croaked. It was the first word he had spoken since he had awoken.

"Luka... my boy. My son... I'm so glad you're awake." Vanessa ran her hands through Luka's blond hair.

"I am so glad you're alive," Luka said, his voice still rasping. "I didn't know if..."

"Oh, darling. Oh, Luka. I'm okay. We're alive. Me, Amelia, and Milo. We made it out of the city. We were worried you would never wake." She caressed him more tightly.

"How long..." Luka trailed off and then tried again. "How long have I been asleep?"

Vanessa frowned, but then said, "Today is the twentieth day."

Twenty days. Luka could just as easily believed twenty days, or two days, or even two hundred days. It would take a great deal for his sense of time to return to him.

"What has happened since I've been out? Did anyone catch them?" Luka asked. He didn't need to clarify who "them" was.

Vanessa put her hand on Luka's arm. "Oh, Luka. I don't think now is a good time. You've only just woken up."

"Please, Mother. I need to know. It won't help if I lay here and wonder."

His mother relented. It took almost an hour for Vanessa to fill Luka in on the state of affairs. Luka said little and strained to concentrate. At times it felt like the description of a nightmare. He wished that it was.

Vernikport was decimated. The bulk of the damage came from the flames from Privus's magic staff. Vanessa struggled as she described how rubble and ash was all that remained of the once-bustling city.

She explained where Luka was—a large farm estate just west of the hills outside of Vernikport. It was about a half-hour ride and just under two hours walk. Sir Jesec had died defending them so they could escape to the farm. Another person for Luka to grieve.

Luka clenched his fist tightly as his mother described the movements of the Zlikrej brothers, who now marched north along Vulture Road, inflicting damage to the cities along the way. They had assembled an army of formidable size, estimated to be between three thousand to five thousand men. Prior to the invasion, they had recruited mercenaries and soldiers from all across the country, as well as from the out-island country of Stranaka, who gathered in Sastavi to join forces with the Zlikrej. Little was known about their ultimate destination, but the popular theory was Canyon City, their former home before they were exiled.

Messages about the fall of Vernikport and the true location of the Zlikrej Army had been sent to General Warwick. It was unclear if he had received the news, but it would be soon if he had not. Admiral Mormar and the Royal Navy had reached Eastport, only to find nothing there. They were still docked there, awaiting new orders. The Navy's prowess was neutralized while the Zlikrej were so far inland.

Vanessa explained that her brother, Lord Donte, now ruled as Acting Regent. He would hold the position until the Lords and Ladies of Estravia could convene to elect a new king. However, no one was willing to meet until the Zlikrej conflict had been resolved.

"That meeting will never take place now," Queen Vanessa said. "You are the rightful king."

The sentence was alien to Luka. It did not sink in properly. He reflected on all of the nights he dreamed of being king, thinking he would be the best at it. He thought he would've given anything to somehow be firstborn and be the next in line for the throne, instead of feeling like an afterthought in Estravian politics. Now he only wished he could trade everything back to see his father and brother just one more time. Agonizing guilt tore at him.

Vanessa continued to fill Luka in on the ongoing conflict, but his eyes began to droop. She stopped for a moment and suggested that Luka sleep. Luka insisted that he could stay awake, but before he knew it, slumber came, and he returned to the fog.

*****

Hours later he woke again just as dusk had set in. This time he didn't wait for the revolting memories to return to him. He rose with all his strength and stepped outside his small cottage. A guard stood there, surprised to see Luka on his feet. "Your Highness, I was told—" The soldier began to say, but Luka brushed past him.

"Forget what you were told. I'm going to see my mother." The guard followed awkwardly and didn't protest any further.

Luka's legs felt like thin, fragile pedestals holding up a heavy statue, but he fought to keep his balance. He managed to cross to the other side of the farm without collapsing. When he reached the main cottage, one additional royal guard stood in front of the entrance. The two most important people in Estravia were staying on this farm, and these two soldiers were the summation of their protection. Luka entered, leaving both guards outside.

Inside, his mother sipped tea in the dining room. Pametan, Amelia, and Priestess Teya sat at the table with her. They turned to him with surprise. He felt a flicker of warmth within him at the sight of their faces.

"Luka!" Vanessa exclaimed, nearly spilling her tea. "What are you doing? You should be resting."

"I've rested more than enough," Luka responded obdurately, though he knew his ability to remain standing was deteriorating rapidly. He quickly eased himself into one of the seats.

Vanessa called for a servant who promptly fetched Luka a cup of tea and three pieces of warm bread. Luka devoured the bread and croaked for more. The servant returned with an entire loaf this time.

When he was finished stuffing himself, Luka asked, "So, what will we do? What are we planning?"

"Planning?" Pametan asked.

"Yes. How are we going to defeat the Zlikrej brothers?" asked Luka.

The others shared a glance of concern. Vanessa responded. "General Warwick should be receiving notice of the events soon."

"And so, in the meantime, we will be waiting here doing nothing?"

"With any hope, they will be stopped before they can progress any further north," said Pametan.

"By whom?" asked Luka, almost in a snarl.

"We hope that Privagrad should have enough fortifications to stop them," Pametan said.

Luka's eyes went wide. *Serena*, he thought. They had to do something.

"You are using the term 'hope' quite a lot, Milo," Luka said, with resolve returning. "Hope will not help Privagrad. As much faith as I have in Lord Tomkins and those defense towers, the enemy has thousands of soldiers now. We couldn't stop them when they only had a few hundred. I'd prefer it if they fled for safety.

"Maybe if we hadn't been misled and sent our entire army away we could have stopped them," Luka said, filling the silence after no one responded to his previous comment. "How could this have happened? How could we have been fooled so badly?"

"We do not know, Luka. We are praying for answers," Vanessa said.

"We no longer have the letters themselves to prove it, but we believe the reports of the Zlikrej advance were forgeries. The attack actually came from the west and not the north," Pametan explained.

"How could we fall for such a simple ruse?" Luka asked.

Pametan responded, speaking slowly and gently, "Your Highness, you yourself were in that room when we made the decision. You had the same information we all did, and you cast the deciding vote."

Luka lowered his head slightly, his face draining of color. He couldn't refute anything that Pametan had just said.

"We all would reverse our decision if we could, Luka. The guilt is not yours to bear." Pametan added, hoping to soften his words.

Luka stayed silent for a moment longer. Then he turned towards Priestess Teya. "What about you, Priestess? I thought you were supposed to be able to see this coming with your powers? Why couldn't you have warned us?"

Priestess Teya shifted in her chair slightly. "I foresaw troubled events on the horizon but could not tell what they were."

"That's bloody helpful then," Luka said acidly.

"Luka, do not say such things!" Vanessa said. "Teya has been working diligently on healing you while you rested. She's the one who knew you were alive. You'd still be in the rubble if not for her."

The priestess did not say a word, her bright blue eyes fixed calmly on Luka. He felt disarmed under her gaze and looked away, but his frustration did not simmer completely.

"Since no one has a plan other than sitting around drinking tea and 'hoping,' I will hunt them down myself. I am going to avenge Father and Xander. I am going to ride up Vulture Road and slay these scum where they stand. When I am done, I will rule this kingdom from a suitable throne, while we rebuild Vernikport, exactly the way it was before."

Luka finished his tea in a big gulp and then slammed the mug down on the table. "I leave at dawn," he declared.

The others rose in protest, but Luka's mind had firmly settled. He reiterated that he was now The King, that those were his orders, and they were final. The debate was over when Luka marched out of the room.

As Luka reached the cottage's front door, an extreme lightheadedness came over him. His arm shot out for the doorknob but missed. A massive headrush overwhelmed him, and he lost balance completely.

He was unconscious before he fell to the floor with a loud thud.

Chapter 15
The Blood Oath

Athick fog rested on the farmland several mornings later. Through the mist, Priestess Teya could see a silhouette standing before two stone obelisks. She approached the figure, but she did not have to get close to know who it was. The young king had abandoned his declaration to leave on his quest the other day, but the priestess knew it was only a matter of time.

When Teya could finally see his face, Luka seemed almost lost staring at the two stone markings. The obelisks stood in the corner of the farm, away from all the animals. One was marked "Var Vernik" and the other "Xander Vernik." There was nothing on the graves to indicate their royalty save for their last name.

"Where are they now? My father and brother?" Luka asked when he became aware of the priestess standing near him.

"All souls need cleansing from sin and evil after death. It takes a great deal of time before a soul is ready for the afterlife. It feels like a long time to us as mortals, but it is nothing compared to an eternity," she answered.

"So, they are in the spiritual baths?" asked Luka.

"That is what many call it, yes," she said.

"For nearly my entire childhood, I sat through your sermons, believing much of what you said was a load of grucknickshit," Luka said. "But now, I have no idea what to believe."

"That feeling is understandable. It can be difficult to accept the mysteries of this world and the next one, but faith will only be a friend."

"When was their ceremony?" Luka asked, his gaze still fixed on the graves.

"It was nearly two weeks ago. We would have preferred you to be awake for it, but we feared you would not rise for a long time."

Luka cursed under his breath, seeming to chastise himself for his own weakness.

"You should not blame yourself, Your Highness," the priestess said.

"But I was powerless... Powerless to even be at the funeral, powerless to stop them in the first place. I've spent my whole life training to fight only to fail when it mattered most. What good am I?" Luka's voice quivered on those last four words.

"It is expected that you would feel so broken, Luka, but it will do you no good to doubt your worth. You are at your best when you are confident in your ordained abilities. This country needs you at your best," Teya remarked.

"When I regain my strength, I will use everything in my power to hunt them down," Luka said, almost as if no one were listening. "I'll kill them all."

"Be wary of your soul, Luka," the priestess cautioned. "Vengeance can destroy you as much as it can your enemies."

Luka merely grunted disapprovingly. He seemed to break away from the conversation, towards a blaze of hateful thoughts. Teya could sense that her words would do no further good. She quietly bid him farewell.

*****

Luka stayed behind, looking upon the structures before him. There were no bodies buried beneath the graves. The stones were merely symbolic.

Kings and princes always had glorious funerals with hundreds in attendance. Members of the Vernik family were buried in the grand family cemetery, but that had been wiped away along with the rest of

Vernikport. Var and Xander would never get that privilege. Instead, they were honored with unadorned graves on an anonymous farm, with only a handful of people witnessing it. A number that did not include Luka.

A single tear traced its way down his cheek. He longed to surrender to the grief, to let it consume him entirely, but he couldn't. Perhaps he was still too numb. Or perhaps a lifetime of training had taught him to bury every trace of weakness.

After a time, Luka wiped the solitary tear away and left the graves. His steps were not as arduous as they had been several days ago. He decided that he felt well enough to venture beyond the confines of the farm.

Beyond the enclosure, Luka reached the first hill. From there, it took nearly three hours to reach the top of the final hill. When he reached the pinnacle, he wondered whether he had any energy left to return to the farm.

At the foot of the mountain lay what Luka needed to see. The fog had lifted, and the morning sun now shone on what used to be the great capital city of Vernikport. Where palaces, luxurious mansions, and bustling shops formerly stood, there were only ashes, debris, and death.

Luka sat down on the ground, his gaze fixed on the desolation below. An uncontrollable swelling of emotional pain began to run through his bloodstream. This had been his home. This was where he and his ancestors had lived for generations. His body trembled, tears building up behind his eyes.

But Luka did not succumb. Instead of sorrow, he could feel something else swelling within him, and he latched onto it. Rage.

This was not fair. The injustice of three strangers appearing one day, taking everything, and then walking free was damnable. Luka stood up and screamed at the top of his lungs, like a wolf's howl in the night.

Violent anger seethed within him. He would not accept these circumstances. He looked again at his fallen home that lay beneath. *What you did to me, I will do to you thousands of times over.*

Luka's eyes fell on a thorn bush nearby, and he tore a stem from it. He remembered an ancient tradition from before the unification of Estravia that he learned about in his childhood studies. It was a time of bloodshed and rivalry as the many divided houses competed for power. Warriors who lost the lives of loved ones would swear blood oaths, vowing vengeance on those who wronged them. Before Sila and his agents, the oath-taker would pledge his entire life to the pursuit of revenge. He was not to rest until his targets were dead.

With the thorns he had just plucked, Luka cut an "X" on the back of his left hand—the infamous "Mark of the Blood Oath." Red liquid trickled down Luka's wrist and arm. He did not remember the exact words of the Oath, but he thought it mattered little.

With resolve, he chanted, "Before Sila and his agents, in the name of the Holy Land of Estravia, I, Luka Vernik, the first of his name, the rightful King of Estravia, vow to avenge my father, King Var Vernik, my brother, Prince Xander Vernik, and the people of my once-beautiful city of Vernikport. I will not rest until Privus Zlikrej, Drugi Zlikrej, and Omarius Zlikrej, the three sons of the tyrant Lord Diocretin Zlikrej, are all dead. This I swear on my life, on my soul, on my honor, and on my family's noble name."

After taking this vow, Luka tossed the stem off the mountain in the direction of the ruins of Vernikport. A dark, vengeful energy now flowed through his body. He did not have to stop to rest a single time on the journey back to the farm.

*****

A pile of maps lay in front of Luka early the next morning, but his focus centered on two that were most relevant to him. The first map displayed the nation of Estravia in its entirety. The other was a skinny vertical map of Vulture Road, depicting intricate details that included every single city and landmark along the way.

Post-unification, Vulture Road was not as dreary as its name would suggest. It served as a vibrant artery and trade corridor. It ran through the middle country from the capital city of Vernikport through the bustling city of Privagrad, towards the edge of Lake Zachary, and ended at the mountainous city of Exeter. Scores of small, yet lively cities sat in between, at least the ones that had not yet been decimated by the Zlikrej brothers.

Yet, this road was not always a thriving thoroughfare. Its dark history earned it a grim nickname. Centuries ago, it was overrun with criminals, more than any other place in the country. The very qualities that make it ideal for merchants today once made it a haven for outlaws. Those who dared to travel its path often met tragic ends.

The famous poet, Milo Juric, coined the term on a journey from Exeter to Vernikport. He spotted a wake of vultures feasting on a pair of dead human bodies lying in the middle of the road. His infamous poem titled "Vulture Road," was accidentally left behind in Vernikport and published sometime later. Tragically, he was murdered on that same road by bandits while traveling back home to his family in the north.

Now, the road would surely once again be home to danger as the Zlikrej moved north, conquering territory. The maps would be valuable to Luka as he pursued them.

"Hello, Luka." Queen Vanessa's voice interrupted Luka's strategizing. Luka had not even noticed her come into his room. "I've just come to check on you. What are you working on?"

"Just looking over some maps," he answered, shuffling around.

"For what purpose?"

"Just to get a sense of how far the Zlikrej have gone. I need to plot out our attack."

"Shouldn't you be resting? There is no need to strain yourself in your current condition."

"I told you, Mother, I've done enough resting," Luka replied, looking up from his maps. He wanted to shift the conversation away from this topic. "How about we take a stroll? I still have yet to talk to the farmer who owns the estate, and I'd love an introduction."

"Yes, of course," the queen replied, a bit surprised.

After walking around the farm, they approached a large barn where nearly a dozen horses grazed on feed. The animals neighed as they drew near. The largest of the stallions was a light brown horse with a thick mane and a muscular body.

Luka was drawn to this steed and went to fuss him. He picked up a handful of hay and held it out. The beast eyed Luka suspiciously before gobbling up the offering.

"His name is Velico," came a rough voice behind them. "He's perhaps the biggest steed I've ever raised."

The speaker was a man in rugged clothes with a thick beard. "Luka, this is farmer Ivan," said Queen Vanessa. "He owns this farm. He has graciously provided us with refuge."

Ivan bowed. "It is my honor to serve you, Your Highness. I am humbled to be able to assist in any way I can after the terrible tragedy that befell you."

Luka waved the bow away. "I cannot thank you enough, kind sir. You are an outstanding citizen. It does pain me, however, to ask one more thing from you."

"Certainly, Your Highness. Just speak your wish, and I will do what I can."

"I would like to borrow Velico."

"Luka, you should not be riding a horse!" Queen Vanessa jumped in. "Where on earth do you plan on going?"

Luka did not address the question. He waited for Ivan to respond to him first.

"Yes, My King. Of course," Ivan said hesitantly. "All of my horses belong to you, should you require them."

"Luka! Where are you going?" Queen Vanessa repeated.

"Mother, I cannot stay here forever. Not while they are still out there," Luka responded.

"You would be mad to leave now. You are in absolutely no condition."

"I have recovered a great deal."

"You could hardly walk just the other day!"

"And now I *can* walk. Besides, I am not going to leave quite yet. Just soon."

"How soon?"

"As soon as I am able."

As the conversation gradually became more intense, Farmer Ivan quietly slipped away.

"Luka, please don't be reckless. You are all I have left."

"I am not speaking of recklessness, Mother. I am speaking of bravery. I am speaking of justice. I must avenge Father and Xander," Luka responded.

"Justice and vengeance are not the same, Luka."

"Don't you want those bastards to die?" Luka screamed.

"Of course I do! But I wouldn't *dare* sacrifice my only living son for that to happen. You must not let rage cloud your judgment. They have an army now. They have magic that could have only come from Vragr himself."

Luka raised his left hand and showed Vanessa the red "X" he had cut on himself the day before. "I swore an oath. No army, no magic, not even my own broken body will stop me now. I have a duty to uphold."

Vanessa's eyes became glassy with the threat of coming tears. "Luka, please. Please don't do this. This country needs you alive. *I* need you."

Luka could not bear the sight of his mother crying. He relented. "Mother, fine. I won't leave just yet, but you must know that I can't remain here forever. I have to do something about this at some point."

That seemed good enough, for now.

*****

Sweat and terror greeted Luka the next morning. The sharp ache in his head and the relentless ringing in his ears began the moment he opened his eyes. Even with all of those symptoms, wakefulness was welcome. In his slumber, he had witnessed his father and brother dying over and over again, Luka powerless to stop it each time.

The last thing he remembered before he awoke was Privus mocking him. "You are pathetic. You couldn't stop us from killing your family the first time. What makes you think you can stop us now?"

Not even in my sleep can I escape my pain.

Luka tried to expunge the poisonous thoughts in his mind, replacing them with images of him fighting back. Picturing his sword slicing through Privus's throat. Of butchering Omarius's big head like a piece of meat. Even of killing Drugi, who was just as guilty, though perhaps not as effective as his brothers.

I can't stay here any longer, Luka realized when he rose from bed. He marched to the main cottage with conviction, knowing that this was his last sunrise on the farm.

Only Amelia and Farmer Ivan were awake at that time, preparing a large, hot breakfast together. Her movements were slow and ancient for someone of her age. She was alive, but her soul seemed to be buried back in the rubble of Vernikport.

"What are you making?" Luka asked

"We are making Socan eggs! A fantastic batch," Ivan exclaimed happily. "They are nearly done."

The thought of Socan eggs sounded delicious. The large flightless birds produced eggs that were far superior in both flavor and nourishment to chicken eggs. The only downside was they required lengthier preparation.

"Would you like some bread and tea while you wait, Luka?" Amelia asked. She tried to maintain her usual friendliness and politeness, but her words were lifeless.

"Yes, that would be lovely." Luka took a seat while his sister-in-law went to fetch him the food and drink. Admittedly, he had not thought a lot about her since awaking. Amelia was likely grieving just as much as he was. Guilt filled Luka at this thought. He smiled warmly and thanked her when she returned.

Vanessa joined them at the breakfast table as Luka was nearly finished with his bread. She patted Luka's shoulder and gave it a quick, affectionate rub. Ivan dropped off Luka's plate of eggs at his place and then went to fetch breakfast for the queen as well.

Luka swallowed a large helping of Socan egg and decided now was as opportune of a time as he would have to make his announcement. "I must let everyone know that I have decided to leave tomorrow after sunrise."

Vanessa threw her hands up, nearly knocking over the food that Amelia was about to set down. "Absolutely not, Luka!"

"I am going, Mother," he replied staunchly.

"Where are you going?" Amelia asked.

"North along Vulture Road. To hunt down the Zlikrej brothers," Luka said, jamming his fork into another helping of eggs.

"Luka, we discussed this. You could hardly walk just the other day!" Queen Vanessa said.

"But I can walk more than well enough now, and I can most certainly ride. My strength grows each day."

"Luka, this is madness. What do you possibly hope to accomplish?" Vanessa pleaded.

Amelia also interjected. "Are you certain you are feeling well enough?"

"I am certain." Luka finished his eggs as Pametan followed by Priestess Teya joined the party for breakfast. He sensed an all-out debate brewing and did not want to battle the entire room. There was no need. "I will consider your remarks, but if I still feel this way in the morning, I will leave—and no one will stop me."

He spent the remainder of the day surreptitiously gathering supplies from around the farm. A sack of preserved meat and grain. A standard issue infantry sword from one of the guards, taken with no explanation. Light leather armor from one of the shacks. Clothes from Farmer Ivan's house. And a saddle that was specifically fitted for one special horse.

*****

"Luka, you really mustn't leave tomorrow," his mother begged once again, later that evening. Her cheeks bore the faint ghosts of tears that had been wiped away. They sat in the light of a flickering candle, glasses of wine in their hands. Dinner had finished, and all the others had gone to sleep.

"Mother, please just let this drop."

"Promise me you won't leave tomorrow. Give it just a few more days, Luka. We can think of an alternative. You're in no condition. You really need to—"

He cut her off. "Fine, Mother. I promise I will not leave tomorrow."

"Really?"

"Yes. Really."

"Well, I am very pleased to hear that." With both mother and son seemingly satisfied by this, they shifted the conversation to lighter topics while the wine in their glasses slowly dwindled.

"Do you remember the centennial ball a few years ago? You and your brother both looked so dashing. Your father, too," Vanessa said.

"I do remember, Mother. It was probably the first ball that I actually rather enjoyed."

"I'm sure that was because you had Serena with you," Vanessa pointed out.

Luka's cheeks flushed. "She was certainly an enjoyable companion. Brooks of Marlinus is a fortunate man."

"You can stop it, you know," Vanessa said.

"What?"

"You can stop their marriage and wed her yourself. You are The King now. Once this settles down, you can choose your queen at your will, as long as she is worthy. It was a mistake to ever deny you this right."

Luka nodded, the idea sinking in at the worst time. "Assuming she survives this. They are headed for Privagrad as we speak."

Vanessa remained silent and took a big sip from her glass. It was clear she preferred to dwell on the pleasant past rather than the wretched present. "Oh, and Xander and Amelia were so happy together," she added. "I knew then and there that they would make an incredible prince and princess."

"I did too, Mother. I know she made Xander very happy."

They spent hours reminiscing as the flame gradually ate the candle away, and the wine bottle emptied out. When they were done, Luka led her to her bedroom and hugged her. "Goodnight, Luka. See you in the morning," she said.

"Goodnight, Mother." *See you in a long time– after I have avenged Father and Xander.*

Luka waited patiently that night until he was sure everyone else was sound asleep. Then, he carried his things into the field and began to saddle Velico. The horse was a mighty steed, well suited for the long journey ahead of him.

As Luka was about to mount Velico, he heard his name. He froze, and his heart raced for a moment. "Luka," the female voice repeated. He turned to see Princess Amelia, standing with her arms folded across her chest.

"Amelia, um…"

"Luka, are you leaving?"

The idea of lying crossed Luka's mind, but he realized the effort would be futile. His intentions were fairly transparent right now. "Yes, I am leaving," he admitted. "I am well enough, and I must do something to avenge Xander and my father. Please do not raise trouble about this."

"Don't worry, Luka. I understand. I will not stop you. Just promise me two things."

Surprised, Luka nodded and waited for her requests.

"First, promise me you'll kill them all. Promise me you'll kill the bastards that took my Xander from me." Her voice nearly broke off at the end of her plea.

"I promise, Amelia. I swear it to you, as I have already sworn to Sila and his agents."

Amelia nodded in gratitude, but she was too choked up to speak.

"What is the second thing you would have me promise you?"

She took a deep breath before answering. "Do you remember how Xander always used to talk about magic?"

"Yes, I do. Sometimes, I would think he was off the moon when he would talk of it. I wish I could tell him he was right."

Amelia nodded and continued, "He would talk of a special place called 'The Magic Tavern' near Jetsac. I always thought it was another myth, but now I think it might be real."

"Xander once mentioned that to me as well. Are you suggesting I can acquire magic at this tavern?" Luka asked, his eyes widening.

"Xander said there was an old wizard there who would put on shows for the customers. His name is Gabbitt. He can summon the elements at his will. He may be able to help you."

At first, the idea seemed absurd to him, but he caught himself. The world was obviously not as he thought it was.

"Promise me you'll go there. You can't fight magic if you don't have magic of your own. Promise me for Xander."

Luka thought for a moment and then agreed. "I promise to go there and see what I can find."

With that, Luka rode off towards the Road of Vultures.

Chapter 16
Vulture Road

The smell of ash lingered in the air. Even as dawn arrived, the sky remained gray and gloomy, thick clouds blanketing the sunrise. Ruins of small villages lined the beginning of Vulture Road, a trail of destruction left behind by the Zlikrej brothers. Luka followed the trail as it weaved north.

Along his journey he had encountered only desolation. He had seen abandoned weapons, fresh corpses, and a stray dog, squealing in search of its long-gone owners. Each time the wind passed through, it carried the scent of death.

Luka traveled all through the night without stopping. Velico held the pace as well, living up to Luka's expectations. His horse was perhaps the only conspicuous thing about him. Dressed in plain clothes with his hood drawn up, he blended into the shadows. The blond stubble covering his face and his longer, unkempt hair further obscured his identity—just the way he preferred it.

After riding for a full day and well into the next night, Luka finally stopped to rest. He found a stable just off the road, one of the few structures that remained standing. Candlelight was absent from the windows of the adjacent house, a sign that the owner was sound asleep. Luka snuck in and led Velico into one of the open stalls. He offered his horse food and water before they both lay down to sleep. The air was filled with the horrid scent of manure, but Luka was so exhausted that he drifted off to sleep in spite of it.

The next morning, Luka awoke to the sound of an avian hissing and squawking nearby. Despite the rancid smell reminding him of where he was, he resisted the urge to get up, hoping for just a few more minutes of rest. That hope died when Luka heard the squeaking of a nearby door swinging open.

Peering from around Velico, Luka watched the stablemaster slowly exit the building, only meters away. Luka braced himself, thinking of how he could explain his trespass. But the man did not notice Luka or the new massive horse that was housed in his stables. Instead, he turned in the other direction and walked away, oblivious.

Luka did not waste another second. He led Velico out of the stables and rode off. A few horses neighed as Luka left, but the stablemaster would not have time to check on the disturbance before he was gone.

When Luka was safely past the stables, he looked up at the sky to see a cloud of thick black birds swirling around to the west. He had a dismal feeling that the wake of vultures was waiting to eat something other than a dead animal.

As the days wore on, the journey became tiresome and lonely. He quickly adapted to the hefty amount of riding and the sparse amount of sleep. He had a much harder time adjusting to the pure solitude. There was little to distract him when nightmarish thoughts of Var and Xander appeared in his head. The best he could manage was to shift his thoughts to slaughtering the Zlikrej brothers in many different, creative ways.

On Luka's sixth day of riding, or at least Luka believed it was his sixth day, he encountered a man dressed in a ragged robe colored in emerald and sable. He was sitting with his legs crossed in the middle of the road. Luka pulled Velico to the right with the intent of avoiding him.

"Oi!" the itinerant called out.

Luka ignored him. He was never enthused about engaging with a stranger on the street, but that was truer now. His mission depended on anonymity. Perhaps his greatest asset was that his enemies believed he was dead. He wasn't going to risk that here.

"Oi, sir, you ride such a great steed," the itinerant repeated. "Where did you come about such a horse?"

Again, Luka said nothing. He was almost past the stranger at this point.

"I'd wager the Zlikrej brothers will take that horse. They've taken everything else around here."

"They will not take this horse," Luka replied, abandoning his intent to ignore the man.

"You look familiar, sir. My name is Ijim," the itinerant said, now that Luka was looking at him. "Have we met before?"

"I'm fairly certain we haven't." Luka giddied Velico along and away from the itinerant. He glanced back once to see the stranger staring at him eerily as he rode away.

Following that encounter, Luka kept off the main road as much as he could. He trotted Velico out to the grassy fields alongside Vulture Road, and they traveled north that way, keeping the road parallel.

The green fields beyond the road were absent of people. He was able to maintain a consistent, satisfying pace, already passing by several small cities, including Lansoj and Wilma. Luka had cautiously investigated those two cities, finding them almost totally destroyed. The citizens who had survived had still not had the chance to clear away all of the dead bodies.

I'll kill the ones who did this to you, Luka thought. But that was all he could offer them as he rode away anonymously.

Several days after Wilma, Luka spotted a pack of massive creatures feasting on the carcass of a dead horse. The creatures were hog-like with dark-brown hides, but they were several times larger than any pig. Two pairs of long tusks jutted from beneath their snouts, giving them a menacing appearance.

Grucknicks, Luka realized ominously.

Velico noticed them, too, quickly becoming agitated. Luka tried to calm his steed and veer to the left, hoping to slip by unnoticed, but his effort was unsuccessful. The beasts grunted violently when they saw him, quickly charging towards him as a pack. They were much faster than they looked, forcing Luka to urge Velico to move faster. The horse's gallop turned into an all-out sprint. Once in stride, their speed was more than enough to get away from the Grucknicks. The creatures trailed them for a time but eventually gave up as they drifted off into the distance.

Later that evening, he took extra care to survey the land around him. If Grucknicks were roaming the area, then sleep would not come easy. With his guard up, Luka gathered sticks and logs and repeatedly struck his flint rocks against each other until the sparks gave birth to a gentle bloom of fire.

As the flames danced, Luka pulled out his preserved meat and cut a small chunk off with Xander's dagger. He could eat it cold, but it was far more pleasant when warm, though even after being cooked, it was a chore to chew.

After the bland meal, Luka fed Velico from the pouch of grain. The horse devoured his food. *He's enjoying his food more than I'm enjoying mine,* Luka thought.

In the loneliness of the night, Luka stared into the fire, watching it flicker as images of the destruction he had witnessed over the past few days of riding flashed in his mind. Vulture Road was now a skeleton of itself, as were all the cities along it. So many innocent lives had been lost, but Luka knew he would only encounter more of that ahead.

He pulled out his two maps and examined them under the dim firelight. By his estimation, the Zlikrej were likely closing in on Privagrad now, which meant that the Tomkins family would be in danger. Luka thought about Serena as he held his gaze where Privagrad was marked. The distance between them gnawed at him, but he was powerless to do anything. He could only hope that she had fled for safety.

As the fire died out, he lay back and looked up at the stars glistening above. There was nothing he could do for her, or anyone else, until he caught up with his enemies.

Chapter 17
Unwelcome Visitors

A distant commotion interrupted Serena's late-night reading. Hearing faint screams, she tossed her book aside and peered out her high bedroom window. The air of Privagrad was filled with smoke, and a devilish orange glow lit the sky.

The sounds drew nearer and grew loud enough to make out the distinct galloping of war horses, the marching of soldiers, and the clashing of steel. It could only be one thing—the Zlikrej were here, just as they had feared.

Serena grabbed a dagger hidden in one of her clothes drawers and departed her room. She made way for her parents' bedroom on the far side of the palace's highest level. Halfway across the floor, she came across her mother, who was frantically rushing in her direction in her nightgown.

"They're here! They're here!" her mother shrieked.

"I know! Where is Father?"

"He was with the security council! We must find him! We can try to sneak through the tunnel. Where is your brother?"

Before she could answer, a thunderous bang vibrated through the palace. The sounds of broken glass and screaming traveled all the way up to them from the ground floor.

"You go find him, Mother! Search for him in his room first," Serena said.

"Wait, where are you—" but Serena was already off, heading down the stairs. She knew danger was at hand, and she knew what she needed to fend it off.

Four floors down, only one above ground level, she found the room. Typically, at least one palace guard held a position outside the door. Tonight, that guard was obviously preoccupied.

The door gave after several attempts to barge through. A glass case sat in the center of the room, displaying one of the most famous blades in Estravian history—*Strujaza*. The sword had been used by Branitej Tomkins, one of the foremost allies of Okupi Vernik the Uniter during the Great Unification. The legends written of it were volumes long, but its most notable reputation was for its speed. It was often called the "Lightning Blade" for this characteristic. Serena was about to test that.

She took her dagger and hurriedly fiddled with each lock until they gave way. With careful precision, she removed the legendary blade from its case. Small sapphires adorned the pommel, gleaming faintly in the dim light. The silver blade caught what little illumination the room offered. The weapon was larger and longer than she was accustomed to, but it still felt shockingly light in her hand. Leaving the scabbard behind, she went down the main stairs to face the source of the commotion.

On her way down, she noticed two men in black cloaks and leather armor on course to intercept her. Serena did not have to guess their intentions. Instead, she prepared to grant them a steel greeting.

The two enemies seemed surprised by the speed of Serena's first strike with Strujaza. Serena was amazed herself.

The first strike flashed like lightning, cutting the nearest man in his ribs before he could even conceive of a defense. The blow itself was not fatal, but it sent him tumbling down the tall set of stone stairs.

The second soldier struck less than a second later, but Serena was able to meet the parry with blistering quickness. As her opponent thrust forward with another attempt, she struck first, cutting underneath his attack. The soldier cried out and then tumbled down the vast staircase, joining his compatriot at the bottom, incapacitated.

Serena hurried down past the bodies. On the ground floor, the hallway was wide and filled with commotion. Scores of palace workers and servants screamed, running in all directions. Some were subdued. Some were able to escape. Some were cut down by the invaders.

The enemies were numerous. Odds of any sort of victory were slim, but a sense of hope began to fill Serena, who felt exhilarated by her triumph over the first two combatants. The sheer speed and deadly pleasure with which she could wield *Strujaza* only added to that thrill. She pressed forward into the chaos. Someone needed to defend her home, after all.

Three Zlikrej soldiers closed in on her immediately. With her blade, she outmaneuvered each one, cutting them down in a maelstrom of silver flashes that her enemies could not counter.

The flow of battle enveloped Serena. She felt as though her identity was indistinguishable from her blade's as they spun through the room. In this spirit, she moved towards the next group of enemies, this one four men strong. The first three fell in a familiar manner. A sharp, shrill voice interrupted her flow before she could eliminate the fourth.

"Serena! Wait!"

The voice belonged to her father. She glanced over only for an instant, seeing him on his knees with a blade at his throat. The speed of *Strujaza* could not compensate for her lapse in attention when she turned back to her opponent. The soldier knocked the blade from her hands. An armored boot followed, smashing into her stomach and knocking her onto the floor.

A quick order from across the hallway spared her life. "Don't kill her! Bring her to me." The soldier above her obeyed the voice, sheathing his sword instead of swinging it down on her.

Several pairs of black-clad enemy arms seized Serena and took her away. They threw her unceremoniously on the ground next to her father. Though stars obstructed her vision, she glanced up and could make out the serious but smug face of the man who had given the orders.

"Well met, young lady. My name is General Klacan, and I must say you are fierce. It was rather refreshing to see a noble family put up a fight. Even though it ultimately amounted to nothing, you can consider me impressed."

He turned away momentarily, barking orders and waving his hands at his soldiers, but he quickly readdressed her. "Now let's see what your new masters think of you."

*****

Privus strutted his way through Privagrad Palace. Throughout the hallways of the castle, his men cheered for him as he passed them by. He waved to them with his left hand, still clutching his staff in his right. Thanks largely to his weapon, the victory had come easily, and Privagrad now belonged to Privus and his brothers.

Even though the city was on high alert, they were easily overpowered. It took only a few blasts of the fearsome elements for the soldiers to realize surrender was the wisest move. It was a far more popular choice than being burning to death or being impaled by ice shards.

With Privagrad conquered, the Zlikrej forces now controlled a highly strategic location right in the middle of the country.

As Privus neared the lord's throne room, General Klacan approached, holding a stunningly beautiful sword. It gleamed from far down the hallway, making him stop in his tracks.

"General, what is this beautiful treasure in your hands?"

Klacan smiled. "This is the legendary *Strujaza*, My Lord. It's the family blade of the Tomkins family. You will never guess who was wielding it."

Klacan handed the blade over to Privus and let him examine it. "Who was wielding this?"

"The daughter of Lord Tomkins. Her name is Serena. Surprisingly remarkable skills for a noble lass."

"Very interesting," Privus said, his eyes still affixed to the weapon. "Was she killed in battle?"

"No, sir. She had slain quite a few of our men, but I used her own father against her. The family has now since surrendered, and they await their fates inside," Klacan said, motioning to the two black double doors behind them. "Where are Omarius and Drugi?"

"Drugi is collecting arrows from the watchtowers for his collection," Privus said matter-of-factly. "Omarius asked me to deal with the Tomkins family. He is recruiting some of the Privagrad city forces to join our ranks. Although I am not sure how many of those men I want in our army. Their resolve was weak against us."

Klacan nodded. "Very well, My Lord. Let's go inside."

Dozens of Zlikrej soldiers held control of the room. The air was thick with the prisoners' fear. In the back, bound in chains, were the Tomkins family and several members of their court. Their faces were pale as they looked up, dread flickering in their eyes when they saw who had entered.

Privus scanned them briefly, then turned to Klacan and said, "Is the executioner ready?" He made sure his words were audible for the captives.

"Yes, My Lord," Klacan answered in the same volume.

"Very good," Privus said, then he turned to the prisoners and announced, "I am going to make this quick and simple for all of you.

All who wish to stay alive will swear fealty to my brothers and me, the new Archlords of Estravia. Those who do so shall be given the great privilege of serving in our new regime. Those who do not wish to stay alive... Well, that is a poor choice, but one I am content to grant you."

The prisoners seemed to turn even whiter than before upon hearing this. Only one reacted in defiance. A knight, bearing a thick white mustache above his lip, rose to his feet. "I'll never serve a usurper! My loyalty is to My Lord, to the throne, and to my country."

Privus's men tried to shove him down and shut him up, but he waved them off. "You talk of a throne. Just what throne would that be exactly?"

The knight hesitated before responding, "The true throne of Estravia. Lord Donte, the Acting Regent, now sits upon that throne."

Privus laughed, throwing his head back in an exaggerated manner. "Lord Donte! What a jest!" He paused for a moment and then turned his tone graver. "This is actually quite a shame, though. You seemed like a wise man, but you have chosen to die. You did not have to make that choice, but as I said, I am content to grant you your wish. Send in the executioner!"

At Privus's summons, a large man wielding an axe entered the room, a black cloak concealing most of his other features. For a moment, Privus considered ordering the executioner to use Strujaza for this deed. It would be fitting in a certain way. He glanced down at the legendary blade he held and then back at the axe. *Too much of an honor for this imbecile,* he thought. He signaled to the executioner to proceed as-is.

Two soldiers grabbed the defiant knight by his arms and led him to the axeman. The knight struggled to escape, wriggling and writhing about, but he was no match for the Zlikrej soldiers. They threw him to his knees beneath the massive axeman, who was casually cleaning his tool.

Privus scanned the faces of the rest of the prisoners, their visible terror causing his lips to stretch into a thin smile. Lady Tomkins was sobbing on her husband's shoulder and wouldn't even look at what was going on. Then Privus noticed their daughter, the elegant Lady Serena. She was afraid, like everyone else, but she would not look away. Her eyes darted from Privus, to the axeman, and to the knight. Privus remembered what Klacan had told him about her. Sudden excitement rushed up within him.

"Wait," Privus called out to the executioner. "Take this into another room and do it."

"Which room, sir?" one of the men asked.

"I don't give a damn which room you choose. Any room. Just come back when it's done." The two soldiers took the knight again by the shoulders and carried him away. The executioner followed, almost dragging his axe behind him.

Privus strolled back to the prisoners, heading directly for Serena. He crouched down so he could meet her at eye level. Her black hair was messy from the chaos earlier, but it still shone with beauty. She looked up at Privus with her ferocious brown eyes, which only appeared more intense and arousing up close.

"You must be Serena Tomkins, are you not?" Privus asked.

"I am," she said, without breaking her gaze. "Are you going to kill us?"

"No, Serena. I think I have a much better idea. I am impressed by what I have heard about you."

He paused before delivering the next part. "You are going to become my wife."

Surprise flickered on her face briefly, but then she turned combative. "Piss on that," she retorted.

"Now, now, Serena, that is no way for the Lady of Exeter to speak." Privus knew that would pique her curiosity, and he was right. "Yes, you heard me correctly, dear. My brothers and I still have much conquering to do. But when it is over we all will rule Estravia from three seats. My seat will be in Exeter, and as Lord of that great city, I will need a great lady at my side."

"I would never go with you," she spat back. Her curiosity had vanished quickly. "You are a monster. My husband will be Brooks of Marlinus. And even if he wasn't, I would still *never* marry you. I wouldn't even want to be in the same room as you! You're a murderer!"

Privus clenched his jaw, his expression hardening. Rising to his feet once more, he turned his gaze on both Lord Tomkins and Serena. "Understand this—you are coming with me. You will be my bride at a wedding in Exeter. It will be a great honor for you, and I will give your family mercy in return. More mercy than you all deserve. Your father and the rest of your family will be allowed to live so long as you behave, obey me, and fulfill your duties as my wife."

"Not only that," Privus turned to face Lord Tomkins, "As part this arrangement, I will allow you to keep your seat as Lord of Privagrad, albeit under my command. I will even leave you with *Strujaza*. It could do great good in the hands of my men, but as a gesture of good faith, I will leave it with the Tomkins family, where it belongs.

"You will write a letter to the Lord of Marlinus," Privus continued. "You will tell him the wedding to Brooks has been canceled. In this letter, you will also order them to fall in line and swear fealty to my brothers and me. So long as you do so, your daughter shall live a long, good, and rich life."

Lord Tomkins was stunned and had no answer.

"I am granting you an incredible opportunity with this offer. It's an offer that won't ever come again—I can promise you that. I implore you to accept. Think of your family."

Lord Tomkins shook his head. "I can't serve you," he whispered. "I could never serve you."

Privus gritted his teeth again. At that moment, the two Zlikrej soldiers and the executioner returned. "It is done, My Lord," bellowed the executioner. He had not cleaned the dead knight's blood off his axe, and it dripped down onto the floor.

Privus nodded. Then he turned back to Lord Tomkins and said, "This is your last chance. Everyone here, including your daughter, can be spared."

Lord Tomkins just shook his pale, sweaty head.

"Fine! Have it your way. *She* dies first." Privus yanked Serena from the ground. She screamed and hit him repeatedly, but he was unabated. The axeman readied himself to do his job again.

"Alright! Alright!" Lord Tomkins yelled. "I accept!"

The commotion finally stopped, and the room fell silent.

"A very wise choice," Privus said, grinning devilishly.

Chapter 18
Glazben

The humble city of Glazben sat in a small valley at the foot of two hills. Vulture Road ran between the hills and through the heart of the city. Glazben didn't boast the same size or population as some of the other cities along the road, but it had just as much vibrancy and character, mostly thanks to the wise and careful rule of the Laz Family, who had presided over the city for centuries.

Maintaining his distance from Vulture Road, Luka approached from the east. He guided Velico to the top of the rocky and jagged hill. When he reached the peak, the city of Glazben came into view in the golden afternoon sunlight.

To his dismay, Glazben had been reduced to a husk of its former self. Many buildings had been partially or completely destroyed. Black Zlikrej banners flapped above a few of the structures that were still standing. The Lord's grand quarters appeared untouched, looming over the debris, but there was little else. It was a sight of devastation—not as total as Vernikport, but sickening all the same.

Luka tightened his grip on Velico's reins and gritted his teeth. The Mithacor flags gave him the feeling that the city housed his enemies, but he felt an urge to investigate. The reward did not cover the risk, but he needed to know if Lord and Lady Laz were still alive. They could be allies to Luka's cause, but more than that—they were always great friends to the Vernik family.

It had been nearly two years since Luka had last seen them, when the entire Laz family was present for Xander's wedding. The event was glorious. Hundreds were packed into the Vernik Temple for the ceremony. Luka had never seen his brother so happy. He and his new bride seemed as if they were shining that day.

Amelia, all I can do for you, my sister, is fulfill my promise and avenge him, Luka thought.

Carefully, Luka proceeded down the hill. Soon he was amongst a cluster of rubble and a few houses that were fortunate enough to still be standing.

The only person to be seen was an old woman washing clothes in the ruined street. When she noticed him, she ceased her chore and stared at him. Luka rode over. "Madam, what happened here?"

She regarded him with suspicion before she replied. "Same thing that's happened everywhere else. The Zlikrej brothers and their army rode into the city. This is all that is left," she answered.

"What happened to the Laz family?"

"Held as prisoners. They are lucky their children were not in the city. Lady Laz is also lucky that she is old, like me. Otherwise... well, they've done some horrible things to some of the girls in this city. At least the ones who are still alive and haven't managed to flee."

A red wave of anger flashed across Luka's face. "Where are the prisoners being held? And how many Zlikrej men are still in this city?"

"They are holding the prisoners in the Hall of Justice. There are perhaps three dozen soldiers in this city, maybe more. They spend most of their time in the Lord's quarters."

Before Luka could press for more information, a lone, black-clad soldier appeared from around another building. "Oi, curfew starts in a few minutes. You best make sure you're inside by then, you old hag," he called out. Then, his gaze shifted to Luka, eyeing the hooded rider atop the imposing steed.

"And who are you?" he asked.

Luka did not respond, his body tensing.

"Oi, you better answer me! I don't like the looks of you." The soldier began to approach as Luka dismounted.

"You want to know who I am? So be it. I am Luka Vernik, rightful King of Estravia." Luka's sword made a hiss of steel as he drew it from its scabbard. Weapon ready, he walked towards the first enemy he had seen since Vernikport.

"What..." the soldier said confused, drawing his own weapon in turn. A flicker of faint recognition crossed his eyes when they stood face to face. "Oh, it would be great if you bloody *are* Luka Vernik."

"Not for you," Luka replied.

The young king struck with dumbfounding speed. The soldier feebly parried the blow, but the next attack was already on its way, doubling him over as it connected with his rib cage. A final stroke across the soldier's neck sent him collapsing, a fatal amount of blood pooling out quickly beneath him.

Luka wiped his sword clean before sheathing it.

He expected the kill to be more satisfying, but one less Zlikrej scoundrel in the world was not nearly enough.

"My, you really are Prince Luka! I can't believe it!" the old woman exclaimed.

"I am the *King* now," Luka corrected, the words still a shock to himself. "The crown has fallen to me, but you must promise to remain silent about this. It was foolish of me to disclose that, even to someone who wouldn't live to spread the information. It is to my obvious advantage that all continue to think me dead. Especially my enemies.

"Now, please do me the favor of hiding this body. I am also going to leave my horse with you. Take good care of him, and do not let anyone steal him. I will be back shortly."

The woman seemed stunned at the request but obeyed his orders. She took Velico and disappeared around the side of her house. Luka was gone before she came back to tend to the fresh corpse.

*****

Two black-cloaked spearmen guarded the entrance to the Hall of Justice. Of course, at present, that was a misnomer—the building was devoid of any justice while under Zlikrej control. Luka, peering from behind a half-standing house, was determined to change that.

When he was sure there were no other enemies in the area, he sprinted toward the two guards, sword drawn. They saw him and readied their spears, pointing them at their oncoming foe.

Luka angled to one side, bringing a rapid assault upon one of the spearmen. His speed and momentum forced his opponent onto the defensive, neutralizing the length of the spear as an advantage. Their weapons clashed twice before Luka closed the distance. He drove his knee hard into the man's stomach, causing his grip on the spear to loosen.

Sensing the second guard behind him, Luka spun around to block. He then used his right elbow to incapacitate the first guard and engaged the other with his sword. Again, Luka moved in swiftly until he was in close. With the position secured, Luka thrust his blade through his enemy's heart.

As the second spearman bled away, the first soldier slowly began to stir on the ground. The elbow attack had left the man pained and dazed. Luka prepared to kick the soldier in the head, leaving the man fully unconscious. In that moment, he saw flashes of Var, Xander, and more recently, what the old woman had told him about what these men had done to the women of Glazben.

There would be no mercy.

Luka kicked the man in the mouth instead. Two teeth and a gush of blood spurted from the impact.

He stood over the man and waited for him to turn over and meet his gaze. When he finally did, Luka studied him briefly, seeing only an average young man who chose to serve in the Zlikrej cause. His eyes seemed to glow with a mix of hatred, anger, and fear. For a flash of a moment, the eyes went wide, fear surging above all else as Luka brought his sword down.

With the guards dispatched, he went inside.

A horrid, nauseating smell greeted Luka when he entered—the scent of many unwashed bodies and human feces left to rot. He tried not to gag as he surveyed the scene.

People sat chained together on the benches beneath the pulpit. Some of the prisoners craned their necks around the constraints to see who had entered. None got a clear look.

After a wide scan, Luka could not see Lord Laz amongst the ranks. He approached a boy at the end of one of the benches. "Hello there," he whispered, crouched down next to the boy. "Can you tell me where Lord Laz is? Is he being kept here?"

The boy's eyes were wide, his body trembling when he replied. "He-he's downstairs, in the dungeons."

"Thank you, lad. What's your name?"

"T-Tomas."

"You're a good man, Tomas. You will be free of this soon." With that, Luka hurried away.

Down in the dungeons, the stench was far worse than above. Rotten death and decay lingered in the air, nearly causing him to retch.

In total, there were six cells in the dungeons. Lord Tristus and Lady Petra Laz resided in one of the middle cells. The other cells, save for one, were filled with key servants or knights who served the Laz House. Directly across from the Lord and Lady, a single cell stood apart, its floor piled with lifeless bodies of all ages. A wave of nausea rose within him, the urge to retch intensifying.

"Tristus," Luka said when he came to Laz's cell. The lord was sitting next to his sleeping wife with his legs crossed on the floor. His head hung down, his eyes fixed to the ground. Astonishment flickered across his face when he looked up.

"Do my eyes deceive me?" he spoke aloud.

"That depends. If they see a friend, then they do not deceive you."

"Luka... it's you, Luka..." They embraced haphazardly through the prison bars.

"Luka, you're alive... What a blessing. I can't believe you survived... I thought they killed everyone."

"I have survived, as did my mother. But most did not. Including Xander and my father." Luka swallowed hard before continuing. "I see the citizens of Glazben have endured their own share of brutality. What they have done here is damnable."

"Your mother survived too? The Queen is alive?"

"Aye. She is safe. Along with Princess Amelia and a few others."

"Oh, blessings! All hope is not lost!" Laz exclaimed. Up until this point the conversation had been quiet, but prisoners in other cells now could overhear.

"You're correct. Hope is not lost," Luka said, bringing the volume of the conversation back down. "Now, how do I get you out of here? It is time to take back this city."

"The guards have the keys. They come multiple times a day to taunt me or bring another corpse for me to stare at," Laz responded.

"Might the guards outside the hall have those keys? I slayed them to gain entry here."

"They may, but I can't say for sure," Laz said.

"I'll go check."

Luka hurried back upstairs and outside. He rummaged through the two dead bodies until he found a set of keys. He smiled as he jingled them in front of his face.

When he returned, he tried each key until, finally, the door to Tristus Laz's prison cell flung open. By this point, Lady Laz was awake now, too. Now, they embraced properly, with no barriers between them.

"What do we do next?" Lord Laz asked. Then he added, "Your Highness."

"We free everyone else and expel the intruders. I have a plan, or at least a rough idea of one." In quiet detail, Luka explained his strategy and then went back to the main level, leaving Laz to unlock the rest of the cells in the dungeon.

Upstairs, Luka attended to the civilians who were bound in chains. Fortunately, the restraints were weak, breaking easily under a strike from his sword. Once freed, each person was ordered to stand by, obeying with hopeful yet nervous confusion.

Luka did not identify himself to any of them. He could hear them whisper to each other. Some surely recognized him, but with his ragged and changed appearance, no one could be certain who he was. Luka preferred to keep it that way.

When Luka was finished, dozens of citizens stood in the pews, unbounded and awaiting orders. Lord Laz walked up the stairs from the dungeon with his wife and a score of the other freed prisoners trailing him. He nodded to Luka and walked up to the pulpit. The crowd erupted in applause.

"My good citizens," the lord said, "For the past few weeks, we have lived under the control of some of the vilest beings to ever walk Estravian soil. Today, that will cease. We have been liberated by someone sent from Sila and his agents."

Laz looked to Luka, seeking some form of acknowledgement, but Luka shook his head. Laz understood and did not address Luka's identity further.

Continuing his address, Laz said, "We will not waste this freedom. Zlikrej rats still infest this city. But we now have numbers. We will overwhelm them and take back our home! And when Glazben is ours again, we will start rebuilding our humble and beautiful city into the place of joy that it always was."

Laz then proceeded to loosely explain the plan to surround the Lord's quarters and overthrow it. He made it sound like a legitimate military operation, but in reality, it was little more than a riot. But that was the best they could do, and the numbers were in their favor.

In a fervor, people gathered what little weapons were available or tried to make arms out of any object they could find, including the chains that had previously bound them. Then, the riot commenced.

*****

Officer Gnusa tapped his fingers against the bar while he waited for one of his soldiers to pour him another ale. The Zlikrej men had filled the living room inside the castle with several barrels of the best ale they could find. Gnusa smiled when the drink came. Without thanking his subordinate, he took a sip and enjoyed the fresh amber liquid, one of many he had consumed that evening.

Nearby, one of the soldiers jumped up from a table with a loud cheer, celebrating a win of a game of Table Dragons. Three pieces remained on his side of the board after he had claimed his opponent's last one.

"Oh, Sila's wrath. I want a rematch," the loser said.

"We both know you would just fall to me again," the victor replied. "I'm getting an ale." He walked past his comrades toward the barrels, with smugness on his face. Nearly all thirty or so of the Zlikrej occupying forces were congregated in this room.

"Officer Gnusa, would you like a game?" the loser asked.

Officer Gnusa took a sip of his ale before answering. "I suppose so. But be ready for an arse beating. If you can't beat Weilos, then you most certainly won't beat me." As he climbed into the seat across from his opponent, he heard a loud knock.

"Ugh, what now?" Gnusa waved one of his arms in frustration. "Oi, Private Davies! Go check on the door."

One of the soldiers got up from his seat to attend to the castle entrance. A hooded young man, Lord Laz, and a horde of Glazbenite rioters were there to answer the door. The hooded man's blade was the next thing to greet Private Davies, finding its way straight through his stomach.

The riot then quickly burst into the castle and into the living room. Gnusa hastily grabbed his sword to defend himself, but most of his men did not have their weapons handy. He cut down a few rioters who charged at him armed only with chains, only to come face-to-face with the hooded man.

Gnusa did not recognize his adversary, but it was clear he was facing an adept swordsman and a formidable opponent. Gnusa's heavy buzz made him slow in defending, and within a short time, the man's sword was buried in his stomach, too. Gnusa could barely tell what had happened to him until the blade was pulled from his belly. The pain was far greater on the way out than on the way in.

Gnusa died in a rapidly expanding puddle of blood, entrails, and spilled beer.

*****

The rest of the rioters quickly enveloped the remaining Zlikrej soldiers like a swarm of hungry carnivores. The sheer numbers overwhelmed them, dragging them to the ground in a storm of stomping, punching, and even biting.

Luka scanned the room and noticed Lord Laz, in defiance of his age, tackling a soldier into a Table Dragons Board, breaking the table in half and sending pieces flying.

Laz ended up on top of an obviously drunk soldier, alternating punches with each hand and yelling, "You bastard!" each time a fist connected with the man's face.

Luka rushed over and intervened before the Zlikrej soldier could harm Laz, pushing the lord aside and stomping hard on the soldier's forehead.

The skirmish was over shortly after that.

Hours later, the castle was emptied of Zlikrej men, and the dungeons were now full of them. The new captives had survived the skirmish but were left badly beaten and bloodied.

A celebration broke out in the living room. The victorious Glazbenites made an even better use of the barrels of ale, emptying them all in under an hour. Luka allowed himself a cup of ale, but he stayed in the corner with his hood up, taking it all in. A few people approached him and complimented him on his swordsmanship and thanked him for his role in their rescue, but he was wary of engaging in deeper conversation, lest he be discovered.

It was surreal to him. Technically, these people were his subjects, and he was speaking to them as if he was an anonymous warrior, unable to tell them who he really was. Rumors would surely start, but Luka hoped he had concealed himself enough to prevent them from spreading. Either way, it was worth it.

Lord Laz noticed the young king after a while and went over to relieve him, leaving Lady Laz to celebrate with several other close friends. "C'mon, lad. Let's go upstairs." He led the way up a dark staircase with Luka close behind. Laz took him into one of the bedrooms, which was messy from Zlikrej occupation.

"I will try to get one of my servants to clean this, but this room is for you to sleep in, My King," Lord Laz said. "You look like you are in dire need of rest."

Luka considered protesting, but instead simply said, "Thank you."

"I can't thank you enough for what you have done for me on this day. I meant it when I said you were an angel sent directly from Sila's agents to aid us. Giving you a proper room for the night only the beginning of my repayment to you."

"Tristus—"

"Think nothing of it. I thought all was lost, not just for me, but for this country. And now we have hope again.

"I am so sorry for your loss, Luka. I miss your father and brother dearly. But I cannot help but feel immense pleasure that you and your mother are still alive."

"I am alive," Luka replied. "Because I have a mission. I will not stop until Privus, Drugi, and Omarius are all dead. All of them. And I need to make sure word does not spread of my survival. My enemies should not know I am hunting them."

Lord Laz put his arm on Luka's shoulder and nodded. "Aye. I understand your request and will honor it if that is the course you wish to take. For now, I think it best that you rest."

Luka glanced at the bed longingly. He had not slept on a proper bed since he left Ivan's farm.

When the servants were done cleaning the room, Laz soon left him alone. He extinguished the lamps and sat on the edge of the bed in darkness. He began to undo his boots, feeling the relief in his worn soles. In the quiet, a memory came back to Luka. He was unwrapping a gift, a wooden toy horse, with his mother, father, and brother around him. It was pleasant and warm at first, but it quickly morphed into an acidic reminder of what he had lost.

He paused with one boot untied, feeling uneasy. He did not like the stillness. Distress, sadness, and rage began to overtake him. He immediately retied his boot, relit one of the lanterns, and wrote a few messages. He snuck out of the room and departed the castle undetected. Many Glazbenites were still celebrating their freedom and didn't notice him.

Luka retrieved Velico from the noble stables, where the horse had been moved shortly after the success of the riot. Nevertheless, he was grateful for the old woman who had cared for him earlier.

After mounting Velico and preparing to depart Glazben, he thought again about what the old woman had said about the vile deeds the Zlikrej soldiers had committed against the citizens, particularly the women, of the city. He thought about the piles of bodies that had only recently been cleared from the dungeons. And he thought about his own city, now in ruins, with the Zlikrej soldiers here having played a part in that, too.

For a moment, he hesitated, turning his head towards the Hall of Justice visible from across the city. A raging, murderous urge burned through him. They didn't deserve imprisonment—they deserved painful deaths. He envisioned grabbing the executioner's axe and letting their heads roll around in the dungeons like tossed dice. But then he stopped himself, not thinking of mercy, but rather of timing.

"They are not the mission," he muttered, his fists clenched tightly. He spared one more hateful glance in the direction of the dungeons, and then turned away, resuming his journey along Vulture Road.

Chapter 19
Martial Law

Thick beads of sweat ran down Luka's face in the early morning light. He wiped his forehead with his sleeve, panting. That was all the rest he allowed himself before resuming his assault on the tree. The bark grew chunks and gashes at an increasing rate.

He had departed Glazben without a goodbye, leaving only a note, just like how he left his mother. Remorse tugged at him when he thought of that. *I have a mission. I swore the Blood Oath,* Luka reminded himself, forcing the guilt aside.

He broke his fast afterwards with preserved beef. It was dull, as always. He tried hard not to imagine what kind of food he could have been enjoying had he woken up in Glazben Palace instead of a lonely field.

The ride held to a good pace later that day. Luka and Velico rode for hours without pause. When his steed's breaths became more labored, Luka slowed down and veered back towards Vulture Road, eventually coming across a small village—seemingly untouched by war.

Looking down at one of the passersby, Luka asked, "Excuse me, ma'am, would you mind telling me what town I find myself in?"

The lady looked right up at Luka, spiking fear that she would recognize him. Fortunately, she did not, her eyes showing only a cold indifference. "This is Ophir," she said, ending the conversation right there.

Ophir. That meant that he was only a few days' ride from Privagrad. He had indeed made good progress since leaving Glazben. Pleased with himself, and his stomach growling at him, he decided to treat himself to a proper meal, tying Velico to the lone Ophirian Tavern.

He sat near the corner of the room where he would be surrounded by as few people as possible and waved one of the serving men over. "What would you like, sir?" the man asked.

"A half-dozen chicken legs, with sauce if you have it."

"And to drink?"

"A full cup of well water."

The server nodded and then asked, "Where are you traveling from, good sir?"

Luka scratched his fuzzy blonde beard and said, "From the south." And then he looked away, making it clear he wasn't interested in elaborating.

While Luka waited for his food, he again thought ahead to Privagrad, and Serena, who lived there. Images of her shiny, long black hair and deep brown eyes filled Luka's mind. Her gaze could flash a fierce intensity and then return just as quickly to a wondrous warmth. As teens, she was one of Luka's most challenging and confident opponents when they sparred. Unfortunately, Lord Tomkins did not think swordsmanship was a behavior befitting the daughter of a nobleman, and Serena began to train only in secret.

The last time they had seen each other was nearly two years ago. He reflected how they had snuck off while both their fathers were discussing some political matters in Vernikport. He could picture the quiet old training arena where they sparred for nearly an hour. When the sparring ended, the heat between them had not. One moment, they were catching their breath—the next, they were tangled together right on the arena floor.

All the time they wondered whether the secret training or the secret intimacy would make more trouble for them if they were ever caught.

"Your chicken legs, sir." The server snapped Luka out of his daydreaming. Luka thanked the man and devoured his food, ripping the tender white meat off the bones like an animal. He left three pieces of silver Novaks on the table when he was done and departed briskly.

As he drew within a handful of steps from Velico, a man intercepted him. "Prince Luka! Prince Luka! You must help!" He was right up in Luka's face and screaming loud enough for the entire village to hear him.

"Sir, I do not understand what you are talking about. I am merely a traveler." Luka tried to step around the man, but he was holding firm.

"No, you are not. I know you to be Prince Luka. You have his face. I need your help."

"I assure you I am not the late Prince Luka. I wish I could help, but I must go. Please move, sir." Luka glanced around and could see that a potential disaster was brewing. About a dozen people had completely stopped what they were doing to watch the curious spectacle.

"No, no, no. I am not fooled," the man continued. "I need your help. My wife and boys were in Vernikport the night of the attack. If you are alive, then so might they be. Please, please tell me if they are alive. Help me find them."

Empathy welled up in Luka as he grasped the depth of the man's sorrow. Placing a hand on his shoulder, he met his pained gaze and spoke gently. "All I can tell you is that Vernikport is in ashes. They destroyed every inch of that city, and there were almost no survivors. There is nothing that can be done. If you wish to go see with your own eyes, then do so, but understand you will find only rubble. I am sorry for your loss. You are one of many people who lost a great deal that night."

Luka moved the man aside forcefully and stepped past. The man just stood there with his head hanging low and said nothing. Luka untied Velico and mounted. "So you are not Luka Vernik?" the man asked once more.

He rode off without answering the question.

*****

General Warwick led the two captives back up the mountain that the army had just descended. A dozen soldiers and a handful of servants joined along for the short but grave expedition. Warwick made sure they would not be seen by the rest of the ranks. News of the attack on Vernikport had crushed their spirits. The general could not afford for them to be dispirited any further. He also could not afford deserters.

One of the captives tried to whisper to the other as they traversed higher. Warwick cut him off. "You will have the right to your last words, but until I call upon you to utter them, you shall not speak." To Warwick's satisfaction, silence followed. The only sounds that filled the dusk air were the crunching of boots on the ground and the strained breaths of the hiking men.

They reached the mountain's peak as the last remnants of the sunset vanished and nightfall arrived. Servants set up a wooden block on a flat stretch of ground, just beyond the other side of the mountain. The soldiers held the perpetrators tightly as they watched. Below them, in the distant valley, flame lanterns marked the location of a small village.

As Lieutenant Baciti read aloud the sentence for deserting to the two troubled men, the general considered the grotesqueness of this procedure. He was hardened now, but one never became fully accustomed to death. Tonight, he could feel something unpleasant in his stomach, but he pushed that down. It had been a frequent occurrence since he had heard the news of the attack on Vernikport. But he remained strong. He had to. There was a void of power in the world—the very throne of Estravia was at stake.

To add to that, the conflict now extended beyond the mere borders of the kingdom. Estravia's own sovereignty was threatened. According to reports, the Stranakans were now on Estravian soil. Even if the country itself had not declared war, it was clearly inevitable. The Stranakans had been Estravia's adversary for hundreds of years, though there had not been a real conflict in many decades.

Warwick hated the Stranakans. They were a vile country, and he believed that vanquishing them was the only course of action to protect Estravia for the long-term. Long ago, he and King Var had spent many hours reviewing hypothetical invasion scenarios, though they never materialized. Warwick resolved that when everything was settled with the Zlikrej brothers, he would make sure to wage war himself. He now had every reason to do so.

"Who shall go first?" Lieutenant Baciti asked. The question was directed at Warwick. It brought his attention back to the matter at hand.

"They may have the right to decide," Warwick responded.

"Very well," the lieutenant said, turning to the deserters. "Which of you wants to do this first?" No volunteers raised their hands.

The officer picked the closer of the two deserters and pulled him in. "Looks like you're the winner." The deserter resisted, nearly breaking away, but the force of other soldiers joining quickly subdued him.

"There is no escape from this," Baciti said. "You knew the consequences of your choices."

The soldiers pressed the man's head down onto the block, his neck fitting perfectly into the central indent. Another soldier unlatched a great axe from his back and readied it, awaiting the general's signal.

"Now is your time to speak," Warwick said. "Do you have any last words?"

"Please. Please don't do this. I can still be a good soldier. Spare me. Please. I-I promise I can fight for you," the man uttered.

"I shall not have you make a fool of me by giving you the chance to desert twice, setting an example for others to see," Warwick replied. "Are those truly your last words?"

"No! I have more!" the man pleaded. He was choking on the few breaths he still had. He fought to calm himself, seeming to think of something to say. "Please don't tell my father that I deserted. I can't have him know of this. Please tell him I died in battle."

General Warwick considered the request. "The glory of dying in battle shall forever be reserved for the souls brave enough to actually do so. That honor will never be bestowed upon you, even in the minds of those closest to you. However, I can do you the favor of sparing your father the true details of your cowardice and betrayal. I can give him the gift of ignorance."

With the deserter appearing to be satisfied, Warwick signaled to the executioner. He carried out his task, and the deserter's head rolled away. The dead man's co-conspirator watched in horror.

As Baciti pulled him in for his turn, he said, "People always assume it is worse to go first. They want to try to last just that much longer. I think it's better to just get the bloody thing over with. That must have been hard to watch."

The deserter's eyes were wide. In his fear, he could not respond. He quickly found himself with his neck lying on the same board, now wet with fresh blood.

They repeated the same process with the second man. In his last words, he did not bother asking for his life to be spared. He did ask that his dishonor not be disclosed to his family.

As he did for the first man, Warwick obliged. Then, he gave the executioner the signal.

When it was done, the servants gathered the bloody wooden block, and they departed back down the mountain. By this time, most of the lanterns in the valley village had gone out.

It took them just under an hour to return to camp. Save for a few men still up playing Table Dragons, all the soldiers were sound asleep. Warwick retreated to his tent and studied a map, tracing the army's intended route. A knot of worry formed in his chest—they might have to change course. They were headed for Privagrad, where their enemies would soon be arriving. But Warwick knew it would be too late. In the timeframe needed to reach that city, the Zlikrej brothers would have already conquered it and passed through.

Their trajectory would have to shift north. It was the only possibility. Only Sila knew how much territory the Zlikrej would conquer in the meantime.

He would inform his men in the morning. He changed into his night clothes and readied himself for bed.

At the top of the mountain that stood behind the camp, two severed heads and their former bodies lay in their permanent sleep.

Chapter 20
Privagrad

Sixteen pointed watchtowers stood tall in the orange sunset sky. That sight marked the city of Privagrad, and it was a welcome one to Luka, because it meant that it was still standing. The watchtowers stretched higher than all other buildings, and each had several watch posts set at different heights to allow for scores of marksmen to defend the massive city. He sincerely hoped that the archers in the towers would be friends and not foes today.

If the Zlikrej have already passed through, then I fear what awaits me here. They had left behind a few dozen soldiers to try to keep control of Glazben. If they had done that, then surely they would have several times that amount in Privagrad.

In spite of the risk, he pressed forward into the city. He needed to find Serena. He couldn't pass through without knowing her fate. Did that mean he loved her? He found himself wondering but he pushed the question aside without resolution. He at least cared for her. It was enough to risk a trip into the city. There was no denying that.

As Luka approached the city limits, he kept an eye on the watchtowers that stood above him. The watchmen should not be alarmed by a lone man on horseback, but the towers were menacing tonight, like silent monsters willing to devour anyone who came close. Despite his nerves, Luka kept his pace unhurried to be sure to avoid suspicion. The watchmen never paid any mind to Luka as he slipped through.

Within the urban sprawl, Luka weaved his way through back alleys and side streets, avoiding any main thoroughfares. He hadn't seen any signs of Zlikrej control so far, but the sun had now set, and the city was dark except for the lanterns that hung outside citizens' houses.

Finally, Luka reached Zamka Square, where the tight buildings ended, and the wide-open promenade surrounding the palace began. Privagrad Palace made everything else seem miniscule beneath it, jetting up into the sky in several sections.

He kept a close watch on a handful of sentries guarding the main entrance. It was clear that they were Tomkins's men, but Luka's instincts steered him away from a direct approach.

He dismounted and tied Velico to a building in one of the alleys. Staying hidden, Luka circled around the palace until he found the Privagrad Temple. The temple was a more modest structure compared to the palace. To Luka's great fortune, it was also unguarded.

Xander once mentioned to Luka that there was a secret underground passageway that connected the temple to the palace, constructed for the convenience of priests needing to travel between the two structures. It was exactly the type of thing that Xander would conjure up for fun, and Luka had fallen for his antics far too often to believe him.

"Alright then. Why don't I show you myself?" Luka remembered Xander saying one night when they were staying in Privagrad as teenagers. He had led Luka through the temple and behind the altar, where a small nook and a hidden door awaited them. Xander's boastful smile when he opened that door remained transfixed in Luka's mind, as if he was gloating all over again.

You cheeky bastard, Luka thought fondly.

Inside the temple, gold was the dominant color. Priceless sculptures and paintings filled the room. At this hour, the temple was also completely absent of people. He figured that an evening service had not yet commenced, if one was even scheduled for tonight.

Luka wandered down the main aisle, made his way past the altar, and just as he remembered, there was a wooden door in a small nook in the corner. He looked around to make sure no one was watching him. When he knew he was in the clear, he went through.

Several stories of small dusty stone stairs led downward in a tight spiral. Luka kept one of his hands on the wall to steady himself as he descended. A dark tunnel awaited him at the bottom. From memory, he knew where the lanterns were, and he felt his way along the wall until he found one. He ignited a spark and walked down the tunnel, guided by the dancing light of his torch.

At the far end of the tunnel stood a wooden door. As he pushed it open, it let out a loud creak, the sound echoing through the tunnel. He ascended another spiraling staircase until he finally reached the end of the passageway.

Luka came out on the other side of a hidden door in a small palace living room. He took a moment to reorient himself with the layout of the castle. Lord Tomkins was likely in his chambers or his study. Either way, Luka would need to climb the palace's main staircase, where he knew he would be exposed.

As he peered out, he could see four guards congregated around the bottom of the stairs. Seeing this, he immediately tried to turn around, but he had been noticed. "Oi! You there! What are you doing in here?"

Luka froze.

"You! Who are you? What are you doing in here?" The guard repeated. The four guards started down the hallway while Luka remained paralyzed, not seeing any options. The guards took hold of him.

"I am Luka Vernik," Luka said as they grabbed his arms. "I survived the attack on my home and am now the rightful King of Estravia. I have come to speak with Lord Tomkins. As your King, I command you to let me go and lead me to him."

The guards stood dumbfounded for a minute, trading glances with each other and scanning Luka's face.

"Do you think it could be him? I do actually see a resemblance," one of the guards said.

"I see that too," acknowledged another.

"We cannot be certain. It could also be a trespasser simply trying to talk his way out of the situation," said a third. "If that's the case, we would have hell to pay for this."

The lead guard then said, "There is only one way to determine this. We will bring him to Lord Tomkins, and he can decide his fate."

The other guards nodded in agreement. Luka tried to protest as they took his sword and dagger from him and began to escort him towards the lord's chambers. He was going where he wanted, but he was getting there as a captive.

The guards were rough with Luka as they led him up the grand staircase and into a room on the next floor. A large table surrounded by dozens of chairs stretched from end to end.

Lord Tomkins sat in the center of the table, facing the doorway. His eyes were bloodshot, his face carrying days-old stubble. A number of Privagrad knights and advisors that Luka vaguely recognized were at the table with Tomkins. There were several other guards in the purple and yellow of House Tomkins. Two more guards in black and gray robes flanked Tomkins on either side of his chair. There was no Mithacor on their chest, but the colors they bore belonged to Luka's enemy. Luka stiffened at this sight but was still unsure of what to assume.

"Lord Tomkins, sir," interrupted one of Luka's captors, "We found this man sneaking through the palace." The guard hesitated before saying the next part. "He claims to be Luka Vernik."

Nothing could have been more effective at getting the attention of everyone in the room. They looked at Luka with other-worldly shock.

Lord Tomkins's jaw dropped, his face turning even paler than it already was.

"It *is* me, Lord Tomkins," said Luka. "I need to speak with you in private."

"I don't believe it…" said Tomkins finally. "You're alive…"

"Aye, I am very much alive," Luka said. "I am glad to see that you are alive as well. Is the rest of your family alright?"

Tomkins nodded, almost absently.

Luka continued. "That is most fortunate. Now, would you please have your men let go of me? I'd like to have a civilized conversation and see no further need to be treated like an intruder."

Lord Tomkins gave a confused, stymied look—like a cow with its jaws open and a clump of grass hanging from its mouth. Then he nodded to the men holding him, and they let him go. At Tomkins's ushering, Luka took a seat, sitting across the table from the lord and his men.

"Luka, this is most unexpected. How did you survive the attack? It must have been a miracle. A true miracle," Lord Tomkins asked.

"It doesn't much feel like a miracle to me. It feels like a nightmare."

Lord Tomkins ran his hand through his hair nervously. "I am sorry for your loss, Luka. I have been mourning them, and until this point, you as well. I'm assuming no one else survived?"

Luka nodded, silently weaving the lie that would protect his mother. "I am riding north, not only to avenge my family and the citizens of Vernikport, but also to protect this country," Luka said. "Help me enact my revenge and honor the lives of my father and mother, who were your dear friends. Provide me with soldiers who can join my offensive. It will not be long before General Warwick and the rest of our army join alongside."

Lord Tomkins cast a hesitant glance at the two officers in gray, as if seeking their guidance. The men stiffened but remained silent, leaving the decision to him. He swallowed hard, his complexion growing even paler as he cleared his throat. "I am afraid I cannot do that, Luka. I really want to help you, but I cannot. You see, the Zlikrej brothers took my daughter, Serena. I know you two were close. She is to be wed to Privus. My loyalty now lies with him and his brothers, Drugi and Omarius. I must respect their wishes in order to keep my daughter safe. I am sorry. It pains me to do this, but I don't have a choice."

A flare of shock came over Luka, as if he had been stung across every inch of his skin.

"I'm sorry, Luka. I hate myself for this, but I have to do what is best for my daughter. I must protect her. I am sorry. I will do what I can to make sure you are not harmed," Lord Tomkins said. "Guards, take him to the dungeon."

A foreign hand appeared on Luka's left shoulder. He acted swiftly, grabbing the hand and yanking it downward onto the table and bringing the man down with it. Luka raised his elbow up and slammed it down like a hammer over the back of the guard's exposed head, leaving the guard motionless on the table.

The next guard enveloped Luka in a formidable chokehold. At once, Luka felt the air being squeezed out of him. Unfettered, Luka put both his legs up against the table and heaved backward with all his lower body strength, sending them both tumbling backwards. The guard knocked into two others as he went down. To Luka's pleasant surprise, one of the guards had dropped Xander's dagger in the fall, which he immediately seized from the floor.

The two officers in gray leaped over the table and produced poniards of their own. They slashed at Luka almost simultaneously. He was able to deflect only one of the attacks with a quick parry. He attempted to dodge the other strike, but he felt a hot, sharp slicing of his skin as the blade cut his right side. He cried out and recoiled, retreating away from the doorway and into the corner of the room. Lord Tomkins and his advisors merely watched as the combat unfolded.

Luka kicked a chair out in front of the two officers. As one of them moved it to the side, he struck like a viper and lodged Xander's dagger in the man's neck. A geyser of blood shot out when Luka removed the weapon.

The other officer pushed through his bleeding comrade and slashed at Luka, who jumped on the table to evade. Lord Tomkins and his advisors continued to stare. Luka glared at them with hate and disgust and then jumped off the table at the other end near the doorway.

Luka barreled through the two guards blocking the exit and burst out into the hallway. He sprinted to the nearest staircase and rushed down. Noticing the other gray officer in pursuit close behind him, Luka leaped downstairs almost a half dozen at a time.

Fighting the pain in his side, Luka shifted his focus to finding the room with the secret passageway. He raced down the hallway on the next floor, darting his head left and right, looking for the room he needed. He spotted it, just as he had run a few strides past by mistake.

Luka halted his momentum and turned around. Just as he did so, the surviving gray officer reached him. He now stood between Luka and the escape route. Luka gripped Xander's dagger, grateful to have it, but against the officer's longer poniard, he was at a disadvantage.

The Zlikrej officer gave his blade a twirl before launching his attack. He aimed a stab at Luka's chest, which he deflected easily. After parrying several more attacks, one cut the back of Luka's right hand, causing Luka to cry out in pain. He kept his grip tight on the dagger in spite of the agony. His life depended on it.

Angry and hurt, Luka took the offensive now. He employed a flurry of alternating sideways slashes. They were not precise, but they were fast. The officer was able to defend each one, but each block pushed him another step back and disrupted his balance. Capitalizing on this leverage, Luka slashed, kicked, and then tackled the officer to the ground. Both men's weapons clattered on the marble floor.

With his left hand, Luka began punching the officer who lay underneath him. The officer fought back, his fist connecting with Luka's cheek and nose several times.

Ignoring the pain from the blows, Luka attempted to grab the man's throat, but with the cut on his hand, he could not grip firmly enough, and the officer was able to throw Luka off of him.

Luka rolled to within a short distance of Xander's dagger. He rose and reached for it, but as soon as it was within his grasp, the officer grabbed his legs and tripped him. Within less than a second, the officer jumped on top of him.

Luka reached up with the dagger, holding it in both hands, trying to cut the officer's neck, but the officer grabbed Luka's wrist, trying to wrestle it free. Both of them strained to pry the weapon away from the other. When it looked like the officer was close to winning the power struggle, Luka heaved to the side. The maneuver threw the officer partially off of him and set Luka's wrists free.

With his enemy's neck exposed, Luka jammed his blade in. Blood spattered onto Luka's face and into his left eye. He pulled the dagger out and pushed the now limp body off of him. Rising up quickly, he wasted no further time heading for the exit, wiping his eyes as he ran.

As Luka opened the wall, he could hear shouting in the hallway. They had found the Zlikrej officer's corpse but could not figure out where the killer had gone. Undetected, Luka closed the secret door behind him and proceeded down the same staircase he had taken less than an hour ago.

This time he did not bother to light a torch, instead feeling his way hastily along the tunnel and then back up the narrow stone stairs. He burst through the hidden door behind the altar, sprinting out into the temple—only to find it no longer empty. A priestess stood by the altar, leading a group of citizens in evening prayer.

"Oh, Mighty Sila, we look to you for signs to guide us. We look for omens during these dark—" The priestess stopped her prayer abruptly at the sight of the bloody hooded man appearing from nowhere and running through the chapel. The congregation looked on in shock.

No one awaited Luka outside of the temple, and he was extremely grateful to find Velico still tied to the same post he left him. *Praise Sila,* Luka thought as he mounted his trusted steed.

He took a route that weaved through the back alleys, heading north outside of the city. Soon Privagrad would be on high alert, but the message had not spread fast enough. Still, Luka had to make haste with his escape. *It won't be long until the whole country knows I am alive now,* Luka thought.

The bottom of one of the northeastern watchtowers pressed close, a sign that Luka was finally at the outskirts of the city. When he passed it, he saw a mostly open field ahead of him. He urged Velico on as fast as he could go.

After a moment of riding, he glanced behind at the hostile city he had just departed. There seemed to be a handful of men holding torches underneath the watchtower. They appeared to be pointing in Luka's direction. That meant only one thing.

Shit, Luka thought. He urged Velico to increase his pace.

An arrow whizzed through the air and landed a meter in front of Luka. Velico nearly threw Luka off of him, trying to swerve around it.

Luka glanced behind him again, seeing marksmen in every post in the tower holding their massive long-range bows. A flock of deadly black streaks darted towards Luka against the late dusk sky.

A small storm of arrows crashed down all around the horse and rider. One bolt grazed Velico, and another shot right past Luka's face, mere inches from a fatal landing. "Ya! Ya!" Luka screamed, trying to keep his panicked horse on track. Luka's heart pounded in his chest and in his side wound, as the horse sprinted and zig-zagged through the death raining down on them. With Luka's increasing distance, he knew his odds were improving, but his adrenaline continued to rise.

After several more terror-filled moments, the arrows began to land farther and farther behind them. It seemed as if they were finally out of range.

Luka did not turn around anymore. He eventually stopped hearing the slick thudding sound of the arrows landing in the ground, and he assumed they were safe. But he still could not stop. They would send scouts on horseback in pursuit, forcing Luka to put more distance between himself and the city.

After several more minutes of riding northeast, Luka veered off and headed directly east. They kept top speed until they reached a small, wooded area.

Velico was slowing, running low on energy after a long stretch of vigorous riding. They would need to stop somewhere soon. The horse had done well, but he could not sprint forever.

Luka dismounted, grunting as the movement strained his wounded side and hand. He tied Velico to a large pine tree and rummaged through his bags until he found his small supply of medical equipment. He sat on the ground with his back against the trunk of the tree and began tying a bandage around his right hand. The cut on his hand appeared as though it would heal on its own without stitches. That part was welcome.

Luka then carefully removed his hooded cloak and shirt. There was blood on the cloak, but it was mostly concealed by the dark brown color. Luka's white shirt was not so lucky. The entire right side of the shirt was completely red and damp. This part was not welcome.

The cut ran down the top of Luka's right rib cage, almost ending at his waist. Other than the initial point of impact, it was not deep, but Luka feared it would require medical attention. In the meantime, he wrapped the bandage around his entire torso, wincing constantly, until the cut was properly covered. He desperately hoped the bandages would hold. Treating these two wounds alone had nearly exhausted his supply.

Luka lay on his left side and closed his eyes. His heart was pounding as if a hundred blacksmiths were hammering the same anvil. He considered that if rest would not come, maybe he should continue to ride.

But what would be the point? *I'd just be riding to my own death,* Luka thought. *I'm lucky they haven't killed me already, and I'm not even remotely close to facing the bastards who did this to me.*

And now they have Serena, who is betrothed to Privus, he thought with disgust.

In a few short weeks, I have gone from a prince and a champion, to a lonely, bleeding idiot in the middle of a forest.

Another thought struck Luka—one he should have realized much sooner. *I can't do this alone.* If he could join General Warwick, he would do it, but the general was still far away. No—he needed an ally much sooner than that.

He remembered what he promised to Amelia about the wizard in Jetsac. It sounded mad, but Luka decided he would go there next. He was desperate enough to try almost anything.

Chapter 21
The Archlord and Archlady

The carriage rolled forward as time dragged on, each moment identically miserable to the last. Inside, thoughts plagued Serena Tomkins—thoughts of her family, of the life she had left behind, and of the seemingly bleak future ahead of her.

She sat mostly in silence, though she wasn't alone. Two of her servants from Privagrad rode with her, but it wasn't nearly enough to make her feel at ease.

At some point in the middle of the day, the carriage made an unexpected stop. Serena peered outside and noticed that all the other carriages, horseback officers, and foot soldiers were still marching forward. Only her vehicle had stopped.

The back flaps of the carriage opened, and Privus climbed in, immediately dismissing the servants. "I wanted time with my bride," Privus said with an unsure grin when they were alone. Serena frowned and looked away. Privus pretended to ignore this and continued with the pleasantries.

"How does today find you?" he asked.

"I want to go home," Serena responded.

"I have told you this before—your home is now with me. You must realize that I am giving you a far superior life than what you would have had before. A life full of limitless luxuries and endless power."

"I don't want any of that! I hate this!" Serena shot back.

"You must stop this sulking!" Privus responded, abandoning his coolness. "Every day, you complain despite my generosity. This behavior *must* cease."

"You're a killer!" Serena shouted. "I want nothing to do with you."

Privus grabbed her arm and yanked her closer to him. "I am a *warrior*! This is a *war*! If you did not know, killing is *part* of war."

Against her own will, tears began to well in her eyes. He relented and let go when he saw the effect his flash of violence had on her. "I am sorry. That was no way for me to treat a queen."

The last word made her pause. "What do you mean 'queen?' Why would you say that?"

He seemed to take note of her sudden, keen interest. "You see, my brothers and I are going to rule Estravia together, as equals. We shall not call ourselves kings, though. The age of one, single, corrupt ruler is over. My brothers and I will be 'Archlords', like in the ancient days before the tyrannical Vernik regime began. Since neither of my brothers have brides in waiting, you will be the first and only Archlady in Estravia, after we are wed. That would make you the highest woman in all the land. An honor equivalent to a queen."

"I'd rather be a nameless peasant than be a queen with you," Serena spat.

"I am not certain you really mean that," Privus responded calmly.

He reached towards a satchel behind him and unveiled a bottle of red wine and two glasses. The bottle looked suspiciously like one from her father's wine cellar.

"I am not going to ask you to have a drink with me, because I know what you will say," said Privus. "Instead, I am going to *demand* that you drink with me. You should do so. For your father's sake." He let the veiled threat hang in the air as he poured each glass steadily.

Privus handed one of the glasses to Serena. She stared at the dark liquid inside, swirling it gently as the thin dark-red line at the top traced slow circles. He watched her intently, his gaze unwavering. After a brief hesitation, she took a sip. There was no denying it—it was rich, smooth, and utterly delicious.

As they both drank together, Privus asked, "Have you ever aspired to be queen before?"

"I must confess that I have. But I think almost every noble girl dreams of that—and don't think for a second that I would have ever wanted *this*." Privus ignored the latter part of what she had said, instead continuing to ask her more questions. Soon, the conversation shifted to her childhood. She opened up little at first, but each sip of wine seemed to bring a longer answer to Privus's questions. Before she knew it, she had drunk nearly half the bottle herself, while Privus had yet to finish his first glass.

With half the bottle gone, she found herself almost blabbing as she recounted the many pressures and responsibilities required of a lord's daughter. Privus listened intently as she spoke.

"I never got to experience any of that," he said when she paused. "By the time I was old enough to retain memories, Canyon City was far behind me, and both my parents were dead," said Privus.

Yes, and that is because your father was a tyrannical lunatic, Serena thought, though she was still sober enough to keep that to herself.

"What were some of the things that you were asked to do as a child?" Privus asked, shifting the conversation back to her.

"The worst of it was that my parents were impossible when it came to my training, especially as I became older. I always had to practice in secret." Her words reminded her briefly of one of the sparring sessions she had with Luka, who never judged her for her gender or anything else. For a split second, she thought her stomach would rupture in sadness.

"In Exeter, I will make sure you get every training accommodation you could possibly require," Privus said. "You'll never need to worry about that again."

Serena frowned. *Maybe you and I can have a go at it. We'll use real steel, and you can really make me happy*, she thought.

In the empty silence that followed the remark, Privus became visibly uncomfortable. He filled the void with the sound of more wine pouring into each of their glasses. They both took a sip, and Privus spoke again. "Was a sword always your favorite weapon?"

"Oh yes."

"Hmm, in that case, perhaps I should have allowed you to bring *Strujaza* with you on your journey with me. I heard incredible things about what you did with it. Well worth losing a few men for that. I find fierceness in a woman to be particularly arousing," Privus said.

The thought of arousing Privus in any way made the wine in her stomach want to propel outward.

"Perhaps I can get you a different blade at another time," he suggested. "You could even have mine if you wanted it. My preference is my staff now, anyways."

Serena's ears perked slightly. "How does your staff work exactly?" she asked. That weapon had been her first exposure to magic—and a harrowing one at that.

Privus unlatched the staff from his belt and held it out in front of her. "I found the staff in the wasteland when I was still a young man. It didn't work at all at the time, but I knew it was special. I believe it is a gift from the spirit world. Sent to me from the divine. I was wise to keep it, because several years later, I became acquainted with an elemental wizard who offered to 'fuel' it with his magic. Now, I can use it to summon the powers of fire, water, earth, and wind. It makes me quite unstoppable."

"Show me," she said.

"Anything for you."

A light burst of wind shot out from the staff in all directions. The breeze gently blew back Serena's hair and ruffled against the inner fabric of the carriage. Then Privus ignited the head of the staff with a flame and held it in front of her like a candle. He waved it around her for effect, Serena's eyes following in astonishment.

"How does it work? How did you make it do that?"

"I have to concentrate on what I want it to do. I am no sorcerer, but the process by which I use the staff is similar. If I want to produce fire, I have to imagine fire and focus my energy and willpower into the staff."

"That is astonishing."

"Quite." Privus reached for his wine glass, which had only a little remaining. As he was finishing the last drop, Serena snatched the staff right out of his hands and aimed it at his face.

Privus's eyes flickered briefly, but his body showed no other reaction. Setting down his glass, he fixed Serena with a cold, detached stare. He let her struggle in vain for a few seconds before effortlessly reclaiming the weapon from her grasp.

"That was dispiriting," he said. "I thought we were having a nice time." He left the carriage silently, leaving her all alone.

Chapter 22
Prayers of the Widows

Steam rose out of a cup of tea and into Queen Vanessa's face. The steam partially obscured her vision as she stared out the window, eyes glazed over. Beyond the glass, cattle slowly roamed across the farm. The scene was peaceful but unengaging. Without a potent distraction, mental flashes assaulted her.

Flashes of a kiss on the beach, shared with her late husband. Of the miracle of when she first laid eyes on her first-born son. When she woke up one morning, and her second-born had left her.

The flashes were not just contained to the past. She pictured fallen cities, burning fields, and mothers all across Estravia who were now bearing the same fate that she was. She felt like a failure as a queen. They were her people. She was supposed to support them. An acidic, expanding pit formed in her stomach.

Far worse, however, was the thought that she failed as a mother. Despite everyone's assurances to the contrary, she blamed herself for losing Xander. Unimaginable guilt filled her every cell—a pain that was only exacerbated when she let Luka slip away. Things were bearable when her only living son was still with her. Without him, she felt so alone.

A pond of tears accumulated in her eyes. She hurriedly wiped them away, not wanting to break down again into fits. She'd already spent hours of the day crying, not gaining even a hint of relief in the process.

Vanessa cursed aloud and let out a piercing scream. In a sudden burst of frustration, she grabbed her full cup of tea and hurled it to the ground. The black ceramic shattered on impact, fragments scattering across the floor in a steaming pool of liquid.

The queen cursed again. This would attract attention, but she wanted to be left alone.

As expected, a servant girl and a guard burst through the door. "Are you okay, My Queen?" The servant asked.

Obviously not, Queen Vanessa wanted to reply. *I've never been less 'okay' in my life.* "Yes. I am fine. My tea merely slipped from my hands."

"I am sorry, My Queen. Shall I fetch another?"

"No. Bring me some wine instead."

The servant girl returned shortly after with a wooden chalice and a bottle of red wine. "Very good," said the queen. Then, the servant knelt down and began to clean up the mess that Vanessa had made. "No, do that later," the queen said, dismissing the servant.

When she was alone again, Vanessa sat back down and began staring out the same window. Now, only one brown cow was in view, munching lazily on a patch of grass. Vanessa drank her wine at a fast pace. She did not care if she appeared to be drunk at Priestess Teya's noon ceremony later. Perhaps she would not even attend.

Midway through her second glass, knocking interrupted Vanessa's thoughts. She rolled her eyes in annoyance, even though the distraction was a benefit to her—saving her from yet another string of torturous thoughts.

"Who is it?"

"It's me, Milo," Pametan's voice came through the door. "I have a message. It's from Luka."

Vanessa was out of her chair and at the door in a blink, swinging it open with haste.

Pametan stood before her, letter in hand. Before he could speak, Vanessa snatched the piece of parchment from him. She turned away and began reading the letter, hanging on to every word her son had written.

"Dearest Mother,

I am writing you safely from Glazben. When I arrived this morning, the city was under Zlikrej control. I will spare you the details of the atrocities that the citizens were bearing, but you can rest assured that they are free now. Lord and Lady Laz are also both alive and safe. They have shown me great hospitality.

In only a few moments, I will continue my journey north. Undoubtedly, more horrors lie before me along Vulture Road, but as king, it is my duty to undo the enemy's damage and save the people of Estravia. It is also my duty to avenge Father and Xander. They are constantly in my thoughts, as are you, Mother.

I hope that you are still safe on Ivan's farm. I also hope that your spirits will soon lift, as I wish the same for Amelia, Teya, and Pametan.

You need not distress over a reply to me. I do not know when or where I will be able to receive a message next.

I hope to see you soon, victorious.

With love,

Luka"

When she was finished reading, Vanessa clutched the letter tightly against her chest. She held back heavy sobs.

"What does it say, My Queen?" Pametan asked.

"Oh, please, Milo. I know that you screen these letters."

"Not this one, My Queen. I swear it."

"Luka is alive and safe. He said that he freed Glazben from Zlikrej control. Now he's marching north again," Vanessa explained.

"Ah. That is consistent with these letters." Milo Pametan handed her several more pieces of parchment. "They are from Lord Laz. These ones... I, um, I did screen. I do admit that."

Vanessa read the messages but found the words to be hollow compared to Luka's. They seemed to almost blur away onto the page. The only thing that mattered was her son's letter, with its familiar and neat but unpolished handwriting.

"I also wanted to make you aware that noon ceremonies are set to begin soon. Although, I understand if you do not wish to attend today, of course," Pametan said. He was not blind to the evidence of heavy tears across her face and the shattered ceramic pieces across the floor.

"I do wish to, Milo. Just give me a moment to gather myself, and we shall go there together."

They arrived to find Priestess Teya standing patiently before the altar—a wooden table borrowed from the farm, much like everything else in the holy set up. They took their seats next to Amelia who was sitting by herself on a rectangular bale of hay. Farmer Ivan, his wife Wanda, and his bulky farmhand sat on a bale across the aisle. A wooden arbor stood behind Priestess Teya, the green farmland and distant hills stretching beyond her.

As Vanessa arrived, a pair of orange and crimson wings flew off of the priestess's shoulder. Her pet phoenix, Naka, had burned in the attack on Vernikport, only to be reborn and rescued by Teya weeks later. The bird remained shy, only perching near the Priestess—and often not for very long.

Priestess Teya acknowledged their entrance with a friendly nod and then commenced the opening prayer. Per tradition, the opening prayer preceded a moment of silence. To Vanessa, the silence crawled by like a sea snail. In the quiet, the flashes returned to her.

Var holding her hand. Young Xander waking her up for comfort in the middle of the night. Luka running around the castle as a toddler, tiny wooden sword in hand.

She flinched and tried to take control of her mind. Battling herself, she pushed against the turmoil until Teya spoke again, allowing Vanessa a temporary ceasefire.

"Almighty Sila and your agents, we humbly ask for your blessings on this day. We pray for good fortune in this dark time. The forces of evil have breached from the shadows and invaded our homes. We pray that you, our gracious guardians, fight this evil and restore purity and light to Estravia. We also ask for protection and guidance for Luka, the divine king of our land. The one who now roams these hostile lands alone. We pray that you are with him, offering your warmth and goodwill."

As Teya continued her incantations, Vanessa's thoughts trailed off again. Suddenly, everything around her seemed so absurd. Sitting on a bale of hay, relying on prayers to faraway gods for their grace when only weeks earlier, mere mortals had taken everything away.

Why should I ask the divine to protect Luka? They couldn't protect Xander or Var.

For a moment, guilt radiated over Vanessa for her mental blasphemy. But she couldn't stop questioning.

I can't leave Luka's fate to the whims of Sila and his agents while my arse is sitting here on a bloody farm. It was time to act. She sat through the remainder of the ceremony with her resolve crowding out her grief.

Her daughter-in-law was not so fortunate. "Oh great, Cuvar," The Priestess spoke, referring to one of Sila's agents and the Guide to the Afterlife, "Watch over the souls of our beloved as they journey to the land of peace. Let them know of our love and that we are—"

An eruption of Amelia's sobs drowned out Teya's words. The farmers on the other side of the aisle looked away awkwardly.

Vanessa put her arm around the young princess. She did not tell her to stop crying. She understood how futile that would be better than anyone.

Even after Amelia had gotten her crying under control, it was clear that the ceremony would not be able to continue—not like this.

Priestess Teya rushed through a brief final prayer and went over to the hurting princess. "My Queen, might you allow me some time with Amelia to myself?" she asked.

Vanessa nodded and turned to Pametan as they rose from the hay. "Milo, come with me. I have something I must discuss with you at once."

*****

Amelia cried uninterrupted for their entire walk but felt gentleness and lack of judgment as Priestess Teya stood by her side. They now faced the makeshift graves, looking directly at the one marked for Xander.

She gazed blankly and painfully at the grave, as if she was staring into a dark void. It was impossible to believe that all that was left of her husband was a name on a stone. It wasn't just the loss that hurt, it was the senselessness of it. How could she possibly accept that this was real?

Amelia was grateful Teya was with her. It wasn't much, but it was all she had right now. Her own mother had fallen to sickness many years ago, while her father had remarried and lived as a retired lord near Eastport. Right now, Vanessa and Teya were the only family she had.

"Is it real, Teya? The spirit world?" Amelia asked after long moments had passed.

"Yes, precious Amelia. It is very real."

"So, I will see Xander again?"

"Yes, my dear. You will see him again one day—reunited in the land of Sila. In the spirit world."

190

"What's it like? The spirit world?"

"It is nothing like our world here. In this world, we have our five senses. In the beyond, we experience things differently, without even a true concept of time. When you reunite with Xander, it would be like you never left him."

"I never did leave him."

"Sorry, I did not mean—"

"Maybe I should join him now."

"No, no, no!" Teya interjected quickly. "You must never do that. Death is never the answer, least of all when it is brought on by ourselves. No matter how much pain you are in, please do not say that, Amelia."

"I don't see a reason...," she choked up again "A reason not to."

"My precious, Amelia, I can sense your soul, and it is one of the most beautiful and pure souls I have ever known.

"You do not deserve what happened to you. It was an act of utter evil, and I know it has caused you great misery and anguish. But you survived. You still have your life. Please take care of yourself. You know that is what Xander would have wanted."

Amelia nodded, slowly accepting the priestess's words. Xander would have wanted her to be happy. She pictured his grinning face and recalled his free spirit and sense of humor. The nascence of a smile nearly formed on her lips, in spite of herself.

Amelia's hand drifted subconsciously to her stomach, anxiety fluttering beneath her fingertips. There was perhaps even another, more important reason to live. She had missed her last cycle. Her next one would be due in only a few days. Could it mean what she thought it did?

She wondered whether Teya would be able to tell whether another soul was inside her. The thought sparked both hope and dread. A piece of Xander growing inside of her, but a journey to motherhood she would have to face alone. It was too much to handle—she set the idea aside. It was probably nothing. She had experienced late cycles before.

The princess and priestess walked back towards the house together, with Amelia eagerly peppering Teya with questions about the spirit world. With patience, the priestess answered as best she could, easing Amelia's pain ever so slightly with each response.

As they were about to enter the cottage, Queen Vanessa burst out the front door.

"We are leaving for Glazben. At once."

Chapter 23
The Healer

Blood seeped slowly but continually from Luka's side since he had escaped Privagrad two days ago. Each breath sent a dull ache through his ribs, while he would find himself light-headed from the loss of blood. He'd taken to wrapping spare clothes around his waist, but the makeshift bandages were soaked through. He was in dire need of a doctor.

After multiple days of painful riding, the town of Bolnica finally came into view. It was small and remote, likely lacking any Zlikrej presence. Luka also assumed that word of his survival had not reached this place, so he did not bother with much secrecy.

The town had small, stone buildings and dirt roads. He approached a man sweeping the porch of a small, run-down shop. "Where is your town's doctor?"

The man furrowed his brow and glanced at some of the blood stains on Luka's clothes. "This town has no doctor. We go to Privagrad for that."

"Sila's wrath," he muttered under his breath.

"If you need immediate care, we do have someone in town. She is a healer, of sorts."

"Is she any good?"

The man shrugged and resumed his sweeping.

"Wonderful endorsement," Luka said aloud. "Where can I find her?"

The man gave him the directions, which Luka followed to the healer's small home. The building resembled a box more than a house, with ivy concealing much of the stone exterior. He knocked on the door with low hopes.

The woman who answered had a lightly wrinkled, leathery face. Her hair was dark but streaked with gray. "What is it?" the woman asked.

"Are you the town healer?" Luka asked.

"My name is Merriweather. I provide healing, among many other services. What do you need?"

"I need your help." Luka pulled up his outer shirt and revealed the blood-drenched undershirt he had wrapped around his torso. She ushered him in without reacting and led him to a bed.

He pulled off the shirt and lay on his back, causing the old woman to grimace. "Oof. That looks grim. Knife or sword?" she asked, reaching for a potion.

"Poniard, technically," Luka answered. "What's that potion?"

"You have the beginnings of an infection. This will stop it." She poured a light red liquid directly onto the wound without warning. Luka howled in agony. The wound felt like it was being ripped open by a pair of hot metal prongs.

Before he could faint, the pain subsided into a duller sensation. His heartbeat pounded where the wound was.

"What the bloody hell was that?!"

"I stopped the infection. I thought you wanted my help?"

"You couldn't give me a warning? Or something to stop the pain?"

"Here," she said, handing him a small glass of blue liquid. "Drink this."

"What the hell is this now? I'm not drinking it unless you tell me first. I don't want my innards to burn too."

"That will numb the pain. It would interfere with the infection potion if I gave you that first. Then, I'll need to stitch you up. Unless that is too painful for you as well?"

"Fine." He sipped the pain medicine. It tasted like death, and he was barely able to resist the urge to gag it all back. Fortunately, the medicine did as it was intended. When Merriweather went to stitch him up, he felt nothing other than a slight tingling sensation.

"Do not take the stitches out for six days. Be careful of having them ripped out. Avoid further combat," Merriweather advised when she was finished.

Avoiding further combat may not come so easily, Luka thought. He thanked her and paid her seventy Novaks for her services. That seemed expensive to Luka, but he did not want to haggle. He was familiar with the price of a sword or a fine bottle of wine, but he had no idea how much a visit to a doctor actually cost. Not that she really was a doctor.

As Luka was heading out the door, he turned and asked, "Merriweather, have you ever heard of 'The Magic Tavern' in Jetsac?"

"Oh yes," she chuckled. "Quite a show they have. You must see it for yourself." She did not elaborate further.

Now that Luka was healed, he had another issue to address—he was still swordless. He had left the standard-issue infantryman blade he had been using back in Privagrad. Bolnica would likely not feature the most attractive blades in Estravia, but he was anxious about the prospect of continuing his journey without one.

When he found the town blacksmith, the pleasant, familiar smell of burning metal rushed into Luka's nostrils. As expected, though, the inventory was scarce and unpromising. Only three swords were on display. They looked sharp, but Luka could tell instantly that the quality was inferior compared to what he was accustomed to.

"Are these all you have?" Luka asked.

"Yes, sir," the shopkeeper replied.

Luka frowned and went over to examine the selection more closely. He could wait to look for a better option later down the road, but each day he spent swordless was a day he was needlessly vulnerable.

He pulled one of the arming swords off the wall and tested its weight, but it felt wrong—awkward and unbalanced in his grip. Frowning, he set it back and reached for another. This one felt better, its weight more agreeable, but the metal seemed flimsy—too fragile to trust in a real fight.

He tried the third sword and believed he could make do with it for long enough. The hilt was short and a bit unusual, but Luka liked the blade's weight and flexibility. "How much for this one?" he said, showing it to the blacksmith.

"Two hundred and twenty Novaks for that one."

"I'll buy it for one hundred and fifty. It's not worth any more than that."

"Don't be absurd, I'd never sell for that low," retorted the blacksmith.

"Well, I'd best go somewhere else then. Best of luck finding another eager customer in this part of the country," Luka put down the weapon and turned to walk out.

"What about one hundred and ninety?" the blacksmith called out when Luka was at the doorway.

Luka had gotten him to budge—the opening he needed in their duel of price. Turning back around, he said, "I did say it was not worth more than one hundred and fifty, but I suppose I would be willing to pay an extra ten Novaks, since you're being receptive."

The merchant countered again. "I can do one hundred and seventy then. Final offer."

Luka paused for a moment and then shook the blacksmith's hand. It was a deal. He paid the negotiated sum of coins and walked out of the store with a new weapon.

Only a block away from the blacksmith's, Luka immediately spotted four soldiers, armed with spears, questioning passersby. They wore the purples of the Tomkins House, but of course, that meant they were now Zlikrej men.

The soldiers stood between him and where he had tied Velico. He turned in the other direction and walked away with his hood up. Disappearing into a crowded outdoor market, he pretended to be an inquisitive shopper. Some of the goods *were* actually appealing to Luka, especially all of the aromatic spices that filled the air. *Maybe they could make my meat not taste like sand*, he thought.

He spotted the four guards entering the market at the edge of his peripheral vision. He doubled his efforts to stay inconspicuous and picked up a tomato at one of the shops, acting as though he was examining it closely. From the corner of his eye, he watched the soldiers question some of the shopkeepers. His heart leaped when he noticed a merchant pointing in his direction. The soldiers all turned to face Luka and then headed straight for him. Remaining calm, Luka lowered his hand to the hilt of his new sword and waited.

This will almost certainly make my stitches tear out, Luka thought.

The men were walking with a business-like pace towards their target. Luka tightened his grip on his sword. This market was about to get messy.

"There he is!" one of them exclaimed.

Luka braced himself for battle. Right as the soldiers came within striking distance, they veered off to the left to a shop stand just behind Luka. "It's the vanilla cake merchant that she was talking about." The soldiers all cheered and ordered several basketfuls of vanilla cakes.

Relieved, Luka quietly put down the tomato, tucked away his sword, and left the marketplace.

Chapter 24
The Rasko Inn

A sizable trade caravan slowly approached the mammoth outer walls of the City of Exeter. The walls were the tallest man-made structure in Estravia. The black-cloaked man peered out of his carriage to get a glimpse of the colossal wonder. From the outside, Exeter was just as grand as he remembered it.

Just beyond the city, the Ekron Mountains loomed large and overshadowed Exeter, their peaks tucked in the clouds. The towering structure of the city just below the nearly incomprehensible mountains made for one of the most wondrous spectacles in all of the country.

When the caravan reached the city gates, they waited for a few moments while a group of city officials questioned the merchants, conducting a search of the carriages. No one with military-grade weaponry was permitted inside the city. The shadowy man was unarmed, and the inspectors found no weapons with any of the other merchants or riders.

After the inspection process concluded, the giant portcullis groaned as it lifted from the ground. With the gate open, the caravan passed through the city's sole entrance and exit.

Nearly everything within the walls of the city was built from stone, including the streets and houses. As a result, the city was dominated by gray. The caravan rode through the pristine stone streets and passed the many busy Exeterians out and about. Even though it was not located near a major port, the city's perceived safety and location at the northernmost point of Vulture Road made it popular for traders and businessmen.

The black-cloaked man exited the caravan once it reached the central commerce square and made his way toward an inn. Even inside the city, it was impossible not to look up. Instead of the typical two-, three-, or four-story houses that littered most cities, Exeter consisted of stone towers and buildings that were twice that size. A single building could house more than a dozen families—or three or four wealthy ones.

He walked through several city blocks until he came to the Rasko Inn, among the most expensive accommodations in the city. The Rasko's lobby matched its reputation. The floors, walls, and ceilings were all built with black and white marble. A crystal chandelier containing dozens of candles hung from the center of the ceiling. A band of four played soft music in the corner, even though there were few people there to listen.

The innkeeper stood behind a thick wooden desk. He looked up at the shadowy man. "How may I help you, sir?"

"I'll be staying here for some time," the shadowy man replied.

"How long will that be, sir?"

"At least two weeks."

"Would you like to purchase a room for two weeks with the ability to extend thereafter?" the innkeeper asked.

"That would work."

"Very good. And your name, sir?"

"My name is Vatren of Scotsgrad."

"Well met, Vatren of Scotsgrad. Your name is in the books." He bent down and began opening a cabinet from under the desk. He stood back up and placed a copper key on the counter. "Sir, your room is on the top floor. Your rate will be one hundred and ninety Novaks per night. For a two-week stay, you will need to pay two thousand six hundred and sixty Novaks."

Vatren nodded, beginning to place large stacks of gold and silver Novaks on the counter. When he was done, the innkeeper thanked him and gave him the key to his room.

A long climb of eight flights of stairs led the way to Vatren's accommodations. It was one of the largest rooms in the building—palatial, matching the marble decor in the lobby, and featuring a breathtaking view of the city. *Divine forces that I do not understand led me to this point*, he thought to himself, as he took in the sights.

Shortly after Vatren had settled, servants came up carrying his things, some wine and a small tray of food, and offering to send private entertainment to him. He merely accepted the wine and took it out onto his grand porch.

The people in the streets below seemed small, but lively. This city had not been touched by war, though a light tension hung in the air. Above all, Vatren thought, was a certain complacency. Exeter's walls had never been breached by a hostile force before. They assumed that would remain the case.

If Vernikport had the same natural and man-made barriers that Exeter had, it might still be standing. Of course, with enough creativity and ambition, any city could be conquered. All the people below, thinking their lives were safe forever, had no understanding of this knowledge. Even after the capital city fell—with everyone's admired leaders now dead—most Exeterians still believed that their way of life was safe. *They have no perspective on the true dangers in this world*, Vatren thought.

Vatren turned his attention from below to above, where the Ekron Mountains towered—too high to be concealed by the surrounding walls of the city, nor the tall buildings inside of it. The mountains were so tall, in fact, that only on the clearest, cloud-free days could their peaks be seen. Fortunately, today the sky was clear, granting him a rare, unobstructed view of the snow-capped summits.

For some, the Ekron Mountain range inspired fear. They were known to be home to many dragons. It was the main reason that Exeter was built purely from stones with hardly a trace of any flammable wood. This design happened to bless the Exeterians with a city that protected them from human threats as well. And in fact, humans were the real threat. The dragons preferred to live deep in the wild, unpopulated mountains, rarely interacting with humans. Exeter had not been visited by the creatures in almost a century.

After finishing his wine, Vatren began to imagine himself defeating a dragon. Only four men in history were known to have ever done it, with hundreds of fools killed trying. Drunk on wine, it seemed like a fun challenge. Even one dragon scale could fetch thousands of Novaks from collectors.

People fear dragons because they can breathe fire. But they do not realize that humans can do this as well. Some humans, at least.

Vatren let heat build inside his mouth for a short while, until it became uncomfortable. Then he opened his mouth and released a giant puff of steam from his lips and nostrils. He put down the empty wine glass and produced a fireball in his right hand, pulsating it in his palm.

Maybe deep down, I am a dragon, he thought.

Chapter 25
Reflections of Power

General Warwick flipped the page on his favorite book—*Reflections of Power in War and Politics* by Lord Serja. It was perhaps his fortieth time reading it.

Lord Serja was not as well-remembered as Zachary the Fierce, whom he advised for years. Perhaps one in every three Estravians knew anything meaningful about Lord Serja, though everyone knew about Zachary. But Warwick admired the former far more, thanks mostly to the cynical brilliance in Serja's book.

Serja was the mastermind behind so many of Zachary's unlikely conquests. He managed to survive the defeat at Seveka when Zachary had been captured and executed. He ended up serving the Sevekans after swearing his loyalty to them—the only way to spare his neck from an axe's sharp edge. From there, he went on to enjoy an illustrious military and political career, completely eradicating his reputation as a rebel. To Rory Warwick, the writings were like a religious text, containing hallowed wisdom on every page.

The book was a helpful guide for Warwick in many things in his life. Now, he was facing the death of his best friend, upstart warmongers trying to take over the country aided by magic, and the Stranakans assisting in the efforts.

Warwick hated the Stranakans. Obadiah, his mother's lover and the closest thing Warwick ever had to a true father, always warned him of that country. Even though Estravia and Stranaka had maintained a distance from each other for nearly two hundred years, Obadiah warned that they would be back one day, on Estravian soil. Obadiah was right. His foresight would have been admired by Lord Serja himself.

Warwick paused from the book and remembered the day that he had to accept that Obadiah was gone—and then the day it all came surging back. He had almost entirely put Obadiah out of his mind when—as a new general—he came across some shocking military records. The documents referred to Kriz-La 19, Obadiah's special unit in the Vernik military. Their entire unit disappeared off the coast of Stranaka, not long after Obadiah had left Rory and his mother.

There was no direct mention of Obadiah in the records, and the cause of the disappearance was not given. But to Warwick it was obvious. The Stranakans had attacked. They had killed Obadiah and taken him away from Rory forever. He never forgot it.

Warwick shuddered and turned back to his reading. Back within the pages of the book, Serja explained the process that he used to persuade his captors to spare him from prison or death after the loss at Seveka. Mid-page, a young officer interrupted Warwick's reading, and the carriage stopped.

"General, sir, we have a problem. We are uncertain of what to do." Warwick could not remember the young officer's name.

"What is it?"

"Sir, a large number of men have become violently ill, and it is spreading."

"How many men?"

"Nearly fifty men now, sir. We fear it will spread to dozens more."

A mere fifty men out of thousands. I do not want to slow down for this. "Where is Lieutenant Baciti? He should be handling matters such as these."

"I do not know sir."

"Bring him to me." The young officer left and returned a few minutes later with Lieutenant Baciti, a lanky, eager aide who was officially number three in the military—behind Warwick himself and Lieutenant Alexander—though he transparently sought to be number one. Warwick thanked the officer and dismissed him, leaving the other two alone. "Lieutenant, what is happening?"

"Um, sir, about fifty or so of our men have become infected with a horrible illness. They have been vomiting ceaselessly."

"Is it fatal?" Warwick asked.

"No sir, but some—"

The general cut him off, "If it is not fatal, then I am not concerned. You should not have let this issue reach my attention. I want you to be more involved in matters like these. Sending me an officer to simply pass your troubles up the chain does not help either of us."

"I—," Baciti began to speak, but Warwick stopped him again.

"Under no circumstances are you to let this slow us down. It is merely Traveler's Sickness, most likely. Are any of these men our best?"

Baciti tilted his chin upward and considered. "No, sir."

"In that case, you have permission to dismiss them from the march if they threaten to slow our pace any further." The lieutenant's mouth hung slightly open. "Do you understand?"

"Y- yes, sir."

"Take more responsibility for this next time. Dismissed."

Warwick went back to his book. *I am quite possibly the most powerful man in the country right now. I would have hoped to not have to deal with such trivial matters at this stage of my life.* When battle came, he would be much more engaged, but for now, the story of one of Serja's most brilliant maneuvers awaited him back in the pages of the old book.

*****

Loud commotion pulled Privus to the edge of Vulture Road. With Exeter still two weeks away, any delays were unwelcome. Before him stood General Klacan, the formidable leader of the Zlikrej military, overseeing a massive merchant caravan of more than three dozen carriages laden with supplies and cargo. Around him, soldiers moved in a flurry, swiftly unloading goods. Nearby, a small group of merchants knelt before the general, their faces mere inches from the sharp tips of leveled spears.

"We captured this merchant transport, carrying some supplies and armaments," Klacan informed Privus. "We seized their contents for our own efforts, and I offered these men the ability to serve in the Zlikrej army. Unfortunately, some of them have found that offer to be beneath them."

One of the men turned to Privus and said, "I would never serve you, Zlikrej scum!"

Privus smirked and folded his arms across his chest. "If you will not serve us, who is it that you *do* serve, pathetic merchant?"

"I serve Luka Vernik, the rightful king." The response was matter of fact.

Privus and General Klacan looked at each other, smirking before they burst into laughter. "That is most strange considering the fact that he's dead," Privus said. "Were you headed to Vernikport to serve his smoldering carcass?"

This time, it was the merchant's turn to laugh. He laughed hard and long, making every effort to be insulting to his captors. "Is the idea of your prince lying under his city that *I* turned to ash comical to you?" Privus asked, no longer smiling.

"Y- you, you must not have heard!" said the merchant in between laughs. "He's still alive! Luka survived and is now the rightful King of Estravia. And I hear he's riding up this very road to come and kill you!"

Privus and Klacan exchanged a different kind of glance now.

"In all my years, that is perhaps the most absurd thing I have ever heard," Klacan said. "Do you think you are some sort of court jester?"

The merchant pulled himself together and elaborated. "We ran into some other traveling merchants who spoke of King Luka. They had been questioned by some of Lord Tomkins's men who were looking earnestly for him. Now tell me, why would Tomkins's men be questioning people of this?"

The color flushed away from Privus's face as he realized the man was serious. It could be just a rumor, but the pit that had formed in Privus's stomach made him think this was real. Privus ordered Klacan to question the merchants extensively and then stormed off.

*****

Within his carriage, Omarius used hot wax to stick small emblems of the Mithacor onto his large wall map of Estravia. He now had them over Glazben, Privagrad, and a few smaller cities that were worthy of the mark. A thick black "X" indicated where Vernikport used to be. When the map was up to date, Omarius admired it in silence, enjoying the visual representation of the progress they had made, as well as the territory they still had to conquer.

Amidst his admiration, Privus and Drugi climbed into the carriage and sat across from their eldest brother, who turned away from his map. Privus relayed the news he had just learned.

"Do you believe these merchants?" said Omarius, dispassionately.

"I have had Klacan question the men intensely, and they tell a consistent story. Apparently, some of Tomkins's men have been searching for him. It sounds ludicrous to me, but I am beginning to believe it."

"Remember, Omarius," Drugi chimed in. "We never checked on Luka to see if he was really dead. Privus blasted him far backwards into that building, but we can't completely rule out the possibility he survived."

Omarius said nothing at first, merely putting his fingertips together and leaning back. After a moment of thought, he said, "If this is true, then it shall not be long until we receive official word from Tomkins or someone else. Frankly, I am frustrated we had to hear this from random merchants before we received an official report. Regardless, we must act immediately. We will treat this as if it is real and take no chances. We will send men south, perhaps two dozen, who will scatter and act as assassins. Have these men put out a reward for information as well as they search."

Omarius detected unease in his younger brothers. "Brothers, even if this is true, we have nothing to fear from this one man. Maybe, if we are fortunate enough, we will get the chance to kill him all over again."

*****

The mood amongst the Zlikrej men had shifted noticeably. Serena interacted with them little, but she could tell that something had suddenly gone wrong. The arrogance and excitement that normally covered their faces was now gone. Instead, she could see confusion and concern amongst them.

An announcement had been made that the march was scheduled to resume in ten minutes—just enough time to investigate. Soldiers buzzed around her, heading back to their stations. She strained to hear what she could, but the men grew silent when they noticed her.

She continued to wander amongst the commotion. She picked up words and phrases like "not dead," "still alive," "coming back," and she swore she heard them say "Luka." Her heart began racing. The five-minute warning was announced.

She slipped beside a supply carriage and crouched behind it. The two soldiers assigned to load the supplies hadn't noticed her—too absorbed in their own conversation—their voices carrying clearly through the air.

"If Luka really is back, I don't see how that changes things."

"How does it *not* change things? He would be the bloody rightful King. The whole point was to eliminate the entire family."

"Yes, but what can he do? He's out in the middle of nowhere. They say he's coming straight for us. He'll be dead before he can even sniff any of us."

"Why would he sniff any of us? We smell like shit. Especially you."

"I just mean it doesn't matter, because he'll just get killed again."

"You don't understand anything about politics."

"Yes, I do! And you obviously don't understand anything about battle."

"I killed more men than you, you cheeky bastard."

"That's not true! That's a load of Grucknick shit!"

Serena knew she was out of time as the men continued to bicker aimlessly. She slowly snuck away and went back to her carriage. Her heart continued to race, and some measure of hope entered her soul.

Luka was alive. This could change everything.

Chapter 26
The Magic Tavern

A morning fog rolled over the fields as Luka continued his ride northwest. It was a sign that he was nearing his target. Lake Zachary, which lay alongside the town of Jetsac, would provide a steady supply of mist on days like this.

It was nearly evening when Luka finally arrived. Fortunately, there was no Zlikrej presence waiting for him. Jetsac was a strategic point providing access to the sea through the lake and the adjoining rivers. If it wasn't too far west off of Vulture Road, Luka was sure the Zlikrej would have sacked it.

Luka detoured along the shores of the lake. It was the first time Luka had seen a proper body of water since he left the Vernikport area. He greatly missed the sea and considered staying long enough to watch the sunset. Since the shore faced west, the sunset would glow marvelously along the watery horizon, turning both the sea and sky a mystical blend of orange, pink, and red. But Luka denied himself the pleasure. He had already wasted too much time on the shore, instead of focusing on his mission. He could not justify waiting anymore.

Luka rode into the town of Jetsac and found The Magic Tavern. "Well, Xander, let's see if you were right," Luka said to himself.

The tavern was merely one half of a three-story house, divided vertically. From the front, it looked miniscule, but as soon as Luka entered, he could see that the establishment stretched far back. A bar ran along the right wall. A modest stage lay in the back of the building, overlooking a scattering of tables placed in the middle of the space. The tables were all full of patrons.

The atmosphere buzzed inside. The thick scent of alcohol—mostly ale—filled Luka's nostrils. The air vibrated with conversation and liveliness.

Luka quickly scanned the establishment but did not see any wizards. Luka's only leads were one frazzled serving lady and one frustrated barman. Luka decided to try the serving lady.

"Excuse me," he said, hastily trying to get out in front of her. "Could you please tell me where I can find the wizard?"

She was on her way to another table and said to Luka with her back to him, "Gabbitt gets on in just a little bit. We haven't any tables left, but you can wait at the bar."

She had already rushed off to another table before Luka could ask a follow-up question, so he found one of the open barstools. The bartender, a man who was a full generation older than Luka, had dusty brown hair, wavy and graying around the ears, and a trimmed beard of the same color.

The bartender's blue-green eyes met Luka's. Luka expected him to come over and take his drink order, but the man instead poured himself a tall glass of ale and took a big swig. Luka continued to stare at the man, unsure of what to do. From the corner of his eye, the barman noticed Luka's staring. He finished his sip and wiped the wetness off his mouth.

"Oi, you want a drink? Is that why you keep looking at me?" the barman said. Luka ignored the snark and ordered the same ale that the bartender had just poured for himself. The bartender scanned Luka intently as he poured it, so much so that he spilled a few drops onto the bar.

"Oops. That tends to happen once in a moon," he said.

"Quite a bit more than once in a moon!" exclaimed the serving lady, whizzing by.

"Quiet, Tanna! I don't pay you to mock me!" he shot back at her, but she was already well out of range before he finished his retort.

The bartender placed the glass in front of Luka and asked for several bronze coins in payment. As Luka dropped the money into the man's palm, he asked, "You pay her? Are you the owner of this tavern?"

"Aye, I am the owner, for better or for worse. Usually, it's for worse."

"So, if you are the owner, can you tell me about this wizard? Do you let him perform his magic here?"

"Well, yes indeed, the arrangement is something along those lines. Why do you ask? You've never even seen his show before."

"I would very much like to talk to this wizard. I need him for something very important."

"Oh, you're very important, are you? Everyone seems to think that about themselves, yet strangely, almost no one actually is. Why should you be any different?"

Luka desperately wanted to grab the tipsy barman by his messy shirt, pull him in, lower his hood, and show him that he was the King of Estravia. *But would this fool even recognize a king?* Luka wondered.

Instead, he said, "You truly talk to your patrons this way?"

"Just the shitty ones, especially after they've already paid." The barman took another big sip of ale, keeping a prying gaze on Luka. "Let me guess—you must be highborn."

"N-no, I am not highborn," Luka said, stuttering out, surprised at the observation.

"That seems like a lie to me. Running a tavern for nearly fifteen years, one can learn to spot a liar with ease. I do appreciate your particular falsehood quite a bit, though. Typically, we have lowborns pretending to be highborns, not the other way around. This is a nice bit of variety." He took another big gulp of ale. "So, what young lordling do we have hiding under this hood here?" The barman reached for Luka's hood, but Luka swatted him away.

"I am no one," Luka said. "Don't touch me."

The barman shrugged off the fact that he had just been slapped. "Well, 'No One,' you may or may not be highborn, but if you are seeking the wizard to help you with some silly power struggle, then best of luck to you. I can guarantee he will not join your cause. All he cares about are whores and drinks, and I can get him just as many of those as any lord in Estravia.

"So, what I would advise you, 'No One,' is to stay here, have some more drinks, preferably expensive ones, and watch the magic."

Luka resolved not to purchase anything more from this insolent man. He sat steaming while he listened to him go bother someone else, at last.

Many minutes later, Tanna, the server, hushed everyone and directed their attention towards the stage. From a back room, a mysterious figure emerged—a man with long, disheveled gray hair, draped in a black robe.

The crowd gave him an enthusiastic round of applause, and he gave an awkward wave back. He gestured, indicating the start of the show. After a brief pause, he held out his palms. Nothing happened for an uncomfortable moment, but suddenly, his hands ignited, brightening the room with two fireballs—one in each hand. He moved the fireballs around with his arms in a fiery dance to the "oohs" and "ahhs" of the crowd.

Luka had to lean to the left on his barstool to watch the performance. He didn't share the crowd's reaction to this. The magic fire reminded him of the flames that had burned his home to the ground. He had seen magic in its cruelest form. These people only knew of magic as entertainment. He shuddered for a moment but then forced the feelings away.

The fire vanished suddenly, and a soft breeze appeared, blowing gently through the crowd. It was pleasant and comfortable, until the magician increased the power and transformed it into a strong gust. The wind was powerful enough to slide the customers' drinks backwards an inch or two. A few glasses spilled off tables in the audience. Luka wagered that they would not receive refunds for that.

Next, the wizard summoned two tendrils of water and made them slither in the air above the crowd. He conducted this routine for a few minutes until the tendrils dissolved into a light rain over the middle of the crowd. A few customers complained about getting wet, but most were entertained.

Based on Luka's understanding of elemental magic, he assumed earth had to be next. He was correct.

The wizard held out his hands again, although nothing happened right away. Only a second later, the ground beneath them started to shake. It was mild at first, feeling like a light vibration. But once again, the wizard increased the intensity. Luka instinctively grabbed one of the legs of his barstool to steady himself while the building visibly shook. More drinks spilled onto the ground.

The wizard's next act was combining elements. He cast fire and water out into the air simultaneously, making them collide to create a thick cloud of steam that filled the tavern. The two elements made a loud hiss when they connected.

The wizard then took command of the steam and moved it at his will, swirling it up and around the room, ostensibly with the power of the wind. He compacted the steam onto the top of one table where four attractive young women sat. They watched wide-eyed as he turned it into an innocuous mini tornado that rose gradually all the way to the ceiling.

Then, the magician released the hold of his tornado and allowed it to dissipate. The crowd began clamoring in desire of more tricks. The wizard obliged after several moments of chanting.

To cap off his performance, the wizard launched long streams of fire into the air with both hands, quickly churning them into the shape of a dragon. The fire dragon glided around the room, above the mesmerized crowd.

When the dragon's aerial dance was finished, it vanished, and with that, the show concluded. The wizard bowed, as the crowd stood and erupted into thunderous applause. This was Luka's moment—he sprang up from his chair and began to rush over to the wizard.

As he was about to sprint through the ovating crowd, a crossbow bolt whistled past Luka's ear and shattered a bottle of brown whiskey at the bar. If he had not stood up from his stool at that exact moment, the bolt would have gone straight through his neck.

The room burst into a collective panic as Luka turned around to see who the attempted killer was. Two men in dark coats stood at the door. The crossbowman was already loading another bolt into his weapon. The other man charged straight towards him with a dagger at the ready.

Luka hastily drew his new sword while frantic customers ran past him towards the exits. When his attacker closed in, Luka swung at him. The man ducked, lunging for Luka's lower abdomen with a swift stab. Luka narrowly avoided the strike, then landed a hard kick to the man's crotch, sending him staggering backward.

Unfortunately, that left enough room for the crossbowmen to have a clean shot at Luka, who was now exposed with his hood down. Before he had any time to react, the bolt was already on course for his skull.

The bolt never reached its target. A potent blast of wind—fired back from behind Luka—knocked the shot away.

Luka was pushed a half step forward, but he was saved. Only the bartender stood behind him when he glanced back.

As the bewildered crossbowman began reloading, the barman conjured a ball of fire, seemingly the same way the wizard had done earlier on stage. He grinned as he hurled it at the assailant. The crossbowman cried out as the fireball knocked him over. The flames quickly started to envelop his body. He wouldn't be alive for much longer.

The daggerman was startled but didn't relent from his target. He attempted another charge at Luka, but the barman intervened again. He summoned an orb of water and threw it at the attacker. The ball expanded into a bear-sized block of ice, which collided with the daggerman, crushing his bones and knocking him unconscious.

At that point, nearly everyone had cleared out of the tavern. Luka turned to the crossbowman's flaming corpse, the daggerman's injured body, and then back to the barman in disbelief. The two looked at each other in mutual incredulity until, finally, the bartender broke the silence.

"Sila's wrath! You're the bloody King of Estravia!"

Chapter 27
The Wizard of Jetsac

"Some ale for you lads?"

Luka sat across from the mysterious tavern owner, too stunned to respond to Tanna, the serving woman. The chaos had now cleared away, leaving the establishment empty save for the three of them.

"Ale? After all that? Not bloody likely, Tanna. We need something *much* stronger."

"Your golden rum, then?" she asked.

The tavern owner nodded. "That'll do nicely." She returned shortly with two glasses, each containing a heavy pour of golden-brown liquid.

"Oh, and please dispose of the burning body. Both bodies, actually. You'll need to figure out what to do with the one who is still alive."

Tanna groaned and said, "You don't pay me enough for this!" But she went off to take care of the grotesque task.

"Maybe I need to have a new policy against assassins in my tavern," the man said as if to himself. Luka didn't respond.

Swirling his drink, the tavern owner watched his employee until he was satisfied that she had a handle on the situation. Turning back to Luka, he said, "Your Highness, Luka, I hear you are now the true King of Estravia. Rumors reached my tavern just a few days ago. I could scarcely believe them.

"Never would I have imagined I would have a king in my tavern! I knew you were highborn, but I had no idea you were *this* highborn!"

Luka still didn't know how to respond, simply watching the strange man across from him.

"So what, um, what brings you here?" he asked after a few moments of awkward silence.

Luka lowered his head and looked at the table for a long second, gathering himself before responding. "Someone close to me told me of this place and of the wizard who performs here. But... it seems there were actually *two* wizards here—where did the other one go?"

The man smiled. "The other one wasn't a wizard. That was Gabbitt—just some fool who works for me. Looks like he ran off during the commotion, but he'll turn up again shortly.

"My name is Reishi Milsi of Westgard. But you can just call me Reishi and not bother with the rest. *I* am the *real* wizard here."

"Well met, Reishi," Luka said, "But if you're the wizard, then how did that other man perform all of that magic on stage? There was literally fire and water shooting from his hands. I don't understand."

Reishi's smile stretched wider. "I'll get to that shortly. Right now, I'm much more interested in you. What makes you want to find a wizard? I could wager a guess, but I'd rather you spell it out."

Luka took his first sip of rum. It filled his mouth with heat at first, but quickly smoothed out and left a sweet, sugary aftertaste. He sighed when he finished the sip. He didn't want to tell this strange man about the loss of his home. And he was even less enthused about asking for his help. But he took another sip and told his story, recounting the horrors Privus Zlikrej was able to inflict with his magic staff.

"And that is why I have come to find a wizard. I have tried facing this journey alone, which has been hard enough. When I face them again, I must have some magic of my own at my side."

The wizard had emptied his glass during Luka's story. He waved for Tanna. "Just bring the whole bloody bottle this time." When she did so, he filled his cup and then went to Luka, who was hesitant to accept more. "C'mon then, drink now. That's my best rum. It's truly fit for a king!" Luka relented, and his glass was full again.

"I am sorry for your loss," Reishi said. "I met your father briefly once. I know he would not have remembered it, but I do. He was a good man.

"A horrible thing to happen to Vernikport as well. I hear it is in complete ruin."

The wizard must have seen the flicker of pain in Luka's eyes, so he stopped himself. "I am no stranger to tragedy myself," he said. "And I know that no words will do you any good, so I will say no more of it.

"But I do also remember Lord Diocretin. He was a vile worm. The stories told in this very tavern about him…" Luka could see Reishi stifle a shudder, not elaborating further. "Your father did a great thing for this country by ridding it of him. Just wish he was able to keep his three sons at bay. They look determined to take their father's murderous ways and expand them nationwide, all with the help of an elemental magic staff."

Luka leaned forward, his eyes wide. "Do you have any idea how they got this magic staff? Do you know how we can beat it?"

"I can only guess where they obtained it," Reishi said, answering only the first of Luka's questions. "It is possible they purchased it or hired a wizard to make it for them."

"A wizard can make that?"

"Yes. Well-trained and powerful wizards can focus their own energies from their bodies—the magical force that flows through them—and store them inside certain objects, like these," he held three transparent orbs of varying colors in his palm. "These are how Gabbitt, my silly performer, does his shows. I supply the magic and leave the showmanship to him. The wizard who made Privus's staff must have poured weeks of his own force into it."

"So anyone can use magical objects made by a wizard?"

"Everyone can use simple objects like my orbs, which usually just need to be thrown. A magic staff is more advanced and requires some skill. Not everyone can use those kinds of objects."

Luka found himself astonished. Magic had been taught in his studies, but only briefly during certain history lessons—stories of wizards fighting against entire battalions, especially during The Pre-Unification Age. But none of those studies were ever to this level of detail.

"I'm going home now," Tanna said, standing near the exit, interrupting their conversation.

"Are the bodies taken care of?" Reishi asked.

"Yes. The survivor is chained up in the basement. The dead one is lying in the horse waste."

"Right where he belongs!" Reishi laughed. "Well done and thank you, Tanna. See you tomorrow."

Luka turned around as well to say goodnight, but she was already out the door. "Reishi," Luka said, turning back to the wizard. "Can you teach me about magic?"

"Um... teach you? Like get you to throw fireballs and such? I-I sincerely doubt it."

"I just want to know as much as you can tell me. This is all new information to me."

A pair of meows sounded from somewhere in the room before Reishi could respond. Luka turned to see a big black cat with large yellow-green eyes approaching their table. Reishi held out his hand, the cat meeting it with a forceful, affectionate nudge.

"This is Buchan. She's the real owner here," said Reishi. Luka tried to reach down and pet the cat, but she reeled back and avoided him. "She'll let you pet her when it suits her." The cat jumped up and settled in Reishi's lap.

"Anyway, back to your magic question," Reishi said as he petted a purring Buchan. "You must know, at least, that there are four kinds of magic, correct?"

Luka shook his head. "I did not know there were four. I think I may know of two. Obviously there's elemental magic, and I believe that there is some sort of spiritual magic as well."

Reishi shook his head. "It's good our drinks are full because I clearly have much to teach you."

Luka leaned into the conversation, anticipating what would follow.

"There are four kinds of forces in this world," the wizard began. "A wizard is only able to gain mastery over one force, never two.

"As we both know, the first kind is the elements. An elemental wizard can summon the powers of fire, water, wind, and earth at his will, like me, and like what you saw from Privus with his staff."

Luka nodded and the wizard went on.

"The second force is the mind. Wizards who practice this magic can learn the ability to control the thoughts and minds of others."

"That seems rather frightening," Luka said. "There are really wizards who can control people's minds?"

Reishi nodded. "Mind wizards gain their power from manipulating the minds of others, but at a great cost to them. They often find themselves in situations of isolation or secrecy. The ones who don't go insane, at least. If you come across one, they're not likely to let you know."

The wizard continued. "The third force is the soul, which I suppose you already know of. Soul wizards are essentially opposite to the mind wizards—they have no hesitation in telling you all about their powers and taking on a public role. Most of them ultimately choose to serve as priests. The members of the High Temple all possess remarkable soul magic abilities."

"Our family priestess, Priestess Teya, I think she has these powers," Luka said.

"Did she survive, too?" Reishi asked.

Luka didn't know whether to reveal the truth, but he realized that it was probably implied from the way he had just spoken about her. "Yes, she survived," he said.

"That is well and good," Reishi said, nodding. "I'm familiar with Priestess Teya, by the way. She is famous for turning down an offer to join the High Temple, instead choosing to serve your father and mother directly."

"She turned it down? I never knew that. Why?"

"Something about 'her calling.' You can ask her yourself if you're interested. Soul wizards are strange, Your Highness, so it's best not to wonder too much how they think. Leave the matters of 'Sila's Will' and the weight of souls to them. I have little interest in that. Just don't make the mistake of disregarding their powers. A soul wizard may not draw the same level of fear as an elemental wizard on the battlefield, but their powers can go well, well beyond healing."

Reishi sipped once again from his rum before continuing. "The last force is the most powerful and also the rarest. And that is time."

"Time?" Luka asked. "As in past, present, and future?"

"Exactly," Reishi said. "It may not always seem like it, but time controls us more than any other force. Everything in our life is dictated by it. We are born at a given time, we live for a time, and then we die at a time. We do not know when those times will be. We cannot give ourselves more time than we are fated. We cannot add more or even take away time from a day.

"Without magic, humans can fractionally control the other three forces. But time can't be affected in any way by normal humans. No matter what we do, the arrow of time will fly forward at the pace it chooses. We can't slow it down, influence it, and certainly can't stop it or change its course. That's why magicians of time are the rarest of all. Many talented men and women have tried to learn the magical art of time in the hopes of living forever, and ironically, wasted all their life on this insurmountable pursuit. Some even claim time magic is a myth—that no such magicians ever existed."

"And you say that they are real?" interjected Luka.

"I *know* that they are real," answered Reishi, "The ancient texts have mentioned three magicians of time. All three were born as humans hundreds of years ago, and all three now live as immortals by controlling time."

"They can really live forever?" Luka asked. Reishi gave a firm nod. "So where are they now?"

The wizard chuckled. "It is not a question of *where* they are—it is a question of *when*."

Luka continued to press the wizard for knowledge as the rum bottle became emptier. Several of the candles burned through their wick and went out over the course of their conversation, dimming the lighting in the quiet tavern. Their discussion lasted for nearly an hour before Luka finally realized he had gone too far off course. His mission was recruitment—not education—despite how interesting the latter had been.

"Reishi, good wizard, I thank you for sharing your knowledge, but I must have your help in a different manner. I need someone with your power and knowledge of magic on my side against the Zlikrej," Luka said, getting to the point, though some of his words were beginning to slur. "Come join me on my quest to stop them and avenge my family."

Reishi's expression darkened after Luka said this. He stared silently into his cup, swirling its contents around.

"Reishi," Luka repeated. "Will you come?"

"I knew you would eventually get around to asking me this." The wizard looked up from his cup and met Luka's eyes. "I opened up this tavern, because I was sick of my life of conflict and fighting. Joining you in your quest for revenge would only send me right back into the world that I left."

"I thought you said you hated the Zlikrej? I thought you agreed that they were dangerous and deserve to die?"

"Aye, they most certainly do deserve to die. Many people deserve to die. It's just not my responsibility to enforce that."

"There will be great rewards. Money, titles, whatever you would desire."

"Those are not the incentives that you think they are. I'm more than happy staying here and satisfying myself with rum. Not a lot of things I'd rather do, quite frankly."

"Do you even hear the madness spewing out of your lips?" Luka asked, his voice now raising. "I am offering you unimaginable amounts of money and power. And all you want is to drink?"

"Yes. What's wrong with that?"

Luka stewed for a moment. He did not have optimal control over his faculties. The continuous golden rum drinking was running its course. He pressed on, despite lacking any sense of strategy or subtlety. "I order you to join me! I am the King of Estravia! I order it!"

"Oh, you bloody order it? I don't care what you're the king of. You're alone, you're in my bar, and I am a bloody *wizard*! No *title* makes you more powerful than me in this situation. You can't tell me what to do."

Luka stood up, enraged. "How dare you!"

"Oh woo-hoo. The King is mad. All must fear the King! He said, 'How dare you.' Oh no!" Reishi taunted.

"Your insolence will not go unpunished, foul wizard!"

Reishi shrugged. "The only thing that should be punished is your inability to hold your liquor."

Red anger filled Luka, to the point that he considered striking his counterpart. The wizard just stared at him, seemingly amused.

"So be it! I don't need you!" Luka yelled at last. "I'll face them on my own!"

The last thing Luka remembered from that night was storming out of the tavern.

Chapter 28
The Meadows

Serena waded through the tall grass that covered the open meadow, enjoying a momentary illusion of freedom. The air of a departing summer and arriving fall felt fresh and cool.

An hour prior, a guard had told her the caravan was stopping for a quick break and that she was allowed to leave the carriage and wander for a bit. She would be monitored from afar, but could go wherever she pleased, within reason.

It was one of the few conversations Serena had with any person since she had grabbed Privus's staff. She had spent the last few weeks in almost pure isolation. Privus had not checked on her a single time. Her servants said little and rotated away frequently. The solitude had started to weigh her down, and she craved both liberation and company.

She spent much of this time daydreaming about Luka. The notion of him rescuing her got her through many of these days. Unfortunately, as time marched on, her logical side began to deconstruct this fantasy. Even if Luka was alive, he had little chance of overcoming the Zlikrej army and Privus's staff on his own. The Vernik Army was still hundreds of leagues away. Even when they arrived, she would be sealed within the walls of Exeter if Omarius's plan worked. And even if there was some small hope for rescue, she feared for her family's safety. Her duty now was to make sure they were as safe as possible, and that meant obeying her captors' every command.

Out in the vastness of the meadow, Serena pretended that her restraints were absent. The freedom was only temporary, but it was the best she had felt in weeks. Exeter was only days away now, and the Ekron Mountains had begun to rise on the horizon—faint silhouettes against the sky.

Minutes later, she noticed the tops of a half dozen metal helms approaching. The grass lowered itself as the men walked through it. This likely meant her frolicking time was over. She sighed but tried to remain grateful for the time she had.

One guard arrived shortly before all the others. He immediately grabbed her by her left arm and squeezed tightly. Serena's eyes went wide. "What in the hell do you want? I wasn't going anywhere."

"Hello, *Archlady*," the soldier said with a ravenous grin. Five other soldiers soon joined and stood near her, predatory hunger burning in their eyes.

"I've never had a lord's daughter before," another soldier said. "I've always wondered what it would be like. Bet it actually isn't any different from any other wench off the streets."

Serena's face went white when she realized what was happening. Terror rose up within her as her heart raced.

"I bet noble ladies are much better! That's what my wager's on," came one of the other soldiers.

"Only one way to find out," said another. They laughed as if her life and her dignity were nothing more than a joke. She felt like prey amongst a pack of starving wolves. They started upon her and began tearing at her clothes.

She would have none of it. She reached for the first guard's dagger in his belt and used it to slit his throat. His lifeless body released its hold around her. Another guard noticed this and tried to seize the weapon, but Serena cut his hand and then his throat as well.

With skill and swiftness, Serena stabbed the next guard in the stomach, his innards spilling out when she withdrew. The fighting began to feel good. The exhilaration began to conquer the panic. It was a rare opportunity to feel like the warrior she was always forbidden from being.

Unfortunately, the next two guards grabbed her simultaneously, each taking hold of one of her arms and tackling her backwards. Their dog-like panting and sweaty soldier stench pressed right up against Serena's face as they pinned her down. The sixth, and only remaining man, stood above her amongst the tall blades of grass. Both rage and arousal emanated from his face.

The man descended on her, ripping her cream-colored dress off in large tears. Serena tried kicking, but it was hardly a deterrent. A wave of despair began to wash over her. She screamed at the top of her lungs repeatedly until a sweaty hand came over and covered up her mouth. Oxygen instantly became scarcer.

Suddenly, a wave of heat came over Serena. The sensation was clearly not coming from her own body. The two soldiers clutching at her sides lessened their hold. The soldier on top stopped his assault and peered around his shoulder.

"Lord Privus—" the officer said, but the man choked on his words as an ice shard pierced his skull.

The two men at Serena's sides seemed even more shocked than her, giving her a chance to wrestle herself away. When she got free of them, she saw Privus with rage burning across his face, his staff raised and pointed at his own men.

One of the men spun around and looked at Privus. "Sir, I-I... What is...," he began saying, but Privus silenced him with another blast of fire.

The other man seemed to be trying to speak but said nothing. It took Serena a moment to figure out that Privus was using his staff to suck the air from his lungs. The man's face became strained and began to turn purple. After several agonizing moments, the soldier succumbed to the lack of breathing. At last Serena was safe. She pulled herself to her knees and burst into tears.

Privus rushed over and clutched her gently. "I'm sorry. I'm so, so sorry about this, my sweet," he muttered. "I'll never let this happen again. I promise I will keep you safe. I'm so sorry…"

Serena leaned into his embrace and continued to sob.

*****

Hours earlier, Omarius had decided to stop the convoy. He almost never did this, as the insurgency's pace was of the utmost importance. "Take this as an opportunity to relax," Omarius had instructed his youngest brother. "Perhaps you can even spend some time with the Tomkins girl. Make her feel more at ease. You need to connect with her, if you are truly planning on taking her as your wife."

"She is a difficult puzzle to solve," Privus said.

"She will not be that way forever," Omarius assured him.

"The last time I tried talking to her, she took my staff and tried to use it against me."

"And you've kept her in isolation ever since?" Omarius asked.

Privus nodded.

"I suggest you change your tactics."

"Tactics with war is one thing, brother," Privus said. "Women are another thing, altogether."

"You'll work something out," Omarius said. "You need to gain her trust, not crush her spirit."

After he had thought it through, Privus called six of his men for a private meeting. "I am growing tired of my bride-to-be," he began. "I know this is rather early to tire of a woman, even for the lowest of standards, but she just cannot appreciate the fortunate position she has been given, and I cannot bear another complaint.

"I intend to find a new wife. I am going to be the Archlord of Estravia, and I am entitled to any woman that I choose. I no longer choose this one. I am done with her.

"Since we are on break, I want you, all six of you, to enjoy her. Consider it a gift for your loyalty against such extreme odds. Wait until she's wandered off far enough and then have her in whatever way you wish. My only condition is that you tell no one of this. Now or after."

Privus had not enjoyed saying some of those words. He could feel the bile lingering in his throat, but he stayed the course. This method was distasteful, but he knew it would serve his purpose.

The soldiers needed an uncomfortable moment to process what they had just been told, but as soon as they were convinced the offer was serious, they rushed off.

Then Privus waited.

Chapter 29
The Warrior and the Wizard

A wicked headache greeted Luka as he stirred awake. When he opened his eyes, he found himself in a bedroom that he did not recognize. The space was messy, with piles of books stacked around the room. With a wince, he lifted himself from the bed and pulled the curtains open, only for the sunlight to jar him like an arrow to his forehead. He closed the curtains instantly and crashed back down into the bed.

He tried to think of where he could be, but all he could remember was an argument with the wizard and lots of rum. Evidently enough rum to drown his memories.

A scratching sound interrupted Luka's thoughts. An adamant meow followed the noise, coming from outside his bedroom. When he opened the door, he saw a big pair of yellow eyes staring up at him. It was Buchan, the wizard's black cat. That explained where he was.

The cat entered the room, chirping. Luka reached down to pet her. This time, she allowed him to. 'She'll let me pet her when it suits her,' Luka repeated in his mind. *She has no idea that I am the King.*

A gag suddenly rose up in Luka's stomach. He suppressed it, distracting himself by petting Buchan on his bed.

"Looks like the King can make new friends after all."

Luka looked up to see Reishi leaning against the wall outside the room.

"Reishi," Luka said hoarsely. "How did I end up here?"

Reishi laughed and entered the room. "Well, you see, there was this very kind wizard and this very disagreeable king. The disagreeable king was yelling at the kind wizard who had saved his life and offered him lots of good rum. At one point, the king stormed out only to come back a few minutes later looking for his sword. He looked all around the wizard's tavern until he forgot what he was doing and passed out. A most embarrassing look for a king, indeed."

"Did you poison me?" Luka asked, seriously.

Reishi laughed again. "In your state right now, you are actually making me wonder. My golden rum is certainly strong, but you obviously do not have the stomach to be worthy of it."

The words "golden" and "rum" triggered a gag, and this time Luka could not resist. Buchan sensed the oncoming retch and leapt away. A puddle of vomit formed in the middle of the floor with Luka hunched over it.

"Ugh," Reishi groaned. "I suppose that will give Tanna something to do, at least. She'll need it while I am out on my silly adventure with you."

The comment did not register with Luka right away. He was too busy staring at his own vomit in shame. "What did you just say?"

"That's right, Luka. We will fight the Zlikrej brothers together. I think it could be quite fun.

"I'm not doing it for free, though," Reishi quickly added. "You mentioned money as an incentive last night, and I definitely want payment. Ten thousand Novaks should suffice."

"I can't believe it..." Luka trailed off as excitement and possibilities filled his hampered mind. A wizard on his side—a level playing field against Privus and his magic. But then he remembered his pride.

This was the same wizard who had insulted him just last night. Though his memories were fuzzy, he remembered the arrogance and defiance of this man—the way he had mocked him.

"I'm not sure I can bring someone who doesn't respect the throne," Luka said somberly.

"What do you mean?"

"Last night, you said you did not care that I was the King. You did not want to come, and you refused my orders."

"You should consider the fact that I don't respect authority the way others do to be a good thing," Reishi replied.

"How so?"

"You can trust my intentions. I won't be joining you because you're ordering me to—I'm joining because I *choose* to. When you reconnect with your army, you'll be equipped with no limit of subordinates. It will be nice, but it will do no good against the magic that the Zlikrej possess."

Luka sat quietly for a moment. The wizard's words seemed to make sense, but with all the clouds in his mind, he could not be entirely sure. "Well enough," he said at last. "What made you change your mind?"

Reishi took a moment before answering. "I've been running this tavern for more than a decade. It was originally an escape for me. In my younger days, I used to employ my abilities for good, trying to make this land a better place. In the end though, I think I just caused more trouble than anything, especially for myself. Coming here was my way of removing myself from the Table Dragons board.

"In truth, I know I am not destined to be a fake barman for the rest of my days. I have abilities, and I must use them for good again. I at least need to try. I'm no priest, and I don't know if I believe in signs from Sila, but if the King of Estravia came into my bar seeking my help, and then I just went on living the same damn life..." he began to trail off.

Luka nodded. There was more to this wizard than he had first realized.

"It's that and also the financial reward I mentioned," Reishi added. "I've been bleeding Novaks ever since the Zlikrej invaded. Last night was a good crowd, but they've mostly dwindled in the past weeks. Conflict has not been good for business and running this tavern is not cheap, you know."

Luka nodded again. "I will personally ensure that funds straight from the crown's purse are paid to you if you help me. There is no question of that."

"There is one other thing you ought to know, however," Reishi said, shifting his gaze to the floor for a moment. "I am not the wizard I used to be."

"What do you mean?"

"When I was younger, I was much more effective. My skills were sharper. Now... the magic doesn't come to me quite so easily. I need to warn you that when it comes down to a crucial moment, I can't promise you that my magic will save us."

"That's bloody helpful then. Why should I even bring you if I can't rely on you in crucial moments?"

"Do you happen to have a better wizard?" he retorted. "I will do my best to regain my top form, but understand that I needed to warn you and be open with you. I do not know if the Zlikrej brothers have a wizard still on their side, but if they do, I fear I may not be as capable as he is."

Luka again had to fight through the clouds in his brain to think of a response. "Understood," he said, almost in a groan. "When it comes down to it, I expect you to do your best and win."

"I promise you I will do my best. Just be warned that my best is not the same best I had in my youth."

"Well, you have time to practice."

"Right. Now that's out of the way, let me get my things in order. I need Tanna to get here so I can tell her to watch over my tavern and my cat when I'm gone."

Tanna arrived nearly an hour later, greeted by a slew of Reishi's rapid-fire instructions. "Make sure the 'Closed' signs are displayed prominently. I don't want anyone popping in here. If they ask, tell them the wizard is away. You'll also need to check on Buchan every day. Actually, twice every day. Three times would be even better. She needs food and water. There's plenty of meat in the pantry for her, just make sure to chop it into small bits. Give her attention as well. Lots of love and attention. She needs it."

Tanna stood there, unreactive, waiting for the barrage of directions to end. Luka felt dizzy as he overheard this, greatly admiring Tanna's patience. There likely were few people out there who could tolerate such an eccentric steward.

"Is that too much to handle?" he asked.

"Quite frankly, that is far better than dealing with your customers every night. And you," she said with a bemused smile.

"Good. Well... I'm not quite certain that is good, but so be it. Just make sure you get it all done every day. Buchan will be very upset if not. And I will know." Tanna rolled her eyes.

"Oh, and one more thing," Reishi added. "Gabbitt can take some time off. Just keep an eye on him. Write me if you notice any unusual behavior." Tanna nodded in understanding.

Reishi then finished up his packing, which included a few flasks, a dagger, a bag of clothes, a small pouch of money, and another full of trinkets and miscellaneous items.

When he was ready, the wizard turned to his cat for a farewell. "Tanna will take great care of you. If she doesn't, then tell me when I get back, and I'll be rid of her." Reishi gave her one last pet and was ready to go.

After a long time of watching the wizard prepare himself, they finally mounted their horses. "At this point, the Zlikrej brothers will be near Exeter. We'll need to continue to follow Vulture Road, but until we hear of something different, Exeter is where we're headed," Luka said.

"Lead the way, My King." Reishi gestured with his arm out, leading forward. On that cue, Luka urged Velico onward. He still had a long journey ahead of him, but now he wasn't riding alone.

Chapter 30
The Invasion of Exeter

Privus sat atop his warhorse and gazed at the awe-inspiring sight ahead of him. The city of Exeter lay in the shadows of the mountains—the peaks hiding in the clouds. The glorious city seemed to shine to him like a trophy, and it would soon be his new home. His new throne. All they had to do was conquer it.

"Get in formation." Omarius's thunderous voice rang out when they had reached their position. Officers and commanders echoed it in a flurry of orders that cascaded down the chain to the remaining men. The force of nearly four thousand soldiers formed a vast crescent moon perimeter less than a thousand feet from the colossal city gates.

With the siege formation in place, an eerie level of quiet filled the field. Only the low murmur of soldiers preparing, the creaking of leather and metal, and the whistling of a mountainous breeze filled the air.

Privus rode away from the formation to the staging area behind, making his way to Serena's carriage. She greeted him with caution and reserve—but not with disdain. That was how she had been since he had "saved" her from the incident in the meadows. It was a marked improvement. He held out his hand, allowing Serena to climb up and mount the horse, sitting in front of him. He enjoyed this arrangement, able to admire her shiny black hair and slender figure from up close. Together, they rode to the edge of the siege.

Over the last few days, they had traveled together in the same carriage much of the time. Privus remained gentle with her, but made sure that several updates about Lord Tomkins were delivered to him in front of her. She needed to be reminded—without being explicit—of how her behavior could affect her family's safety. The veil of that threat would still be critical in controlling her, but he didn't have to be the one to deliver it.

On their own in the middle of the grassy field, they gazed ahead at the spectacle of Exeter. "This city has never been conquered in all its history. Now, I will change that. Do you believe it?" Privus asked.

"I do believe it," Serena replied candidly. "I know what you are capable of with that magic staff."

"I am not a barbarian or a fiend," Privus said, not sure if he had detected disapproval in her voice. "My intention is to keep this affair as efficient and bloodless as possible."

"I don't want *any* blood," Serena said. "So much has been shed already. We used to have peace in this country."

"Peace?" Privus hissed. "I never enjoyed the peace that you speak of. Var Vernik killed my father and mother. He exiled me when I was an infant. All I knew as a boy were the walls of the prison city and the dry wastelands around it.

"You might say that Exeter does not deserve the conflict we are about to bring upon it, but I ask you—what did I do to deserve *my* exile? I don't care what sins my father may have or may not have committed. That has nothing to do with me. Do you know how miserable it was to grow up in that dark, cold world?"

"No... no, I'm sorry, I didn't mean..."

Privus felt a fire building up within him, but he suppressed it. He did not want to take it out on his bride-to-be. His enemies would be the ones to suffer that soon enough.

"Do not worry, Serena," Privus said, exhaling. "I know this is difficult for you. This entire situation. But change is inevitable. It is a river that never stops running. Some try to resist the river. Most people are swept up in it. But throughout history there have been a precious few who shaped it. We are the next river shapers, Serena. And you are part of that.

"People forget that this country used to be divided into separate city-states, Canyon City among them. Then the Verniks changed that at the cost of great bloodshed and chaos. But that is the nature of change."

Serena nodded, no longer seeming interested in debating him, but her back remained stiff, her jaw clenched tight.

"Soon this glorious city will be ours, Serena. Not mine. *Ours.* The route between Exeter and Privagrad will be highly protected. We will be able to visit your family frequently. Life will be good."

"I would certainly appreciate that," Serena said, her grip on the saddle seeming to ease. "It's hard being apart from my family."

"After this is over, you will see them again. But first, we have some matters to attend to," Privus said, his hand moving to his waist where his staff was latched. "When the signal comes, we take Exeter."

*****

The commotion started to spread through Exeter as a flurry of hushed whispers. Vatren, with his black hood up, listened as he walked through the city's western market near his inn. Around him, citizens muttered in a low-vibration worry.

Is that true?

Can they actually breach the walls?

I've heard they have magic that can burn down the walls.

What should we do?

How do we know this is true?

I can ask my friend Zigra if her son has heard anything. He works up on the walls.

Vatren grinned. It was starting to happen. He just needed a little bit more confirmation. He could only give the signal once without attracting attention. He needed to be sure.

Soon, the flurry of whispers turned to a blizzard of panic. A group of hurried Exeterian soldiers ran past, only to be followed by several more. They were headed in the direction of the wall. Citizens began to rush inside to their homes, slamming doors and locking them behind them.

As Vatren walked back towards the Rasko Inn, he noticed a number of citizens being prayed over by a priest outside of a temple. *Prayers will not help you today*, he thought. He felt an impulse to mock them, but before he could do so, a young soldier tripped and landed next to him, his unit pushing on ahead.

Vatren went over and extended his hand to the young man.

"Thank you," the soldier said as he pulled himself up using Vatren's arm. His eyes momentarily drifted to the red scar marks on Vatren's wrist and forearm.

Before he could rush off, Vatren asked, "Is it really true? Are the Zlikrej here?"

The soldier hesitated, so Vatren pushed again. "Please. I have two young daughters, for Sila's sake!"

The soldier sighed and said, "It is true—they are here. Get your family to safety. Thank you again for helping me." Then he rushed off to join his unit, having given Vatren the confirmation he needed.

Back in his hotel, Vatren stepped out onto his balcony and raised his right arm. A bright fireball formed at his fingertips and launched high into the air, high enough to be seen from anywhere inside or outside of the city. That was the signal.

Moving to his second task, Vatren ventured to the inner perimeter of the city walls. He consulted his map until he found the correct point. He glanced around to make sure there were no onlookers, and then he placed his hands on the walls and concentrated. The stone beneath his fingers began to crack. The small chasms spread rapidly, and soon chunks began to fall away. Shortly a hole emerged, wide enough for several people to walk through. It would remain open only for today's purposes. After that, Vatren would close it back up.

Three silhouettes appeared and walked through the tunnel. When they were through, Privus, Drugi, and Omarius Zlikrej greeted their wizard friend, embracing him one at a time.

"Thank you again, Vatren. We are looking forward to conquering this great city with you," said Omarius. "This is providential. Just as the divine and the spirits willed it."

"Indeed. I have been looking forward to this day for a long time," said Vatren. The four men proceeded towards the city entrance, ready to open the gates from within.

The gates of Exeter were governed by a lever that was housed within a small hut built into the side of the wall. Dozens of guards surrounded the hut. A hush came over them when they noticed four figures approaching. Vatren knew that the Zlikrej brothers would be instantly recognizable with their distinctive weapons and distinguishable vigil of the Mithacor emblazoned on the center of their chest.

"Allow me to handle this," Vatren said, stepping forward and holding out his arms. A red and yellow blaze came forth, engulfing the entire street and swallowing up the Exeterian guards. The men screamed in agony for a few seconds until a total silence followed.

Vatren held out his arms again, bringing a torrential rain down on the street, putting out the fires that he had created. Puddles appeared, and clouds of steam now rose from where the fire had been—the path now clear. When they were inside the hut, Privus immediately went to the lever. He pulled it down and waited. Moments later, they could hear the great iron gate screech open.

*****

"Lieutenant, behind you!"

For the better part of two hours, Lieutenant Smece had kept his eyes fixed on the mass of soldiers below him. At the shout from one of his officers, he turned around, pointing his gaze inside the city.

When he turned, he saw a ball of fire ascending into the sky, somewhere above the middle of the city. A sense of dread came over him. "It's some kind of signal," he said.

Somehow the Zlikrej had a contact already inside the city walls. He sent two soldiers to investigate the source of the signal but kept the rest of his resources on top of the wall. The priority was the enemy below.

After remaining steady for nearly an hour and a half, the congregation of forces began to slowly creep towards the city. The signal must have prompted their movements, but Smece could not figure out why that could be. The gate was closed—the soldiers below wouldn't be able to breach the walls. He had well over one hundred archers perched on the walls, equipped with thick and deadly long-distance bows and arrows. The army below them was large enough to easily withstand that over a short period of time, but they would die slowly as they failed to penetrate the defenses.

The mass of soldiers halted their advance once again, closer to the city, but just out of range of the Exeterian archers. They were clearly waiting for something—probably another signal. Smece began to pace as the moments dragged on.

Then, cutting through the silence, came the slow, grinding sound of metal gates rising. The noise echoed across the field. Terror swelled inside of Smece. How could the gates be lifting?

Thinking fast, he pulled in two additional soldiers. "Go straight to the palace and alert Lady Dija of this," he commanded. "She needs to know that our city has been breached."

They sprinted away and headed to the palace. The rest of the archers turned to him, waiting for guidance. "Steady!" he said.

When the first bodies were in range, Smece gave the command. "Fire!" He watched as most of the arrows fell short of the advancing enemy. A few men went down, but the adversarial mass continued its pace, undeterred.

Smece gave the order once again, and a second round of arrows was released. More Zlikrej men went down, but they were merely removing drops of water from a tidal wave. They wouldn't be able to stop them at this rate.

More waves of arrows followed, but by this time, the first line of the enemy force had breached through the gate and entered the city. This battle had to be fought on the ground. He gathered a few of the archers and a few foot soldiers and gave the order for the rest to continue shooting arrows at the enemy below.

As he descended hundreds of stone steps, Smece tried to ignore the bubbling panic in his insides that was compelling him to flee. His instincts were telling him that near-certain death awaited him. Only his decades of training could help him resist that urge.

An ongoing battle scene greeted them when they finally reached the ground. Exeterian foot soldiers traded blows with Zlikrej forces near the city gates. It was heavily congested, but among the foes, Smece recognized the great war hammer he had heard so much about. The weapon swung about in the air, flattening soldiers in its way.

Despite all of his prior fears, he now had an opportunity to kill the leader of the invasion. Omarius Zlikrej, covered in thick black armor, was only a few strides away. It wouldn't be easy, but killing him would strike a huge blow to the Zlikrej campaign—perhaps even end the conflict altogether. Maybe Sila's agents had smiled upon him after all.

Smece engaged, sword drawn. He moved into an opening created just after Omarius had struck down two Exeterian soldiers. He had half a step on the large warrior, landing several strikes against his thick armor. Another soldier joined Smece, and they took Omarius on two-on-one.

Together they maneuvered around the large warrior as their silver blades clashed against his armor. All the while, they ducked and dodged the wide black flashes of the war hammer. Though it was such a massive instrument, Omarius could wield it as quickly as most swordsmen wielded their much lighter blades. They managed to evade for several moments as the space around them began to fill with more bodies, both dead and alive.

As Smece landed a direct strike, the hammer swung away from him, connecting with the arm of the lieutenant's partner. Smece could see his elbow at an angle that seemed not humanly possible, his forearm seeming to dangle off the joint. The final strike came down right after, crushing the soldier's body like an insect under a boot.

In anger, Smece leaped and tried to land another powerful blow. As he was airborne, a force of air smacked him from the side. His bones crunched as the city walls connected with him next. Stars swam around his eyes as he lay on the ground, tackled by an invisible force.

Smece tried to feel with his fingers and strained with his eyes to see. He saw the blurry figure of Privus Zlikrej standing above him. The man grinned for a moment before bringing down a fatal flash of silver to his head.

*****

Two young soldiers came rushing into Lady Dija's quarters. From her open window, she could hear the commotion as she nervously twisted her grey, curly hair with her fingers. She could venture a guess about what they were about to say.

"There is nothing we can do now," Dija said after they had given the report. "We have no way out of this city. Our defenses have failed. Now they only serve to trap me here. I suggest you both hide, so that your lives will be spared."

"What about you m'Lady?" asked one of the messengers.

"I cannot hide. I must stand by my city and negotiate for the best possible outcome."

The two soldiers tried to protest, so Lady Dija snapped and told them to get going, her voice sharp and final. She watched them disappear down the hallway.

Lady Dija took a longing look at her bedroom. It was large enough to house a dragon and was decorated with diamonds and rare paintings collected over many lifetimes, including a portrait of her late husband on the back wall. She sighed, knowing it could be the last time she ever set foot in here again, and walked downstairs.

Dija didn't have to wait long for her enemies to arrive. Privus was the first one to walk in through the grand front door of the palace. He was followed shortly by a dark, cloaked, mysterious man, his two older brothers, and dozens of soldiers. They poured into the atrium, filling the space and making it feel icy and crowded.

"Lady Dija," Privus said, grinning excitedly. "How kind of you to welcome us."

Chapter 31
The Sova Woods

It took very little time for Luka to discover the challenges of riding with Reishi.

The wizard constantly stopped their ride to urinate because of how much he drank. Luka imposed limits on this after the first day. When they weren't stopped, Reishi's horse was slow compared to Velico. They had been traveling at a fraction of the pace that Luka had when he was by himself. After being lonely for so much of his journey, Luka now wondered if he preferred solitude after all.

It was only when Reishi shared his knowledge of magic that Luka was reminded about why he had recruited him in the first place. The wizard had countless stories to tell and a vast understanding of things that were completely alien to Luka.

"I don't think that just anyone can learn magic," Reishi said in answer to one of Luka's questions. "People appear to be predisposed to certain types of it. I started to notice my own abilities not long into my third decade. From there, you have to practice and train properly."

Reishi paused to take a drink of rum from his flask. Luka thought about chiding him but decided against it. "How long did it take you to learn magic?" Luka asked.

The wizard wiped his mouth before answering. "It took me many years. I first went to learn by going to the monks in the..." Reishi paused for a strange amount of time before continuing, "Tatran Mountains. I spent nearly three years there, developing my skills. They put me through rather grueling studies, starting before sunrise and ending well after sunset.

"But that grew old to me. I thought that I no longer needed my teachers. The monks were good and wise people, but far too closed-minded. Although sometimes I wonder what would have happened if I had stayed..."

"What makes you say they were closed-minded?"

"Well, they greatly discouraged the use of magic for external purposes... Or for profit for that matter," Reishi chuckled to himself. "There was no fun in it. Almost no application of our abilities. They wanted everyone to use their magic for its own sake as if it was some kind of art, all in the isolated confines of their temples. I say piss to that. Speaking of which..."

"No, no, Reishi. Absolutely not. We literally just stopped an hour ago. You know the rules," Luka cut in quickly.

"Fine then. I'm honestly not sure I can make it that long. If it starts to smell like urine, your ridiculous rules are to blame."

"If it wasn't for my ridiculous rules, we'd still be in Jetsac."

The wizard seemed to say something under his breath, but Luka didn't press on that. "You said you trained in the mountains hidden away with the elemental monks. You also have speculated that an elemental wizard may be aiding the Zlikrej brothers. Is it possible you were in the mountains with him at the same time?"

The wizard paused a while before answering. "Reishi?" Luka prodded.

"I suppose it's possible, but I can't imagine who it would be. I haven't kept up with anyone there in years."

"You don't have any ideas on who it could be?"

"No, but I suppose I can think."

Just over an hour later, as the sun hung low in the sky, the two came across a small village. They were staying a safe distance west of Vulture Road, so they had not seen any towns in some time. "They have an inn!" Reishi exclaimed, pointing to one of the buildings in the village.

Luka noticed the inn as well. It was diminutive, only two stories. A few of the rooms were lit from the inside by a set of candles. The inn's comfort and coziness were alluring to Luka, but he resisted. "We still have many hours in the day left to ride. I don't want to stop here."

"Luka, I mean, Your Majesty, with all due respect to you, you look like Grucknick shit. You haven't had proper rest in ages. I know you want revenge, and I know you want it as soon as possible, but that won't do you much good if you're exhausted as all hell."

Luka relented. After paying the innkeeper, they separated, going to their individual rooms, planning to meet each other in the tavern for dinner shortly after.

Luka's room was minuscule, but it had something that seemed like a forgotten comfort—a bed. He sat on the corner and began to remove his clothes down to his undergarments. He ran his finger over the ugly scar on his side. The bumps where stitches had been were grotesque but painless.

Enjoying the blessed quiet, he lay back in the bed and sighed.

*****

"Oi, Your Highness!" A half-remembered voice called out to him.

Luka was swimming in the ocean and looked around, confused. Xander swam next to him, but he had not been the source of the voice. Deanna, their caretaker, was standing on the shore, but clearly, she had not said it either.

"Oi! Time to get up!" the voice came again.

Luka felt a shake on his shoulder, and on the third "Oi," he began to piece it together. His heart sank as the refreshing ocean, the view of

Vernikport, and his time as a child with his brother all faded away. When he opened his eyes, he saw the bearded, smirking face of Reishi.

"There's the King! I was beginning to think you had actually died," the wizard said. Even startled awake by the wizard, he felt his eyes beginning to shut again. "And this is the same person who tried telling me he didn't want to stay at the inn! C'mon now, it's past noon."

"Noon, you say?" That got him up. Luka jumped out of bed and began to put his boots on. *How can I have allowed this to happen?*

Reishi nodded. "I'm a little annoyed you went straight to bed instead of joining me in the tavern downstairs. No matter, though. I won more than sixty Novaks playing Pula from some of the tavern folk. I've never collected so many tokens from my opponents so quickly."

Damn, I missed Pula too? I would have surely beaten anyone this fool could beat.

Luka wasted no more time, getting his things in order and checking out of the inn. They resumed their journey in the early afternoon, making a good pace for many hours.

Their momentum soon slowed when the trees multiplied around them. They had come upon a dense forest. Luka looked at his map and then back up at the green mass ahead of him. It had to be the Sova Woods, likely an impediment, but also a marker that they were even farther north than he had expected.

Luka mentioned the good news to Reishi. The wizard did not share the same sentiment with Luka. "I do not like the look of this forest. This is a bad, bad forest. Bad forest. And I bet there's Giant Werdals in there."

"There won't be Giant Werdals in there," said Luka.

"What makes you so bloody sure?"

"Why are you so afraid of a Werdal? Shouldn't your magic be able to beat one?" said Luka.

"Maybe one, but not fifty!"

"There is no chance we'll come across fifty Werdals in there. Come on, let's go. Stop being a craven." Reishi finally relented, but let Luka go in first.

Inside the forest the tall canopy of trees restricted the afternoon light. Only a few rays of sun managed to penetrate the leafy branches—otherwise it was dark. With leaves and shrubbery covering the forest floor, each step their horses took had a pronounced crunch. Luka and Reishi were not alone in the woods. The forest teemed with flying Squevas gathering nuts, jumping around, squeaking, and chasing each other up and down various tree trunks.

"Buchan would love it here," Reishi said, observing the nature around him. "I bet she'd be able to catch a Squeva if she tried."

Luka did not think that comment merited a response. He stayed silent and concentrated on the forested path in front of him.

Reishi opened his mouth for another quip—but froze as heavy rustling broke the quiet. It was unclear exactly where the noise was coming from, but they stopped to listen. As the rustling grew louder, they were able to figure out its origin—directly ahead of them, where a few thick bushes shook violently.

"I swear to Sila's agents, Luka. If that's a Werdal...," whispered Reishi.

"Shush!" Luka shot back. The bush stopped shaking, the forest going completely silent for a moment. Luka noticed that his heart was racing again, causing him to curse his own nerves.

A large figure finally emerged from the bush, its black snout pointing out. The creature's mouth hung open, letting out a thick glob of drool in between several dozen razor-sharp teeth. On top of the snout were two horns, one sitting in front of the other, both with the ability to impale. Underneath the beast's muzzle was a long, bushy brown beard, which retained much of the slobber that dripped out of its mouth. It had two wide circular eyes that darted around. The creature's massive body was bigger than a bear's, lined with thick armor plating.

It *was* a Giant Werdal.

As the Werdal came out of the bush, Luka and Reishi noticed another bush start to shake nearby—revealing *another* Werdal. Its long, thick tail flapped aggressively. The two beasts grunted to each other in grotesque harmony.

Luka and Velico remained frozen. Reishi began fishing in his bag for something but his horse lost his composure before he could get it. The mare neighed loudly in fear, reared back, and dashed off, throwing Reishi all the way to the forest floor and scattering his belongings.

The wizard gasped loudly in pain as his horse fled from sight. "Ahh, my back," he groaned.

The Giant Werdals had heard the commotion, their gaze fixed directly at them. They rushed towards their newfound prey in haste.

Velico remained still and disciplined, even as the Werdals began to approach. Luka turned to Reishi. "Climb on! Hurry!" Reishi tried to stand up but cried out, falling back to the ground.

Reishi tried again only to get the same result. The Werdals were now only seconds from devouring the wizard alive. "Go, Luka! You need to run!" he pleaded.

Luka watched Reishi turn away from him, stumbling to his bag, retrieving a dagger and some glass orbs. As the beasts came within feasting distance of the wizard, Luka urged Velico forward and intercepted them.

"Get out of the way, you fool!" Reishi yelled, but it was too late.

The lead Werdal lunged at Velico, trying to bite off a large chunk of horsemeat. Velico hitched hard to avoid the teeth and successfully evaded a devastating bite. In the process of this, the Werdal tangled up with Velico, sending horse, rider, and predator into a tumble. Luka landed first, falling hard on his side on the forest floor and rolling several times, narrowly avoiding being crushed by Velico, who fell right next to him.

One of the Werdals got to its feet quickly, eager to try to feast on Velico. Luka's horse managed to kick the Werdal in the snout twice, but the Werdal dove in to bite, undeterred. It closed its titan jaw, but instead of the juicy taste of flesh, it tasted the cold steel of Luka's blade.

The beast grunted furiously, releasing its mouth from the sword. Luka slashed immediately, striking the Werdal on the side of its mouth. The attack drew blood but didn't stop the beast. It pounced on Luka, throwing him to the ground. Bucketfuls of slobber dripped down onto Luka's face as the Werdal roared at him.

The noise was a mix of an angry dog's bark and a reptilian growl. The beast was heavy, and all of Luka's strength would barely even get the creature to budge.

Out of the corner of his eye, Luka spotted Reishi finally managing to bring himself to his feet. Two glass orbs shattered in his palms, releasing twin fountains of water that spiraled outward before freezing midair into long, sharp icicles. He launched them towards the beasts.

One of the frozen projectiles connected with the Werdal that was only seconds from devouring Luka. It pierced the creature's eye, the entry point into its skull. Blood and some other colorless liquid spat out onto Luka as the creature finally became still.

The other Werdal was the recipient of the second icicle, but the beast's armor plating protected the creature. The frozen spear shattered on impact, bursting into a harmless flurry of snow and ice.

The surviving beast turned its attention towards Reishi now. Luka tried to get out from under the dead creature on top of him, but made little headway.

He watched as the wizard reached into his pouch. Three fireballs ignited his palms soon after. He threw them at the Werdal, but his aim was poor. The first two exploded way off to the right of the beast, creating a small fire. The third hit the Werdal in the armor, wounding the beast again, but not causing nearly enough damage to defeat it.

Reishi cursed, reaching into his bag again. This time two great bursts of wind emerged from the orbs. Each knocked the creature backwards and flipped it over, but it got up both times and resumed its march.

Retreating, desperation and panic began to cloud Reishi's face as he rummaged through his bag another time. The orbs he threw at the Werdal turned into giant boulders—but the throw was too weak—the beast simply dodging the first boulder. The second struck the Werdal in the face, prompting a pained shriek, but only impeding it for a moment. The beast climbed over the rock and landed on the other side.

The Werdal quickly closed the gap between the wizard. With only seconds left, Reishi reached into his bag and pulled out one more orb with his right hand, his dagger ready in the other hand. It would be his last defense, otherwise he would be a meal.

At that moment, Luka finally wiggled free of the dead creature on top of him. He sprinted over towards his magical compatriot.

Before the Werdal could bite Reishi's face off, Luka leaped in front. Like he did with the first Werdal, Luka blocked the beast's mouth with his sword. This time, the Werdal easily ripped the sword away and turned back to Reishi once again. Just as it did so, however, Luka impaled it with a long, bloody ice spear that he was holding in his other hand. The frozen weapon, which Luka had pulled from the first Werdal, went directly through one of the creature's eyes and out through the other.

The beast lay dead less than a second later.

Reishi fell backwards in relief and lay on the forest floor, catching his breath. Luka gasped as well, standing over Reishi and watching him. Neither said anything for a long moment.

When he was ready, Reishi sat up cross-legged and extended his arm out. Luka pulled him up. Reishi stumbled immediately after getting up, but Luka caught him. He helped support the wizard as they walked back to where Velico stood.

The steed was unharmed and standing proudly, unlike Reishi's horse, which was long gone now. "Your horse wasn't a worthless craven like mine," Reishi said, between gasps. "I'm rather impressed."

"That's right," Luka said.

"Yeah, you know—" but Reishi stopped himself, realizing something. "Oh no..."

"What is it?" asked Luka.

"We're going to have to ride together. On the same horse..."

Chapter 32
Rumors Travel Faster than the Wind

Beyond the reach of the woods, Luka and Reishi's new one-horse travel arrangement was as contemptible as they expected. Reishi sat at the back end of the saddle, holding on to whatever he could to stabilize himself—other than Luka's body, which the young king had explicitly forbidden. Up this close, Luka could feel Reishi's breathing on the back of his neck, bringing a constant sense of frustration each time he felt the exhalation.

Working their way back towards the road, they noticed a small village on top of a hill. A score of other small mountains lay beyond it. The terrain was becoming increasingly alpine as they drew nearer to the Ekrons.

Luka referenced his maps. "I think the Brojna Hills are ahead," Luka said to the wizard behind him. "We should go into the town and find a horse trader."

"Oh, yes please! As much as I love breathing down your neck, I think it's high time for my own horse again," Reishi said.

As they rode through the town, Velico kicked up a small cloud of dust on the unpaved dirt street. The small village was quiet, and the few pedestrians they passed did not make eye contact with them.

Halfway through the town of Brojna, they still had not spotted a stable, but Reishi did point out a tavern. Smoke rose from its chimney, and an old man sat on the porch of the building, rocking in a chair back and forth.

"I'll run in there and inquire about where the stables are. I can also see what I can gather on the latest Zlikrej movements, if tavern patrons are aware."

Luka craned his neck around to glimpse Reishi's face. He seemed far too eager for Luka's liking. "Maybe I should go in."

"Your Highness, you are a known figure in this country. You'll be spotted, risking chaos and unwanted attention. The last thing we need is more assassins after us."

He considered protesting, but decided to stand down. "Fine, go in. I don't want you drinking while you're in there. Get the information we need and get back to me." Reishi shrugged him off and went into the tavern.

To avoid the sight of the old man, Luka pulled around to the side of the building. He waited there for longer than he had desired, but Reishi finally emerged from the establishment. Luka stood next to Velico with his arms crossed. "I told you not to have a drink," he scolded, smelling the ale on him.

"I just had one ale. Calm your king's teats," Reishi responded, beginning to mount Velico. "The horse stables are just at the bottom of the hills here."

"Good. We'll head there at once. Did you gather any other information?"

"Yes, and it's not good," he said, his voice suddenly devoid of its usual flippancy.

"What is it?" Luka pressed.

"Exeter has fallen to the Zlikrej. They were able to breach with the help of a wizard named Vatren. He must be the one who gave Privus his staff."

Luka muttered a string of curses under his breath as he joined Reishi atop of his steed. Exeter was supposed to be impenetrable. "Are you still sure you don't know this Vatren?" he asked. They began to ride out through the town and down the hills.

"Never heard of him. Suppose I'll find out more in ten days when we reach Exeter ourselves."

Luka didn't like that response. He felt like the wizard was hiding something, but he didn't know how to press the issue—or if he even should.

They descended the hill and found the stables sitting amongst a quiet valley settlement. After some bartering, Luka purchased a tan-colored jenny for several hundred Novaks.

They departed and resumed their journey north, now riding on separate horses next to each other. "That expense is coming out of your payment at the end of all of this," Luka grumbled.

"Oh bloody hell. If you insist," Reishi said.

"Ten days' ride, you say?" Luka asked.

"That's what the barwoman said inside. She even said small teams of Zlikrej troops pass through every week or so, but they don't stay long."

"Point is," Reishi continued. "We're getting close now. What's your plan for when we actually get there?"

"To kill the Zlikrej brothers. Make them pay for what they did to me, along with every single one of their followers."

"I think you just described your desire, not your plan. I already knew that part."

Annoyed, Luka said, "I don't know about a full *plan*. I haven't got that far. My army should be there soon."

"They don't know you're alive yet, right?"

"I don't know that either. Rumors seem to travel faster than the wind. I have to imagine that they'll find out soon." Luka turned to address Reishi directly. "No army has ever breached the walls of Exeter in history. Only the Zlikrej have, and it was because of that wizard.

"I may not have a plan yet, but one thing is clear—you're going to have to defeat that wizard," Luka said. "Can you do that? I ask, because I am beginning to grow concerned, Reishi. Against the Werdals, you appeared to use only premade magic orbs. You didn't summon any magic of your own. Am I wrong about that? Did my eyes deceive me?"

The wizard frowned and looked down. "Remember when I told you that I am not the wizard I once was?" he said. "I warned you. I used to be able to summon my powers at a moment's notice. Now... I need long moments of concentration to ready myself. I didn't have that time against the Werdals."

"And it's almost certain you won't have that time against Vatren and the Zlikrej forces, either. War doesn't grant favors like that."

"I'll be alright. I can do this. And if not, the worst that will happen is that I'll be killed."

"And that is acceptable to you?" Luka asked.

"Well, not much I can do about it. That's the logical result."

"I do not find that comforting, Reishi."

"Don't forget," said Reishi, "We will have the element of surprise. They won't be expecting a wizard at all."

"The element of surprise has never covered up for *total* weakness," Luka replied.

Reishi frowned again, this time staying silent.

*****

Glazben buzzed with activity. The clamoring of hammers rang out against crumbling stone walls, echoing through the streets. People of all ages scurried about removing debris and carrying new materials. They had made commendable progress in their attempt to rebuild the city, but Glazben was still a shadow of its former self.

Vanessa and her companions rode through the throngs of workers. It wasn't the signs of renewal that struck them most—it was the devastation that had already happened. The last version Glazben they had seen was a small and peaceful city, not a ravaged site trying to rebuild itself.

"Oh my, oh my," Pametan kept repeating to himself, scanning the destruction. Priestess Teya whispered prayers under her breath. Amelia instinctively held her hands over her stomach when they passed a ruined school building, which caught Vanessa's attention—though she couldn't think about that now.

The castle was protected by two sentries standing at the entrance. They regarded the travelers with suspicion as they approached. "Who goes there?" one asked.

"We must speak with Lord Laz at once," Pametan responded, keeping his voice low.

"I asked you who you were, not what you wanted," the guard replied coldly.

Pametan fidgeted. "We must speak with Lord Laz. He knows us."

"The only one you'll be speaking to is the jailkeeper if you don't comply," the second soldier said.

"Oh, for Sila's sake, Milo. We can tell them who we are," Vanessa said impatiently towards Pametan. Then she addressed the sentries. "You are speaking with Vanessa Vernik, Queen of Estravia."

The guards looked at each other wide-eyed, unsure of how to respond. Before they questioned any further, a voice came from behind them. "Your Majesty?" They turned around to see Lord and Lady Laz returning to their castle, donned in robes of red and white. A handful of guards and advisors trailed them.

"Petra! Tristus!" Queen Vanessa shouted back with joy. She dismounted from her horse and ran over to embrace the old couple.

"Oh, wow," Vanessa could hear one of the guards mutter from behind. "That really is her."

At the behest of the Laz's, the sentries were waved off, and Vanessa and her group were soon escorted into the palace. They were led into the great hall, where an impromptu feast was thrown together, the servants hard at work to cook what they could. The hungry travelers devoured pieces of bread until steaming duck was brought out as a main course.

During the meal, both Tristus and Petra recounted how Luka had rescued them and helped reconquer the city. Vanessa beamed at every single heroic detail she heard about her son.

"We are just so happy to see you," Lady Laz said, once the stories were over and their bellies were full. "We hated the idea of you staying on a farm. You will be much better off here."

"Yes, well, actually," said Queen Vanessa, "While we are grateful for your generous hospitality, we can't stay here long. We are going to find Luka. We're headed north after this."

Tristus Laz's mouth hung open; Petra nearly choked on a sip of water. "You're going north?" the lord exclaimed.

"Yes, I am."

"We know where her son gets it from," Pametan chuckled. Vanessa shot him a glare, causing the minister to deflate back in his chair, his smirk vanishing immediately.

"You can't!" Lord Laz protested. "The way north is controlled by our enemies. Privagrad has fallen! Exeter has fallen! It's far too dangerous."

"We are going to pursue an alternate route," Vanessa said. "The Zlikrej won't have a presence far east of Vulture Road. We'll be safer there."

"My Queen, I know you want to join your son, but you could be of much value if you stay here," Tristus said. "Your brother is in dire need of assistance in gathering support from other cities. Having the authority of Queen Vanessa, alive and stationed out of Glazben, would rally them."

"I understand and appreciate the suggestion, Tristus, but my duty is to my son. He is the King, anyway. I must support him."

"Tristus," Pametan added. "We've considered that, but we ultimately believe that announcing the Queen's presence publicly is too great of a risk right now. We'd rather remain undetected."

"But what's your final destination? Do you know where you will even stay?" Petra Laz asked.

"We're going to go wherever the conflict takes us. We'll be safe when Luka rejoins the army," Vanessa answered.

"And what if Luka never finds them?" Lord Laz pressed.

Priestess Teya answered. "We are praying that will not happen."

"We will join you in those prayers," Lady Laz said. "But we do hope you reconsider. Our castle is intact. It is safe here. You will be much more protected if you stay."

"I'm not sure that anywhere in this country is safe," Amelia said quietly. The group at the table traded glances with each other, but the conversation died there. No one could argue against that.

*****

Clouds covered much of the early sunrise, leaving the morning dark and gray. Reishi opened his eyes to see Luka cooking a rabbit over a small fire. While Luka had been hunting, Reishi had been sitting upright in a meditative state, trying to quiet the demons in his mind. He had many more inner battles to fight, but he was content with the results from this morning's bout.

"What were you doing?" Luka asked as Reishi sat down next to him.

"Little concentration exercise that the monks taught me," Reishi answered, but his voice made little more than a croak.

"How was it?"

"Not the worst thing, thank you for asking."

"Are your abilities back to their form?" Luka asked.

"Hmm, let's see." Reishi held out his hands theatrically and shook them. Nothing happened, and he shrugged. "Suppose not, but it certainly helped."

"You're making me nervous, Reishi. We're only a few days away from encountering Vatren."

"If my magic fails me in the moment we need it, you can't say this was for nothing," Reishi said, resisting a smile.

"Oh? Tell me why exactly," Luka asked, handing him a few pieces of the cooked rabbit.

"Because I have kept you great company. And you needed me to push the pace on your journey. You simply were not moving fast enough until I joined you."

Luka seemed ready to jump up and throw the wizard in the fire at this joke. "You're a real scoundrel, Reishi."

"Jesting aside," Reishi continued, pleased with himself, "I know what you need from me. And I know the odds that we're both facing. My job is to help even them—to help you vanquish the Zlikrej brothers. I am *not* here so you can scold me about pissing every few minutes. Trust me."

"I will admit you would have to be rather mad to follow me this far with no magical abilities, only to end up dead," Luka said.

"Exactly. Now you're getting it." Reishi took his first bite of the cooked rabbit. Though the food was a welcome change from the dry beef they typically ate, it was gamey, each bite a labor under their jaws.

"I wish I could have a drink to wash this shit down," Reishi said.

Luka, whose mouth was full and dueling with the chewy meat, handed him a flask. Reishi impulsively reached out to take it but then resisted. "No, I can't. Nothing besides water for a while. I need to have my mind sharp. Even though I certainly want it."

Luka raised his eyebrows in surprise and put the flask back down. Reishi had stopped drinking a few days ago, the ale in the Brojna tavern his last sip of anything. Now he beginning to feel the adverse effects of his abstinence.

His head constantly pounded. At random points, his vision would blur, and bouts of extreme dizziness assaulted him. The sum of these effects was clouding his mind, but Reishi knew that when it passed, he would be clearer than ever. It would be any day now before Reishi would feel like his normal old sober self. The problem was that he hated that person, and pieces of that person were flooding in, without the protection of rum or ale to block them.

The pain was necessary, though. Drinking for so many years had blunted his powers—a welcomed side effect—but not the primary thing he was trying to numb. It wasn't that he couldn't use his powers, it was that they were inconsistent. He wasn't able to fluidly control his abilities. Techniques he used to be able to master in his younger days were foreign to him now. And he was certainly not combat ready. The Werdals had proven that. If he had to face Vatren directly in his current state, he'd be incinerated.

That's what the meditation was for. That was why he needed to remain sober until the battle had passed. *I'll reward myself if I win*, Reishi thought, perhaps using the wrong motivation, but he needed something to get him through.

"I've heard people who drink too much go through something called 'the Dry Sickness' when they stop. I hear it's rather awful," said Luka.

"I would not know of that. I feel great." He knew Luka would not believe the lie, but he did not want to give him the satisfaction that would come if he admitted to it.

"I don't mean to mock, Reishi," Luka said, shifting his tone. "I do appreciate your commitment to this cause. If avoiding the drink helps your powers, then you are doing the right thing."

"Thank you, Luka," Reishi said. He didn't say that his powers and doing the right thing hadn't always gone hand in hand. Once he started using them again regularly, there would be no going back.

*****

Only about a week of riding separated Warwick and his army from their target as they arrived at a small city known as Roda. Reaching this point meant that soon Warwick would be able to lay rest to this saga. But it also meant the battle loomed nearer, and it didn't sound as winnable as it had when they first set out. In fact, nothing was as it had seemed compared to when they first set out.

Roda was an elegant town that crested around a small lake. Fishermen wandered about, carrying nets and spears, some dripping wet. They regarded the Vernik forces with surprise. As the army rode into town, the smells of freshwater fish filled their nostrils.

"We can camp here," Warwick said. His lieutenants bore a look of shock on their faces.

"Are you serious, General?" Lieutenant Baciti said.

"Have you known me to jest?"

"No, sir."

"We have made good progress," Warwick said. "We can spare one afternoon in the confines of this village. We ride out at dawn, though. Make sure all your men are ready. Do not let me regret this decision."

Warwick himself took the opportunity to relax, his lieutenants following him to a tavern. They sat in a dimly lit corner in the back.

Dozens of Vernik soldiers had already filled the establishment, and the buzz of ale-fueled conversation permeated the room.

When the server came over, he took the lieutenants' orders first. They ordered ales. "One for you too, sir?" the server asked the general when it was his turn.

"No ale for me," Warwick replied. "Show me the whiskey you keep here."

The server returned with one bottle, which bore no label or distinguishing mark—a quarter full of brown liquid. "This is all we have, sir."

Warwick motioned for the server to hand it over. He removed the cork from the bottle and sniffed it. He did not speak or react. After a moment, Warwick removed the bottle out from underneath his mustache and handed it back to the server.

"This will not do," Warwick said. "Just some tea for me."

The server stifled an eye roll as he walked away. Soon after a few ales and one steaming tea sat on the table.

"I feel as though I'm running out of things to say to my men about this wizard," Lieutenant Alexander said, wiping some ale off of his mouth. "I know they're all scared, but I'm tired of the chattering."

Warwick nodded. "Since the reports of the attack on Vernikport, we have known that our enemy was equipped with magic. As I have tried to explain before, it makes little difference to our objective if they can claim a wizard in their ranks."

"If it is even true," Lieutenant Baciti chimed in.

"I do think it is true," Warwick replied. "We are lucky we heard those reports when we did so that we can prepare appropriately."

"These reports likely won't make their way to Lord Donte—I mean Regent Donte—for some time," Alexander said.

"Aye, and that is a good thing," Warwick said.

"A good thing, sir?" Baciti asked.

"That's right," said Warwick. "We already know what our destination is—Exeter. And barring a surprising action from the Zlikrej brothers, our course will not change. We are the decisive ones. We know what we need to do, and we don't need to be taking orders from Lord Donte, as much as I respect him, at this stage in the conflict.

"The fate of the country lies with us, the ones on the battlefield. Not with the orders of someone who is thousands of leagues from the nearest arrow or sword."

Baciti praised the general's words, but Alexander remained silent. Though Var was dead, and few Estravians respected Lord Donte the way they had the late king, Donte was still Acting Regent. He was the highest authority in the realm. Warwick knew his words lacked reverence, but he cared little.

A thin, young-looking merchant interrupted the discussion before it could progress further. Warwick had noticed him earlier—he was one of the few patrons in the establishment before the army arrived. "Excuse me, but are you General Warwick?"

Warwick nodded. "Aye, and as General, I seldom take conference with strangers."

"I'm sorry sir, I was just wondering whether you had heard the news yet. It only reached Roda yesterday."

"Yes, we know the bloody news," Baciti said, trying to shoo the merchant away.

"Well, I am, uh, just frankly a bit surprised about your reaction. You seem displeased," the merchant said.

"Why in Sila's wrath would you be surprised about that?" Warwick asked. "We're facing an enemy that is protected by the defenses of an impenetrable city, and boasts a wizard in their ranks, and we're supposed to be *pleased* about that?"

The merchant smiled. "Ah, so it seems like you only know the *old* news. I was referring to something quite different."

"And what would that be?"

The merchant's smile seemed to stretch wider before finally delivering the message. "Well, it seems as though Luka Vernik is *alive*."

Three sets of jaws nearly dropped all the way onto the table.

"It's true," the merchant continued. "He survived the attack on Vernikport and is riding up Vulture Road. He was spotted by Lord Tomkins, the traitor, in Privagrad."

Warwick stood up from the table now. "This had better not be a jest," he said.

Because if this is not a jest, then it changes everything.

Chapter 33
Holy Matrimony

Serena grimaced as two servants cinched a restricting corset around her torso, each tug on the laces biting at her rib cage.

"Sorry, m'Lady," one of the servants murmured, noticing her discomfort. Serena did not know if she was capable of summoning the breath for a response.

She had already spent most of the day with the Exeterian servant ladies, diligently preparing for the grand wedding. Now, there were only a few hours remaining before the ceremony—time that would be spent with only partial access to her own lungs.

She had always imagined she would spend the hours leading up to her wedding with her mother and closest friends—eagerly awaiting her walk down the aisle to Brooks of Marlinus by the altar. Instead, she found herself surrounded by strangers, getting ready to be married to another stranger.

I must be strong for my father. I can endure this for his sake.

Her father had once told her to keep her mind on the good of a situation—that even when all seemed dark, there was always some light to be found, even if it was small. She put that exercise to the test, focusing on the fact that she was about to be the equivalent of a queen. Another positive was that Privus's behavior was much more caring lately. The sight of him no longer made her bristle, at the very least.

Maybe they would be able to get past all of the violent history with time. Part of her actually hoped so. Part of her detested that she would even think that. Part of her wondered if the violence would never go away. She kept overhearing Privus and his brothers expecting a battle right outside of Exeter, against Luka and his forces.

Would she have to choose a side if that happened? Thinking about that made her stomach churn and her mind twist. It was too difficult to think about him. Too confusing. Too hopeless. She was locked within this city now, within this fate. Better to focus on other things. Keep the mind on the good.

Painful tugs on Serena's scalp brought her back to the present. They continued working on her, straightening and removing knots from her hair. All the while, a bulky guard stood at the doorway, silently watching this all unfold, his face concealed beneath a dark helm.

It was undeniably an invasion of privacy. She was almost completely naked in front of all these strangers for most of the time. Yet, it wasn't the exposure that troubled Serena the most. It was the stark reminder that she wasn't free—not even on her own wedding day.

Keep the mind on the good, she reminded herself. But in some moments, that felt impossible.

*****

Privus's nerves seemed to dance around his body as he paced about his new grand bedroom, which had formerly belonged to Lady Dija. Now, it belonged to him, and it would serve as the place where he would consummate his marriage.

Despite all the festivities that awaited him, he felt unease from fears that he could not shake away, like leeches stuck to his body. He was getting married tonight, and he still could not be sure of his wife's true intentions. Luka was still alive, causing a stir throughout Estravia. Perhaps he was proof that Privus was not strong enough to truly crush his enemies.

Privus also sensed that his bride was closer to Luka than she let on. Perhaps they were good friends, perhaps something more. The thought was disquieting to Privus.

Serena may be strong and fierce, but I know she will be dutiful. If not to me, then at least to her family. I am in control here, he told himself. *I am in control.*

Pacing within the confines of his room became too constricting, even with its high ceilings and wide walls. He made his way to the courtyard, where he was greeted by fresh air and beautifully designed stone columns. He was also greeted by his middle brother. It was a rare sight to see, but Drugi actually looked like he was doing something important, hurrying through the palace.

"Privus, what are you doing out here? Shouldn't you be getting ready?" Drugi asked, when he noticed his brother.

"I needed some air. To be frank, Drugi, I'm a bit nervous."

"Brother, what have you to be nervous about?"

"I'm... it's just a big day, is all."

"She's very beautiful, Privus. You made a good choice. She'll be a tremendous archlady."

"Aye, I think so. I just hope she warms up to the idea a bit more."

"She will, Privus. You are a good man. Just give her some time."

"Thank you, brother."

"And don't forget," Drugi added. "You are giving her a magnificent palace to live in."

Privus nodded. "True, brother. I am pleased with how we have divided up the country. Exeter is a glorious city. No one from a wasteland prison village could dream of something so grand."

"I am pleased too, Privus. I am happy for you and your bride. I am also looking forward to the day when Zachary becomes mine."

"Yes, and you need to ensure you are capable of managing our imports when you arrive," Privus said, his finger pointing commandingly at his older brother. "When Omarius leaves for Canyon

City, overseeing the receipt of new forces and supplies will be your sole responsibility."

"Yes, yes, Privus. I've been told thousands of times," Drugi said, fidgeting a bit. "I'm sorry to run off, but I really must be going now."

"What are you up to?" Privus asked. "Are the voices in your head bothering you again?"

"They are not voices—they are spirits," Drugi said. "And you know they are real because they led me to your staff. And helped us find Vatren."

Privus shrugged dismissively.

"I was actually assisting with something for the wedding," Drugi continued. "The priest of Exeter is refusing to do the ceremony. Omarius sent me to tell him that he has one chance to change his mind."

"What happens if he refuses?" Privus asked.

"Well, um, he will die."

"No, no, of course he will die. That's a given. I meant, who will be leading my ceremony?"

"Well, I think Vatren said he would do it, even though he's not really a priest."

"He is absolutely not a priest." Privus preferred a proper priest at his wedding, at least for his bride's sake. "Let me come with you."

Drugi hadn't exactly agreed—he had simply resigned himself to the reality that his younger brother was now tagging along. A few dark-armored guards trailed behind as they departed the palace grounds and made their way to the prison. The building loomed ahead, cold and unwelcoming—a lifeless gray box devoid of warmth or mercy.

The priest's cell was on the lowest level, five stories below ground, the same level that held Lady Dija. She could prove to have her use in the near future, just as Lord Tomkins had his. So, she would keep her life, at least for now. The former Lady of Exeter lay asleep on the cold, hard floor as they went past her cell. The cell contained no bed or other comforts—nothing save for a waste bucket in the corner.

The priest was in the middle of a prayer in the adjacent cell. Privus interrupted with a bark. He waited until the priest met his eyes to speak. "My brother tells me you refuse to preside over my wedding today."

The priest glanced at both brothers before replying. "Your brother is correct. I will not partake in such a malevolent ceremony. I would never be able to stand before Sila's agents and justify myself again."

"Right now, you stand before *us*, not Sila's agents," answered Privus. "You know what your choices are. You can be a good sport and officiate my wedding, or you can simply die."

"If serving you is all I have to live for, I do not think my choice is difficult," the priest said.

Privus turned to Drugi and said, "The more I consider it, the more I think Vatren could make a fine priest for the day. Don't you think, brother?"

"Yes, I imagine he would be adequate," answered Drugi.

"I agree. Brother, would you be so kind as to kill this man? I hear it's bad luck to kill someone on your wedding day."

Drugi was not pleased with the request. "Um, I, uh, Omarius said—" he stuttered.

"What?"

"Omarius said he would get an executioner over here to do it."

"What, you don't want to do it? C'mon now."

"No, I, um, don't need to..."

Privus rolled his eyes. If his brother did not want to do something, it took a force strong enough to move mountains to motivate him. For the sake of expediency, Privus unveiled his staff from underneath his black cloak and pointed it at the priest.

"Privus, no! It would be bad luck to kill someone on your wedding day!"

"Well, you said you would not do it. And I don't see why we should wait any longer, quite frankly. He just said he has nothing to live for."

Only Drugi was shocked by this. The jailed man remained perfectly calm in the face of imminent death.

A blast of fire emitted from the staff and burst through the metal bars. The priest shrieked in pain as the flames enveloped him, alerting everyone in the cell block. The fire danced in Privus's eyes as he watched the insolent zealot melt away. He briefly glanced at his brother, who watched on as well, seeming contemplative.

They departed, walking past the cell of Lady Dija, who was now awake. "You monsters! I've known him since I was a girl!" she screamed and rattled the cell barriers. "You are a plague on this world!" She continued to fire curses at them as they walked away.

"That was hurtful," Drugi whispered to Privus. "She has no right to say that to us."

"You are lucky we kept you alive. You should be grateful to us," Privus hissed, doubling back to address Dija. "We can take away so much more from you than your ladyship and your city."

She cursed them again. Privus grinned and pointed his staff at her. A powerful gush of ice-cold water shot through the cell barrier and knocked Dija back on the cell floor. She hurled no further curses at them after that.

Privus and Drugi left her as she lay in a freezing cold puddle, choking water out from her throat.

*****

Serena stood in her long, bright dress, waiting outside the Temple of Exeter. The building stood tall, blocking the afternoon sun and casting a shadow over her and her attendants, which included nearly a dozen Zlikrej soldiers. Serena knew that when she next stepped outside that great structure, her whole life would be different. She inhaled deeply before the servants opened the door and escorted her in.

The center aisle, which lay between two sets of more than a hundred rows of packed benches, was covered with a blue carpet. Flowers plucked from the lush gardens of Exeter filled the walls and sat on the ends of every single pew. Statues of Sila's agents stood above a large blue banner that circled the inside of the temple. They were massive and awe-striking, looking down and judging those in attendance.

At the very end of the hall and next to the altar, stood Privus, in his black silk suit, embroidered in shiny silver—a look that Serena admittedly found handsome. Vatren, who Serena had only talked to briefly, stood next to him, holy book in hand. She knew him enough to know that he was no priest.

The thought of escaping the whole endeavor on a technicality occurred to Serena. If there wasn't a real priest, maybe the wedding wouldn't count. But she quelled these unrealistic thoughts, because it would take a miracle—not a technicality—to get her out of this. Either way, she knew she had to be strong for her father, and thinking about escape wasn't useful anymore. Her only choice was to accept her new life.

From across the temple, Vatren spoke the opening incantation, reading directly from a book. Every priest would have this memorized, but Vatren, of course, did not. Since he was looking down at his book, his voice did not project all the way to the back. Serena could not make out any of the words properly, but she had been to enough weddings to know what Vatren was saying, or at least what he was supposed to be saying.

When he finished speaking, everyone's heads turned back towards Serena, and one of the servants beckoned her to move forward. It was time. Her heart sank a few inches, her stomach fluttered. A grand orchestra played triumphant music as she elegantly strolled up the aisle. Serena held her head up high and took deliberate, graceful steps toward the altar.

Halfway down the aisle, a wave of despair rose within her, threatening to spill into tears. This was all wrong. Her father should have been the one by her side. The ceremony should have taken place in Privagrad—not distant Exeter. Her family and friends should be surrounding her—not these unfamiliar faces.

Serena stopped in place, immediately feeling the anticipation and concern from the audience bearing into her. She turned her head ever so slightly, ready to run in the other direction, but the impulse was fleeting and futile. She gathered herself and donned a convincing fake smile, proceeding forward. The crowd eased in turn, seemingly believing that she had been overwhelmed with joy.

When she reached her destination, she stood across from Privus and before the hundreds in the audience. Omarius, with Drugi next to him, was impossible to miss from the front row.

"Hold each other's arms," Vatren read from his book. Serena held out her hands, Privus taking them gently. "Man, please state your name."

"I am Privus Zlikrej of Canyon City, Liege of Exeter, and Archlord of Estravia."

Vatren did not need his book for the next part. "Woman, please state your name."

"I am Serena Tomkins, noble daughter of Privagrad."

"Privus Zlikrej and Serena Tomkins," Vatren said, "Today, you are both to be wed before Sila, his agents, and these witnesses. Your lives will be forever connected, but more importantly, your souls will be bonded in a manner that transcends our mortal lives.

"Love is the greatest gift Sila and his agents have given us on this earth. It is through this gift that we all have come into existence, and it is through love that you both are here today. Therefore, it is expected that for the remainder of your lives, you will both honor each other in recognition and appreciation of this gift.

"After today, all titles, money, property, and land will be combined and owned as one. This is final and irreversible. It is not a contract, but a permanent blessing.

"Privus Zlikrej," Vatren continued, "do you understand this, and do you agree to abide by the divine, binding laws of marriage?"

"I do."

"Serena Tomkins, do you understand this, and do you agree to abide by the divine, binding laws of marriage?"

"I do."

"And Serena Tomkins, do you agree to become, Serena Zlikrej, Lady of Exeter and Archlady of Estravia, relinquishing your previous titles and being a loyal and faithful wife to your husband, the people of Exeter, and the people of Estravia?"

Serena Zlikrej, she thought bitterly. *The Archlady part sounds good, at least.*

"I do."

"Very well," Vatren said. "By the power vested in me by Almighty Sila and his agents, I pronounce you husband and wife. You may now seal the ceremony with a kiss."

Serena closed her eyes and leaned forward. Privus's lips were dry, and the embrace was long. Her attention faded out amid the thunderous cheers from the audience with shock and disbelief. Now, it was official. But it was not final. There was still more to come that evening.

From that point on, the night became a blur, with the celebration feast commencing immediately after. The copious wine and liquor Serena consumed only amplified that feeling. Speeches and toasts and food and partying whirred by in a frenzy. Almost mercifully, it left her no time or capacity for emotion or reflection.

Out of seemingly nowhere, Serena realized the crowning ceremony was taking place. She and Privus were led up to the front of the great hall, where all the heads at each table turned to them in between courses.

Two golden crowns sat next to them prominently on a silver cloth. Omarius stood behind the table and bellowed with his great voice for everyone to quiet down. "Now," he called out. "I have the great honor of bestowing these crowns on my youngest brother and his new lovely lady." Rowdy applause followed.

"As we all know, my brother is one of the Archlords of our great country, with Exeter serving as his seat. Serena is now his lady and will also serve our country and this city faithfully. These crowns are to honor this occasion and remind us all of their important roles in our new regime. Congratulations to the new Archlord and Archlady!"

Omarius took the bigger of the two crowns and gently laid it on Privus's head. With his size, it was shocking to see him do anything gently. He smiled proudly at his youngest brother and embraced him. Serena could hear Privus nearly wince from the force of it.

Then Omarius turned, picking the other golden crown up and approaching her. She gulped in anticipation of a moment she had fantasized about as a girl. *But why did it have to happen like this?*

Omarius stood directly in front of her, eclipsing the view of everything behind him with his mountainous frame. He smiled—an alien sight—and bent down slightly so he could meet her at eye level. With even greater care than he had done with his brother, Omarius placed the Archlady's crown on Serena's head. It felt metallic and stiff on her head.

When he was done, he put both hands on her shoulders. Again, he was gentle, but the sheer weight behind his arms intimidated her. Only a man such as Omarius could make gentleness seem indistinguishable from power.

Then he looked at her right in her eyes and smiled. "Congratulations, Archlady Serena," he said. A nod was all she could manage.

Once the ceremony ended and both Privus and Serena were crowned, the night resumed its whirlwind of movement and energy. In hindsight, it would all blur together—she would barely remember so much of it.

Finally, the guests dissipated, and the night was ready to reach its climax. Serena walked silently up the stairs with Privus who seemed to be rushing up in anticipation. He pushed open the double doors to the master bedroom. "Welcome to your new quarters, my lovely Archlady," he said.

The room was spectacular, its vast dimensions faintly illuminated by the flickering candlelight. Privus unlaced his shoes and took off his jacket. Serena fidgeted as she watched him. He began unbuttoning his shirt and then seemed to notice his new wife's hesitancy.

He motioned with his index finger for her to approach. She did, but slowly, hesitantly. When she was within reach, he held her gently but began to kiss her passionately. As a reflex, she resisted for a moment, but then she stopped. She relaxed her body and kissed him back.

In the Exeterian moonlight, Serena gave in to Privus, ultimately and completely.

Chapter 34

Rys

"So, when did you learn to fight?" Reishi asked as they traversed along the rocky terrain, north of the Brojna Hills. Light gray clouds held the sun back even at midday.

"My father tells me I first picked up a sword when I was three," Luka responded. "By the time I was five, I was taking the odd lesson here and there. Won my first tournament when I was nine. That was also the first tournament I ever entered."

"Well, they couldn't have let anyone defeat the Prince of Estravia, now, could they?" said Reishi.

"Are you suggesting they let me win?" asked Luka, stiffening his body.

"Oh, seems like a possibility. I've known it to happen to sons of lords before."

"Well, it never happened to me. Everyone I've ever fought has tried like hell to beat me, and almost no one ever has."

"They may have taught you to fight, but clearly, no one has ever instructed His Highness in the ways of humor," Reishi said. Luka ignored that.

"What is the name of that town ahead?" Luka asked, pointing to a meager village before them.

Reishi fiddled for the map and squinted when he pulled it out. "Looks like it's the town of Rys. Are you thinking what I'm thinking?"

"That we need to stock up for more food?"

"Precisely," Reishi said. After weeks of riding, the two unlikely companions were now a few days from Exeter, but they had finally run out of beef.

"We'll go into Rys, but we don't have time for nonsense."

"I don't like that implication," Reishi said. "I provide the least nonsense out of anyone I know."

"Must be a short list of people then."

Before they reached town, they assessed the potential for Zlikrej presence. They had now crossed Vulture Road and rode on its eastern side, where the areas controlled by the Zlikrej forces lingered much more closely. Spotting no enemies, they rode into the center of the village with their hoods up.

To their benefit, the market was alive, with dozens of vendors lining the town square. Around them, the air was filled with the sounds of the continuous humming of buyers and sellers bartering. The butcher was not hard to find. They followed the alluring scent of meat to a stand in the center of the village.

"Do you have any preserved beef for sale?" Luka asked the butcher. The vendor was slender and wiry, unlike most butchers Luka had seen, though admittedly, he hadn't interacted with all that many as prince. Either way, it made him wonder if this man's meat was any good. *Shouldn't butchers be fat?*

"I've got dried meats. Dozen Novaks per Mark," the butcher said, still working with a bloody cleaver as he spoke.

"Luka, I don't want dried meat," Reishi complained. "The preserved shite we've been eating for weeks has been bad enough."

Before Luka could scold the wizard, the butcher interjected. "Luka, did you say? Are you Luka Vernik?" The vendor seemed to crane his neck to look under Luka's hood for a better view. Shoppers and other vendors nearby overheard this, heads suddenly turning in their direction.

Luka looked to each side, accepting that the attention was unavoidable now. He lowered his hood, letting his face be seen unobstructed. "That's *King* Luka Vernik," he said. "'Your Grace' or 'Your Highness' will do."

Gasps echoed through the market. "It really is you..." the butcher said. The gasps turned into whispering and quiet chattering. Luka began to absentmindedly tap with his foot, fearing the possibility that this attention could turn hostile.

From across the market, an unkempt man carrying a basket of vegetables called out to him. "Oi, King Luka!"

Every eye turned to him. Luka's hand moved instinctively to the hilt of his blade.

"Thank you!" the man said and started clapping. "Hail to King Luka! Hail to the King!"

The market erupted now, applause bursting from all directions. The citizens of Rys joined the man in his cheers, shouting "Hail to King Luka!" over and over. Luka beamed, unable to repress his smile.

"Good people of Rys," he said, addressing the market when it was finally calm enough to be heard. "Good people of Estravia, I am here to save you. My mission and my duty are to vanquish the Zlikrej brothers and restore order to this country."

The cheers erupted once again. Luka nodded to himself, taking it all in.

"Yes, yes, that's all very wonderful, but can we buy some beef now? Not the dried stuff?" Reishi asked, trying to resume the task they originally set out to do.

The effort to buy beef was interrupted once again. Commotion, coming from somewhere outside the city, made its way to the market.

*****

"Lieutenant Alexander, tell me what village lies ahead," General Warwick commanded his nearest subordinate as they approached a settlement just off Vulture Road.

After unfolding the unwieldy piece of parchment, Lieutenant Alexander said, "That looks like Rys, sir."

"Let's avoid it then. We'll veer north," Warwick said. "No sense in passing through. It will only delay us even more."

The officers and riders at the front led the way, changing the army's direction slightly and avoiding the small town altogether.

*****

Luka listened closely and heard the words "big," "army," and "royal." It was enough to make him leave the market, in spite of all the praise he was receiving.

The sounds of thousands of footsteps marching just outside of the small village met Luka's ears. His view was obstructed by the assortment of stone buildings in the village. He weaved around them until he got a clear look.

Sure enough, a massive army marched through the grass fields just beyond the village. Though the flags were too small to accurately see from that distance, he knew they carried the sigil of his house. He knew there was a mighty golden phoenix depicted on the crimson cloths flapping in the air. Excitement and disbelief welled inside him.

His army was here.

Luka turned around and rushed to the post where he had tied Velico. He was close to a full sprint. Reishi was waiting there for him, eating a kebab of steaming beef. "What's going on?" he asked between bites.

"My army is here. I must join them," said Luka, hurriedly untying Velico. Before Reishi could even look at the rope that was tied to his horse, Luka was off. He assumed that Reishi would follow him, but he didn't look back to check.

Luka rode towards the front of the march, which seemed to stretch for miles. He kept a watchful eye as he passed, making sure that he didn't draw the arrows of any archers who deemed him a threat. No such thing happened, but he saw a small scout team of three officers on horseback peeling off from the march and heading his way. He slowed down slightly, allowing the officers to reach him without any fear of a chase.

"Oi! You there, identify yourself!" The lead officer called.

Luka brought Velico to a halt so he could address the men directly. "I am King Luka. I am here to rejoin my army. I command you to take me to General Warwick, at once."

Once he said that, their look of suspicion morphed into recognition. "Yes, Your Highness. We will bring you to the general at once."

As he was escorted, Luka spotted Warwick from a distance. When the general noticed him approaching, he gazed intensely in his direction, an element of uncertainty in his eyes, likely working through his sheer disbelief. The gaze softened and turned into deep warmth when Luka came closer.

"Sir," the officer began, "We have—"

"I can see who you have." The general cut him off and headed towards Luka.

"General..." Luka was unable to find the rest of the words. It was like getting a family member back. And those were precious commodities to Luka these days.

"Luka, this is miraculous! It is wonderful to see you. I heard you were alive, but I almost could not believe it. Words simply cannot describe how pleased I am that you are here." They dismounted and embraced.

After a moment, Luka said, "We have much to discuss, General, but first, I should probably let you know that I am not alone. I have a, um, 'friend' with me. He should be here any minute."

Chapter 35
The Queen's Journey

Vanessa rode through undisturbed hills and vast empty landscapes with her small team. Glazben was now days behind them, and each day of riding lessened their desire to go back. Though they did not have the comforts that Glazben could have offered them, they had felt safe so far as they rode northeast.

Right now, Vanessa's sole focus was on finding her son. What lay behind was no longer of concern. He needed her. Or perhaps it was truer that she needed him.

On the fifth day of travel, the group came upon a cluster of barracks nestled at the bottom of a hill. No flag flew above any of the buildings. They sat there anonymous but unfriendly.

"Are those our men?" Vanessa asked as the group halted.

"I cannot be certain, My Queen," Pametan replied. "We are not far from Lord Tomkins's territory. These could be his men, and thus under Zlikrej control. I think the risk is too great to approach."

The minister's logic was met with agreement. They kept a great distance away from the barracks, veering their course much farther east.

That evening, they rode for an hour after the sun went down, trying to squeeze the waning bit of light from the day. When it became dark, they settled down for the night. A fire was lit—partly to cook their food, partly to ward off the creeping chill. Autumn had arrived, bringing crisp breezes and dry night air. They gathered around the flames, trading stories and passing a bottle of wine from Glazben. All except Amelia. She sat slightly apart, occasionally pressing a hand to her belly. Vanessa watched her in silence, a mix of excitement and unease stirring in her chest. Was there a bump? She couldn't be sure—but the question refused to leave her mind.

"Everyone..." Priestess Teya interrupted one of Pametan's stories. "I sense danger and foul spirits drawing near."

"Where?" asked Queen Vanessa.

The priestess stood up and scanned the surrounding area, like an animal searching for a scent. After a moment, she pointed to the south, in the direction of where they had come from. Soon enough, four figures on horseback holding torches appeared at the crest of a hill. The threatening shadows stood still, their shrouded faces staring down at them.

"Put out the fire!" ordered Vanessa. They rushed to extinguish the flames, but it was too late. The figures descended the hill and rode towards them. Pametan reached for his sheathed sword and strapped it to his belt. Queen Vanessa rushed to grab a crossbow from her bag. She quickly loaded it and placed it on the ground behind her, out of sight. Amelia and Teya were unarmed, taking cover behind the horses.

The shadows grew nearer, becoming visible in the moonlight. Their faces were stern, scanning Vanessa and the group beneath their helms.

"Tell us who you are and what you're doing out here," demanded the voice of one of the soldiers.

"We are merely travelers. Why should our business be of any concern to you?" said Pametan.

"That one's got a sword," said one of the other soldiers in the back.

"Thank you, *Jon*," the lead officer replied. "We could all see that the short old man has a sword, but your observation has been noted. Now, back to my question—"

Another soldier cut in and said, "Don't these people look familiar?"

"What do you mean? Who do you think they look like?" said another. The lead officer glared back at his men, who continued their side conversation.

"I can't help but feel as though I've seen them before. In Privagrad, I think. Doesn't that one right there look like Queen Vanessa before she died?"

Vanessa tensed up but remained silent.

"Which lord do you serve?" asked Pametan, trying to deflect attention away.

The three soldiers in the back went quiet. The lead officer spoke up again. "Oh, I suppose you're asking the questions now?"

The officer divulged anyway. "These men have served as scouts under Lord Tomkins of Privagrad for many years. But now they serve the new Archlords of Estravia—Omarius, Drugi, and Privus Zlikrej. And we expect that you do, too. We are on patrol in our territory, and we demand that you report your identities to us."

"We are just travelers," Pametan pleaded.

"I really think that's Queen Vanessa," came the same soldier in the back again. "I mean, I really can't let the idea go."

"Hmm, you may be right," the leader finally admitted, "If that scoundrel Luka survived, why couldn't his mother have as well? After all, we never found her body." The officer's face now stretched into an anticipatory smile. "I think I sense a wonderful promotion ahead for me. Let's get a closer look." He dismounted and walked over to her, removing his helmet for the sake of a better view.

Queen Vanessa reached behind and sprang up with the crossbow in hand. She aimed it at his unprotected head and fired from close range. At the last second, the officer jerked to the side. The bolt made a metallic clunk as it connected with his spaulders.

Recovering from the surprise and acting quickly, the officer shouted, smacked the crossbow out of Vanessa's hands, and seized her, crushing her arms under his grasp.

In that moment, Pametan charged at the soldier with his sword drawn, only to be intercepted by the spear of one of the horseback soldiers from the back. The counterattack knocked the sword away, while Pametan fell backwards onto the ground.

The armored Zlikrej lead officer caressed Vanessa's head and moved her blonde locks out of her face. "I really think you *are* Queen Vanessa. You are certainly beautiful enough to be her." Vanessa struggled to resist, but the man was overpowering. Despair came over her, realizing the peril of the situation—outmatched against four enemy warriors in the middle of nowhere.

*****

Several meters away, Priestess Teya walked out from behind her equine cover. She inhaled deeply and scanned the souls of the four men who were confronting them. As expected, the lead officer's soul was almost entirely black, making it a dead end for her. She moved to his three underlings. They all had young souls—they could not have been much older than twenty.

None of these young men were pure evil. They all were facing conflict, fear, duty to Lord Tomkins, and greed for power that drove them to serve such a vile man. For two of the young men, Teya knew she would not be able to get far enough to make a difference in such a short time. Jon, the soldier in the back, however, had a severe conflict in his soul, and the priestess knew she could exploit it.

From a field of view that blended this world and the next one, Teya watched her powers take effect. In the midst of the chaos, Jon's soul reacted to an outside force, his body and mind interpreting it as someone's voice.

"My son..." It was faint and Jon assumed it to be his imagination. "Jon, my son..."

Father? Jon thought, audible to Priestess Teya and the source of the voice.

"Yes, Jon. It is me."

Father? Where are you? Am I going mad?

"No, my son. You are not going mad." Jon became separated from himself and the situation before him. He now stood in front of his father in a dream-like state, in the living room of his childhood home.

"Father!" Jon exclaimed, now fully immersed in this new world.

"Jon, my son. It is wonderful to see you."

"It's wonderful to see you too. It has been so long. Can you tell me what is going on?"

"Jon," his father said with resignation. "I am speaking to you from another world. I know you have many questions, but we won't have time for them. I need something very important from you."

Jon nodded, still adjusting to what he was seeing.

"I know you yearn for justice," His father said. "I know you no longer want to serve these traitors."

"Yes, father. I hate it. I wanted to be a soldier just like you, fighting for the crown and for honor."

"Well now, son, you have a chance to do just that—on a scale far more glorious than I ever did. That woman *is* Queen Vanessa. You swore an oath to protect her and her interests. Now it is time to fulfill that oath."

Jon nodded again, this time his eyes full of tears. "I miss you, father. What's it like? The afterlife?"

"I must not answer that, my son, other than it is great but well beyond comprehension. For now, you must focus on your duty to your queen. Go now. It is wrong for you to stay here for too long." Then he added, "I love you, my son."

To Jon, the house faded away in a white smoke. Priestess Teya stepped back, satisfied. She knew that her magic had accomplished its intended effect. She would not have to use the Light of Sila or some of her more dangerous powers.

*****

Jon slowly came to his senses, realizing he was back in the field. He drew his sword and rode towards his officer, whose head was completely exposed. "Jon, back off. Deal with the others," his officer commanded, not turning to look. But Jon did not back off. He swung his blade down, lodging it deep into his superior's skull.

Jon removed the blade and turned his horse to face his two comrades as Queen Vanessa came free of the dead officer. "Jon! You bloody fool!" said one of them.

Both soldiers charged at Jon, one close behind the other. Jon defended, hitting the first soldiers squarely in the chest. The force of the blow hurled the man from his horse—he hit the ground hard, his neck snapping on impact.

The second soldier came upon Jon swiftly, landing a blow of his own. The strike threw him from the horse, the stiff earth swallowing him up. He lay there, winded with stars dancing across his vision. He didn't dare count how many bones he had just broken.

After a moment, he was able to rise slowly. His vision cleared in time to see his former comrade turning his horse and charging back to finish the job. Jon had no options or defenses. His sword lay much too far away, and his legs would not allow him to reach anywhere in time.

"Sir, here!" said a man's voice, it was the "old man," who tossed his sword over to Jon. The young soldier caught it just as his enemy was there to strike him down. He evaded the attack and spun, striking the soldier in his back—the blow causing his opponent to lose his balance and topple from his horse

With heavy agony, Jon walked over to face the man he had unhorsed, sharp pain jabbing him with every step. His opponent removed his cracked helmet and tossed it aside. "Jon," he said, "You're being a fool! You're committing treason!"

"No. I *was* committing treason. Now, I am making it right."

Their swords connected. After several even trades of steel, his former ally broke through his defenses with an uppercut slash. The attack pierced the chain mail under Jon's sides, drawing blood and causing him to lose grip of his sword. He was hit again in succession, breaking through the chain mail on the other side. Jon fell to the ground. He tried to fumble for his weapon, but his opponent kicked it away.

"Jon, I *have* to kill you for what you have done." He continued to hack down at Jon, piercing more chainmail and drawing more blood.

Jon started to feel his life fading away. His consciousness only jolted back into focus at the sound of a voice.

"Stop it! Leave him be!"

The soldier finally stopped hacking at him, turning towards the source of the voice. He looked directly at the queen, who stood only a few meters away, pointing the crossbow right at his face.

Queen Vanessa did not miss this time.

The last soldier fell back, with his eyes still open, looking right at the bolt that was lodged in his forehead. The armored body made a loud thud when it connected with the ground next to him.

"Are you okay, My Queen?" Jon could hear the old man ask.

"I'm alright. We need to check on the soldier who helped us." The four travelers came over to him, gathering around. He strained to keep his eyes open so he could see them.

"What is your name, good sir?" asked Queen Vanessa.

"My name is Private J- Jon... My Queen."

"We are so grateful for you, Private Jon. You acted heroically. You came to our defense."

Jon stretched his mouth into as much of a smile as he could muster.

"Do you think we can get him to a doctor?" he heard one of the younger women whispering to the other woman. There was no audible reply—Jon knew what that meant. He felt a sense of peace, even amongst the physical pain. He was standing on the edge between life and death, ready to leap, knowing he had done his duty. Knowing he would see his father again.

The queen and her group stayed with him as the darkness clasped all the way around him. He did not die alone, and he did not die in vain.

Chapter 36
The Cavalcade

The air in the courtyard was absent of the humidity that had lingered over the past few months. A pleasant, cool breeze passed through, brushing across Serena's skin. Autumn had arrived, pushing summer into the past.

The new Archlady was stealing a moment to herself, only a few days after her wedding. They shared a bed together every night, but during the day, Privus spent little time with her. He preferred the company of his brothers, planning the next steps in their war, or patrolling the city with his soldiers.

She wasn't sure if she preferred it that way. In this unfamiliar world, Privus was the person she knew best. Without him, she felt utterly alone—surrounded by nothing but strangers. She yearned to go home, but her husband had made it clear that would not happen until the conflict was resolved.

She found a bench in the courtyard in a patch of sunlight and sat down, opening a book. Soon, she'd be expected to appear in public as part of the departure ceremony for her two brothers-in-law. Omarius and Drugi would be leaving with two-thirds of The Zlikrej Army.

The quiet of the courtyard slowly became overtaken by buzzing outside the palace. Hundreds of people were beginning to gather for the parade. Serena knew that much of the excitement was contrived. Every citizen of Exeter was required to attend. They would applaud as loud as necessary to avoid punishment.

She looked up from her book to see a servant approaching. It was time. She followed the servant back to the palace antechamber, where dozens of black-clad soldiers waited. Her stomach knotted into a tangle of vines, realizing that she was about to appear in front of her subjects for the first time as their Archlady. It was not only her nerves that were unsettled—something in her soul whimpered. Her husband had seized this city by force. Would the people accept her as the Lady of this city? Should she even want them to?

Privus and his brothers approached from a palace hallway. "You will have plenty of men at your disposal here. Not to mention you have the most fortified city and the aid of magic at your side," Omarius said, his words audible from that distance.

"Do you think that the Vernik boy will alter the expected behavior of the army?" Privus asked.

"I do not," Omarius said. "I am confident in our strategy, and our timing is optimal. We will be weeks ahead of the Vernik army's arrival. That said, if he does appear, please do make an effort to capture Luka and not kill him. Send word when you do. Drugi and I will make time in our conquests to return here and execute him properly."

"Of course, my brother. We will share in that pleasure."

Serena repressed the urge to shudder when she caught them saying this. It demanded all her strength to act as if she had not heard anything.

The conversation broke off as they reached the antechamber. Omarius and Drugi acknowledged Serena with a short greeting. Privus came over and embraced her. "Hello, my lovely Archlady," he said, an excited smile still on his face. Serena leaned into his arms and let him kiss the top of her head. "Are you excited for this momentous day?"

"I am, Privus. It is an honor to appear at your side today," she said dutifully.

"As it is mine. Come, dear. It is time to start the parade." He took her hand and led her to the starting line.

Outside, Omarius and Drugi's share of the forces awaited, already in formation. Silver helmets and the glistening points of swords and spears stretched hundreds of rows back. Serena followed her husband and his brothers to their place at the front of the cavalcade. They climbed on top of a pearly white carriage, stolen from Lady Dija, which would be driven by six horses.

When everything was in place, Privus raised his golden staff above his head and launched a bright fireball high into the air. When it exploded, the three brothers started trotting forward. The mass of soldiers followed.

On the roofs along the street, Privus's best marksmen watched everything below. They would make sure that the three lords would be safe while they marched in the open. Along the sides of the procession, the citizens clapped, obeying their instructions. Privus's thousand or so men were interspersed amongst the crowd. Out of the corner of her eye, Serena thought she noticed a soldier beating a citizen on the street, presumably for noncompliance. She diverted her glance and kept her face forward, continuing to smile and wave. She understood her duty.

The parade moved at a slow pace, each stretch feeling monotonous to Serena. More stone buildings. More people forced to cheer. Halfway to the city gates, her eyes locked with a little girl in a bright yellow dress in the crowd. Serena smiled directly at her, hoping to inspire some form of hope or joy. The little girl's face remained blank and confused. The girl's mother stood next to her. Only fear and sadness could be found in her eyes.

They see me only as their captor, she thought. For the second time that day, Serena suppressed a shudder.

At her side, Privus's face was still covered with his wide, cocky grin as he gestured exuberantly to the citizens below him. Drugi waved as well, his manner more awkward than his brothers. Omarius waved every now and again, but for the most part, stood stoically, one hand always resting on his war hammer.

The carriage finally reached the city gates, signaling the end of the parade. They disembarked and made their way toward a wooden platform where Vatren stood waiting. Serena avoided his gaze as she ascended the steps. The stage gave them an elevated view above the ocean of military helms and soldier heads. This part of the parade was meant for the Zlikrej ranks, composed of mercenaries, loyalists, and even Stranakans. Few Exeterian citizens were in the crowd now.

Privus let go of Serena's hand and stepped forward, ready to speak first. "Great men of the Zlikrej Army, good people of Exeter, it is my honor to address you today, as Liege of this magnificent city and Archlord of this country. This is a day of celebration. A chance to relish in our continued prowess and dominance. But it is also a somber day in a sense. Today, we must say goodbye to my brothers, Archlords Omarius and Drugi Zlikrej." Privus yielded the stage to his two older brothers as applause thundered out.

Omarius stepped forward and spoke. "Thank you, Privus. I know the city of Exeter is in great hands," he bellowed. "I wish you and your men could continue with us, but this city needs a powerful leader, and the center of Estravia needs a great Archlord to watch over it. You will fill that role better than anyone."

Omarius turned from addressing his youngest brother to the crowd again. "About two months ago, we gathered in a field far south of here. All of you great warriors had just begun to embark on our bold quest together. It is important we take moments like these to reflect on our progress. We have even more audacious goals for the months ahead, but we can embrace these ambitions with the confidence that we have gained from so many victories. Few men in the history of this country have been able to conquer as much territory as we have, and certainly not in such a short period of time. Take pride in that!"

The loudest uproar so far filled Serena's ears. Somehow, she was able to hear Omarius turn to Drugi and say softly, "Do you wish to say anything?" It may not have even been worth asking. Drugi simply shook his head.

Omarius turned back to his audience, "Priest Vatren," he said unironically, "We ask your blessing."

Vatren stepped forward with a piece of parchment in his hands. Just like the book at the wedding, he read straight from it, only this time, he was the one who had written the words. He asked Sila and his agents to bless both the men who would depart and the men who would stay behind and watch the city of Exeter. Then he said a sloppy prayer for the handful of soldiers who had died along the way. More reverent, less enthusiastic cheers ensued when the makeshift blessing was over.

After that, Privus reclaimed the stage and concluded the ceremony, "Please join me in bidding my brothers goodbye!" He then raised his staff high above his head and blasted three more fireballs into the air.

With the ceremony over, two servants appeared to take Serena away. Privus caught her before she left. "Thank you for your presence with me today. I think it is important for my people to see a beautiful lady at my side and to know that we are united."

"Yes, it was lovely. Thank you, Privus."

Drugi came over to her hesitantly and said, "Well, I guess this is goodbye for now."

"Yes, goodbye, Drugi. I wish you the safest of travels."

Omarius came over to her next and swallowed her up with his embrace. She felt small and meager against his cold armor and his hulking frame.

"Treat my youngest brother well," Omarius whispered in her ear. "You know the consequences if you do not." With that, he let go, letting the servants take a shaken Serena away.

*****

Privus, Drugi, Omarius, and Vatren stood to the side as they watched General Klacan lead the next campaign of soldiers outside the city. When the last few units were slowly filtering out of the city, Privus spoke up and said, "I really never thought this would happen. I never imagined we could make it this far in our quest for vengeance. I could only ever dream of ruling such a place."

"We rule many cities, Privus," Omarius reminded his youngest brother.

"True, but this..." Privus gestured to the massive city that lay behind him, "This is unimaginable."

"Let it remind you of what you are capable of," said Omarius.

"We wish you were coming with us, Privus," said Drugi. "You too, Vatren. We'll miss having elemental magic on our side." Vatren nodded.

"Yes, but Vatren will fuel Privus's staff as he needs it," Omarius responded. "And he will be instrumental in bringing the Vernik Army to its heels. As you know, more magical aid awaits us soon."

"Part of me still wants to come as well. I quite like conquering cities," Privus said.

"Once the Vernik Army arrives and is defeated permanently, that will resume. That will be the job of you two," Omarius motioned at Privus and Vatren. "Part of me even wants to swap places and defeat all of them myself, but I can't afford to waste any more time that could be spent conquering more land. That, and I want to go home."

Privus nodded. Canyon City. He had no memory of it. He was not even a year old when he was exiled along with his mother and brothers.

Drugi claimed to recall fragments and faint impressions. Omarius, on the other hand, remembered it clearly.

"When the dust of war has settled, I'll make a point of coming to see it for myself," said Privus.

"Aye, my brother. You should. You deserve to know what was taken from you," said Omarius.

The brotherly trio bid their final farewells to each other and then departed on horseback. The two oldest Zlikrej brothers rode after their great army but were in no hurry. Privus saw Drugi look back twice at the city and the brother he was leaving behind. Omarius kept his head forward.

Privus watched his brothers become smaller in the distance as the giant gates slowly came down. After a long moment, they were out of sight, and the city was closed off.

Chapter 37
The End of the Road

It was midday when the fog had cleared enough for the Ekron Mountains to come into view. They sat like a dark gray beast, patiently waiting for its prey to arrive. The sight was only a shape, a mass on the horizon, as the Vernik Army rode through the green plains. Given how high the mountains stood, they could be seen from forty leagues away.

They had now intersected with Vulture Road and were riding north, with only the last fraction of the journey remaining. Their travels would last just a few days more.

Luka rode alongside General Warwick, at the front of the army. "It is certainly a given that we vastly outnumber them," Warwick said. "That is our key advantage. But you have to remember, our men have traveled across this country, from its southernmost end, to its easternmost end, and now all the way back to its center. They are weary. The Zlikrej forces have had time to rest in the fortified confines of Exeter. Remember also, even if we did find a way to get in, Exeter is designed to turn the advantage of a large army against itself. If our units are forced to filter into small units in tight spaces, then the advantage would rest on their side."

Luka grunted. "We'll start by laying siege, then. We'll have to devise a better strategy when we get there."

"Indeed. And our strategy will also have to account for the magical capabilities on their side. That complicates things several times over."

"Yes, well, that's what Reishi is for. He will even the scales. Perhaps even tip them in our favor, given the element of surprise."

Warwick frowned. "Yes, in theory. In practice, it may be that he presents his own kind of risk. He could disrupt our side as much as theirs. Have you even seen his powers? The only things *I've* seen from him are his bad-taste jests and irreverence."

"Well, you should be grateful that he is not drinking for the time being. I have actually found him to be displaying much better behavior. And to answer your first question—yes, I have seen his powers. He saved my life from a pair of assassins." Luka thought briefly about Reishi's struggles against the Werdals but said nothing. It would not help his case to air his own doubts about the wizard.

"Hmmm," Warwick responded. "If his powers are effective, then perhaps he can neutralize the enemy's wizard, but I am not comfortable making any plans that depend on him."

"I have a feeling we will *have* to make plans dependent on him," Luka said.

"Well, I don't think—"

Luka cut Warwick off. "General, it is my choice to deploy Reishi how I please."

For the first time, Luka had the satisfaction of overruling his mentor as Warwick fell silent. The noises of horse hooves against gravel filled the air for several long moments.

When the general spoke again, he changed the subject. "Luka, I never mentioned this to you, but this Zlikrej threat dates back further than you know. Perhaps now is a good time to speak of it."

Luka turned to the general, his ears perking up. "Explain, Rory."

"Not long after we had executed Lord Diocretin, we discovered correspondence between him and the Stranakans. He had been attempting to enlist their support and stage an uprising for years.

"When I saw this, I advised your father that the Stranakans were not quite the dormant entity we presumed them to be. Their communications with Diocretin showed enthusiasm for his plan, although of course it did not amount to anything at the time."

"I was never aware of that," Luka said. "I find that quite concerning."

"It is concerning. Omarius is carrying out the very plan his father crafted decades ago. If we had dealt with them at that time, perhaps this would never have happened," he said.

"Perhaps," Luka said, stewing.

Warwick continued. "At present, we have the conflict of the Zlikrej before us, but after we defeat them, you, as king, will have much to think about regarding how to handle the Stranakans. Their involvement could be considered an act of war."

"My understanding is that the troops here are private citizens, not government-backed," Luka replied.

"Of course, the emperor would make that claim. But let's not fall under any illusions that their government is oblivious to thousands of their citizens entering into a military campaign against their greatest rival."

"Fair point," Luka acknowledged. "But as you said, for now, we should remain focused on the Zlikrej brothers. I hold them alone responsible. I will have their blood before I have anyone else's."

Warwick nodded, seeming content with that response for the time being. They rode on and continued to strategize, this time planning real military operations rather than theoretical ones like they used to.

The next dawn, as the army began to commence its march, Warwick appeared in Luka's tent with Lieutenant Alexander and a servant behind him. The servant carried a large wooden box and a sword that slept inside a crimson sheath. "What is it, General?" Luka asked.

"Your Highness," Alexander responded. "A few of us noticed you were carrying a commoner's sword, and that the light leather armor you wore did not meet a standard suitable for a king. We wanted to remedy that. We've found standard-issue knight's armor, as well as a Vernik Army lieutenant's blade."

"You are both a king and great warrior, and I want to see you with the proper armaments," Warwick said. On cue, the servant handed the blade to Luka and proceeded to unbox the armor. Inside the tent, the metal coverings shone, even with sunlight restricted. It was new armor, never previously worn, with a color of untarnished silver and crimson pauldrons, stripes of gold running down for further adornment.

For his months-long journey, Luka had been equipped with whatever equipment he'd been able to scrap together—all of it below what he was accustomed to. Now, he was immensely grateful for the upgrade.

Luka donned the armor and held the sword in his hand. "How do you feel?" Warwick asked.

"Dangerous," Luka replied.

*****

"Why are we doing this?" Reishi groaned, as Luka came to wake him up before sunrise.

"Because, if we leave now, we can reach Exeter tonight, ahead of schedule," answered Luka.

"What's wrong with keeping the schedule we had?" the wizard said, rubbing his eyes.

"I don't want to delay justice any longer. Get up." Luka left Reishi, who eventually arose and found his horse.

With their target so close by, Luka rode silently next to Warwick for most of that day. He found himself constantly fidgeting with Velico's saddle and rubbing the "X" mark on his left hand, which had grown faint since he had sworn the Blood Oath.

Throughout the silence, Luka's thoughts would drift to the ambush at Vernikport. He had gotten used to straining to push those thoughts away, but today he decided he would not do that. He reflected on his loss, his heart hurting as he mourned for Xander and his father.

The reflection inevitably turned into rage, which built up inside him like thick fumes. With the mountains getting bigger, they had never meant as much to him as they did now. Luka believed that the location of all three of his perpetrators lay at the foot of those giant bodies.

Hours later, the sun had sunk past the horizon in the west, painting the cloudless autumn sky in vibrant orange and pink. In the shadows of the mountains, the great city of Exeter came into view. A few lieutenants suggested setting up camp with the city now in view, but Luka rejected the idea. He wanted to get closer.

They settled several hundred paces away from the city. The majority of the soldiers hurried to bed. That did not apply to those selected for Luka's reconnaissance unit, as he called it. He gathered one hundred soldiers along with General Warwick and his highest-ranking lieutenants.

"Poor bastards," Reishi said aloud as he began to turn in for the night.

"You're coming too, Reishi," commanded Luka.

"Sila's wrath! Why?" asked Reishi.

"I need you at my side in case we encounter Vatren."

Reishi groaned but relented and joined the unit.

The pack rode a few extra minutes along the final stretches of Vulture Road until they reached the foot of the towering city gates. Weeks ago, Luka had set out at the southernmost point of the road, just beyond the ashes of his homeland. The Road of Vultures now ended here, at the gates to the most fortified city in all of Estravia.

Above, archers and watchmen on top of the walls examined them and then left their posts, ostensibly to inform their leaders. Luka rode right up to the gate. Eight dreadnought soldiers in thick armor, wielding large, two-handed greatswords, stood at attention on the other side. They did not waver when they saw him. He dismounted from his horse and drew his new sword. He walked right up to the gate and clanked at the portcullis with his blade, meeting each guard with a menacing glare.

Addressing them, he said, "You tell your bastard leaders that vengeance is here. They can come out and face me like proper men, or we will force our way inside. Either way, they will die."

One of the guards scoffed. "You fool. You will never break through here. You're wasting your breath."

"We will get in. I swear it," Luka said. Then he turned around and went back to the pack.

When Luka had circled his way back towards Reishi and General Warwick, the wizard said, "Well, General, I hope you taught your men how to climb giant, sheer walls."

Chapter 38
The Siege

Warwick delivered the bad news to Luka in his tent two mornings after they had set up their camp. During that time, the city remained dormant even as scores of army scouts constantly searched for any sign of an opening. Luka could feel his face twitch under the gaze of the general and the high-ranking officers. The air began to feel scarce in the room as he fell quiet, stewing on the information.

The silence broke when he slammed both fists down on Warick's wooden table. Dust that had been hiding in the general's many maps shot upward, forming a cloud. "How can this happen? Omarius and Drugi are *gone?!* How far away can they be by now?" roared Luka.

"We do not know, but it is likely a long way. Our estimates suggest that they have about a two-week head start on us. Privus still remains in the city," answered the general. "We can divert a portion of our forces to pursue them, but I would suggest staying on course and handling Exeter first."

"The other two could get *years* ahead of us while we deal with this bloody city! I can't believe this!" He found an empty ceramic mug and flung it to the ground. The mug exploded in a high-pitched clank, scattering shards around the tent.

The others stayed quiet as the young king stormed around. He ran through estimations of distance and time, as well as dozens of other scenarios, tangled up like a jungle in his mind. It only made his frustration grow further.

"Privus stayed behind, you say?" Luka said after a while.

"Yes, sir. He is in the city with Serena Tomkins, who, as of a few weeks ago, is now his wife."

Luka's eyes went wide as he felt his hot rage turn to icy hate. He fell silent, pondering which piece of news was worse—Omarius and Drugi departing, or Serena marrying Privus. Two successive punches to his stomach. After a long silence, Luka said, "We will stay here and lay siege to Exeter. All of the Zlikrej brothers will die. Privus will just have to die first."

Warwick nodded. "We will commence our siege at once."

*****

The wind whipped around Privus as he stood atop the outer walls overlooking his enemies. He could see them approaching in siege formation, ready to surround the front part of the city. With only one entrance, the Vernik army had effectively blocked any possible flow into or out of the city from their siege point.

Privus did not find the large numbers of enemies to be intimidating. The upper hand lay with him. *If any one of them enters this great city, it shall only be as a prisoner or as a corpse.*

There was a plan, devised primarily by Omarius, that would ensure Privus's victory. He would have to drag the siege out for some time, but that would allow his older brothers to make as much progress as possible. That was critical in case they abandoned their siege and instead pursued Omarius and Drugi. The probability of that was much higher with Luka back in the fold, even though it was still low. Luka was more unpredictable than the general.

Privus descended from his vantage point after he had grown tired of looking at the enemy below him. A dozen guards trailed him as he walked back to his palace—a luxurious place to rest and wait out the pathetic siege.

*****

Ever since Serena heard the news of the army's arrival, the twisting and nausea in her belly would not subside. She was only just beginning to accept her new life, trying to embrace its apparent stability. Now this new threat, and a reminder of her past, had just arrived outside the city gates.

Possibilities—or delusions—of being rescued by Luka gave her no comfort. They did not seem realistic, but moreover, she didn't even know if that's what she wanted anymore. The idea of Luka dying in battle was terrifying to her—even though she had already mourned his death once before. The idea of Privus dying was another matter. If Luka slayed him, would she really be happy? She had spent so much time with him, slowly getting used to his presence. What would she do if he died? More importantly, what would happen to her family if that happened?

"A siege has started, Archlady Serena," informed one of her servants, Mila, who brought in some tea and bread. A welcome interruption to her spiraling thoughts.

"So, I've heard," she said. "How long do you think it will last, Mila?"

"I do not know, m'Lady. Sieges can last for ages. We have a lot of food in this palace. It could be years before we run out."

"And what about the rest of the citizens?" she asked.

Mila frowned. "You must worry about yourself, Archlady Serena. The citizens will be fine for a time."

The servant had hinted at what was already obvious to Serena. If food supplies ran low, it would be the common folk who would suffer first. This thought angered her. It made war seem like a silly game, where the masses suffered the consequences. She felt rage towards *both* Privus and Luka, two prideful young men playing the game of Exeter.

These feelings only added to the twisting and nausea in her stomach. She wished she could do something, but she couldn't see any options. Even a subtle attempt to persuade her new husband could be seen as a breach of her loyalty, and her father would pay the price.

"Mila," Serena said, addressing her servant who was putting clothes away in the corner of the room. "Can you fetch me some more books?" Further distractions were needed.

"Of course, m'lady." She returned several minutes later, leaving a stack of books on the living room table. She picked up the first book— a compilation of poems. A few of the entries in the volume were elegant, but not captivating. She needed something far better.

She picked up the next one, a work of fiction titled *Lola's Journey*. The first few pages sucked her in immediately. The tale described a wealthy woman from the city of Buvara who fled from her unfaithful husband. She went on to travel the breathtaking land of Estravia on her own for years. Serena was tantalized and envious of the protagonist's freedom.

The life of Lola helped Serena forget about her own for a while.

*****

Sister... this is so reckless of you. Lord Donte set down the letter and let his face fall into his palms. A deep sigh filled his lonely study. The contents of the letter had informed him that Vanessa was traveling hostile lands with almost no protection. The letter was likely written at least three weeks ago, which meant that she could possibly be dead or captured at this point.

The news of his sister distracted Lord Donte from the host of other issues that he had planned on addressing that day. He was in the midst of negotiations, or at least attempted communication, with Lord Tomkins, the traitor. He wanted to win Tomkins back over to the crown's side but had only received disheartening rejections and threats in response to his messages. Many of them were clearly crafted with Zlikrej supervision.

Donte was also attempting to raise support from nearly a dozen cities in the southern region of the country. He wished to consolidate their individual forces so he could lead a separate front on Privagrad and the territory they controlled. Given the chaotic and treacherous environment of this new world, other lords and ladies were hesitant to help. They had only responded with reluctance and reminders that they needed their own armies to protect themselves. Their city could be next, they would always say.

All of those problems were exacerbated by the recent reports that Stranaka was considering a full-fledged invasion of Estravia. They were mere rumors for now, but the threat was severe enough to challenge the lord's ability to sleep even more than it was already.

All the while, the Zlikrej conquered more land, with Luka and Vanessa rogue in the middle of a hostile country.

If only Vanessa would help lead *instead of running on this crazy adventure,* thought Donte. *These cities would listen to her. Or Luka. But not me.*

Estravia needed unity now more than ever.

*****

Queen Vanessa and her travel companions were fortunate to avoid any additional enemies in the days since their encounter with Lord Tomkins's men. The difficulties of their journey persisted, however, as they faced natural barriers instead of human ones. Low, rocky mountains continuously arose in their path, making it difficult, or in some cases, impossible for the horses to climb. They wasted hours going around boulders or sharp stony hills that they first tried to scale.

At noon that day, they came upon another wide and rocky hill, directly in their path. Vanessa groaned when she saw it.

"Should we try to go straight through it, Your Highness?" The priestess asked.

"I don't see a point in that anymore. Let's just go around."

They headed west, around the hill. The obstacle seemed to continue to stretch forever, not yielding any opportunities to get through. Vanessa grew increasingly frustrated as each minute passed by.

Finally, the mountain gave way to a clearing, allowing them to ride north again. Unfortunately, they had also journeyed farther west—that much closer to Vulture Road and all of its perils.

At her side, Amelia, who was quiet as always, seemed especially pale, her hands twitching at her sides. "Amelia, what troubles you, my dear?" asked Queen Vanessa.

Amelia looked at the queen with uneasy eyes. Vanessa could see there was clearly something on her mind. Something that had lingered with her for likely this entire journey, and Vanessa needed to press her on it.

"It's okay, Amelia. You can tell me anything," Vanessa said encouragingly.

After a long moment, Amelia said, "I-I-I'm pregnant. I am bearing a child as we speak."

"You are pregnant with Xander's child?" Her words contained more surprise than she actually felt. She had already suspected it but wanted to feign ignorance.

"Yes—please do not be angry. I do not want to be a burden on this journey."

"No, no Amelia, my sweet daughter. Why would I be angry? This is wonderful news!"

"Indeed, Amelia. New life is a blessing—something to celebrate. Not to fear," Teya chimed in.

"Yes, Princess. Teya is right," Pametan added. "Not to mention, the Vernik bloodline is in great jeopardy. Your child will be of high importance to our country, should Luka—"

Vanessa cut him off. "Milo, enough of that. You are making this about bloodlines and politics, and the baby has not even left the womb. This is not about that. This is about the fact that Amelia will be a mother soon. And I will get to be a grandmother!" she said excitedly.

Vanessa could see the color return to Amelia's face from their reactions. She rode now exuding confidence, without the weight of a secret.

When the celebration of Amelia's news had died down, they all seemed to come to the same harrowing realization. They were now traveling with another life. They had a renewed sense of urgency to reach their destination. Neither time, nor Amelia's baby, would wait for them.

*****

Luka had always found sieges to be boring to learn about, but that paled in comparison to how boring it was to actually *live* through one. He sipped heavy amounts of cheap wine while listening to plans with the general and nearly a dozen lieutenants. The buzz from the drinks helped the seemingly meaningless hours pass by. This was the sixth such meeting, and this time Luka took a backseat inside the crowded tent and zoned out while others did the talking.

In the first few meetings, Luka had taken the lead with great enthusiasm, trying to devise all sorts of plans, but each one met the same fortified dead end. Now, nearly identical talking points were being discussed, only disengaging him.

During an extremely granular conversation about siege formation shifts, Luka noticed Reishi step through the tent and linger by the entrance. With a subtle motion of his head, the wizard beckoned him over. The general glared at the wizard, most of the other attendants following his lead.

Luka rose and walked over to him. In a guarded whisper, Reishi said, "I have a plan."

Chapter 39
Reishi's Plan

Luka loved Reishi's plan. It was by no means perfect, but it was aggressive, and Luka was desperate for aggression. Better than anything, the plan gave Luka a clear path forward, something the never-ending siege did not.

"I had to be sure my powers were back, and that I could reliably control them before we could execute this plan," Reishi added when he had finished explaining.

"Have you been practicing?" asked Luka.

"Oh yes, for a while, but I haven't had much consistent success until earlier today."

"What happened?"

"That is not important right now. What is important is that I teach you how to use these." Reishi held two magical orbs in front of Luka. "These have the elemental power of the earth. They are the cornerstones of the plan, as you know."

"I still do not understand why you are comfortable fighting another wizard, but not opening a hole in the wall yourself," said Luka.

"As I said, it is a matter of timing. We need the element of surprise. My assumption is that Vatren will ride out to meet our challenge. I'm not completely sure I can overpower him, but I know I will surprise him. And that should be enough to defeat him."

Luka replied, "You really can't just open those gates yourself? As in right now?"

"I may be able to, but even if I could, Vatren should be dealt with before the army enters the city. He could simply stand inside the gates and burn the entire army as they try to filter through. Not our best bet," said Reishi.

"And what if Privus does decide to be the one to accept my challenge? I won't be able to face him myself," Luka asked.

"Put yourself in Privus's shoes. Would you take that risk when you have your own wizard to send out?"

Luka agreed. "The chances are slim. But if Privus comes out, and you can defeat him, you need to incapacitate him, not kill him. Then you make sure I am alerted as soon as possible."

Reishi nodded.

Luka, content with the risk, scratched his beard while pondering the strategy further. Reishi's plan appealed to him emotionally more than it did logically. He recognized that, and he knew he had to be cautious. It seemed brilliant, but it also seemed like suicide.

Moments of facial-hair-scratching and foot-tapping passed by. Finally, Luka came to his decision. "Alright, we will do your plan. Now show me how to use your magic balls."

*****

"I need some paper and a quill. I am going to draft an invitation for a duel. I can no longer dally in an interminable siege," Luka said, practically bursting into General Warwick's tent.

Warwick had been caught off guard by Luka's entrance but replied after gathering himself. "Luka, who are you going to challenge? I hope you know Privus will not come out. There isn't the slightest chance. It would be foolish of him."

"That is exactly what I anticipate. The language will request a challenge against their strongest combatant. I presume that they will send Vatren out, which is what I want."

"You intend to fight a wizard all by yourself?"

"I don't intend to be the one doing the fighting. I am going to have Reishi handle it. He will be my champion."

"Do you think he can actually beat this wizard?"

"He says he can. He has no incentive to lie about that. He'd suffer greatly if he faced Vatren and lost."

"That means little, Luka. What if he is wrong? If our men see that, they could be demoralized. Even if he does win, someone could get injured as a bystander. There's a lot more to consider than your wizard friend. We may even have to surrender, depending on the terms of the agreement you're drafting."

"I'm not concerned with those things. We need a chance to remove Vatren from the table before we can do anything else. After that, we are going to be able to get into the city."

"Luka, sieges take a long time. Patience is what—"

"No!" Luka cut him off. "We don't need more patience. We need *action*. Time is short. I'm going to draft this right now. You can help me with the language, or not, but this challenge will be sent no matter what you choose."

The general begrudgingly helped Luka with some of the formalities and nuances of the letter. He made a few disapproving comments as the quill moved along the parchment but otherwise complied.

An hour later, Luka watched from a distance as a messenger surrounded by six officers carried his carefully written letter to the gates. When the messenger reached the entrance to the city, he handed the letter through the iron grid to the Zlikrej sentry.

Now it was time to wait.

*****

"This was not a part of the plan, but I suppose that we can make this work in our favor. It's a way to bring their pathetic resistance to an end even sooner than we anticipated," said Privus after reading the letter from Luka.

"What did it say?" asked Vatren for the third time. "May I read it?"

Privus hesitated but finally relented, handing the letter to the wizard as if it were a fragile baby bird. Vatren, on the other hand, wrangled the bird in a rush so he could learn of its contents. After reading it, Vatren asked, "Are you going to go?"

"Absolutely not. *You* will go. Imagine the look on Luka's face when he's expecting to face me, and you appear. It will be glorious. Just keep the bastard alive and bring him to me when you're done. I could not have him die before anyone else's eyes but mine."

"I would very much like to see that look on Luka's face. I'd do it as soon as today if I could," said Vatren.

"Let us not rush this. Remember, we are trying to give my brothers more time to progress onward. Let's have Luka and General Warwick wait this out for a while. Remember, if I send you, you *must* capture Luka alive and bring him in. It won't be right if I don't get the chance to kill him myself. I would even hope to hold him prisoner long enough so my brothers can be present."

*****

Privus did indeed wait for a considerable time before responding. Luka had expected it, but it didn't ease his restlessness. The message arrived days later. It was short:

To Luka Vernik, the Arrogant Boy Masquerading as a King,

We have read your request for a duel. We have no incentive to agree to this, as we will be safe from your pathetic siege for a long time. That said, I am no coward, and I do not fear combat with you. We will meet your challenge on your terms. The duel will begin at high noon, one week from today. In the impossible scenario in which you win, we will agree to open the gates. If we win, you and your army will surrender to me, and the entirety of your forces will swear their fealty to me and my brothers.

-Archlord Privus Zlikrej

"What's it say?" asked the general, craning to read over Luka's shoulder.

Luka passed the message over. "The good bit is that he agreed to a duel. Bad bit is he wants to wait a bloody week."

*****

Reishi had thought of his plan many days before he outlined it to Luka, wandering meditatively outside the camp. That day, a chilling breeze ran through the air, causing Reishi to put his hands in his pockets. *I can't believe I left my mittens in Jetsac,* he chided himself. Glancing at the city of Exeter, it was hard to imagine that it was any kind of target, hiding all sorts of enemies inside. It stood still and strong, a beautiful spectacle.

Reishi wondered how much damage could be seen inside the city. The Zlikrej had only just conquered it a couple of weeks ago. He also wondered how much more damage would be done once they got inside. Of course, getting inside was a big assumption—one that hinged on Reishi himself.

He had not yet divulged to Luka that he had two magic earth orbs that were powerful enough to penetrate the city walls. The young king was overzealous and would rush into the battle, where they would be outmatched by Vatren's magic. He would need to even the odds himself. And to do that, he needed full command of his own magic.

After weeks of practice, he was close to being able to master his skills again, experiencing several moments of lucid ability. Yet the capability to summon his powers consistently had still not returned. Years of blunting and keeping his powers dormant had weakened him. He did not want to siege forever, but he was grateful that it was buying him a little bit more time.

"What are you doing over here, wizard? Out for a magical stroll?" The unfriendly voice came from behind him, interrupting his ruminations. Two officers on horseback rode towards him and pulled their horses alongside.

"Any stroll I take is magic," he responded. He turned his back on the officers and tried to continue his walk, but they continued to ride alongside him.

"We'd love it if you could do some magic for us," the other officer said.

"I charge for that privilege, you know. You're more than welcome to come to my tavern, but you'll have to pay like the rest of my patrons," Reishi responded. He stopped walking now and engaged the officers directly.

The officers snickered at this. "You *perform* magic at a tavern? As in, like, a show? What are you, a private jester?"

Reishi rolled his eyes. The mockery continued.

"Wait, wait. I'll pay, wizard," one of them said in between snickers. "I just want a little free sample. C'mon now. Show me a little bit of something," the other officer said.

Reishi had plenty of retorts left in him, but he could see his counterparts were not acting in good faith—and it wasn't worth his time. "To be clear, I'd *never* do anything for either of you dirty ratwaggers. You don't deserve it. You don't even deserve the privilege of talking with me right now."

"Oh no, Max, I think we upset the wizard. Do you think he'll go cry to his mother?"

"No, Ollie. You want to know why? Because she was crying for *me* last night!" Their laughter had transformed into absurd guffawing now.

"Time to teach you filthy scoundrels a lesson," he said, inaudible due to the volume of their laughter. He took a deep breath and reached outward with his mind. Neither of the men had any awareness of what he was doing.

To his utter delight, the ability came easy to him, running as smooth as an unimpeded river. He was able to access the minds of Ollie and Max, reading all their thoughts. He could feel the emotional joy they were getting from their ridicule as if he was experiencing it himself.

Time to change that. Reishi brought his mind like a large wave over the consciousness of his targets. He drowned out their tomfoolery, replacing it with extreme fear and terror. Neither officer had any idea why they suddenly felt like their lives were in danger, but both began to sweat and shake, and both felt like turning away.

But Reishi was not nearly finished. He leaked through their memories, searching for repressed moments. Ollie had an unfortunate memory of having his pants fall down in front of his fellow cadets during training. Reishi forced that to the front of Ollie's mind, making him relive it on a loop for as long as he desired.

Max had a far more recent memory of a major blunder, only a year ago, that cost him a promotion to senior officer. It was the kind of embarrassing memory that made the whole body cringe. Reishi gleefully made it repeat as well.

All of this mental maneuvering had happened in just about ten seconds. Reishi now had complete control of these men, with so many entertaining possibilities before him.

He forced Ollie to jump off his horse and lie face down in the grass while Max watched with confusion. Reishi then made Max do the same thing, right on top of Ollie.

The two officers then began munching blades of grass on the ground, under the false idea that eating the grass would make the memories stop. Now it was Reishi's turn to guffaw, tears of laughter forming in his eyes from the absurd sight below him.

"Why are you two eating grass? That's so strange!" he cried out in between chortles.

Reishi's laughter was a response to more than just the humor of the situation—it was also relief. He was *back*. This was proof that Reishi was capable, once again, of using his true powers. The powers of a mind wizard.

Chapter 40
Plan in Motion

The sun hung near the center of the sky, causing the morning chill to depart. It was bright but obstructed by a scattering of clouds. The clouds also covered the Ekron Mountains, hiding their peaks from view. On the ground, ten thousand men stood at the ready. Of that number, only a handful knew what the true plan was. And only one knew what was truly about to take place.

Reishi stared at the fortified city, deep in reflection. In a short period of time, he would become known to the world. But if his plan went as he thought, his true nature would remain hidden, and his lie could be sustained.

The lie was like an uncomfortable coat in the winter. He hated it, but he had to keep it on when he was outside in public. It protected him. And when he was back in the warmth and privacy of his own home, he could take it off.

Being a mind wizard was a liability. Old memories reminded him of why he chose to keep his true magical powers a secret. The fear and horror of the townsfolk who shunned him and drove him away. The way his own loved ones disconnected from him. He fought back a shudder at these thoughts, just as Luka approached.

It would be much easier to take the coat off and tell the world who he really was. Even to just tell Luka. But the risk was too great. He had to keep up the appearance of an elemental wizard. They were a marvel. People did fear them, but their fear was a healthy, natural fear. Fear of something they thought they could understand. It was much different for a mind wizard.

Reishi extinguished any fantasies about revealing himself as Luka came closer. He would continue with his lies as long as he could—and with his plan, he could continue them quite a bit longer.

Luka was clad from toe to neck in polished armor, the sun partially reflecting off the shiny chest plate. His helmet lay tucked under his left arm. His face bore a new level of focus and seriousness, ready for the coming conflict.

"Are you sure you want to do this?" Luka asked when he came upon the wizard.

"Certainly," said Reishi.

"Your powers will work? You're sure of it?"

"They will work, Luka." He briefly reached out with his mind, feeling Luka's own worries. They were twofold—one that Reishi would fail against Vatren and embarrass the army. That would create a great risk for Luka, although that was offset in his mind because he would still have an opportunity to kill Privus. The second was a worry for Reishi's own life, something Luka would never admit out loud. That made Reishi happy.

He washed a sense of calm over Luka's mind, leaving him with confidence that Reishi would be successful. He quickly retreated from his mind after that. Out of respect for the king, he wanted to keep his mind meddling to a minimum.

"Good," Luka said after a moment. "If you have assurances, then I do as well."

"Are you sure *you* want to do this?" Reishi asked, though he knew what the answer was.

"I'll admit this is risky, but I'll feel a lot better when I have my sword in Privus's throat. Assuming your magic balls can get me in there."

Reishi chuckled.

"What?" asked Luka.

"Magic balls. That will always be funny, especially when you say it," said Reishi.

A laugh even managed to escape from Luka's throat. "I'll confess that actually is funny. But it won't be if these balls don't do as you promised. And not just the earth orbs. I need the other ones you gave me to work as well."

Reishi had given Luka all of his orbs, except for two. It was ten orbs in total, including the two earth balls that would be used to penetrate the walls. "My balls will work, don't you worry. Very simple creations. Just throw them and they explode."

The sun inched closer to the center of the sky as everyone continued to wait. Though there was still no sign of Privus or Vatren, there was activity at the top of the city walls, above the gate. Spectators were beginning to gather. The duel was imminent.

Those men are in for an even better show than they bargained for, Reishi thought. He reached out with his mind to see if he could get a sense of them from hundreds of feet away, not expecting much. He was pleasantly surprised to be able to lightly brush against a few minds up on the walls, even at such a distance. A good sign.

"It's almost time," said Reishi.

"Appears to be," said Luka.

Another agonizing quarter of an hour passed, but finally, there was commotion at the city's entrance. Reishi and Luka squinted to see the gates slowly beginning to draw open.

"That's your cue," said Reishi. Luka signaled to two soldiers who were versed in the mission. He donned his helmet and snuck off, the two men following him.

*****

The designated entry point was at least a quarter of the way around the circumference of the city. Luka and his two men trudged a long way to get there.

"How long have you both served in our ranks?" Luka asked the officers who accompanied him.

"Seven years, Your Majesty," the first officer said.

Luka nodded and looked at the other officer. "It will be three years come the winter for me, Your Majesty," said the second.

"Three years?" Luka asked. "And you are already in the Special Infantry?"

"Yes, Your Majesty."

"Most impressive," Luka said. "What was your name again, Officer?"

"Gerard, sir. Officer Gerard."

"And you?" Luka asked the more seasoned officer.

"Officer Fletcher, sir."

"Well met, Officers. General Rory personally recommended you both. I hope you recognize the importance of the mission you have been selected for. Success with this task will mean tremendous things for your careers," Luka said.

"That will be good for my family. My wife will be pleased to hear that, Your Majesty," Officer Fletcher said.

"I'm sure she will be proud," Luka said. "And what about you, Officer Gerard? Any woman waiting at home for you?"

"No, sir. Hopefully one day, should I be fortunate enough."

An abandoned gray house, standing lonely and out of place in the fields marked the approximate point of entry. When they reached it, they moved towards the great wall. They came right up against it, with the behemoth gray mass towering hundreds of feet above.

Luka reached into his crimson-colored pouch on his left side, where only the two earth orbs were held. The other orbs were kept in a similarly colored pouch on the other side of his belt.

He thought about Var and Xander for a moment. For some reason, now, they felt close to him in an indescribable way. *I will avenge you both.* He thought about Serena, too. He had to save her. Maybe she could even help him with his mission. But he would somehow figure that all out when he got inside.

Luka sighed and took a step back from the wall as Gerard and Fletcher looked on. This was where he would find out if his trust in Reishi was well-placed. He reeled back and threw the first orb, just as the wizard had instructed. The orb shattered, sending a ripple through the wall, forming a crater and scattering debris around them. He threw the second one into the center of the crater, the effect duplicating.

When the debris had cleared, Luka could see light at the end of the newly created tunnel. There was a space big enough to fit one person at a time—and that was all that was needed. Luka went in first.

*****

When the gate opened, swordsmen and spearmen poured out by the dozens. Scores of bowmen followed. The group marched in pristine formation for many moments towards Reishi and the army around him. They stopped within one hundred paces of the Vernik Army. They stood with arrogance across from the full weight of ten thousand troops, a number vastly exceeding theirs. There was still no sign of Vatren or Privus.

After an extended pause, Reishi heard the sound of the iron gate being lowered back to the ground. A black hooded figure walked out from underneath it, right before it shut. Two pairs of thickly armored dreadnought knights flanked him on each side. The mass of Zlikrej soldiers parted themselves, leaving an aisle between for the man and his four guards to walk through.

Though there were thousands of soldiers in the area, no one said a single word. In that silence, the sound of the four knights' armor clinking as they took each step was the only noise in the entire field.

When the cloaked figure reached the end of the aisle, the four knights stayed behind at the front of the formation. Soon, the cloaked figure stood before everyone, by himself.

Reishi knew who this was.

On cue, the Zlikrej soldiers fell back into formation, closing the gap between each side, and creating a chorus of shuffling noises. In seconds they were back in place, lined up in two rows behind the black robed man. Reishi knew that the majority of the Zlikrej army was composed of mercenaries, but these men appeared to be highly trained and disciplined. Reishi spent a brief moment scanning the soldiers' minds. In some of them, he saw flashes of innocent civilians dying at their hands. A rage welled up within him that he restrained. He needed to keep his focus on his main enemy.

The black figure took several more steps forward and held out his arms in a questioning gesture. "Where is Luka Vernik, your champion?" he called out.

Reishi waited a moment before slowly walking forward. After several paces, he stood alone, the Vernik Army behind. Thousands of eyes were on him. "We did not specify that His Highness would serve as his own champion."

"And who are you, exactly?" asked the figure, slightly perturbed.

"I suggest you announce yourself first," Reishi said. He already knew who it was, easily able to confirm his identity from his mind. The rest of this wizard's mind was notably hard to navigate, however. *If he has been trained in resisting mental magic, I could easily end up as a pile of ashes...* Reishi thought.

The figure pulled back his hood, revealing short black hair with a thin beard and eyes of the same color. Underneath his left eye, he had a clear burn mark that roughly mimicked the shape of a tear. "I am Vatren of Scotsgrad!" he announced. "I have been given the honor of serving as Archlord Privus's champion." He took off his robe next and let it fall to the ground. Underneath, he was wearing a black, sleeveless shirt, revealing even more burn marks.

Vatren held out his scarred arms wide and summoned fire, wicked flames dancing on each hand. "If the cowardly king will not challenge me, then who are you that would dare take his place?" he said.

The Zlikrej ranks muttered in excitement. The troops in the Vernik Army gasped in fear. Unfazed, Reishi took a few steps forward and responded. "My name is Reishi Milsi of Westgard, and I have been given the honor of serving as King Luka Vernik's champion."

"And why on earth would Luka choose *you?*" Vatren tried to preserve a mocking tone but could not mask his confusion.

"You are not the only elemental magician in Estravia, Vatren," answered Reishi, igniting one of his two orbs he had kept with him. A smirk covered his face, and a fireball of his own danced in his left hand. He had to keep up appearances, after all.

Chapter 41
Into the City

Just inside Exeter's walls, a road circled the city's perimeter. Luka and his two officers planned to follow this outer street back to the gate where the lever was located. They had chosen a small team for this mission, prioritizing stealth over strength. With attention focused on the duel outside the city, they assumed fewer guards would be stationed within. Moving as a group of three would also help them avoid detection.

They ran along the outer walls like the shadow of a sundial edging towards its apex. The buildings to their right were curved, mimicking the concavity of the outer walls. It was a unique attribute of Exeter, but they regarded it only as a guidepost to their target, ignoring its aesthetics.

As they paced towards the gate, Luka found his thoughts yet again returning to Serena. A wave of uninvited images filled his mind. As he ran, he could see Privus grabbing her by the arm, dragging her against her will into an unholy marriage. He couldn't save his father or brother, but he could still save her. And time was running out to do so. Soon enough, the battle would breach the walls of Exeter, and something needed to be done before that.

Luka briefly considered how long it would take to get all the way there, sneak to the lever, and then head to the palace. That timeline was not satisfactory anymore. He stopped running and stood in place, his officers halting and following suit.

"Officer Gerard, Officer Fletcher. You know where the lever for the gate is, correct?" Luka asked.

Both officers stuttered for a moment, as if they had been given an unexpected test. "Little hut near the gate," answered Gerard. "About one hundred paces away."

"That's right," replied Luka. "Do you recall how to get there?"

Fletcher answered this eagerly. "Just keep our pace along this outer road." He pointed to his left. "It should be coming up shortly."

"Correct as well. I need you both to go there on your own now. Our expectations are that there will only be two or three guards at most. I am expediting the plan, and I know you are both capable," said Luka. "Remember, they will not be expecting you. Use the element of surprise to your advantage."

They fell silent at that, shock covering their faces. "Where will you go?" Gerard asked after a moment.

"I'm going after Privus. Straight to the palace."

"Sir, the plan was that we'd all return—" Fletcher began to protest.

"I'm changing the plan. After you pull the lever, make sure you jam it, and then you may head back to the front line."

"Yes, Your Majesty," Gerard said. "May the will of Sila and his agents be on your side." They departed, heading in separate directions.

Even with the distraction, there will still be enemy guards surrounding the lever. The entire plan hinges on them getting that gate open. I'll just have to trust that they can handle this, Luka thought. *And if not, I'll kill Privus either way.*

Inside the circumference road, the rest of the city was ordered in a neat grid system. Luka was pleased with the absence of enemy soldiers in this part of the city. Most of their forces were positioned on top of the walls, expecting to witness Luka duel a wizard. The lack of hostile soldiers was especially favorable, because in Luka's shiny armor in the afternoon daylight, he was quite conspicuous, and he was now opting for speed instead of stealth.

As he rushed down the streets and passed by stone buildings, plenty of Exeterians noticed him, but even his noticeable Vernik red and gold color scheme, it would be impossible for them to really know who was underneath the helm. Either way, they had no interest in getting involved.

As Luka hurried his way down the streets, he kept his focus on the road far ahead of him. He was about halfway down the radius of the city when he spotted the first group of Zlikrej men. The soldiers were lightly armored but numbered half a dozen. He avoided them, veering down a side street undetected.

Continuing his journey to the center, he spotted more and more groups of Zlikrej soldiers. He constantly had to adjust his route laterally, which was immensely frustrating. He was on a warpath to the palace, and he preferred that the path stay straight.

As Luka drew only a few blocks away from the center of the city, he came to realize that evading the Zlikrej men was no longer an option. Even with the duel going on, the enemy presence was significant in the central part of Exeter. Ahead, four Zlikrej foot soldiers stood casually at their post. The streets on both of his sides were patrolled by soldiers as well. Retreating was not a consideration.

He unsheathed his sword and thought once again of Var and Xander. He pressed forward purposefully, right towards the four men. The extent of their armor was light leather plating in some areas, and none had their weapons drawn. *This will be much like butchering meat,* thought Luka. He spun his sword once as he approached.

He was a mere dozen paces away when the soldiers slowly turned to look. Only one even thought to reach for his weapon.

The closest soldier, seemingly a Stranakan, opened his mouth as if to ask Luka something. Luka preempted the question by lodging his blade into the man's neck and collarbone. The attack happened in a flash. The next soldier had no time to react before Luka withdrew his sword from the first man's body and did the same thing to him.

The third soldier panicked and tried to unsheathe his sword. Only a couple inches of steel managed to emerge from the scabbard before Luka slashed sideways, cutting through the leather armor and into his ribcage. Seeing that the blow was not fatal, Luka slashed again from the side, this time aiming for the neck. When he pulled the sword away, a fountain of blood shot out from the side of the throat. The man fell to the ground, lifeless.

The townsfolk who witnessed this did not realize what was going on at first, either, but they screamed at the sight of the slaughter. Attention was inevitable now.

The fourth and final soldier had enough of a chance to draw his sword by the time Luka killed the third. He stepped forward and engaged. The soldier struck at Luka with a frightened and desperate attack, going straight for the helm. The strike met a fierce parry, forcing the soldier's blade to the ground. Luka's stab that followed was so forceful that it pierced the leather chest plate as if it were a thin slice of bread. Luka removed his blood-covered sword from his enemy and wiped it on one of the dead soldiers' sleeves. Then he pressed on.

Less than a minute later, Luka glanced backward, mid-jog. About a dozen soldiers were standing near their dead brethren, asking questions of the witnesses. He watched a pair of Exeterians point directly at him. Luka knew that meant it was time to look away and move faster.

It was only a moment later that two light gray palace towers peeked from above the rooftops, meaning he was drawing close. Along the way, Luka also noticed several more groups of soldiers who stood on the edges of the streets. Luka ran right past them instead of engaging. They were slow to react, but eventually began to pursue him, joining their comrades who were already giving chase.

At last, he reached the circular plaza that contained the city's center. A thirty-foot bronze statue of a young, muscular warrior standing on top of a slain dragon was the center-most object in the city. It was built in honor of the legendary Lord Saddiq, who famously killed a dragon that had flown too close to Exeter. The rest of the plaza was open, lined with cobblestone. The palace waited at the other end of the circle but in between stood scores of Zlikrej soldiers.

Luka halted to take stock of his situation. He could dare to stop for only a few seconds, with his pursuers coming for him from behind. In his few available moments, he devised a possible solution. He fiddled in his bag of magical orbs until he found the two orbs that would produce the effect of wind.

One of the orbs is much stronger than the other, Luka remembered Reishi saying. He recalled asking Reishi *which* of the two was stronger, and how he would be able to tell the difference. *Sorry, Your Highness*, Reishi had said. *I really don't remember. You'll just have to cross your fingers and get lucky, I suppose.*

Luka ran forward into the midst of soldiers but didn't bother to cross his fingers. When enough of the Zlikrej men had noticed him and begun converging on him, Luka heaved the orb into the space far ahead. The orb exploded on impact, creating a mammoth shockwave in the air that sent bodies flying as if they were a splashing pool of water.

The blast radius was so large that Luka was caught in it himself, getting knocked down onto his back. For a moment, it brought back the ringing in his head that had plagued him since his coma. *I think I can assume that was the more powerful orb*, Luka thought, amidst the ringing. He quickly got to his feet while his enemies were still lying on the ground, stunned, injured, or in some cases, dead.

The orb had worked perfectly—Luka now had a clear path to the palace.

Just as he was about to enter, he noticed a small group of soldiers who must have been on the edge of the blast radius like him. They were rising to their feet to fight again. They were shaken, but able to identify Luka as their enemy and the source of the blast. The lead man charged at Luka with his sword held high. Luka's parry was so powerful that the assailant lost his balance, completely exposed for a fatal blow—which Luka summarily delivered.

The remainder of the combatants were not foolish enough to attempt the lone wolf strategy. They gathered together and attacked in unison. There were four in total. Luka could handle them in combat but opted for a quicker option. He reached into his pouch once again.

A red fire orb flew through the air and landed right at the feet of one of the men. The burst of inferno was large, engulfing three of the other soldiers, before spreading onto the arm of the fourth. That soldier was too busy trying to put out the rapidly spreading flame to attack, so Luka left him and proceeded to the palace.

When Luka entered, he feared more guards on the other side, but was pleasantly surprised to find only servants in the foyer. They paused and looked at him, wide-eyed and confused. "Where are the Lady's quarters?"

No one answered him, so he repeated his question. Again, he received no responses, so he sheathed his bloody sword and grabbed one of the servants, a short old man, pulling him right up to his helmet. "Where is the Master Bedroom?" he screamed. "Tell me now!"

The servant answered but had to battle through terror and stutter to spell out the directions. Luka let the man go and ran up the grand staircase while the servants scattered in fear.

*****

Serena stopped reading her book, which had scant pages remaining. She heard commotion followed by an explosion that made her nearly jump out of her chair. She ran over to her high window and looked over the city center, seeing a scattering of bodies lying all around.

She had been informed about the battle outside the city. With glee, Privus had told her that Vatren was going to fight and likely defeat Luka outside the city walls. By the looks of it now, though, something was happening *inside* the city. Not only that, but right next to the palace.

From her window, she watched some of the soldiers slowly rise to their feet. A few went to check on their comrades who were still on the ground. By the looks of it, many of them were not able to stand. A group of the surviving soldiers gathered and began pointing towards the palace. They rushed inside, clearly chasing after someone.

In that moment, Serena heard her door swing open, followed by the sound of clanking armor. She turned around to see a knight in shiny armor with red and gold stripes—Vernik colors. The knight's closed helm hid his face underneath an intimidating mask, with only a few vertical slits for sight and air.

"Serena," said the knight. The voice was eerily familiar. He took a few steps toward her.

"Who are you?" she asked, anticipation building within her.

The knight took off his helmet, revealing the now bearded and more mature face of a man she knew well. "Serena. It's me, Luka," he said.

Serena could not muster any words. Her jaw hung open as Luka approached further. Longing was in his eyes as he embraced her. She reciprocated and said, "Luka... I-I can't believe it's you. How did you get into the city?"

"That would take much longer to explain than you would think," Luka said.

*****

Privus watched from the top of the wall as Vatren walked down the formation between the two sides of soldiers. It was difficult to tell who was who from this distance. It took many moments for Privus to realize that the man who had stepped forward to face the challenge was not Luka.

This man was clearly no warrior. Who was he?

Privus was flustered and agitated when he came to realize that a stranger—not Luka—would be the one to challenge Vatren. He was devastated when he saw the figure produce a fireball.

*****

"It's been so long. I can't believe it. I can't believe you're here... in my arms."

"It has been too long, Serena."

They released from their embrace and gazed upon one another, their arms still touching. Serena was as beautiful as Luka had remembered. On the outside, her features shone. On the inside, though, something was wrong. Her eyes seemed like a doorway into a hollow world.

"I'm scared, Luka," she said softly, her eyes falling to the ground. "This feels so dangerous. Battle and bloodshed arrived at my home months ago. Now it feels like it's come back again."

"Serena, this battle will free you. *I* will free you. That is why I am here."

She said nothing, but for a moment she seemed to glow like a shooting star, only for the light to fade away quickly. Sullenness seemed to come over her, and her voice was flat when she replied. "You can't free me, Luka. I don't think anything can. They have my family. No matter what you do, word will reach them, and my family will be in danger."

"We will find a way to save them, too, Serena," he assured her.

"They have guards with my family constantly. They would murder them in an instant if they found anything out," she said.

"You mustn't think like that," Luka insisted. "I will find a way to free them. I found a way to you, didn't I?" She nodded but remained silent. Luka went on, filling the quiet. "Unfortunately, your father betrayed me when I visited him weeks ago. When we return, he will have to face justice, but—"

"Don't you *dare* speak of my father that way," Serena interrupted. "He was just trying to protect me. He had no choice."

"He tried to have me imprisoned! He's a bleeding traitor!"

Serena turned away viciously, seeming to stifle a tear. Luka lowered his face into his gauntleted palms and sighed. *You imbecile*, he chided himself. Bringing up her father's betrayal was foolish. Lord Tomkins would indeed have to face harsh punishment for his deeds but now was not the time to mention that.

"Serena, I am so sorry. I could never have imagined that we would find ourselves together in a situation like this. I always imagined a far different future for us. One that is still possible.

"What happened to you was not your fault. We are both the victims of heinous acts. Evil visited upon us and pilfered us of what we held most dear. We cannot change the past, but we can avenge those we have lost. And we can prevent further damage from being done."

She turned back towards him and nodded, her body still stiff and her face still blank.

Luka continued. "I am here to save you. Not only that, once this is over, I can do so much more. I will have your false marriage undone. Priestess Teya will be able to do that easily. You will be liberated from that bastard."

Serena nodded again. Luka thought about adding one more possibility to that list. He considered telling her that he could marry her instead. He could make her queen. They could be together for the rest of their lives. But he stopped short. Today, that sounded like lunacy. But perhaps one day it could happen.

"Do you know where Privus is?" Luka asked.

She hesitated for a moment, but then said, "He went to watch you duel Vatren from the top of the wall above the gate. But obviously, he is not watching you. I am not sure what he will do since you are not there."

Luka weighed her words for a moment. "What's the quickest way to get there?" he asked. "I promise I will come right back for you after."

"Through the back of the palace and then..." she trailed off.

"And then what?"

"Are you going to kill him?" she asked.

"Yes." The word hung in the air coldly, her gaze again falling to the floor.

Luka furrowed his brow and clenched his jaw. "Serena, you cannot honestly tell me this makes you unhappy? You can't seriously want him to live, do you?"

After more drawn-out silence, she said, "I don't know."

Red stars entered his vision, and the ringing sound returned to his ears. He breathed in deeply and said, "I cannot *believe* you just said that. You don't know? You don't *know* if you want a mass murderer to die? What could possibly be holding you back? Please don't tell me you've *fallen* for this man."

"Luka, he's my husband. This is more complicated for me than you could imagine."

"Your 'husband' is a brutal murderer! A man who kills kings, princes, and innocent men, women, and children, all alike! And smiles, oh, how he *smiles* when he does it! Believe me, I've bloody seen it! There's nothing *complicated* about that."

Her face became ghostly white, and her tear ducts began to fill. "Luka, please do not go to fight him. One of you will die. Or both of you."

"No, Serena. *Privus* will die. Only him. And I need you to tell me that you want that."

She shook her head several times, water now dripping down both cheeks. "Luka, I don't want it. I don't want anything to happen to you. But I don't know what they'll do to my family if something happens to him."

He felt the fury coil inside him and press against every fiber of his being. His voice raised even louder when he spoke. "This is madness you speak of! I came here to save you, and you ask me to protect the man who killed my family? All because your father was too weak to stand up to them?"

She looked at him in a scorching red glare filled with hatred, fear, and resentment all at once. She seemed as if she was about to strike him, but the fire died down, and she retreated to being stiff and still again.

Luka backed up, taking two steps away. The thought of her defending Privus under any circumstances was unacceptable to him. He had come all the way here for her, risking everything just to get to this point. And now it felt as if she was rejecting him. "I just offered you salvation," he said. "Yet you rebuked me. You will never get that offer again. I think you are a traitor, just like your father. I should have known. I should have been wiser." An eerie calm filled Luka as he spoke.

"In a few minutes, if they haven't already, my army will get through the gates to this city. We vastly outnumber Privus's men, and we will defeat them. Before the battle is over, I suggest you run away, as far as you can. I am going to kill Privus and all of his treasonous associates. If you are truly aligned with them, then you should get far, far away."

With that Luka put his helmet back on, obscuring the sight of Serena through the slits. He turned away from her and made for the door. She pursued him, crying, and asking for some sort of mercy, but she never took her words back. She reached for him one last time, only for him to brush her away violently and leave.

The door slammed so hard behind him that a crack appeared on its bottom side.

Chapter 42
The Duel

The face Vatren made when Reishi produced the fireball was thoroughly enjoyable. The dark wizard's entire demeanor went from that of a young cocky champion to a little boy who had shat himself in front of thousands of people. In fact, Reishi thought that there was a reasonable possibility that Vatren did shit himself.

Vatren's surprise lowered his mental guards just enough for Reishi to get farther into his mind undetected. He searched randomly through Vatren's memories and could feel his distress. He was also able to confirm that Vatren did not, in fact, soil his pants. What a shame.

Unfortunately, it would take much longer to gain full control. And he needed to be careful. If Vatren became conscious of what was happening too soon, then he could potentially fight him off. He wouldn't need to have his mental blocks up for very long to incinerate him.

Vatren tried to hide his surprise and disappointment with a fake yet arrogant smile. "You may be a wizard, but you are old and dusty," he taunted. "It's easy to detect a man out of practice."

"Practice?" Reishi replied. "Judging by what you've done to your own arms, you should be the last person to speak of practice. Try not to burn yourself further in this duel, Vatren. Just a suggestion."

Vatren tried to ignore the quip, but Reishi was far enough into his mind to know that he had struck a nerve. That was satisfying. "Well then, Reishi," the dark wizard said. "Why don't we see if your skills can compete with mine?" Traditionally, Reishi was supposed to agree, and the duel would commence, but the Zlikrej champion forewent that formality. He raised his left, open palm and fired a wide blast of fire right at Reishi.

Reishi had read his thoughts and knew this was coming. He was already shifting to his right before the fire was released, allowing him to completely evade the attack. The heat from the fire warmed Reishi as it passed by. As he ran to his right, he jumped and threw his own fireball midair at Vatren.

In defense, Vatren crossed both arms in an "X", producing a wall of wind that met the fireball head-on. The fireball exploded and sent flames scattering out into the air. Vatren was left untouched. Reishi had not expected his last fireball to actually defeat or even wound Vatren, but it did give him an opportunity to observe the mental processes that he had used to command the element.

On the edges of the duel, several spectators stepped back, avoiding the airborne flames. They quickly resumed their positions, not prying their eyes away from the magical battle.

Vatren uncrossed his arms and aimed both his hands forward. *Ice this time*, Reishi knew. He tried to see if he could influence the maneuver somehow. He managed to distract Vatren just enough, but the Zlikrej wizard almost became conscious of the invader's presence in his mind. Reishi withdrew before completely taking control.

A floating aura of water materialized in the air in front of Vatren and immediately froze into ice. This was where Reishi's interference had its effect. Many of the ice shards never fully froze. Reishi braced himself, and when Vatren fired the cascade at him, the ones that hit their mark made only a splash rather than a pierce.

Reishi subtly pulled out another magic orb—his last one. He hoped that none of the soldiers noticed, but he knew for a fact that Vatren didn't, thanks to his powers. Reishi tossed the orb a few meters ahead of Vatren, unleashing a blast of water of his own that he did not have time to dodge. The gushing stream had enough force to knock Vatren back and fill his throat, eyes, ears, and nostrils with water.

Choking, coughing, and gasping for air, Vatren rose to his knees and began to fire blasts of wind in all directions. Reishi held both hands out at the ready, appearing as if he was preparing to unleash more elemental magic, even though he had no more orbs to his name. What he was really doing was examining the mind of his enemy. Each time Vatren fired more wind bursts into the air, Reishi gained more and more influence over him.

Vatren stood up at last, soaked from head to toe. Reishi would have laughed at him, but he was too focused. "Is that the best you have? You'll not last long if it is," the dark wizard bragged defiantly.

"That is not *close* to the best that I have," Reishi replied.

*****

Officers Gerard and Fletcher raced around the outer street at the base of the great walls of Exeter. Suddenly alone, they both bore a much greater burden of responsibility than they had ever anticipated. Fortunately, they did remember where the lever was located and stopped when they came upon it.

About a hundred meters away from the gate, there was a small stone hut built into the side of the city wall. Inside, the hut held a large iron lever and a designated leverman who opened and closed the gate.

Unfortunately, surrounding the hut were more than a dozen men whose job it was to guard it. The assumption that there would only be two or three guards was wrong. Dead wrong.

Had Luka been there, the dozen guards would have been of little concern. The young warrior would likely have been able to defeat them on his own. Gerard and Fletcher did not have nearly that level of skill. Their hearts sank as they began to realize their chances of success and survival were low. Yet the consequences of failure were unimaginably high.

They pulled to the side, hiding behind a house, out of sight. For several moments, they traded worthless ideas, but hopelessness began to creep in quickly. Finally, Fletcher said, "One of us could try to get their attention and lure them away, and the other could go inside and pull the lever."

Gerard nodded. "That may be our best bet." What was left unspoken was who would volunteer to be the distraction—an almost certain death sentence.

Fletcher gulped and said, "I will do it. I will be the distraction. Once I get their attention, you go in." *It was my idea*, Fletcher thought. *It would be wrong to subject him to this fate.*

After a moment of silence, Gerard did not protest. "Thank you, Fletcher. I will not let you down." Gerard offered his hand, Fletcher took it, and they shook.

The elder officer then took a deep breath and said, "It is time."

He sprinted out from behind the house with his knife drawn, Gerard staying behind to watch from the cover of the building. Fletcher sprinted right up towards the nearest guard and buried his blade into his throat. Before any of the others had a chance to react, Fletcher pulled away and ran off down one of the streets, taunting as he went. "Come get me, you whoresons!" He accentuated this by adding a shake of his arse for good measure.

The gesture was effective. All but two of the soldiers impulsively followed after Fletcher with their swords drawn. Surely, Gerard could handle the rest on his own, meaning that he had already succeeded at his job. Now all he had to do was survive.

He darted down a few side streets and created a zig-zag pattern designed to lose the Zlikrej men. Unfortunately, he could never get fully out of their sight, and he was starting to lose breath.

A few of the men were faster than Fletcher, and after chasing him down past several streets, they were upon him. He spun around just as one soldier slashed at his back. The two blades clashed in the air with a metallic clang. They traded more blows as the other soldiers drew nearer to the fight.

Fletcher was stronger and more skilled than his opponent. It only took a few more seconds before he incapacitated the guard, leaving him at his feet. Unfortunately, nine other guards now circled him—bloodthirsty grins stretched across their faces.

The pack converged on Fletcher. So many silver streaks flashed at him that he wasn't sure which ones he was able to parry and which ones cut into his flesh. They quickly overwhelmed him.

Laying in the Exeterian street, with his life evaporating from him, a comfort came over Fletcher. His death had served a purpose. He had created the opportunity for Gerard to get inside the hut. He had fulfilled his mission and served his king and country. Hopefully, his family would understand. Hopefully they would be proud.

Now all Gerard had to do was pull the lever.

*****

Vatren growled and held out his hands another time. Once again, Reishi knew what was coming—earth magic. By this point, Reishi had gone so far into Vatren's mind that there was virtually nothing the Zlikrej champion could do to hurt him. And he was none the wiser.

A giant mass of dirt and stones emerged from the ground, levitating in the air in front of Vatren. Given the proximity to the Ekrons, the terrain was tough and rocky. Vatren could crush an Exeterian building with a mass of earth that size. As expected, Vatren threw the boulder. He thought he aimed it right at Reishi, but it would not end up reaching its mark.

With his mind, Reishi had influenced the magical attack so that it would land short of its target, right in front of him, blocking each wizard from the other's line of sight. The dark wizard growled again, frustrated by his weakness. He focused on the boulder, which now shielded Reishi. The rock began to crack and break apart.

Reishi, whose path into Vatren's mind was not impeded by the boulder, stepped back, aware of what was coming. The boulder broke into smaller rocks, most of them spanning a meter wide. He raised them up and held them menacingly above Reishi for a moment. Reishi looked up at the army of stones dispassionately, before returning his gaze directly to Vatren. He delved further into his mind, grabbing hold of the exact space that controlled his magic.

Now I've got you.

Vatren released the blizzard of rocks down upon his opponent. Reishi held up his arms as if he was trying to seize hold of the stones. The witnesses would see Reishi seeming to stop the rocks above him, suspended in the air. What the audience did not know, and nor did Vatren, was that the dark wizard himself was holding the stones up there—Reishi had controlled the entire action.

The puppet show was entertaining to Reishi. Just like with Gabbitt back in his tavern in Jetsac, Reishi was the only one who knew it was all an illusion. The mind wizard pulled the strings on his new puppet again, making Vatren unknowingly send the stones flying right back at himself. He tried to erect a frozen wall to shield himself, but the rocks came in fast and strong, many bursting through the ice. The attack broke multiple ribs, bloodied his face, smashed his shins, and sent him falling backwards onto the grass.

In that moment, Vatren feared he was defeated. He was immobilized by the pain and demoralized at the fact that his opponent had the upper hand. *If this wizard summons a fireball, I am finished. I don't have the energy to defend myself,* Reishi heard Vatren think. But no fireball came.

Vatren rose off the ground and sat upright, without putting any weight on his legs. He saw Reishi slowly walking closer to him. There was no hurry, and he was not summoning any magic. *That's odd*, the dark wizard thought. *Has he come to gloat? That would be a big mistake.*

Suddenly, Vatren became aware of something strange. He had felt it briefly before but thought nothing of it. But now he felt it again, and he searched his mind. After a moment, he found it — the presence of Reishi hiding in his head like a beetle under a leaf. That explained everything. Vatren fixated on the unwelcome presence and cast it out as if it were a bad thought. *Get out of my head, mind wizard scum!* It was the last thing Reishi heard from the dark wizard's mind.

While seated in the grass, Vatren threw two fireballs at Reishi. The mind wizard did not know they were coming this time, but he had already begun retreating physically as soon as the dark wizard had cast him out mentally.

One of the fireballs fell short by a wide measure, but the second one landed only a few feet from Reishi. When it exploded, it set the left side of his pants on fire. He fell to the ground, yelling in pain. As he rolled around in the grass, he tore at his pants, trying to patter the flames away. By the time he had put the fire out, his skin underneath was charred.

Across the field, Vatren rose to his feet. He began to hobble towards Reishi, one hand clutching his rib cage, the other tossing fireballs. Reishi began to run again, but more and more flames swallowed up the ground around him.

"You vile parasite! You will burn for what you tried to do to me!" yelled the dark wizard.

Vatren switched tactics now. He held out both hands and shot out a mammoth blast of wind. The attack felt like running into a wall, and it sent Reishi skyward. He rolled over on the ground many times when he landed, winded with stars covering his vision.

"There's no escape from this, Reishi!" he screamed.

Vatren had honed his defenses now. Reishi had only seconds left to avoid being turned into an ember.

*****

Back by the gate, Gerard watched as most of the dozen soldiers ran after Fletcher. Only two stayed back. That was certainly preferable to twelve.

He unsheathed his sword and prowled over to the remaining targets. The guards saw him coming, but for the first one, it was too late. He blocked one strike feebly, only for the next attack to stab through his innards. Gerard pulled his sword out just in time to fend off the other guard. This guard was quick, forcing Gerard onto the defensive, retreating as he parried.

Gerard didn't have time to defend against this soldier for long. Shifting the momentum, he lunged forward—all his body weight behind his desperate blow. The soldier's defense was off balance, and his sword flew away. Gerard quickly delivered the killing blow, finally erasing the hut's defenses.

When he went inside, an unarmed leverman looked at him, fearful and confused. "Step away," Gerard commanded, holding his sword's point inches from the man's throat. "And keep silent."

The man obliged and stepped aside, leaving the lever unguarded for Gerard. He tried to pull it back towards him with one hand, while the other held his sword. The black iron handle was heavy, and with only one hand, he could not get it to budge. He put down his weapon, grasping the lever with both hands now.

At that moment, the door swung open, two men with crossbows hurriedly entering. Two bolts launched through the air, piercing his armor. While neither shot was fatal, they were enough to force him back from the lever.

Before the crossbowmen could reload, Gerard grunted and put his hands back on the metal bar. This time, he pulled all the way down, hearing the black iron mass begin to lift off the ground close by. He felt a sweet rush of triumph come over him as he readied to jam his blade into the switch, ensuring the gate would remain open.

Only a second later, Zlikrej infantrymen burst through, barreling straight for Gerard. They tackled him to the ground and pinned him down. One peeled off and grabbed the lever. The guard returned it to its original position, ensuring the gate would close again. It had only come open for a few seconds, not nearly long enough to get anyone through.

With several heavily armored men weighing him down, Gerard knew that the gate would stay shut with Luka trapped somewhere inside the city and the army trapped outside it. He would die believing that the final act of his life was a failure.

*****

Laying on the ground, with patches of fire all around him, Reishi tried to avoid panic. The mental bout had fatigued him, but Vatren continued to draw nearer, unleashing haphazard blasts of fire in his direction. Smoke rose above the field, beginning to obscure the two wizards in thick, dark clouds. Death was approaching, and he only had a single option left.

Straining again to focus, Reishi resumed his mental offensive. This time, Vatren would know it was coming, but he had no choice. He delved into the dark wizard's mind, trying to pry deeply. As expected, the guards were up.

You think I haven't been trained against your kind? Vatren thought.

Not as well as I've been trained against your kind, Reishi returned. He tried to force his way in, past the mental blocks that had been erected. Reishi's mental energy and ability to concentrate now meant life or death for him. All the while, Vatren hobbled closer. Soon, he would be close enough to end him.

347

Reishi made no progress—each time he pushed forward, he only met a mental wall. Both wizards could feel the pressure in their foreheads building. Time was running out, but Reishi kept trying.

When he was in range, Vatren began to turn his attention to summoning another fireball, but the momentary shift in focus allowed Reishi to sneak past the barriers. Now, Reishi had access to Vatren's key memories. He decided to use them.

Reishi forced one of Vatren's most repressed memories out to the forefront of his consciousness. Ironically, a person's most repressed memories were always the easiest to access. Both wizards watched the scene unfold in their minds' eyes.

He was a boy with the same dark hair and dark eyes but lacking the grotesque scars that had yet to develop. Somewhere in a messy kitchen, an old woman—Vatren's aunt—hit him repeatedly with a thick wooden spoon.

Vatren, as he always did when this memory would rear its ugly head, shifted to a memory of him burning her alive with his magic. The thought was comforting, and by being able to bring it up at will, Vatren believed he had retaken control of his mind.

The conjured memory continued as the anguished aunt writhed on the floor with her clothes melted away and her whole body burning. Gradually, though, Vatren's faint memory ended, and Reishi's vivid illusion began. The flames suddenly disappeared. Vatren knew then that he wasn't in control anymore, panicking to try to recapture his consciousness. But the effort was futile. Reishi was the puppet master once again.

The aunt's clothes reappeared, and her eyes opened. She stood up, ghastly, with burns covering her face. She glared at Vatren with her angry, twisted eyes, and pulled out the wooden spoon again. The beating that followed was worse than Vatren had ever remembered. His body felt each blow as if it was real. Howls of agony escaped his throat.

During this memory, Reishi was able to stand back up and walk back towards Vatren. He could see tears running down his adversary's cheek.

At Reishi's command, the nightmare became exaggerated. The aunt grew in size, standing taller than a giant. The beatings continued. She hit Vatren over the head, and each time he felt as if his whole body was crushed. He toppled over, Reishi now standing above him.

It's time to go away for a while, Reishi communicated. Then he switched off the dark wizard's conscious mind, casting him into the blackness of a coma. *And now you will do something for me.* But Vatren did not hear that.

Reishi took control of the unconscious body, making it stand back up with its eyes closed. The soldiers witnessing the duel were utterly confused as to what was taking place, but Reishi assumed that they knew he was winning. The Zlikrej army stood at attention, prepared to strike if needed.

Using his control of Vatren, Reishi emptied the enemy wizard of all the magical energy in his body, unleashing a firestorm towards the Zlikrej soldiers, who had not yet processed the fact that their champion had lost.

Reishi made it appear as if the blast was sent from his own arms, but it did not matter who it came from to his victims. The bright avalanche of fire engulfed nearly all of them, burning many to death instantly. Few survivors were left.

Reishi let Vatren fall to the ground and turned back to the Vernik Army. "Now! Attack!" he commanded.

Almost ten thousand men charged forward towards the city, darting past Reishi and his defeated opponent. Running through the burning grass, they imprisoned or killed any of the remaining stragglers and headed for the city gate, which was supposed to open any minute—not by the Zlikrej, of course—no one expected them to honor the terms of the duel.

Reishi stayed behind for a moment and brought Vatren back to consciousness. Vatren opened his eyes and saw Reishi standing over him, still feeling the poisonous grip on his mind. *Get out of my head!* he tried to demand.

Oh, I will leave your head soon, but you won't like the condition I leave it in.

Who are you? Why are you doing this? Vatren pleaded.

I already told you who I was. And you want to know why I'm doing this? Technically I was ordered, but that's not why. You are a plague that must be vanquished, responsible for so many deaths. Your memories prove your guilt to me. I won't even feel bad about this, Reishi responded.

Gradually, Reishi began unraveling Vatren's mind and body like a thread. Abject terror filled the dark wizard as sensation fled from his limbs and the dark edges in his vision began to close in. Moments later, the annihilation was complete, and there was no longer any mind to connect with.

*****

After Privus saw the mysterious man burn practically all of the men who had been sent down there, he stormed away from his viewing point and rushed back towards his palace. A line of his guards hurried after him while he descended the long staircase that led from the top of the wall back to the ground. When they reached flat ground at the bottom, Privus picked up his pace.

Minutes later, Privus entered through the back entrance to the palace, a much more modest part of the estate. Things were not going according to plan, and he had just lost his most powerful ally. If that new wizard could defeat Vatren, then clearly he could use his powers to tear through the walls.

Where did this wizard come from? And why are they only deploying him now? Why wasn't I alerted to this by my contacts? He steamed, full of perturbation.

Regardless, I must devise a plan to defeat this wizard. I still have my staff.

"Leave me," Privus said to his guards when he reached the palace's courtyard. They disbursed, and Privus continued along the way to his room, which towered over the far end on the other side of the long patio area.

Suddenly, Privus spotted a figure in silver armor across the way. It was not one of his men.

"PRIVUS!" yelled the armored man, charging with his sword drawn.

Ah, Luka. How fortunate. Privus unlatched his magic staff from his belt and pointed it at his oncoming adversary. *Time to finish you once and for all.*

Chapter 43
Rage of the Phoenix

After departing Serena's room, Luka stormed through the palace, barreling past servants in his way. His boots pounded down the tower steps at a reckless and dangerous pace.

He fumed about many things as he sprinted towards his destination, but none stung more right now than his interaction with Serena. She had rebuked him. It was treason in Luka's mind. She had asked him not to spare Privus. There wasn't a single fiber in his being that would accommodate that request.

His route led him towards the back door of the palace, the most direct path to his target. Was Privus up there, watching Reishi win—or watching him fail? He gritted his teeth and cast those thoughts aside. Right now, he could only focus on one thing—revenge.

On his way to the palace courtyard, Luka turned a corner into a narrow hallway. The hallway had no windows, but in the low lighting, Luka saw a half dozen Zlikrej guards who blocked his path.

The men noticed Luka at that same instant, seeming to sense that they were in the presence of a hostile and terrifying force. The soldiers hesitated for a moment, fearful even with their advantage in numbers. Luka did not hesitate and converged on them.

In such tight quarters, Luka had a distinct advantage over the spearman who awaited him first. He pressed in close, slicing up the combatant as if he were defenseless. Luka stepped over the fresh corpse and advanced, unstoppable in his rage.

The second soldier stabbed at Luka, only for his spear to connect with his left bracer, which held firm. Luka's blade then slid through the spearman's exposed stomach, leaving a second corpse to join the first. Entrails spilled out all over the floor.

With a sharp gesture, Luka parried a desperate attack from the next soldier. Their blades clashed and held in midair. At the same time, another soldier tried to squeeze past, attempting to attack from the left side. Luka grunted and heaved against both blades, pushing the two soldiers into each other.

The soldiers had collapsed, but Luka was not finished with them. He swung down at the exposed neck of the nearest one. As blood gushed from the dead man's throat, Luka kicked the next soldier square in the nose. He lay momentarily incapacitated in a pool of blood from his three dead comrades.

Only two soldiers remained standing now. Their terror was palpable as Luka moved in closer to them. He unleashed a torrential storm of silver against the soldier closest to him. Only a single strike met a steel parry. The rest met flesh, carving him up and adding to the collection of corpses.

Before he advanced to the final foe, the soldier behind Luka began to lift himself off the ground, clutching at his shattered nose. Sensing movement, Luka spun and struck like a viper, finishing the kill.

Only one soldier stood against him now, his blade visibly trembling in the dark hallway. For a heartbeat, the soldier hesitated before turning to run. Luka threw his sword at him like a disc. It spun horizontally and clanked against the back of the soldier's armored legs. He fell face forward, sprawled at the end of the hallway.

In only seconds, Luka was upon him with his sword back in hand. They locked eyes for a moment, the soldier's terror gazing back at him through the slits in his helmet. No thoughts of mercy entered his mind—he finished his work.

Luka spared a glance at the carnage behind him. Six men who had stood in his way only moments ago were now scattered across the floor. They had the misfortune of standing in the way of one of the deadliest swordsmen in Estravia. It had been deserved, and it had been satisfying, but the hunger to kill only grew inside him. Only the lifeless eyes of Privus rolling back in his skull would satiate that.

He proceeded through the hallway and headed down another flight of stairs, which led out to the main courtyard. Several distant voices and the clanking of armor rang out from the other end, causing Luka to take cover behind a stone column. Peering around, he saw a man in black and silver armor flanked by a dozen guards. His stomach twisted inside.

The man dismissed his guards and headed in Luka's direction. As Luka watched, a silver Mithacor emblazoned on the chest plate and a golden staff came into view.

Luka had found his target. The source of all of his pain. The creator of his never-ending nightmares. He pictured the smirk on his face only moments before he had blasted Luka into a burning building—and only moments after he had taken his father and brother from him.

He had overcome a coma, ridden alone on a treacherous quest, and taken many, many risks to get to this point. His blood boiled inside of him as he drew his sword and gripped it like an iron vise. This was it.

"PRIVUS!" He sprinted toward his nemesis at full speed, not even slowing down as Privus unlatched his staff and aimed it at him.

A massive emission of flames burst out towards him. The fire spread wide—Luka could only avoid it by dropping down. He somersaulted forward, sparing him from a fatal burn. The fire licked the back of his armor, leaving it charred, but that was the extent of the damage. He emerged from underneath and continued his forward momentum.

"You should have stayed in the ashes of Vernikport with your pathetic family's corpses," Privus mocked as Luka continued towards him. The youngest Zlikrej brother then waved his staff in the direction of the ground. The earth trembled beneath, splitting into a jagged chasm in the middle of the courtyard.

Luka could not stop his pace. His foot fell through the crack, sending his whole body tumbling forward. He braced himself with his arms, but his chin struck the ground, jarring his head. Pain flashed through him as his sword slipped from his grip.

Privus loomed over him, kicking the blade aside. Aware of the glowing staff only inches from his head, Luka lurched forward. He wrapped his arms around Privus's calves at the same moment a tendril of flames shot from the staff.

The fire connected with the back of Luka's pauldrons for a mere second, but long enough to make his armor feel like it was screaming against his flesh. He cried out in agony as he tangled with Privus on the ground.

They wrestled for a moment on the courtyard floor before Privus shoved Luka off of him. The youngest Zlikrej brother stood up and kicked Luka three times in the helmet. Luka rolled away to avoid more attacks, sparkling stars and sharp ringing filling his head.

Before Luka could rise from the ground or retrieve his sword, a flood of water engulfed him and swept him up. The water hit him like a charging bull and then swelled all around him. Privus had unleashed gallons of liquid from his staff, capturing Luka inside and wheeling him around like a puppet. He swirled Luka all around the courtyard, making him dizzy and short on air, as his head bobbed in and out of water.

With a hitch of the staff, the surge of water jarred to a halt and froze solid—Luka caught inside.

In the center of the courtyard, Privus had created a haphazard and chaotic ice sculpture, with sharp ends that shot out in all directions. Within that frozen formation, Luka hung upside down, a few feet above the ground. Most of his body lay entrenched firmly within the glacial structure. He was dizzy, and only his head, left arm, and one of his legs were free from the cold ice.

As Privus walked slowly and triumphantly towards him, Luka exhaled a breath of steam from between the slits of his helmet. He was trapped and powerless in a frost-bound prison. *Is this it? Am I finished?* he wondered, a sense of dread pulsing through his inverted body.

The youngest Zlikrej brother took a moment to stand with his arms at his hips and a gloating smile stretching across his face. "This ended rather quickly for you, did it not?"

Privus drew nearer and put his hands on Luka's helmet. "I want to look upon you before I kill you. This time, I'm going to make sure you are really dead." He did not notice Luka's free left hand, which was fiddling with something at his waist.

The helmet jerked uncomfortably on his scalp before Privus wrenched it free. He tossed it aside, the helmet clanging as it rolled across the courtyard.

Luka's face became exposed to Privus. When they had last met, he appeared far younger, with a slightly boyish, clean-shaven face and short blonde hair. The man that glared back at Privus now had a messy beard and unkempt hair, which was hanging upside down. The boyishness was gone, aged away by corrosive pain and rage.

"It really is you," Privus said, almost to himself, pointing his staff at Luka once again. "You never did get to be a king, did you? Not really, anyway. I did you a favor by killing your father and brother, letting the crown fall into your lap. But then, all you did was come here to die? Pathetic. I will make certain you are remembered as 'Luka the Fool.'"

Luka stared at the glowing head of Privus's staff, bracing for the final taste of fire that awaited him next.

Chapter 44
Battle at the Mountain's Gate

Instead of the organized rush of thousands of soldiers pushing into Exeter, Reishi saw only chaos. The majority of the Vernik forces formed a mass outside the city, stymied by the gates that remained shut. Arrows rained down a few dozen at a time from the walls above. A few frightened Vernik soldiers scattered away.

Panic rose up in Reishi and sat hot in his chest. *Luka failed to get the gate open,* he realized. *My plan was foolish. We did not send enough arms inside to open the lever. Luka rushed in like a mad idiot, and I got him killed.* Reishi picked up his pace now, drawing closer to the army. Then he realized something else. He had given Luka more than enough support in the form of magic orbs. There was no way that he would have been outmatched by the defenses at the hut, equipped with such a powerful advantage. That could only mean one thing.

You reckless bastard, Reishi thought. *You never went to the lever—you went straight for Privus.*

His thoughts were nearly drowned by the sounds of screaming and confusion amongst the soldiers. A corpse nearly tripped him. He looked down, wide-eyed at the dead young man and then up again, as black streaks continued to come down. Instinctively, he threw his hands up in defense, knowing full well it would do no good.

He tried to calm himself, inhaling deeply and reaching out with his mind. He was able to locate General Warwick easily. "Where is that damned wizard!" he was screaming over and over, frantically looking for him. Reishi headed in that direction, squeezing through soldiers and fearing death from above.

"General!" Reishi called out, when he knew his voice would be audible. They met deep in the crowd, anxious soldiers tight around them.

"Wizard! What in Sila's wrath is going on? The gate is supposed to be bloody open! We are completely exposed out here! This is a failure, and I blame you!"

"I don't think Luka followed the plan, General," Reishi shouted back. His response was followed by a pained neigh and dozens of human shrieks. A large warhorse collapsed only meters away.

"I believe that he went straight for Privus. Those soldiers were not able to get the gate open by themselves."

"So, Luka is in that damned city all by himself?"

"Yes, General, but I think I can get that gate open. I just need a few moments alone."

"How can I trust you? At this point, I am more of a mind to retreat. Our army may be large, but it can't withstand this forever."

"I give you my word, Rory," Reishi said. Brushing against the general's mind, he instilled feelings of ease and trust and quickly retreated.

"Very well, Wizard," Warwick said, absent of his earlier resistance. "You have five minutes."

Reishi dashed away, through the crowd, holding his hands above his head for protection. Brushing against the general's mind had left him feeling slightly uneasy. It was a complex place, full of intelligence—but full of pain—much like Reishi himself.

The general's mind was of relatively little concern right now. Much more to Reishi's detriment was the time he spent inside Vatren's mind and some of the Zlikrej soldiers. The results of that weighed heavily on him. It would take a great deal of effort to separate their sick memories from his own. Or he could drown the memories altogether in a bottle of rum—that was his usual method.

Minutes later, Reishi arrived at a spot removed from the conflict but still close enough to be effective. He sat down, his back against the stone Exeter wall. When he was able to find focus, he cast his mind outward into the city. He became aware of the first line of Zlikrej defenses standing near the entrance, eliminating futile battering ram efforts against the great iron gate. He advanced beyond them with his thoughts.

From the information he had gathered, Reishi created an internal map of minds, which he compared to his understanding of the city's layout. If he was fortunate, he could use this to locate the gate switch. He continued to search until he overheard a promising thought pattern.

Reishi plunged into the mind of a young soldier named Huric, who was marching towards Exeter Palace. He silently eavesdropped on the soldier who was in the midst of a conversation with a comrade as they walked.

"What do you think Privus is going to do when we tell him about the two men who snuck into the city and tried to pull the switch?" said Huric.

"He will not be pleased, especially with everything else going on. I am fortunate I am not going to inform him alone," was the reply.

Reishi scoured his captive's recent memories, playing back the experiences he had in the last five, then ten, and then finally twenty minutes. This was where the memory lay. Through the eyes of Huric, Reishi could see Officer Gerard's body, laying on the ground next to the lever, silent and still.

"I, uh, I just realized that I need to turn around and get something," Huric said to his comrade. "I'll be back before you know it." With the unknown influence of Reishi, Huric was off before the other soldier could react.

Seven soldiers now guarded the little stone hut. None of them knew why Huric was headed in their direction, and frankly, neither did Huric. All Huric knew—thanks to Reishi's false memory implant—was that he had forgotten something. He just wasn't sure what that was yet.

"Officer Huric, what are you doing here? You were supposed to go inform Lord Privus of the break-in attempt," said one of the guards.

"Oh, I, um, I just left something in there when I was here earlier. I, um, it was because I was helping apprehend that, um, prune," Huric said to the guard. He still had no idea why he would say something so absurd, and he still could not remember what he had lost in that hut.

"Orders are that no one is allowed in there. Not even us," said another one of the sentries.

Reishi adjusted, briefly letting go of Huric's mind, aiming to latch onto one of the other soldiers. As Reishi withdrew, he was brought back to his own mind, ambushed immediately by chilling memories from Vatren and some of the soldiers from today. It brought an unwelcome and unexpected wave of anxiety over him, stifling him and making him feel dizzy and dazed.

Time was not his ally in this endeavor. Thoughts of archers atop the Exeter walls culling young Vernik soldiers in bunches only added to the pressure. His heart pounded rapidly against the inside of his chest. In the panic, Reishi lost all sense of where Huric and the hut were. His mind became disconnected. The powers of a mind wizard were only as strong as his ability to concentrate.

In the perturbation, Reishi tried to reconnect to the mind he had just left, only for his thoughts to be impeded again and again. Lightning seemed to run rampant through Reishi's bloodstream, causing his hands to tremble. The weight of ten thousand lives seemed to bear down on him—the heaviest life of all being Luka's.

Reishi withdrew completely now. The anxiety was a raging ocean of a storm inside of him. The waves crashed around him, making him feel like he was drowning in the panic.

He took a deep breath, trying to quiet himself. He had been out of practice, but he still knew how to control his own mind. He reflected on a distant memory, something he had come back to many times.

"Fear is for us to overcome, Reishi," his mother said to him, comforting him from a nightmare. "We couldn't be brave without it."

His left eye became wet. Reishi wiped at it and sighed. Then he reached back out with his mind, the ocean still raging inside of him—only now he could navigate against its violent waves.

He regained Huric's location, who was now being verbally berated by the sentries. The young soldier had no answers to their questions. Reishi chuckled to himself and slipped right back inside.

With control of Huric again, he was quickly able to shift around, latching on to the mind of one of the sentries. He cautiously induced him to say, "I've bloody changed my mind. Huric, you can go in for just a moment. No one will mind. Especially since he helped apprehend that prune trying to open the gate earlier!"

Before anyone else could object, the guard hurriedly ushered Huric inside the hut. Huric walked in on his own accord, keen to put this nagging question at ease in his mind. When he entered the hut, he was all alone, and there were no objects to be seen, other than the large black lever. In Huric's moment of confusion, Reishi seized control again.

Inside Huric's body, Reishi walked over to the lever and pulled down on it with all the soldier's strength. It made an unfortunate, loud cranking sound that immediately drew the attention of all seven guardsmen. *Dammit,* Reishi thought. Fear rose up within again, but he remained undeterred.

Reishi turned to an old trick that he had not used in a long time. If he failed at this, then the gate would close again, and all would be lost. He dared not shift his focus to anything else.

He dispatched himself from Huric's mind once again and latched onto the first guard who had entered the hut. He quickly tried to shut the man's conscious mind down and send him into a temporary coma. Without knowing how or why, the soldier's vision began to fade, and he kept feeling the need to pass out.

As the first soldier drew nearer to the lever, Reishi's effort succeeded. The soldier collapsed for no apparent reason. The technique worked very well against those untrained against mind magic.

Reishi moved on to the next soldier and repeated the same maneuver, and then the same to the next one. Each time, it came easier to him. Soon, Huric was standing next to the lever with a full minute of no memories and a batch of unconscious soldiers who had just dropped down right before his eyes.

Reishi took control of Huric one final time, taking the young soldier's sword and jamming it into the lever. He tested the lever and tried to pull the blade back out, but it was clear that it was completely jammed. It would take a great deal of time and skill to repair the switch now.

You're a good lad, Reishi said to Huric, when he was satisfied.

What? What in Sila's wrath is that? Who are you? Huric asked the strange alien voice that had spoken to him inside his mind. Reishi's only reply was to shut the door on him, rendering him unconscious.

*****

"Stand your ground, men!" Warwick commanded. His brave lieutenants and officers repeated the order. "The gate will be open any minute!"

General Warwick decided the next time he spoke to his men, it would be to retreat, even with the assurances from Reishi. Arrows from above continued to strike more and more of them. Those fortunate huddled underneath shields. Many were not so lucky. Warwick estimated that he had lost several hundred already. Even an army of ten thousand could not withstand this for much longer.

A black streak flew right by Warwick's head, finding a landing place on the shoulder of Lieutenant Alexander, who stood next to him. The lieutenant pulled the arrow out of his armor and rubbed his shoulder. "I'm alright, General!" he called out.

This is lunacy, Warwick thought. *It was lunacy from the start. Luka is too young and naive, and neither of us should have trusted this strange Reishi and his ridiculous plan.*

Warwick shook his head and opened his mouth, ready to make the order. As he did so, a loud, metallic noise rang out through the air. Thousands of heads turned in unison to see the large black iron gate rise slowly. On the other side of the gate, Warwick thought he could see fear and shock in the eyes of the thickly armored Zlikrej guards.

Warwick did not hesitate.

"Charge!' He cried out. His men rushed forward in a fervor.

"For King Luka!" soldiers cheered in unison as they advanced.

Warwick watched as the first wave of men swallowed up a line of Zlikrej sentries below the gates. The mass of Vernik soldiers ahead prevented him from taking a position at the front of the offensive. Instead, he shouted orders from the middle of the pack, making sure his swarms were advancing on their target with haste.

The sudden onslaught of the Vernik Army slowed quickly—the gate serving as a filter. Though it was still quite wide, there was simply not enough room for all the men to storm in at once. A bottleneck of soldiers formed instantly, just inside the city gates.

The Battle of Exeter would be largely fought right at the city's entrance. Packs of Zlikrej infantrymen rushed to meet the intruders with spears and swords. The Vernik Army's forward momentum reached a glaring halt. Hundreds of men on the periphery clamored to get into the battle, held up by their fellow soldiers.

Even if General Warwick wanted to, there was no way he could get through the gates. It seemed that not even a tenth of his troops had made it through at this point. Warwick barked words of encouragement at his men to keep pushing through, but mostly it seemed as if they were just pushing each other.

An alien tap on Warwick's shoulder caught him off guard. He swung around, sword drawn, but relaxed when he saw who it was.

"Well done, Wizard!" he commended. "I was wrong about you! You have done as you promised. Now it is time for me to do my job and get my men through these gates."

"There is another opening to the city, General," Reishi said. "As you know, I lent Luka some magical items that helped create a hole in the city wall. It's likely not big. Perhaps one or two men will be able to get through at one time, but it could make a difference."

Warwick fell silent and pondered the possibility. After a moment, he said, "That is what we will do then. Lieutenant Alexander!"

The lieutenant quickly responded to the summons. "Alexander, you are now in charge of the main offensive. It is your responsibility to ensure that as many of our men as possible are able to push through. The wizard and I will lead a flank through an alternate entrance into the city. We will try to relieve the bottleneck as much as possible."

"Another entrance, sir?" Alexander asked.

"No time to explain, Lieutenant. You will have to trust my orders."

Alexander did not protest further. "Yes, sir. We will press on."

Warwick nodded, content. He left his lieutenant with the enormous responsibility of leading thousands of men into the heart of the battle. Warwick departed with Reishi and gathered several dozen infantry men. As they moved out of the mass, Warwick could hear Alexander shout, "For King Luka!"

It took longer than comfortable—time spent away from the nexus of the battle—but they finally came upon the opening in the wall. They were not alone. Looking through the other side of the opening were a handful of Zlikrej men who were investigating the anomaly.

One of the Zlikrej guards emerged from the hole and immediately charged the group. General Warwick met the man head-on. With eagerness, Warwick showed off his swordsmanship and skill, which were impressive for someone of his age. The general defeated his opponent quickly, with several elegant and advanced sword techniques. Several more Zlikrej men emerged immediately after, headed directly for General Warwick.

Miraculously, they dropped before him, one after another.

Warwick turned around and glanced at Reishi.

"Did you do that?" General Warwick asked.

"The power of the wind is quite a wonder," Reishi responded. There were no further questions, and the unit stepped through the breach.

Chapter 45
Vengeance's Burn

From his inverted perspective, Luka's eyes locked with Privus's. Victory gleamed on his face as the staff glowed an ominous red. His mouth stretched into its usual smug smile, oblivious to Luka's fiddling at his side with his pouch of orbs. Luka's fingers closed around one, praying it was a fire orb and praying that it would work in time.

A hiss of steam emitted from the ice, and he knew that his prayer had been answered. The ice melted just enough for Luka to fall free, just as a fireball seared the air where his head had been moments before. A second later, and he would have been incinerated.

Liberated from his frozen prison, Luka rose and hurled his last remaining wind orb at a stunned Privus. The orb struck the Mithacor emblem squarely on Privus's chest plate, sending him hurtling backward across the courtyard. His staff slipped from his grip midair, clattering to the ground as Privus landed with a splash in the water now pooling from the melted ice.

Luka retrieved his sword, his left hand fingers tightening around the hilt as he pulled another orb from his pouch. *I wish I had done this earlier,* he thought.

Privus lifted himself from the puddle, his gaze darting to where his staff now lay—a spot much closer to Luka than to its master. An angry curse escaped his lips.

"So, you have magic of your own now?" Privus said. "You found an elemental wizard foolish enough to join you, I see."

Luka nodded. "Your monopoly on magic has ended, Privus. We both know that you're nothing without it."

Privus bound for the staff instead of retorting further—only to be intercepted by another red orb. When it landed, flames bloomed like a bright orange flower, the explosion knocking him backwards. He thrashed back in the puddle where he landed, frantically trying to extinguish the fire racing up his legs.

Unhurried, Luka strode over to the staff and picked it up, holding the lieutenant's blade in his other hand. Across the courtyard, Privus clawed his way to his feet, finally free of the blaze.

"I don't need magic to kill you," Privus spat. "You'll taste my blade just like your father did." He drew his sword, the blade emerging from its scabbard in a silver arc, its sharp edge hissing as it sliced through the air.

Then he charged.

Luka aimed the staff at his oncoming enemy, hoping to summon a hellish flame that would reduce him to ash. His effort yielded nothing other than allowing Privus to close the distance between them. As soon as he reached him, he was met by a storm of strikes.

After a day of cutting down lesser soldiers all throughout Exeter, Luka was reminded quickly of what a fellow expert swordsman could do.

For several brutal exchanges, Luka held on to both the staff and sword, parrying against metal flashes in his vision. When he gained his footing, now acquainted with the rhythm of his opponent, he changed the tide. He blocked several blows with his sword, able to deliver a successive smack with the rod several times in a row. Each time he connected, he relished the thud of metal on bone. His adversary grew angrier but continued to press the assault forward.

Unexpectedly, the beat of Privus's offensive shifted, and he brought his sword down from high above his shoulder. Luka deflected with the staff, but the sheer force of the blow wrenched it from his grasp, sending it splashing into the puddles below.

Privus lunged again, his hacks harder and stronger. Several of Luka's parries arrived late—unable to prevent two slashes—the first to his right side and the other to his left, cutting through a lighter layer of armor.

Luka hissed through his teeth, retreating a step as blood seeped from the wound.

The enemy did not relent. His opponent fought with a hate that Luka thought he alone possessed. With his surge of vitriolic passion, Privus had taken the upper hand. Luka had survived multiple magical attacks from his staff but now was retreating under the ferocity of Privus's swordsmanship. One misstep and it would be over. The balance of the duel needed to shift back to his side quickly.

Privus slashed again. Luka ducked underneath, the blade slicing through the air just inches above him, close enough to brush his hair. He rose out of the ducking motion and rammed his armored shoulder into Privus's chest. Without hesitation, He followed the blow with an elbow straight to his jaw. Red blood and a white tooth both sprayed from Privus's mouth.

Luka pressed the attack. Privus's blocks began to falter, growing weaker with each clash of steel. He retreated a full step with each parry, Luka's will propelling them both across the courtyard.

Steel rained heavy from Luka's hand, each blow landing with the weight of a mountain behind it. Finally, a powerful downward slash knocked Privus's sword from his grip. He capitalized instantly, slashing at Privus's chest and sending him sprawling to the ground once again.

A hungry exhilaration came over Luka. This was it. He had disarmed and downed his enemy. Now it was time to destroy him.

Vengeful anticipation filled him as he raised his sword for the killing blow. But his strike met only the ground, the jarring impact ringing through the bones in his arm.

Privus had rolled away, narrowly evading the blow. He continued to tumble away from Luka, eventually springing up and sprinting towards his staff. Luka turned to follow, but the distance was already too wide.

Stopping in his tracks, he watched as Privus reclaimed his staff. He quickly turned and unleashed a torrent of wicked blue flame in Luka's direction. The bright blue fire devoured the entire courtyard, capturing Luka in its wide jaw of inferno.

These flames burned far hotter than the yellow and orange flames that had acquainted themselves with Luka already. His skin seared with the feeling of a million stings. His armor became so hot that it felt like it was melting into him. His blade became too hot to grip.

Luka fell to the ground, trying to dodge what flames he could and trying to use the wet puddles on the ground for relief. The dark blue inferno continued to feast on him and the ground around him.

With great struggle, Luka was able to crawl far enough away. He staggered to his feet and stumbled out of the courtyard, wisps of blue flames still clinging to his armor. Most of his beard and much of his hair burned away, filling the air with a horrid smell. His face was singed with black burns. The pain was so strong he could barely think.

Luka's only advantage was that the wide blast would have restricted Privus's vision, giving him the ability to escape. It would only be a few seconds, but those moments were invaluable. He took off down the hallway, leaving behind a melted sword.

Far down the corridor, Luka tried to undo the armor that seared white hot against his flesh. He forced himself to keep moving, knowing that to stop meant certain death. Nothing was more uninviting than more of that blue fire.

After an agonizing effort, he managed to unfasten his bracers, followed by his chest guard, and most of the rest of his armor. The pieces he left behind him were charred almost completely black.

As he rounded a corner, he turned to find three Zlikrej officers rushing in his direction. He no longer possessed a sword, but he dared not turn around.

He took stock of his limited options. He still had Xander's dagger and two orbs remaining. Luka quickly retrieved his last red fire orb and tossed it right at the soldiers. The fire wrapped them in a burning cocoon that they would not escape.

Luka snatched a sword from one of the burning men, ignoring the fresh waves of agony from his own burns that plagued him as he advanced past. He fought the urge to faint with every step, but pressed on, knowing that Privus was close behind and would soon come upon his burning soldiers.

At the end of the next corridor, Luka found a door that opened up to a stone staircase leading both up and down. No matter which direction he chose, he would have half a chance of throwing Privus off his trail.

He only considered it for a moment. As he reflected, images rushed back to him. Privus's sword piercing his father's throat. Xander crushed beneath the hammer. Serena's rejection.

The hot rage inside overtook the sensation of the burns on the outside. Hiding, despite all of the rational reasons to do it, was not a possibility.

Luka turned around.

Back through the same hallways, he retraced his steps. He ran as fast as he could through the infernal pain. With each step he took, every fiber in his skin howled in agony, but he used the sensation only to spur him onward.

At the turn of the next corner, Privus became visible once again, surprise on his face. Luka ran faster.

He threw his final orb, a small glass ball that hit Privus in the shoulder. Bucketfuls of water exploded out, knocking Privus down, soaking his body, and most importantly—sending his staff to the ground before he could activate it.

Luka pounced. His boots, the only armor he still wore, splashed through the puddles he had just created. He raised his commandeered sword high in the air as he charged.

Privus was only able to rise to his knees, blocking from below. Luka's attacks were mighty and violent. With a craze, he struck down again and again. Each connection of steel loosened his enemy's already feeble grip. Eventually, the sword fell aside, leaving Privus exposed.

With Privus splayed on his back, defenseless and powerless, Luka readied himself to deliver the final blow. He coiled back with savage hunger and brought his sword down again.

The blade clanked against the stone ground, missing its target. Privus had managed to roll to his side, escaping death yet another time. A frustrated scream burst from Luka's throat.

Privus rolled the other way now as the blade swung back down, narrowly missing his skull. This time, the stone floor chipped off a large piece of the blade.

After the miss, Privus kicked Luka in the shin, the feeling of the steel boot finding bone making Luka wince. As Luka recoiled, Privus was able to use the opening to regain his sword and scramble back to his feet.

The king and archlord glared at each other for a moment, only a few meters separating them. They held their swords firmly, neither breaking their gaze nor making any movements. They panted like dogs but did not speak.

"This is for my father and brother," Luka said calmly, when he had caught his breath. He pointed to his adversary with the cracked tip of his sword.

"Send my regards when you see them," Privus replied, smiling devilishly. "I think they miss me."

Just then, Privus glanced sideways at his staff, hiding in the peripherals of his vision, not far from his reach. But by diverting his gaze sideways, he had broken his focus, even if only for a second. That was all the time that Luka needed.

Summoning a renewed hate and intensity, Luka brought down his most devastating onslaught yet. His blade flashed through the air like a lightning storm that Privus would scarcely be able to see. Quickly, the attacks started to outpace Privus's reflexes, many blows landing. Each time Luka gashed him, his strength increased and his opponent's waned.

After several wounding blows, Luka slashed again, striking Privus on the ear and cutting it half off.

The youngest Zlikrej brother fell back, a fountain of blood spitting out from the lesion and an inhuman shriek bellowing from his throat. He lay on his back, exposed in the puddle in the hallway.

Luka reversed the grip on his sword and drove it downward at his enemy's face. Privus threw both his hands up in desperation. The blade cleaved through flesh and bone in both arms, causing his adversary to cry out again. Despite the pain, his arms had caught the blade, preventing it from cutting down through his head.

The tip of the weapon was only millimeters from Privus's face, blood dripping down into his eyes. Luka pushed down harder, generating another ghastly shriek. Less than a hair's breadth separated the point from its ultimate target.

Seeming to summon a doomed morsel of strength, Privus shifted his arms abruptly to his right side, forcing the sword out of Luka's hands. Then, once again, Privus kicked Luka in the shins three times, forcing Luka to the ground.

Before Privus could capitalize any further, Luka pounced on top of him, seizing his throat. He tightened his grip, trying to squeeze his neck with all his might. With his hands stuck together by Luka's sword, Privus could do little.

In a desperate ploy, Privus tried to fumble to get better positioning, gradually inching the sword out by pressing it against his body. Luka noticed immediately and let go of Privus's neck with his left hand and drew Xander's dagger.

He jammed the dagger down into Privus's elbow, paralyzing that limb and extinguishing any final chance of escape. He quickly put his left hand back where it belonged. Two blades were now lodged in Privus's arms, and two hands were wrapped around his throat.

Luka looked down now at his enemy, beaten and entrapped. His eyes still displayed defiance, in spite of how Luka had broken him. In spite of the fact that he was on death's edge.

"You think that you are worthy of some conjured-up title," Luka began. "You think you deserve to rule, but you come from a worthless family line. My father should have killed you and your brothers when you were children. Instead, I will be the one to finish his work."

His fingers tightened around his enemy's neck like prey under a predator's jaw. Privus had no air to summon a response.

"I am your reckoning. But I won't be finished after you. I promise that I will do the same to your brothers. I will kill them and make them suffer. You all made a mistake. You should never have trifled with my family, and you should never have left me alive. Your schemes will come to an end at my hand.

"Not you, not Drugi, and not Omarius. None of you will *ever* be archlords, or kings, or anything of consequence. Your only fate is death at my hand. *I* am the King."

The color on Privus's face turned closer and closer to purple. He tried to flinch and wrestle away, but he could do little other than squirm.

On top of his great enemy, Luka relished the sight of life fleeing from Privus's eyes. The corridor and the world around him faded away, time standing in abeyance. His hands seemed more a part of Privus's neck than his own body. A dark and deep power took hold, giving him something very different from happiness, but something very like a sweet satisfaction. He had never felt a sensation more powerful.

At last, Privus's eyes rolled back in his head, and the body fell limp.

Privus was dead.

For good measure, Luka held on tighter for a few moments. It did nothing—his hands were around a soulless corpse, but he had to be sure.

When he was finally finished, Luka released and stood. The world around him came back into view.

Even though he was not the one who had just been strangled, Luka found he still needed to catch his breath. His heart was pounding stronger and faster than it ever had. That was, of course, preferable than Privus's disposition—his heart would never beat again.

For a moment, Luka looked down upon his dead foe. Part of him wished he could revive him and kill him again. But Luka cast this aside, allowing himself to be satisfied with his work.

Nearly three months ago, he had sworn an oath, overlooking the ashes of Vernikport. He vowed not to rest until all of his transgressors were dead. Though the "X" he cut on his hand had faded away, the vow remained as stark as lightning against a dark sky. Already, he had fulfilled a large part of that oath. He had ridden north on Vulture Road, mostly alone, and defeated a seemingly insurmountable enemy. He had collected his debt from Privus.

Privus and his brothers may have killed Luka's father and brother and destroyed his city, but Luka had just proven that Privus could not do that and live to tell the tale. One was dead. Two remained.

He wrenched Xander's dagger from Privus's elbow, wiped it clean, and then hobbled over to retrieve the staff.

It was a weapon of tragedy. Luka would need to ensure that no one ever used it again. Thanks to him there was at least one less person who could use it. That was enough. For now.

Chapter 46
Corpses and Casualties

The stench of blood permeated the air. The bottleneck held firmly just inside the gate, and corpses on both sides were piling up. When they arrived at the scene from inside the city, Reishi, General Warwick, and his men had never seen so many bodies, dead and alive, packed into such a tight area.

The battle had now been going on for over an hour, with the Vernik Army seemingly pushing only inches of ground into the city.

"We should flank from the side streets," General Warwick said. "We would just be adding to the crowd if we continued forward."

A few streets farther in, they reached a suitable point on the edge of the battle. On Warwick's command, his half dozen crossbowmen began shooting into the crowd of unsuspecting soldiers that were focused on the conflict in front of them.

The crossbowmen fired a few volleys into the crowd before they were noticed. The enemy then turned and rushed at them, quickly becoming a deluge of foes. A few of Warwick's swordsmen stepped forward to meet the approaching enemies. They would have been overtaken instantly, but Reishi intervened.

He held out his hands, once again pretending to summon the powers of the wind. Everyone could see his dramatic pose, but none saw how he put a chain of Zlikrej enemies to sleep, their bodies tumbling down one after another.

"How about some fire magic?" General Warwick yelled out from the middle of the combat.

"Too dangerous in these tight quarters, General," Reishi yelled back. The explanation seemed satisfactory.

Dozens of Zlikrej foes continued to rush forward. In rhythm, Reishi was able to incapacitate the vast majority of them. The soldiers that followed had to hurdle the unconscious bodies of their comrades as they advanced.

A few enemies broke through the ranks—General Warwick stepping forward to dispatch them. Reishi's magic was effective, but his mind did not work fast enough to take down everyone. They continued to press forward, the opposition falling in waves.

After defeating several scores of Zlikrej forces, their efforts were beginning to have a noticeable impact on the tide of the battle. The enemy began to give up ground as more and more soldiers pushed through the gates, and more and more men were thinned out by Reishi and Warwick's flank. Soldiers from both armies dropped dead at the front of the pack, but now the empty spaces their deaths created were filled with Vernik forces, who pushed the front line further into the city.

The battle at the gates had finally reached a breaking point. Warwick and Reishi, with a clear path forward, pushed ahead toward the center of the city.

*****

Luka glanced down once more at Privus's corpse. It lay still, save for the blood that oozed from the wounds.

The hole inside him remained a hollow ache, even in victory. He could never get his father and brother back. But he could at least take from those who wronged him.

The air was filled with deep commotion from the conflict that was now clearly within the confines of Exeter. Luka was grateful the army was able to get into the city. He had kept all thoughts of the battle outside in complete abeyance as he fought for his vengeance against Privus. Now he had nothing left to give to that conflict.

A few beads of sweat ran down Luka's forehead and hung right over his left eye. When he raised his forearm to wipe the sweat away, he was reminded of the burns across his body. His skin seemed to tighten on him in an agonizing bind. He had no more motivation to fight through that pain. He gave in and let the beads of sweat sting as they crept into his eyes.

The sound of metal boots running on stone suddenly alerted Luka. The noise was close at hand and approaching quickly. He staggered in pain past Privus's body and turned a corner, back to the hallway that ran adjacent to the courtyard.

The sounds of the soldiers' footsteps drew nearer. Luka tried to take cover behind a wall, but it was too late. A squadron with dozens of Zlikrej soldiers emerged and noticed him.

They charged immediately. Luka held up Privus's staff as the men approached. He knew he would not be able to make the staff work, but he hoped his adversaries would be fooled. Bluffing was the only hope he had.

The men did not fall for Luka's ruse, advancing undeterred. Luka abandoned the staff and held his sword in a battle-ready position with both hands. With almost no energy and no armor, Luka gritted his teeth and prepared for one final act of combat.

*****

The first enemies were finally beginning to drop their weapons in surrender. General Warwick pushed forward to the palace with some of his best men at his side. He strode past Zlikrej soldiers who had thrown their hands up or were going to their knees.

Reishi lagged behind, his pace slowed from the injuries he had sustained in his duel against Vatren. Conversely, the general had made it this far in the conflict practically unscathed.

He watched as Warwick and his men cut down a few desperate holdouts who refused to surrender and pushed forward. Soon after, General Warwick disappeared beyond the tight sprawl of buildings and into the palatial square. Reishi came upon it himself moments later.

The once pristine center point of the city was now covered in bodies, laying at the feet of the statue of Lord Saddiq, as if the legendary lord had slayed them all himself. One man, laying deformed in a haphazard, broken way, caught Reishi's eye. The man's limbs had been crushed under some unknown force.

Well done, Luka, Reishi thought. *You used the wind orb to perfection.*

Ahead of him, Zlikrej men were beginning to line up at the command of Vernik soldiers. Their battles had begun mere months ago when they had been promised the opportunity to take part in a historic military endeavor. Now that was coming to a swift end.

Reishi picked up his pace with a wounded jog across the square. Warwick stayed ahead of him and entered the palace. Dozens of men followed him.

*****

The enemies drew closer to Luka, their weapons drawn and pointed. *This is the end,* Luka thought with resignation. He knew he would not be able to survive, but he was sure he could at least take a few of the bastards down with him.

When the men were several strides away, crossbow bolts rained down on them, seemingly out of nowhere. The soldiers' advance stopped, and they turned around to find a swarm of Vernik soldiers surrounding them. The small Vernik force quickly engulfed the threat, leaving dozens more corpses and saving Luka.

Luka lowered his blade and sighed deeply, the tension in his body releasing. He shook his head in welcome disbelief, savoring the unlikely stroke of good fortune.

A moment later, he looked up to see the familiar face of General Warwick breaking through the crowd. Despite the toll of the last few hours, Luka managed a smile as the general strode over to meet him.

"Luka!" The general extended his arms for an embrace. Luka coiled up and refused the gesture. He briefly explained his burn marks and said that a hug would hurt more than perhaps anything else Sila could conjure.

Warwick nodded in understanding—and perhaps in admiration. "We will get you the best healer in the city as soon as we can. You will be able to rest from this great conquest."

"Thank you. I shall certainly need that." Even speaking those words made Luka wince.

Changing the subject, Warwick asked, "Where is Privus?" Luka gestured behind him and stepped aside.

Warwick peered around so he could see the corpse. His eyes lingered on the dead Zlikrej brother's lifeless form. He exhaled deeply, swelling with relief. "It is done," he said quietly, almost to himself. Then his voice rose in excitement. "We have won! Exeter is ours!"

*****

Serena had seen much of the fighting from her window. Down in the courtyard below, she witnessed Luka survive the wicked blue flame of Privus's staff. She saw Privus disappear down the hallway to pursue him. A squadron of Zlikrej men passed through much later, followed quickly by the members of the Vernik Army. Finally, she saw Luka reemerge, standing next to General Warwick, a look of sullen victory on his face.

Privus never emerged. Her husband was surely dead.

She was free of him now. She felt as though a tight binding around her body had been released. But the absence of the restraints left a lonely ghost of a feeling. She would never be able to see her own husband ever again, whether that was for good or for bad.

She remembered Luka's words: *Run away... as far as you can...* She burst into tears and fell to her knees. Her mind seesawed frantically. Had she done the wrong thing by asking Luka to spare Privus? Was Luka unreasonable to her? Could she go back to him and ask for forgiveness? Was it worth it? The only thing she knew was that none of this was fair.

Unfortunately, she didn't have time to wallow in that today. She had to do something.

Run away... as far as you can... the words echoed again. Indeed, running seemed to be the only option she had. She took only her book, a small knife, and all the Novaks she could find in the room and put on modest, comfortable clothes.

She raced through the palace, her hurried footsteps echoing off the marble halls. She avoided the gazes of the frightened and confused servants with whom she had become so close with over the last few weeks. She stopped for nothing. Escape was her only priority.

Outside the palace, no one questioned her as she sprinted towards the city's exit. Mercifully, the gates were open when she got there. Hundreds of Vernik soldiers celebrated their victory, exchanging merry words near the gate. Many seemed to notice her as she ran through, but no one stopped her, even as she climbed over scores of corpses to reach the exit.

Finally, she was outside the city, no longer trapped by monstrous stone boundaries. The city below the mountains was now in the distance, along with her memories that it contained.

She didn't know if she had made the right decisions, but she knew she now had one thing she had wanted for so long—freedom.

Chapter 47
Battle Scars

Violent squawking marked the next dawn. When Luka pulled back the curtains in his palace bedroom, he witnessed black clouds of vultures and scatterings of crows hovering in the low sky. Dozens more grunted as they feasted excitedly on corpses in Saddiq Square.

Sharp aches and burns began flaring across his body not long after he stirred. Groggily, Luka limped back into bed. He tossed and turned, unable to get comfortable until mercifully the pain surrendered to his exhaustion—casting him into the abyss of sleep.

His dreams carried him to the ghost shores of Vernikport. Var and Xander were at his side. Gentle tides from the ocean licked against the sand near their feet.

His father and brother each placed an arm on Luka's shoulders. They stared at the black silhouettes of two ships sailing away from Vernikport, even with each other as they neared the shimmering horizon.

"I am proud of you, Luka," his father said. "You showed incredible strength and courage. You are worthy of leading this nation."

"Aye, Luka," Xander agreed. "I'm proud of you, too. Not bad for my little ratwagger of a brother."

Luka smiled faintly.

"I must caution you, my son," Var said, his tone becoming more solemn. "I can see your path of revenge is treacherous. You must be careful not to lose yourself in it. You have responsibilities to your people that must always come before a personal quest for vengeance."

"Aye, but don't let those bastards get away with what they did," Xander added. "The other two must die as well. They took me away from Amelia."

Var and Xander looked at each other, seeming as though they were about to argue.

Before the discussion could continue, a sharp knock shattered the dream. Var and Xander dissolved back into the depths of Luka's unconsciousness as he awoke. Disoriented, he rubbed his eyes and did his best to stretch his stiff and pained body. It took a moment for him to notice that the sun had set, an unsettling reminder of how much time had passed.

A second knock brought Luka to his feet. General Warwick stood on the other side of the door, with three dark-robed doctors flanking him and a roll of parchment resting in his hands. "Good evening, Luka."

Luka thought about admonishing his mentor for not addressing him formally as king but decided against it. "Evening, General Rory. What have you awoken me for?"

"I managed to find the best physicians this city has to offer. Let them take a look at you and help you recover properly from—"

"Is that message for me?" Luka interrupted, his eyes focusing on the roll of parchment in the general's hand.

"Um, yes. This is from your Uncle Donte. I had hoped that the doctors would be able to spend some time working—"

"Let me see it."

Reluctantly, the general handed him the letter. Luka rushed to read it, his eyes darting around the page. "Mother..." he muttered under his breath.

A sense of urgency welled up within him as he learned about Queen Vanessa's travels. She had not stayed on the farm, after all. Rather, she had brought Amelia, Teya, and Pametan with her, venturing through the middle of the country, unprotected.

Luka immediately turned to his closet, looking for his shirt and cloak. "I must ride out at once."

The general and the doctors erupted into a cacophony of protests that brought ringing back to his head, but he ignored it all. Nothing could stop him, not even his injuries, as he gathered a small caravan and left the city.

*****

Luka's travels back south along Vulture Road bore little resemblance to his original journey. This time, he rode from the safety and confines of a carriage. Outside, the trees had shed the bright greens of late summer for the yellows, oranges, and reds that marked autumn. The sounds of hooves crunching on fallen leaves filled the air.

In contrast to the constant chattering and jesting from Reishi, Luka's company consisted of a score of skilled officers, plus the three doctors that Warwick had procured. They made for much more reserved travel companions than his wizard friend.

Left to his thoughts, Luka's anxiety grew as the travels progressed southward. Each day meant another day that his mother was unprotected in the south, while Omarius and Drugi continued to conquer more territory in the north.

After nearly two weeks of riding, rumors began to surface. The reliable ones described Luka's mother as being with two women and one man. Some of the reports confused Luka, mentioning a woman who was bearing a child.

Later in the evening, Luka ordered his men to set up camp, leaving them behind as he embarked on a brief stroll. With the treatment of the doctors, he was able to walk with less and less pain, though the damage Privus had done still plagued him. He was a long way from battle condition and even further away from comfort.

When Luka had nearly exhausted himself with his pacing, a shadowy figure on horseback appeared in the distance, heading in his direction. Instinctively, he placed his hand on his sword, another lieutenant's blade that had replaced the one destroyed by Privus.

The singular shadow grew to four figures as they drew closer. His heart quickened. "Luka?" came a familiar female voice, only it wasn't his mother's.

"Who is it?" Luka replied.

"Luka?" came a distinct, second voice. That *was* the unmistakable voice of his mother. A deep well of relief filled him as he started forward.

Out of the shadows came the welcome figures of Queen Vanessa, Priestess Teya, Minister Pametan, and Princess Amelia, whose lower belly noticeably protruded outward. That meant Luka would have a nephew or niece in only a few months. Since Luka had taken the crown before Amelia's baby had been born, his regency would not be threatened by Xander's heir. That mattered little to him right now, either way. A quiet joy stirred in him at the thought of his brother's line living on.

Luka sheathed his sword and ran forward as fast as his wounds would allow. He reached his mother quickly, and they embraced.

"Luka, I am so happy to see you! Words cannot hope to describe—"

"No need, Mother. I have missed you, too. I have much to tell you about."

"You most certainly *do*! You can start with why you left me so abruptly—without even a goodbye."

"Mother..." Luka began, but he could not conjure a proper response.

"I was so scared for you. For weeks, I had to wonder if you were alive or not. After I had already lost so much," Vanessa said.

"I know, Mother. I know. I am sorry. Must we dwell on such unpleasantries?"

She paused for a moment and sighed. "It's alright. We are together again. I missed you so much. All we have left is each other now. You know that to be true." She moved in slowly and wrapped her arms gently around her wounded son.

Luka embraced his mother tighter. "I do."

*****

When they finally reached Exeter, Queen Vanessa was escorted to a grand chamber within the palace. The ceiling of the room stood high, with velvet drapes catching bright streams of sunlight against the window.

They had entered the city with little fanfare, largely undetected. There would be a decree given by Luka, followed by grand celebrations in the days to come, but for now, peace and stillness were a gift.

Across the hall, Vanessa knew that Amelia would also be treated to a beautiful bedroom and much care for her coming child. Her pregnancy would make for a big story in the country and would have lasting repercussions on the Estravian political landscape. More importantly, she wondered whether her first grandchild would look like her firstborn son. She sincerely hoped so.

As she settled into her luxurious quarters, a hollowness and emptiness came over her. No matter where she found herself, her bed would be empty, and her days would be spent without Var.

*****

Priestess Teya waited in the palace gardens, which lay adjacent to the battle-weary courtyard where Luka and Privus had dueled weeks earlier. A pleasant but chilly breeze calmly drifted through the area. After another moment passed, Teya heard the sound that she had come to hear—a happy birdsong echoed through the air and drew nearer. Priestess Teya smiled as Naka the phoenix, only a few weeks grown past a fledgling, swooped down and greeted her caretaker.

"I knew you would arrive today, my sweet," she said as the golden bird landed on her shoulder. Their bond had ensured that Naka would be able to find her, but only when it was safe in Exeter.

"Come inside, Naka. I have managed to procure a suitable cage for you." Priestess Teya headed inside with the bird and into her new quarters, those which had previously belonged to the former priest of Exeter.

With Naka safe and secure in her new cage, she left the room to attend to Luka. The young king was far more receptive to her treatments than before, even going so far as to expel the doctors who had been working on him previously.

Teya had only begun her healing work on Luka for that day, when Reishi knocked on the door of Luka's bedchamber and entered promptly without a response. He found Luka lying shirtless on his belly, with Priestess Teya holding her hands above him.

"Luka! My King! I heard you returned!"

The young king was a bit flustered when he responded. "You heard correctly, Reishi."

The wizard smiled. "Welcome back. I suppose now is not the best time to remind you about my payment?"

Chapter 48
The King's Address

"**G**reat people of Exeter, you are free!"

With his arms raised high, Luka's voice rang out from the palace balcony to the thousands of liberated Exeterian citizens below. Packed tightly together in Saddiq Square, the people erupted into thunderous applause.

For the first time, Luka stood before his people—donned in glimmering golden and crimson robes and a golden crown on his head—as The King of Estravia should be. His mother and Lady Dija stood at his sides, the queen proud and smiling, the lady solemn and watchful.

"It is an honor to address you all as your king," Luka continued, raising his voice over the cathartic cheers from below. "But it is an honor that should never have fallen to me. The crown belonged to my father, after which it was supposed to pass on to my brother. The only reason it rests on my head is because they were taken from us.

"Some have urged me not to dwell on this evil—that I should speak to you all today as your king with an uplifting message. Unfortunately, as king, it is my *duty* to dwell on this. I can never forget what happened to my family. History will never forget it either, so why should we?"

He paused for a moment, the crowd now murmuring instead of cheering.

"I have killed Privus—and along with the good people of the mighty Vernik Army—I have liberated this city. But that does not yet give us the luxury to relax and enjoy a sense of peace. Until the others are dead, there will be no peace.

"We must stand united as a nation. There is an evil within this country that will take every one of us, citizens and soldiers alike, to vanquish. I will—we will—have our vengeance.

"All who dared trifle with this city saw what the consequences of crossing me and the Vernik line are. Now we will show the rest!"

The cheering resumed, and with that, Luka turned around and headed inside. The applause followed him in, as did Vanessa and Dija, who had probably hoped for a more uplifting message from the nineteen-year-old king.

*****

The doors to the council room—her council room, or at least it used to be—swung open. Since Luka and the others had arrived in Exeter, they had made frequent use of the large space for planning purposes. Today, only Luka and Queen Vanessa inhabited it, sitting at the far end of the room. A thick white marble table stretched from end to end, with empty seats all around it. Dija made her way over to them.

"Your Highness, you have called for me," Dija said.

"Indeed. First of all, I would like to thank you for procuring my new crown. My mother told me how you helped obtain it. It is marvelous, and I would not have been able to get one of such fine quality in such a short time if not for you," Luka said. His face was now clean shaven and many of his scars had healed, thanks to Priestess Teya.

"My pleasure, Your Highness. The people of Estravia deserve to see their king wearing the proper accouterments. Especially a crown."

"I hold that thoughtfulness in high esteem, Dija. But that is truthfully not why I asked to speak to you," he said, his words growing more solemn, his gaze shifting around. "There is something that has weighed heavily on my mind for quite some time."

389

A sense of unease came over her. "What is it, My King?"

"You may be aware, but months ago, prior to the Zlikrej invasion, we received correspondence from Exeter. Multiple scouting reports claimed sightings of the Zlikrej brothers just south of the Ekron Mountains. We acted upon those, and due to that, we were left wide open for the subsequent attack."

Dija could feel the color drain from her face and her heartbeat quicken. She tried not to stumble on her words as she responded. "Y-Your Highness... Those reports *never* came from Exeter. I received correspondence from your father asking for verification, barely a week before the Zlikrej themselves arrived." She paused, her throat feeling brittle and dry. "But by then... it was too late."

"Dija, we are not accusing you of anything," Vanessa said gently, reacting to her obvious discomfort. "We have all been the victims of an elaborate ruse. We believe the letters were forgeries. We are just asking if you know of anything, or if you can help us find answers on how this could have befallen us in the first place."

Luka eyed his mother as if he wanted to protest. But the look was only for a second, and he yielded. "If you have no connection to these letters, then we have much more inquiry to do until we find answers. In the coming days, the three of us will meet with Pametan and Warwick. Maybe we can figure this out, as a group. But tonight, let us enjoy the great feast."

"Yes, Your Highness. I swear to help you in whatever way I can." She bowed before she departed, some color returning to her face, but a sense of unease simmering within.

*****

"Mother," Luka said, after Dija had left. "There's something that is bothering me. It's a lingering feeling from back in Vernikport."

"What is it, my son?" Vanessa replied.

"It's Admiral Mormar."

"The Admiral?"

"Yes," Luka said, rubbing his now clean-shaven cheeks. "I remember back in Vernikport, he was the one to receive the initial letter stating the Zlikrej were advancing from the north. It is unusual enough for *him* to receive that kind of military correspondence in the first place."

Vanessa nodded, seeming to digest the information.

Luka continued. "Then, during the meeting of the war council, he was by far the most vocal in support of the military offensive—which was also highly unusual."

Even mentioning the council meeting brought pain to Luka's soul. Xander had been right to be suspicious of the whole thing, and Luka voted against him. *I let you down, brother. But I will find who was responsible, and I will avenge you.*

"You are right, Luka," Vanessa said, her own face tightening with concern. "Those facts paint a strange pattern. If your instincts are telling you this, you could bring him in for questioning."

"Yes, but he is far away, still docked in Eastport," Luka said. "It would take a great deal of time to get him here, and I wouldn't want to disrupt our naval capabilities."

"Luka, the navy isn't doing anything right now."

Luka shrugged in agreement.

"Besides, if you're truly concerned, you can appoint a vice admiral to take his place on an interim basis."

Luka nodded again. "Thank you, Mother. I just may do that. I'll bring this up to General Rory when he comes in, but I wanted to ask you first."

The general appeared only a few moments later, seeming surprised to see Vanessa there, but didn't protest. In his arms were a handful of scouting reports, full of information on recent Zlikrej movements.

"King Luka, Queen Vanessa, it is a pleasure to see you both. That was an excellent speech, by the way. I know for a fact that our troops appreciated it."

Luka turned to his mother with a vindicated, knowing look, but she did not meet his gaze. "Thank you, General Rory," he said. "It feels good to address my subjects. Please have a seat."

The general sat a few seats away from Luka and his mother at the large marble table.

"General," Luka began. "As you recommended, I have questioned Lady Dija."

"Very good, King Luka. What did you find?"

"I find her to likely be above suspicion. It's near impossible to imagine her serving the Zlikrej. There is no clear motive. She suffered greatly under their reign here."

Warwick nodded, then half protested. "Your Highness, I can understand that sentiment, but anomalies persist. Perhaps she is not guilty of collusion with our enemies, but she is likely guilty of a breakdown in communication. The letters, though they may have been forged, bore the official seal of Exeter. It could only have come from someone within this palace."

"I see."

"Allow me to lead an investigation into this matter, Your Highness."

"Fair enough, General. But there is something I would like for you to do first."

"Yes, King Luka. Whatever you wish."

"I need you to summon Admiral Mormar back to Exeter for questioning. His role in this needs to be investigated."

"With respect, Your Highness," the general said, his mustache almost twitching. "The admiral is no traitor. He has served this nation for decades without so much as a sniff of treason."

"Then explain to me why and how the messages came to him of all people, instead of to you or to my father directly? It makes little sense."

"That may be unusual, but it does not implicate—"

"He's not implicated of anything... yet," Luka said. "My intention is merely to question him. He has a lot to answer for. It's awfully convenient that he has managed to avoid this conflict entirely on the east coast. He was also exuberantly supportive of the military campaign that damned us in that council meeting."

"Very well, King Luka. I will summon him at once."

"Thank you, General. At the moment, I'm in no mood to read scouting reports. Please leave the reports on the table, and I will review them later. That will be all."

After Warwick left, his mother kissed his forehead and departed as well, leaving Luka to his thoughts. He felt uneasy, now certain that someone had betrayed him. All signs pointed to the admiral. He knew he had to question Mormar, but he was unsure what it would accomplish. He would have no way of getting inside the man's head. Not without a mind wizard, which, as far as Luka knew, he did not have.

If I can deduce that he is guilty of aiding my family's killers... Luka thought, as he reached for the reports that Warwick had left on the table. *Death may not be a worthy enough punishment.*

*****

Reishi was among the first to arrive at the feast that evening. This would be his final night here, and he intended to enjoy it. When he entered the great dining hall, other guests recognized him, offering him praise and curious glances. He was a man of meaningful celebrity now, accepting their greetings with unsure smiles and subtle waves.

A server approached Reishi with a glass of red wine on a silver tray, which he readily accepted. The drink was splendid. Worth savoring. Reishi finished it in minutes and was already requesting another glass.

This was more than a celebration. He had been sober and clear headed long enough to take him through the battle, but he came away tainted by even more twisted and vile memories from Vatren and the Zlikrej soldiers during the conflict. Now, the wine would drown it away—an effective painkiller, albeit a temporary and harmful one.

Reishi sipped his third glass of wine as the hall began to fill. Priestess Teya, Princess Amelia, Lady Dija, and Minister Pametan entered together and took their seats near him at the head of the table. Over the past few days in Exeter, Reishi had grown familiar with each of them. He'd forged pleasant connections—with all but Teya. Reishi knew she was suspicious of him, but he wasn't surprised. The power of the soul was almost as effective as the power of the mind when it came to detecting liars.

General Warwick trailed in after and sat next to Reishi. "Greetings, General," Reishi said.

"Greetings, Reishi. I trust this evening finds you well."

Their conversations had not progressed beyond the formal, but at least they had progressed past the hostile. They now spoke to each other with mutual respect.

Finally, the last two seats at the table were filled when Luka and Vanessa arrived. The banquet rose in unison at their entrance and only sat back down when signaled. On cue, busy servants hastily covered the table in platters of food and the feast commenced.

In between bites of tender Socan meat, Reishi eyed Luka enjoying himself from a few seats away. His mother and close friends were at his side. It was the happiest he had seen Luka in the few months he had known him. Perhaps he felt whole, at least for one night.

Suddenly, Luka looked Reishi's way and made eye contact. He excused himself from his current conversation and approached.

"I see your brief sober period has reached its tragic end," Luka remarked, standing behind Reishi's chair.

Reishi turned around to face the king, a messy Socan leg in one hand a nearly empty glass of wine in the other.

"Ah, it was just brief enough and doesn't feel so tragic to me."

"I see you are certainly making up for lost time," Luka said with a half-smile.

"Well, I'd say I've earned it, wouldn't you?"

Luka chuckled. "Aye. As much as it pains me to admit, you *have* earned it. You were invaluable to our cause. I'd shake your hand, but seeing that—"

"Nonsense," Reishi interrupted, "Here we go..." He hastily put down his wine and tried his best to clean the Socan grease off his hands.

"I must insist we don't," Luka said, pulling his own hand away.

"Fair enough," Reishi said with a smile and a wave of his hand. "Anyways, I've actually got to empty my well rather badly—if you know what I mean."

"How unlike you," Luka said with an eye roll.

After excusing himself from the table, Reishi hobbled out of the dining hall, cheers and encouragement following him as he passed. He made his way through a maze of marble hallways, towards what he believed to be the waste area. Instead, he found himself outside.

It took a moment before he realized that he had just stepped out of the back entrance of Exeter Palace. Seeing that he was alone, and feeling desperate, he simply found a nearby tree to do the job.

While he was relieving himself, Reishi noticed a hooded figure emerge from the same backdoor of the palace that Reishi had just taken. The two made viciously uncomfortable eye contact before the figure looked away and began to take off.

"Oi! What are you looking at? Why are you watching me piss?" Reishi called out in jest, but the figure was clearly in no mood for play.

Something was wrong with this man. Though it would be laborious while he was inebriated, his instincts told him he needed to use his powers to investigate.

After pulling up his pants, he fought through a thick haze of drunkenness, casting out his mind toward the fleeing figure. Cazin. That was the name of this clandestine man, whose mission was no longer concealed to Reishi.

Cazin was a currier, instructed to deliver a secretive message in the middle of the feast—a time when everyone would be preoccupied.

Be a shame for Cazin to trip, Reishi thought.

Under the wizard's control, the envoy lost balance, stumbled on nothing, and fell onto the stone Exeter street, dropping the scroll to the ground. Reishi wandered over to him in a haphazard zig-zag fashion.

Cazin reached for the scroll, but Reishi picked it up. "W-what have we here?" Reishi asked.

"I can't let you read that." Cazin was standing up now, dagger in hand.

"I can't let you speak to me like that," Reishi replied.

With effort, he focused on Cazin's fist, tightly clutching the dagger. The weapon slipped out of his fingers and clattered on the ground. When Cazin bent down to pick it up again, Reishi induced within him the same drunkenness that he was experiencing. The move was called "mirroring" by the monks—a simple and effective trick. Cazin stumbled and collapsed a second time.

Reishi then dove into his mind like a surgeon. He found the memory of the Cazin being ordered to deliver the message. It was so shocking that Reishi replayed it several times. *This can't be true,* he thought. *Am I really this drunk?*

But the truth was clear. After obliterating the scene from Cazin's mind, Reishi was now the only one who held the messenger's memory. Of course, one other person would have a recollection of that event from a different perspective.

Now that he was safe, Reishi opened the scroll. The words were blurry and danced all over the page. After much squinting and straining, he was able to read the sentences. The words on the page were shocking and appalling, turning his stomach over.

Luka must see this.

But it could not be that night. It was a night of celebration, and Reishi was too drunk. With a sigh, the wizard rolled up the scroll and took it back to his bedchamber.

He would have to give it to Luka in the morning, before he left.

*****

Minutes later, the sudden haze lifted from Cazin's mind. He awoke under the glistening stars of the cold Exeter night, his dagger lying on the ground next to him. Confused, he picked it up and rose to his feet. There was no one else in sight.

Did I not have a mission I had to carry out? Cazin thought to himself. When nothing occurred to him, he shrugged and wandered off into the night.

Chapter 49
Farewell

The parchment shook in Omarius's thick, trembling hands. He wanted to tear the letter to shreds, but knew that if he destroyed it, he couldn't be certain that it was real.

Omarius had led a life of little pleasure and few good moments until his recent conquests. Receiving the news of his youngest brother's death from his scouts was the second worst experience of his life. He began to pace in rapid circles, trying to process the shocking information he had just received. The messenger opened his mouth to speak, but Omarius shoved him violently out of the way.

The noble keep of the western city of Laisuria sat in the far end of the urban center. Its former inhabitants now occupied the crowded, musty dungeons or the even more crowded mass graves. Little foot traffic came through this part of the city, allowing Omarius to have the privacy he needed when he exited the palace. He took his hammer with him and lugged it at his side.

In the middle of an empty street, underneath a tall bell tower, Omarius let out an anguished scream. He screamed several more times and brought his hammer down onto the weathered stone ground repeatedly. Each crash of his great weapon punctured the street and scattered debris. Some of it bounced so high into the air that it hit him in the face, but he paid no mind and kept swinging. It did not give him an ounce of relief or comfort, yet he felt like he could do nothing else.

By the time Drugi came out to see the commotion, Omarius had created a small crater in the street. Sweat and dirt covered his face.

"Omarius, what troubles you?"

The giant man turned and looked at his only living brother. He could not summon a word, so he merely handed him the message. Drugi took the parchment and read it cautiously. "No. No. No... No..." he kept muttering out loud.

Above them, the bell began to toll at the end of another hour, the ringing of the brass echoing against the silent sky. Omarius put his hand on Drugi's shoulder. A solitary tear trickled down his cheek. "They will pay for this. I swear it."

Drugi did not reply. He handed the message back to Omarius and wandered off. Omarius knew that when he was alone, he would cry his soul away.

Omarius would shed no more tears. Later that day, he returned to the temporary study he had set up, where his personal map hung on the back wall. He went over to the Mithacor emblem that marked Exeter and ripped it off.

*****

"Do you swear this to be authentic?" asked Luka, though he recognized the handwriting character for character. The signature on it was undeniable.

"I do, Luka, erm, Your Majesty," answered Reishi. "I wish it weren't."

"And where is this messenger now, you say?"

"I do not know. I know his name was Cazin, but I do not know where he went after our encounter. With some time, I may be able to track him down."

"No need. I can worry about that later. There is a far greater evil that I must address."

"There certainly is."

"Thank you for bringing this to my attention... I can't believe this..." Luka's voice trailed off. "It explains almost everything."

"I am so sorry, Luka."

Luka said nothing for a while. "You don't have to stay for this," he said finally. "You may leave today like you planned but expect that our paths will cross again."

Reishi did not have to guess what the young king would do. He inadvertently saw the images flash across Luka's mind. Even without exercising his mental abilities, the silent, cold rage Luka was emitting nearly made Reishi recoil.

"I- I think that I will leave today, but I am happy to stay if you need my support. We have been through a lot together, and one extra day will not hurt me," Reishi said, after several seconds of silence had passed.

Luka softened. He looked Reishi directly in his eyes and held out his hand. The wizard took the king's hand and shook it. "We certainly have been through a lot, you mad bastard," Luka said, with as much of a smile as he could muster in that moment. "Thank you for everything. I know we could not have done it without you."

Reishi smiled back. "I must thank you as well. You taught me how to hold my bladder for long periods of time. That was the best lesson I learned on this journey."

Laughter escaped from both men.

"Jesting aside, though," Reishi continued. "Thank you for believing in me and allowing me to accompany you in your battles. I know that my days were not spent well back in Jetsac. It was good fortune that you appeared at my tavern. For the first time in many years, I have done something useful."

The handshake turned into an embrace. When they let go, Reishi could see that Luka had turned somber again, reflecting on the news that he had just received. Reishi left him to his thoughts.

*****

Reishi did, in fact, leave Exeter that day. The thought of what he uncovered from the messenger weighed heavily on him the entire journey back home. To distract himself, he chose to focus on happier ideas, such as Buchan, or the view of the lake from his top window. For many weeks, Reishi had been caught up in a war that he originally wanted no part of. Now he knew he must relish any chance for peace he could find. Soon enough, he would be swallowed up by it again.

Weeks later, Reishi arrived home. He felt his excitement well up as he opened the door to "The Magic Tavern". He dropped all his travel wear next to the door and immediately fixed himself a drink—a tall glass of his golden rum.

The tavern chairs were folded upside down and placed on the tabletops. He went over to the same table where he and Luka had spent so much time together the night they had met, months earlier. He flipped over both chairs and sat.

Reishi sighed between sips and allowed himself to take in the memories of his journey. He would only have a few moments alone to himself, because shortly after, he heard an enthusiastic "Mew!"

Buchan jumped up onto the table and greeted her companion with forceful nudges and a flurry of chirps. "Buchan! My friend! Did you miss me?"

The black cat chirped back.

"Tanna better have taken good care of you. Have you been fed enough?" He continued to pet his cat while she circled around the top of the table and came back for more nudges.

"I've got quite a bit to tell you, Buchan," Reishi continued. "First of all—look at all this money!" He motioned to the heavy bags of Novaks that Luka had given him. "And remember the king who was here last time? He and I are good friends now. Oh, and I fought another wizard and beat him in front of two entire armies! I'm a bit of a hero now.

"Gabbitt's magic orbs came in very handy, because the whole time, they thought I was an elemental wizard! They still do!"

A pang of guilt popped into Reishi's stomach as he thought about all the secrets he still clung to. He drowned it quickly with a glass of rum and let Buchan climb onto his lap. Her chirps turned to purrs, both master and pet drifting into a peaceful sleep on the chair.

Chapter 50
The Final Lesson

A cup of freshly poured black tea steamed next to a stack of papers on General Warwick's desk. After much lobbying to Lady Dija, he was given a large study to serve as his war room. Over the last few weeks, he had worked hard to match his new room with the office he had in Vernikport.

Three knocks rapped on the door as Warwick took a slow sip of his hot tea. "Who is it?" he said after putting down the cup. Without responding, Luka stepped into the office. "Luka, to what do I owe the pleasure?"

"You are supposed to address me formally, Rory," he replied icily. "I am The King now." He stood tense at the doorway and did not make eye contact. Something appeared to be wrong.

"Forgive me, Your Highness," Warwick said. "Have you come to discuss our council meeting that is planned for later this evening?"

In the weeks since the victory against Privus's forces, Warwick had been hosting nightly meetings with his lieutenants and highest officers. While Luka was gone, Warwick had full autonomy and had sent small units of the military to some of the Zlikrej-controlled villages near Exeter. Since Luka had returned with the queen, Luka had taken over these meetings. He also insisted that the Queen and Lady Dija be involved for reasons that Warwick did not understand.

"Actually, I have something else I wanted to discuss," Luka replied.

"Well, come have a seat, Your Highness. What is on your mind?"

Luka nodded and approached the general's desk. "How about a drink first?" he said.

"I assume you don't mean tea?" asked Warwick. Luka nodded again. "Well, I have some whiskey here. Aged more than twenty years. It's older than you, actually. Will that do?"

"That will do just fine."

Warwick walked to the corner of his office to where he kept his personal inventory of fine wines and spirits. Many of the bottles had been ones he had owned for years and were taken with him on his long journey across the country.

While the general reached for the bottle, Luka looked around the room sullenly. "This new office is in remarkably good order considering how short a time you've had it," he observed.

"Thank you, Your Highness. My work area is always a high priority to me."

"I can appreciate that," Luka said. "Maybe I'll have to take this office for myself. It looks like a great place to run an army from."

General Warwick chuckled uncomfortably at Luka's comment, which he sincerely hoped was a joke. Brushing that off, Warwick handed Luka a glass of brown liquid and clinked their glasses together. They each then took a hearty sip of the drink. It was delicious, sweet on the palate and delivering a pleasant, oaky burn that lingered for several moments. After their first sip, both men took their seats.

"It is quite fortunate for you that you had the foresight to bring your best bottles with you," Luka said. "If you had left them in Vernikport, they would have been destroyed along with everything else."

"Well, I did lose a few fine bottles back in Vernikport, but yes, I am fortunate to have brought these with me," Warwick acknowledged, but then he quickly changed the subject. "So, Your Highness, what is it that you wanted to discuss?"

Luka sighed and cleared his throat before answering. "You remember our recurring lessons back in Vernikport, discussing old military texts? Well, there is a document that I have come across recently, and I wanted to get your opinion on it. We can discuss it just like in the old days."

"Certainly, King Luka. That sounds like a most pleasant idea. Let's have a look."

Luka reached behind his robe and pulled out a scroll, placing it on the table. The general unrolled it while Luka downed the whiskey.

Warwick recognized his own clear and mechanistic style of handwriting instantly. A bottomless void formed in his stomach as the first word in the short letter jumped out at him.

"Omarius,

I am writing to inform you that I must terminate our agreement. The dynamics of our arrangement have changed since we first made it, and I now believe it is best for me to serve King Luka. It is not my fault that you left him alive, allowing him to return and retake command of this country. With the young king—who is my protégé—at my side, I will be able to embark on the military campaigns that this country has needed for so long.

It does not make sense for me to wait for you to resolve your conquests, while I follow your orders or convince my own men to surrender to you. I know you had promised me that you would betray the

Stranakans one day, but I do not need to rely on your word any longer. I have a legitimate, young king at my side, who can start this process much sooner.

Though you may assume otherwise, I do feel regret for what happened to your brother. Privus was a formidable warrior in his own right.

Nevertheless, this will be the last letter I will write to you in this manner. In future correspondences, should there be any, I will treat you as I would any foe. I know you are likely to be unhappy with this news, but you must recognize the fact that without my assistance, you would not be where you are today.

From this point forward, we will be enemies again but know that I admire your strength. Congratulations on a historic military campaign, but I must inform you that it will be coming to an end soon.

Sincerely,

General Rory Warwick"

Warwick tried to formulate a clever response to the document. He tried to think of some escape route—some way out. But the letter was damning, and no words could rescue him.

Warwick turned to face Luka and was met with a blade to his chest. Luka had jammed a winged dagger into Warwick with such strength that he fell out of his chair, taking the weapon with him onto the floor.

There was no ache at first—just sheer, brutal force of impact. When the pain from the cold steel blade arrived, it was agonizing. Warwick screamed, but his voice was neutered. In that moment, he did not know if he would survive.

Lying on the ground, Warwick's life flashed before him, and memories flooded into his mind. He remembered how it all went wrong, how he had gradually decided to turn on his closest friend.

He remembered all of the times he tried to convince Var to attack the Stranakans, desperately seeking to avenge Obadiah, who had been vanquished by that country. They were weak, Warwick would tell Var but would grow in strength. Now was the time to strike.

But his suggestions were rejected time and time again. Even after it was discovered that their country had potentially conspired with Lord Diocretin, Var would not act. Estravia, under Var's leadership, was weak.

He remembered receiving the offer, poring over it in his private office. His instinct told him to bring it straight to Var. But he resisted. The offer was too enticing. It gave him the opportunity to do what he always wanted to do. The Zlikrej brothers would bring the Stranakans onto Estravian soil, temporarily, at least. They promised that after conquering Estravia, with Warwick's necessary help, of course, that they would appoint him to be their military leader. Thereafter, they would promptly turn against their former allies and formally wage war against the Stranakans.

The campaign would create an even grander empire, and history would bestow glory upon Warwick. Future generations would not know of the arrangement that occurred beforehand, and instead, they would think of Warwick as a savvy man who surrendered to the winning side only to become a war hero again, much like Lord Serja of old.

It was a risky gambit. He would have to sacrifice so much. He still loved Var and the Vernik family. Innocent blood would be shed. And the Zlikrej could turn against him when they no longer needed him. But it became clear it was the *right* risk. It was his best chance at getting revenge against the vile Stranakan Empire. It was his chance to be remembered as the one who wiped them out forever. Something no one before him had ever done.

Then he remembered when he found out Luka was still alive. It was gravely conflicting. Luka was his protégé. A true warrior and a fierce young man. But he would disrupt the whole plan, and Warwick would likely lose control of the military to him. The country was already beginning to rally behind him.

Quickly, though, Warwick began to see the opportunity. It became clear that Luka was now the best option. He was war hungry and young. He would be easily persuaded into a fight with the Stranakans, especially since they had taken up arms already. The path was clear once again. He would change his allegiance back to Luka, without the young king being any the wiser.

Better yet, Luka would not betray Warwick the way he feared the Zlikrej might. His position and his life were safer in Luka's hands. Or so he had thought.

The excruciating, biting pain in his chest brought Warwick back to the present. His choices had led him to this point, with his life trickling out of the wound along with his blood. He had chosen poorly, severely underestimating his own mentee, and severely overestimating his own ability to keep his plans concealed.

Standing above him, eyes ablaze in rage, Luka shouted, "It was you! It was *you* who had those letters forged! You planned all of this all along! How could you betray my family? They died because of *you.*

"Why?! Why did you do it?"

Now it was Warwick who could not make eye contact. He looked at the blade inside him and put his hands on it.

Luka immediately saw this and kicked the general's hands away, knocking the dagger sideways in the process. The blade shifted against the flesh inside his chest, amplifying the pain by an unbearable degree. He winced like a wounded animal. "Why did you do it, *you bastard!*"

It took great strength, but Warwick finally answered Luka. "Power should not belong in the hands of those who are not willing—"

Luka cut him off. "You ungrateful sack of shit! My family gave you more power than you ever deserved! How dare you!"

The general attempted to utter another response, but Luka shouted him down again. "I don't want to hear from you! I don't want to hear from the *weakest* man I have ever known.

"My father and brother were the greatest men this country has ever seen. The history books will remember them. No one will ever remember you."

Luka knelt down beside Warwick and glared. Warwick saw a limitless well of rage looking back at him through his former mentee's eyes.

He wrenched the dagger from Warwick's chest, causing a fountain of blood to spray out. "This dagger was my brother's," Luka said, brandishing the old weapon that was now bright red. "We once had a debate over whose dagger was better. I suppose he was right in the end. I know he would appreciate that it was used to kill you."

Luka rose to his feet and pulled a white cloth from his pocket and began wiping his blade. Soon, the dagger glistened a shiny silver, and the cloth was soaked in red. Luka let it go, the cloth landing next to Warwick in the quickly expanding puddle of blood.

Warwick watched as the young king took one last look at him, dying on the floor. He took a deliberate step over him and departed the room.

The door slammed behind him violently when he exited. The undrunk whiskey in the general's glass swirled about and nearly spilled out onto the desk from the vibrations.

All alone now, he looked at the blood that had been lost and the blood that was still pouring from his chest. Given that sight, he knew he had no hope—perhaps only seconds remaining.

What lay beyond for him? The general's mind spiraled around all the possibilities of how he would be spending eternity and then shifted to one guarantee—his life was over. The decades he had lived were not enough. He had so many regrets. Chief among them was that Luka was right. He would be forgotten. He was a general who spent his career mostly during peacetime. Now he would die as a failure without an ounce of glory from the war that he had helped create.

Despair overwhelmed him. All of the scheming, sacrifices, and betrayals had been for nothing.

Less than a minute passed before Warwick could no longer string thoughts together. The pain became duller, his senses fading away.

At last, the heavy, black curtains of death closed over him.

THE END

Luka Vernik will return.